Hidden Trump

An Amber Farrell Novel
Book 2 of the
Bite Back series

by
Mark Henwick

Published by ***Marque***

Series schedule, reviews & news on
www.athanate.com

Bite Back 2 : Hidden Trump
ISBN: 978-1-912499-14-4

First published in December 2012 by Marque

Mark Henwick asserts the right to be identified as the author of this work.

Cover design: CreativeEdge, Andrew Dobell
Cover model: Maria Askew

Author's note:

Asian names:
Throughout this series, I use the Western sequence (First, Middle, Last Name) to depict names, so as to match with the majority of characters in the books. Most Asian societies would put the Last Name first.

Chapter 1

MONDAY

I was going to be betrayed before the week was out.

The realization seeped into me as I drove away from the Nexus building on the southern outskirts of Denver. SWAT teams were swarming over the building, arresting the surviving members of the ZK criminal gang. And body-bagging the ones I'd shot. Since ZK had kidnapped and wounded their police captain, José Morales, the assault teams were not in a good mood.

But I wasn't running from them. I had taken off to avoid the FBI, who were starting to question how one Amber Farrell, lowly PI, was suddenly involved in so many organized crime busts. And how come I emerged unscathed from situations that would have killed a normal person? Questions I couldn't afford to answer.

Today's scene made it worse. It had started as a routine case for a corporate CEO, Jennifer Kingslund—find out who was trying to sabotage her company. It turned out to be her business rival, Jack Tucker—a seemingly legitimate businessman—and his illegitimate son, Frank Hoben, who ran ZK. And it had escalated into attempted murder, hostage taking, assault weapons, exploding grenades and a hot zone helicopter extraction from the Nexus.

Some days are like that.

I'd achieved my objectives. Hostages rescued. ZK demolished. Tucker dead—though I hadn't intended that. He'd shot himself as the SWAT teams closed in.

Of course, I hadn't done it on my own. I'd had help—just not the kind of help that I could tell the FBI about. Not criminals, but people whose survival depended on staying under the radar. And whose interests didn't necessarily coincide with the FBI's. Or regular humans.

Which was why my adrenaline rush from slam-dunking ZK at the Nexus was cooling off rapidly. It was great to have allies, but they had competing agendas, and their own ideas of what to do with me. I was the weak point, the expendable asset. And I wasn't sure I could trust myself any more than I could trust them.

My eyes flicked to the rearview mirror, and held.

Crap.

The adrenaline spiked back up.

I'd picked up a tail.

That black Cadillac SUV with the tints had been following me since the Nexus building. Black Caddies weren't that unusual, but everyone else was rubbernecking the end of the SWAT operation, with squad cars, ambulances, lights and sirens making a real circus of it. Not to mention the helicopters overhead. The TV people were probably there. Now, who would find following me more interesting than that?

Working on my gut feeling, I headed south out of Meridian and picked up Interstate 25. The Caddy was still there, two cars back. When they followed me off at Castle Pines, I knew my instinct had been right.

What I should do about it depended on who they were.

I guess it said things about me that there were so many candidates, and not all of them outright enemies. It might be the FBI, for instance, or Obs, the army medical unit tasked with investigating me. Or even my paranormal allies.

But my gut told me it was Hoben's crew. And that spelled trouble. Hoben didn't have Jack Tucker's veneer of civilization—he was a vindictive son of a bitch with a fondness for rape and torture. Anger stoked my belly.

I leaned over and got my Heckler & Koch Mark 23 from the glove compartment. It's a lump of a pistol, but I'm used to it from my days in Ops 4-10, the army's most covert special forces battalion, and it has real stopping power. I'd let Hoben get away once—the first time he'd come after Jen and me. I wouldn't make that mistake a second time.

As the roads got quieter and turnoffs ran out, the SUV fell way back. That told me either they were just tailing me to see where I went or they were on their cell phones to their buddies and I was going to find my way blocked somewhere on the empty stretches ahead. Probably the latter, and that wasn't good. I didn't want to be trapped between two groups of them. It was time to party. A pity I'd left the Kevlar vest back at the Nexus building.

I took a bend, temporarily out of sight of the Caddy. The road ahead was clear as far as I could see. It'd been a long day—hell, a long couple of weeks—and the major reason why was right behind me. Hoben had been dogging my heels, lurking out of sight and threatening Jen and me from the shadows. I was done with that.

I popped the emergency brake and spun the car into a one-eighty, lining up to block the lane. I got out and sprinted for the side, sliding into a ditch.

I had a minute to curse myself for idiocy as I got ready. How many people can you get in an SUV? Five? Five armed men against me wouldn't be good odds. This was crazy—I'd gotten careless on the downside of an operation. Exactly the sort of mistake I'd trained people to avoid in Ops 4-10.

But there wasn't any time to change things; I could hear them coming.

By the time they arrived, I was a bit of dusty trash by the road, half-hidden in sand and obscured by the scrub. Not worth their attention, which was focused on the empty car in front of them.

They coasted to a halt and came out of the car cautiously.

Well, crap. Not Hoben, and not ZK either. Then who?

One piece of luck—there were only two of them. But the guy nearest me, from the passenger side, had a shorty shotgun. There were two problems with that. A guy with a shotgun thinks he's invulnerable and any hack can shoot one. They always say close only counts with grenades, but shotguns work like that too.

They crept clear of the cover of the SUV, and they'd soon realize there wasn't anyone hiding in my car. My instant camouflage wouldn't hold up if they looked around and the odds weren't going to get any better. The tension leaked out of me, and my muscles felt loose, ready. It was time.

I came up into a crouch with a two-handed grip on the HK, sand cascading from me like an extra in the Dune movie.

"Drop the weapons now," I yelled. I was twenty yards away. Anyone with any sense would have obeyed. Someone with training, who was desperate, might have tried rolling away to throw my aim off.

Mr. Shotgun just turned and lifted.

At twenty yards, I don't miss.

The driver was slower than his companion, but much smarter. He put his pistol down on the ground, his face slack with shock.

"Back up," I told him, and he stepped back quickly.

I checked Mr. Shotgun. His marque, a brassy scent, told me he was Athanate.

Not a vampire; they're Hollywood and myth. Athanate. The word means undying, but it doesn't mean they—we—can't be killed.

All Athanate have a faint scent and a subliminal presence, which other Athanate can detect and which together make up their marque. Each Athanate House has its distinctive marque. This guy's marque told me he was House Matlal.

Crap, now I had Matlal after me as well. I'd climbed onto his shit list when I'd busted the ZK drug smuggling operation, which was the distribution pipeline from his base in Mexico.

Mr. Shotgun's pulse told me he was still alive. If he'd been human, the .45 round might have killed him straight off. I couldn't feel any sympathy; he'd tried to shoot me first.

I picked up the driver's gun. Sig Sauer 9mm. Nice, compact pistol.

"Kneel," I said. "Hands behind your head."

He obeyed. Sweat glistened in his slicked black hair and his eyes were sharp, taking stock: his friend's body, the road, the HK. I liked that. It would piss me off to have to shoot him too, but he looked smart enough to know trying something wouldn't be healthy.

The shock came as I registered his marque. He wasn't House Matlal—in fact, I didn't recognize the marque at all.

First things first; I took a minute to check the SUV for more weapons. Nothing, but his cell lay on the dashboard. I pocketed it.

Now I wanted answers. I stood in front of the driver. Mr. Shotgun was dressed in a bad-guy dark business suit. The driver was in charcoal gray cargo pants and a rust-colored college sweatshirt, with wraparound, iridescent shades pushed back on his head. Chalk and cheese.

"Who are you working for? Matlal?" I asked.

His mouth opened, but no sound came out. I'd seen that before, people so scared their voice wouldn't work, but I'd thought he was better than that.

"Hoben?" I prompted him.

He nodded. His head dropped and his face twisted in frustration and…anger? What was that all about?

But I didn't have time to mess around here.

"Look at me." I waited till his head came back up, then I lifted the HK slowly and pointed it straight between his eyes. Any firearm pointed at you is frightening. The black hole of the muzzle looks deeper and darker and bigger the longer you look at it. The HK already looks like a freaking cannon. Up close and pointed at you, it's terrifying.

"Are there others up ahead?"

The HK helped him find his voice, even if it was strained. "Yeah, heading towards Parker," he said. Well, that was useful. I visualized the roads. There was a highway coming down to Parker, and then this road snaking through farmland. It would take maybe—

"They'll be here in ten," he said.

A man in fear for his life will tell you more than you ask for, trying to ingratiate himself. So will a smart man. But a really smart man, a really cool operator—he might lie.

"How many?"

"Two cars," he said. "Maybe eight guys."

Too many. So, not trying to lull me into a false sense of security. And I needed to be gone; I couldn't go up against that many people.

"Hoben there?"

"Yeah," he rasped.

Damn.

I tried to think of a way I could ambush him, but I simply didn't have enough time. It hurt, but I was going to have to give this one a miss.

"And what were you told to do? Kill me out here? Capture me?"

"Just follow you. Stop you from getting away. Hold you for Hoben if we had to. Not kill you."

Hoben would want to do it himself. In his twisted mind, every time I'd survived one of his attempts had humiliated him. He'd need to repay me in front of his friends, show them his power over me. It wouldn't be quick. Or painless.

But how come he had people loaned from Matlal to help him?

"And since when does scum like Hoben get his own Athanate to order around?" I asked.

His face twisted in anger again, and his mouth worked before he managed to speak. "We're watching him."

Well, I could believe that. Matlal would be holding Hoben liable for the loss of his drugs in the busted shipment. Things must be tense between them. There had to be an edge there for me to exploit.

But not right now.

This guy didn't seem to have any problems telling me things about Hoben, so it was worth at least one more question.

"Where do I find Hoben? Where's he hide out?"

"Moves around. All sorts of places. Different every day."

Shit. So close. I ground my teeth.

The comms unit in the car squawked, "What's happening, Garcia? Where the fuck are you now?"

Even distorted through the radio, I could recognize Hoben's hoarse voice. Time to go.

"I've got a message for Hoben," I said.

He looked apprehensive. He knew dead men are a strong message—the sort of message Hoben wouldn't think twice about sending.

"I'm coming for him." His eyes widened in doubt. "If he thinks that's not serious, tell him to go check the body bags at Nexus."

I went behind him and hauled him to his feet. There were some cable ties in the Caddy. Probably meant for me, but they'd do just as well for him.

"Wait," he said. He looked over at Mr. Shotgun, and shifted slightly so his back was to his partner. His voice dropped. "Please, take me with you. I want out, Farrell."

What?

I'd been in this position on missions before. I'd had conscripts beg me to keep them prisoner. But surely not this guy? I stood back so I could watch him and the road.

"Out of what, exactly?"

"I'm not House Matlal, for Christ's sake. I've gotta get out."

"Which House are you?"

"I can't say." His eyes bulged as if he was going to be sick. I inched forward with the gun. Sweat started running down his face.

I was having real trouble reading this. One minute, he was a smart operator; the next minute, a gibbering wreck.

"Try again."

"I. Can't. Say." He had to force the words out. His stomach was heaving.

Light bulb moment.

I'm no expert, but I knew just enough about Athanate mental abilities to suspect he meant it; he actually, physically, couldn't say, gun in his face or not.

I was stunned. A House allied somehow to Matlal, but its people so unwilling that Matlal was compelling them?

Could I trust this? And if he wanted out, how could I use that to get to Hoben?

"Matlal's screwed with your head?"

He didn't answer, but his expression told me I was right. I wondered what he could answer.

"Matlal's got you working for Hoben? You can talk about Hoben?"

"Yeah."

"Enough info to allow me to hunt him down?"

He looked more cautious. "Maybe."

I knew then I could nail the son of a bitch. I could work with hints that this guy didn't even realize would give me Hoben.

If he wasn't a real cute way of trapping me.

But taking him with me now was definitely out. It'd alert Hoben. It would be too much to say a plan was forming, but I had an idea. This guy was going to have to work for his way out.

"What's your name?"

"Larry," he said.

"Listen up, Larry. I'm not going to take you with me now. But if you can get away tomorrow evening, without anyone knowing, I'll pick you up. You think you can do that?"

"I think so," he rasped.

There was no time to plan anything fancy for lifting Larry. I needed somewhere open, where I could see anyone trying to sneak up. With people around. I didn't like the thought of others getting in the way, but probably my best defense was that Matlal and Hoben would be wary of getting bystanders involved as well—they couldn't afford the police attention.

"You know Cheesman Park, the one with the fancy pavilion?"

He nodded.

"I'll be there tomorrow, just as it's getting dark. Make sure you don't have anyone following you. I'll have the place staked out." I was lying through my teeth, but he didn't know that.

"I'll be there. I won't screw you around, Farrell."

"See that you don't. You give me Hoben, and I'll protect you."

I made him fasten one hand to the wheel with the cable ties, and I did the other. One eye on the road to Parker, I ripped the comms unit out and tossed it into the trunk of my car, along with their guns and his cell.

Then I smoked my tires and headed back down to I-25 and Denver.

I'd given Larry a tough job, and he'd need some luck.

Now a cool operator, a really, really good operator, an operator with ice in his veins instead of blood, might have come up with all of that to trap me. But that wasn't the thought that was bouncing around in my head—no, that was I'm going to nail that bastard Hoben tomorrow night.

Meanwhile, I was still dressed in the courier uniform disguise I'd used to get into the Nexus building, and now I looked like a hobo, with dust in my hair and clothes, blood splatters under the dust, and my face and hands a mess. And there was scratchy sand down my panties. Eww. I would hardly have noticed it back in Ops 4-10, let alone cared.

I'm getting soft.

Luckily, my gypsy lifestyle meant there was a change of clothes in the trunk. I really needed to find someplace to clean up before I did anything else. Anyplace would do. The hot shower would have to wait.

Chapter 2

I pulled into Park Meadows Mall and managed to sneak into the restrooms without being arrested for vagrancy.

With the worst of the mess cleaned off, changed into fresh underwear, jeans and T, I started to feel better. I leaned forward and checked my reflection in the restroom mirror. I'd brushed the dust out of my auburn hair as best I could. There were dozens of scratches on my face, caused by spalls and ricocheting fragments from the grenade exploding in the stairwell while I'd been rescuing the hostages.

The scratches were closed and healing already, because I was Athanate now, and we healed quickly. There were no other clues to that in the mirror. I had a runner's body because I ran. My face was unchanged. The too-sharp nose was the same one that had always told me I didn't have a best side. The bronze tone to the skin and the green eyes were unusual, but the result of mixed Irish and Arapaho genes rather than any peculiar side effects of my paranormal transformation. At some stage, as I became fully Athanate, there would be changes to my body. Not all something-for-nothing changes, but better returns for effort I put in. My body had already become more efficient. I was faster, stronger and fitter than I had been.

I felt a mild panic as I looked at my reflection.

I'm a freaking vampire.

No, Athanate. Not the mythical vampire that burned in the sun, but a living, breathing person. Just one with a need to drink human blood. I'd get the fangs for it, too, even if they would only manifest for drinking. I'd felt mine a couple of times, but I'd never seen them and I hadn't bitten anyone, yet. I was developing a phobia that they'd pop out and would stay there in plain sight, forcing me to go around with my hand in front of my mouth.

A woman came in and caught me inspecting my gums.

"Oh, my dear, you're so right to check them." She tripped across and laid a card on the surface next to me. A periodontist. My luck. "People can do all sorts of things with teeth, but if you lose your gums, that's it. Come see me for a free evaluation. If you need treatment, you can put it on your accident claim. Don't worry." She flapped her hand. "I've seen everything."

"Ma'am," I said, grinning, "you have no idea."

And I guessed my face did look as if I'd been in an accident. I took my bag of dusty clothes and went back out to the mall to buy a snack and a soft drink. No time for breakfast this morning, and nothing for dinner yesterday, if you didn't count the soup.

While I ate, I turned my cell back on. A bunch of messages from Tullah, my assistant. I felt a pang of guilt. She'd been waiting to hear I was okay. I wasn't used to having people worrying about me.

I gave her a call, but got her voicemail. Things must be busy at work. I told her to meet me at Washington Park. I'd lost Hoben's guys, but they might be watching the office as well as Jen's place, where we'd been working temporarily. Better to meet somewhere they wouldn't be looking for me, and where I'd be able to spot them if they followed her.

The next message was from Bian. This one I couldn't ignore.

Two weeks ago, I'd been fighting against becoming Athanate, and losing, even if I'd denied it. Then I'd met and been adopted by Altau, the Athanate House in Denver. They'd decided I warranted my own subsidiary House and allocated Bian to advise me on what that meant. But until I swore allegiance to House Altau at the formal Athanate Assembly this coming weekend, it wasn't a done deal. And until I got that protection, it was hunting season, with me as game.

Yeah, Altau were definitely my new best friends.

My world hadn't completely been turned on its head. I would still kill myself rather than become Basilikos Athanate like Matlal. One of the two major creeds of the Athanate, Basilikos regarded humans as food.

But the thought of being part of the Panethus Athanate, the alternative creed, wasn't so bad any more. Panethus worked to make their relationship beneficial to both humans and Athanate, and Altau were the leading House in Panethus.

There was a problem here; I didn't have any guarantee what type I'd end up as. I hadn't had enough time to find out very much about the Athanate at all, and nothing particularly about why there was a difference between Basilikos and Panethus. Athanate needed emotional sustenance as well as blood—why did Basilikos feed on fear and Panethus on love? What if I became Basilikos? Was it a gradual process that could happen without my realizing it? I'd seen enough to know your head can play games with you. I'd changed even over the last two weeks, and things felt different to me. How would I know if I was going in the wrong direction?

For that matter, what if I just went completely rogue?

The Athanate survived by controlling their instincts. Even Basilikos were careful not to attract the attention of the normal world. But the sensations were difficult to master. I hadn't experienced them yet, but I'd had plenty of warnings. Athanate, especially new Athanate, were liable to lose themselves in the pleasures, and if unchecked, quickly descended into insanity.

I couldn't face the thought I might become Basilikos. Or rogue. I shuddered. I had to pick up on that with Diana.

Diana was second in command to Skylur at House Altau, and I just felt she was slightly more approachable on this. I couldn't quite figure out where Bian came in the hierarchy. Possibly third. Diana and Skylur were scary as hell; Bian was different. And scary.

Enough daydreaming; I had to talk to her. That presented a Bian-shaped problem all its own. Our last conversation had ended with her leaning through the window of my car, licking her lips and showing fangs. I'd made a joke and she'd upped the ante. Like the best of running jokes, I was kinda nervous about my turn and unsure where the game ended and reality took over.

She answered on the second ring.

"Hello, Round-eye." She sounded as if she'd just woken, but I didn't know what to make of that. I had no idea what her hours were. She'd never failed to answer a call from me at any hour.

"Morning, Pussycat," I said. "Why am I picturing your spotted shoulders peeping out above silky white sheets?" She'd made some tattooist very happy when she commissioned him to turn her neck and shoulders into leopard skin.

"They're silky *black* sheets. Are you calling me for phone sex?" she purred. "Why not just come right on over instead?"

I should have known better than to try and tease her. "I'm calling because you left me a message asking me to."

"Oh, that. It was nothing, just a TV news item with some idiot leaping off a building and hitching a ride on a helicopter like a monkey dangling from a branch. It'll probably go viral on the net."

I winced. I was supposed to be a discreet PI; I didn't want my face all over the news or the net and Altau didn't either. The only good thing was that the press couldn't have been at the Nexus in time to film it; this would be someone's cell phone video, and the picture would be small and jerky. But Bian was head of security for Altau—it was her job to make sure the Athanate stayed under the radar. Which was no doubt why I was getting the sarcasm.

"Ah. Yes, that was me, on Jennifer Kingslund's case."

"Busy girl, Amber." There was a pause, and I expected her to warn me about the danger of drawing attention to the Athanate through my actions. Instead, she said, "Are you okay?"

Before I could stop it, the demon that sometimes takes over my throat said, "Why, Pussycat, I didn't know you cared."

She gave a snort. "I'm supposed to be educating you in your duties as House Farrell," she said. "Imagine the embarrassment if you went splat on the sidewalk during my watch."

This was the Bian I knew and—kind of—liked. "I'm battered and bruised but fine, thanks," I said.

That appeared to be the extent of her concern about security issues. Maybe she really *was* checking to make sure I was okay. Stranger things had happened. "You should stop by," she said. "We can use my special Vietnamese oils for treating bruises."

"Hmm. Yeah." I was pretty sure I knew where *that* would lead. "You may be more interested to hear what happened after."

Something about the way I said it alerted her and the banter disappeared. "What?"

"A couple of Matlal's crew tailed me, tried to capture me."

"Matlal? Why?" All trace of sleep was gone from her voice.

"I think the idea was to capture me for Hoben. It looks like Matlal's loaned some guys to Hoben, probably to make sure he doesn't go underground. Matlal figures Hoben owes him for the drug shipment that was busted."

"You said capture? You mean Hoben wants you alive?"

"Seems so, according to one of the guys. I doubt it would be for a long time."

"Huh. And these Matlal people, how did you get rid of the bodies?" She was all business now, the Altau head of security.

"Ah. I left them alive. Only one was House Matlal. I shot him when he turned a gun on me, but he was still alive when I left. I think the other guy was under some kind of compulsion, so I just tied him up. I wasn't sure what you'd want me to do."

"Uninvited Basilikos in our mantle?" she said. "Bring them to us securely if you can, otherwise kill them and call it in. It's really not helping us to leave them free."

Great. She sounded pissed that I'd let them go.

"That's pretty terminal," I said. "And how wide's that mantle?"

"Say fifty miles of the Capitol. But no one's going to argue about a couple of House Matlal, or their affiliates. They shouldn't be this side of the Rio Grande without special permission."

I'd bet there were more than a couple. If only one of the cars that Larry had mentioned had Matlal people in it, that would still mean a half-dozen of them in all. That was overkill for watching Hoben. What else was going on? If Larry made it to our meeting tomorrow evening, I was going to have to pump him for information.

I debated telling Bian about Larry, but decided to keep our meeting to myself for the moment. The Altau cared about Matlal, and possibly about me, though I wouldn't bet the farm on that. They weren't interested in Hoben—or, more important, in Jen's safety. That was my responsibility. Once I'd extracted the information I needed from Larry, I could turn him over to Bian if necessary. If he even showed up.

"All right, sorry," I said to Bian. "Also, it wasn't just a couple, I think. There were some others. They were trying to spring a trap, catch me between two groups."

"Two plus *some* others? Five? Ten? Fifty?" She muttered something in Athanate. From the tone, I probably didn't want to know what it was. "I know how well you take advice, Round-eye, but tackling unknown odds on your own is frigging dumb. You may be doing well so far, but you could come up against an older Athanate, and you wouldn't know it until it was too late." She made a frustrated sound, almost a growl. "Most times I'd say call a response team, but we haven't any to spare right now. I think you'd better come in to Haven."

Haven was the Altau's secret headquarters. It was a luxurious mansion on extensive grounds, with discreet guardhouses and surprises for any enemies who did manage to find it. Safe, but restrictive. Hiding out there wouldn't solve my Hoben problem, or protect Jen. I hoped this was a suggestion, and not an order.

"I can't go into hiding, Bian," I said. "I can't leave Hoben free while I'm mixed up in the Assembly. And it's not as if Matlal's going to give Hoben people just to chase me. Today's attack was the tail end of the Nexus thing—they were already in position, so Hoben just redeployed them."

"Have you got any leads on Hoben?"

"Hmm." We were back to Larry again. Holding out didn't feel right—I was supposed to be strengthening my alliance with Altau, not giving them reasons to distrust me. But until I was sure my interests wouldn't be subordinated to theirs, I needed to look out for myself. Altau would want to pump Larry for information about Matlal, and going by Bian's comments about being in their mantle without permission, it wouldn't end well for Larry. I don't work like that.

Luckily, Bian didn't sense that I was holding out. "Well," she said, "the next time you get a chance at Matlal's guys, take them out." She was quiet for a minute. "You know, you're not very bloodthirsty for a former special ops girl. It sounds like you were running risks today to keep the body count down."

I made a face, though of course she couldn't see that. "I'm a novice in the Athanate world. Not sure what's justified. And if I start, where do I stop?"

"It wasn't a criticism, Round-eye." She sighed.

Now I felt like a complete shit for holding out.

I gave her the Caddy's license plate and promised to get her any useful information from their cell phones before I signed off.

Bian was absolutely right about fighting Athanate. Those I had come across that day were young, which I thought meant less than twenty years as Athanate. I knew Diana and Skylur were much older, and probably Bian was too, and the thought of trying to fight any of them was frightening. They were too quick, too strong. I didn't know how many of the Athanate were older, or how many of those might be loaned to Hoben. But Matlal wouldn't leave many of them here at Hoben's command. All I'd have to do was get past one or two younger ones and I'd get my shot at Hoben.

I'd have to be careful, of course. And I had to do it before I got caught up in the Assembly. That made it a little harder, but I could handle that. Had to. Now, how?

While I kicked ideas around, I got back on I-25 and headed for Washington Park.

Chapter 3

I walked the circuit while waiting for Tullah.

I was worried that Hoben might already be watching Tullah. And seeing how I was going to have to take the same precautions for Cheesman Park tomorrow, I got myself back into the habits I'd been taught in Ops 4-10. Start by *not* looking at individuals. Look at groups, shapes of groups, movements and immobility. Get a sense of anyone acting outside of the pattern. Then fix on them, rate them 1 to 10 on threat level. Were they alone, in a group, of a type? What were they dressed for? Then take action or move on.

Despite doing all that, I spotted her easily, striding towards me with the sun gleaming on her straight, dark hair. I mix Arapaho and Irish, which can't be that common. Tullah Autplumes-Leung mixed Arapaho and Chinese, and I'd lay good odds that was vanishingly rare. It just worked, apart from the surname. It gave her a fresh-faced, exotic look to match her cheerful optimism. I'd met her at martial arts training, at the Liu Leung Wu Shu Kwan, which her father ran. I'd hired her as a part-time secretary while she finished her degree in criminal law at the university.

It turned out that was a setup. Tullah's mother, Mary Autplumes, was an Adept, a magic user, and she'd wanted Tullah to keep an eye on me. Adepts and Athanate had an edgy relationship at the best of times. Mary had seen I was becoming Athanate and yet, she'd also seen I had a spirit guide, like an Adept. She wanted to know how and why.

Hell, I wanted to know too.

In any event, Tullah hadn't been happy with Mary's deception. When I'd started to get suspicious about a bracelet gift from Mary that turned out to be magical, Tullah and I persuaded Mary that we needed to be open with each other. Frustratingly, it raised more questions than answers. Like what problems a spirit guide might cause with the Athanate.

And that was before we got onto the 'workings' that Mary said she could see in me—long-term magic that was so rare, she didn't even know if it was a blessing or a curse.

This was all yet another thing I hadn't discussed with Altau.

We'd left it that Tullah was going to continue working for me after she finished college. I was happy with that; she handled the bureaucracy far better than I did and her enthusiasm raised my spirits.

But that was a couple of weeks ago, when we thought that somehow I wouldn't end up as Athanate, or at least it was a long ways away. I couldn't predict what Mary would do, and I couldn't rely on it being to my benefit. Her agenda seemed very different from Altau's. Or even mine, maybe.

And what would Tullah do now? She was an Adept as well, and her mother had made it plain she should leave if I changed. And I felt I'd changed.

I wanted Tullah to stay. We were friends as well as colleagues. I would miss her badly, and I doubted I could keep my PI firm going without her, given everything else that I was having to deal with.

There was no sign of doubts about me in her easygoing smile as we met. She was obviously relieved that I wasn't more beat-up than I was. And she'd brought me coffee. She knew me too well.

I gave her a hug and relieved her of the coffee. "Walk a while," I said quietly.

She caught on, and we walked and watched as we spoke. I told her what I was doing and she said the man in the gabardine coat was a spy, of course. I grinned at that, but didn't let it distract me.

I also gave her a summary of what had happened earlier. When I got to the point of Tucker's death I wondered how that was going to go down with her. The circumstances could hardly have put Athanate in a worse light, but I wasn't going to hide the issue.

"He was bitten by an Athanate, his fiancée, Inez Vega Martine," I told her. "She told him he needed to die before he could become an Athanate. Complete bullshit, but he believed it. Vega Martine is House Matlal, and he just decided Tucker had become a liability."

"So he shot himself thinking he'd, like, resurrect as an Athanate," said Tullah.

"Yeah. Even if he hadn't, that bite started the crusis, the critical phase as the body changes. Altau spend months getting Aspirants physically ready to survive the crusis. Tucker wasn't ready and so he would have died anyway. He was already going insane from the effects. That's probably what destroyed his judgment."

Tullah grimaced and shuddered. But she didn't seem to take it as a mark against all Athanate, at least. "So that wraps up Jen's case?"

"No. Hoben's still out there, and he's worse than his father."

Tullah had been part of rescuing a girl from ZK last week, at risk to herself. The girl had been tortured and was about to be gang raped when we'd gotten her out. Tullah didn't need me to press the point.

I turned off the circuit to toss the coffee cup in the trash and took the opportunity to take a long look back the way we'd come. Schools were out and the park had gotten busier. It was harder to make out individuals in the crowd. No one suddenly changed their pattern of movement, or turned around as I watched. That didn't prove anything though, other than there were no amateurs trailing us.

"Tullah, have you ever trained with a gun?"

"What? No."

"Right, starting this week, you put in at least two sessions a week at a range. You can use my Walther, but we'll go find a suitable gun for you. And you'll need to register. And get a concealed weapon permit."

"Whoa, Amber. I—"

"This isn't negotiable, Tullah. You want to be a PI and work with me?"

"Uh, yeah. But this is something else that's not going to go down well with Ma. Adepts aren't supposed to have firearms."

"Well, she should have thought of that before she sent you to spy on me, shouldn't she?"

Tullah gave half a smile. "Will you tell her?"

"Oh no! Your mother, your job."

"Thanks a bunch." She put her hands to her head and squeezed her eyes tight shut in mock dismay.

"How is Mary feeling about everything now?"

Tullah looked away, grimacing. "I don't know, exactly. Not really happy about anything." She shrugged. "She did ask one thing. How did werewolves get involved in all this? If the Denver pack is allied with Matlal and his kind of Athanate, she's going to be really unhappy."

Part of Jen's case had been the disruption of construction at her new resort in the Rockies. I'd proved it was werewolves and gotten them to stand down.

"They're not allied with Matlal." I said. "They just got suckered in to do some work. Matlal knew Tucker needed some sabotage, so he drops into a conversation with Tucker that a longtime contractor of his company, Tucker Beacon, is a Were," I said. "Tucker persuades the guy to take the pack and party over at Jen's resort. Construction work stops and some of the pressure on Tucker's resort comes off, and his business benefits. But strictly a one-time thing. The pack's not going to get caught like that again."

I hope.

"Who's this contractor guy? Was he your contact in the werewolves? How did you get him to lay off disrupting Jen's resort?"

I tried to make my smile secret and knowing, but failed and ended up grinning crookedly. "Alex Deauville's his name. I met him at the charity ball."

Tullah's antennae twitched at the tone in my voice, and she peered at me. "How did you get him to lay off?" she repeated, suspiciously.

"Honey," I drawled, in my best Jen imitation, "I was trying my hardest to get him to lay on, first thing this morning."

Tullah's eyes went buggy. "As in..." She made some discreet little pumping gestures with her fists over her hips and I blushed. Doesn't matter that I have a natural bronze skin color, I still blush.

"Wow, I let you take a weekend off and you're humping werewolves," she said. "I'm going to need all week to catch up."

I laughed, but quickly sobered up. Imitating Jen and talking about Alex. Sigh. The Athanate changes were affecting my body and my mind. They were telling me that all that stuff about being straight didn't necessarily apply to Jen, irrespective of what was happening with Alex. And when and how was I going to discuss this with either of them?

"It's not just last weekend. I'm not going to be able to do much this week. I've got to nail Hoben."

And not get nailed first. There were too many people in the park now. I steered Tullah back towards the way she'd come in, scanning back over the milling crowds.

"Anyway, I can see you're aching to talk to me about our PI business," I said, nodding at the file she'd brought.

Tullah flicked it open.

"We've had a dozen inquiries from people at the charity ball." She looked up and grinned. "Some of them were for honest work."

I'd made a bit of a spectacle of myself at the ball and Tullah had designed some racy new business cards for me which I'd left on my table. Yeah, I could imagine some of the inquiries. She handed over a list of the real cases with scribbles next to the entries.

"I've picked out a couple of simple ones I can do. There's one which is more in the bodyguard line, and I've subcontracted Victor Gayle for that. There's a guy in place already."

Victor ran the largest of the small PI firms in Denver, specializing in security. He was a good friend and it was thanks to his skills flying a helicopter that I'd gotten the hostages and myself out of the Nexus. He also provided security for Jen.

Tullah was looking nervously at me. Last week she'd been a part-time secretary. She'd assumed more responsibility here than we'd discussed. I read through the list and nodded at her.

"Okay, I'm happy with those," I said slowly. "Normally, I'll make these decisions. If I'm not around, and you aren't completely sure you can handle it, yeah, subcontract to Victor."

"Understood." She nodded and pulled out an envelope. "This is a special delivery from the cops. Came in this morning."

I opened it and caught a small USB drive that fell out. A short note said it was a compilation of reports of attacks that mentioned dogs or wild animals. I'd made the case to Morales that werewolves and Athanate should be considered good citizens until proven otherwise. This report might show me how far I'd stuck my neck out on behalf of the Weres.

"Good." I pocketed the drive. "Any other cases?"

"Only one. The guy came through asking for you specifically. Quinn. Said he knows you."

I lifted an eyebrow and Tullah showed me the note she'd taken. The Quinns, Niall and Ruth, were old family friends. Tullah had taken down the address and written 'theft/insurance' next to the name.

We'd reached the edge of the park. My Ops 4-10 training and my instincts were in conflict. The training said this was becoming dangerous, we'd been too exposed too long. The instincts said I should be making more time for Tullah, make sure she was all right and safe.

"I'll call him tomorrow," I said, my attention distracted by color and movement back at the middle gate. Three clowns had come into the park. One was pushing a cart and banging a bass drum; the other two were running around, selling ice cream from the cart.

Classic setup. They were moving too fast. They'd sell more by standing still.

"Come on." I grabbed her elbow and hauled her out of the park and behind the nearest van.

"You got a thing about clowns?" she said.

"I've got a thing about noise and distraction in crowds," I replied. "Maybe just my paranoia, but you never know, one of these nights a clown may try and eat you."

"Eww. You know, you're freaky sometimes, boss. Surely Hoben's not going to be able to do much with ZK gone?"

"Just like he's still free, I doubt all of ZK have been caught. And anyway, he's borrowing people from Matlal, and that's even more worrying." I peered around the van. The clowns were moving in the other direction. False alarm, maybe. "Anything else?"

"Yeah. The FBI want to talk to you." Tullah passed over the last note in her file. "I don't want to be out of line here," she said hesitantly, "but it's probably better to talk to them while they're kinda not sure what they want to talk to you about."

"Hmm." I nodded gloomily.

I knew she was right, but I couldn't imagine any visit with the feds would be pleasant or short. I had a life hedged with secrets. All my time in Ops 4-10 was special access program levels of secret. And of course, I couldn't talk about the Athanate. Or Were. Or Adepts. They were bound to stumble across something I couldn't tell them. In the worst case scenario, they might decide they had sufficient to detain me for obstructing an investigation—while they 'cleared things up'. Or have me restrained under the mental health regulations. That was a big risk for me; I *had* to be free to go after Hoben and I *had* to be at the Athanate Assembly on Saturday.

"Is it okay?" she asked, joining me to look back at the park. "I didn't see anything suspicious."

"Yeah, probably nothing, this time," I said.

"I better get back. I have to leave early today."

She sounded concerned. I raised an eyebrow.

"Talk with Ma and Pa." She rolled her eyes. "Formal. Meet the boyfriend. Then, later, discuss the job. Review my progress as an Adept."

She was trying to laugh it off, and it wasn't quite working.

I retrieved the cell I'd taken at Castle Pines from my pocket.

"If you're seeing Matt, ask him to run his analyses on this cell, please. And warn him I'll want a couple of other little jobs." Matt was her new boyfriend, with the brain of an über-geek behind the face of an angel. He worked for the Kingslund Group.

"You cleared it with Jen?"

"I will."

"Okay." She walked off. I watched her get into her car, and no one followed or even appeared to notice her leaving. The groups of people I'd been worried about were still in the park, even the clowns. My paranoia wasn't always right, but just to be on the safe side, I never went to sleep with a clown in the room.

Tullah was a bit distracted today, whether that was because of her parents, or Matt, or the additional responsibility she'd taken on. I'd have to keep a close eye on that. She hadn't yet taken on any overtly dangerous work for the business, but it wasn't a safe job and it didn't pay to get distracted, working as a PI.

A bit of advice I should pay more attention to.

Chapter 4

I walked back to my car, still checking out the park.

I drove a couple of blocks and found a shady spot to park in a quiet street, behind my old school, South High. I spent a couple of minutes just looking at the buildings with a sense of nostalgia. Damn, I'd thought my life was complicated back then. How wrong could I be?

I hadn't been completely honest with Bian today, and now I'd done the same with Tullah. I wasn't feeling proud of myself. Telling Bian about Larry would have lost me my chance to get Hoben, I felt clear about that. Not telling Tullah I was now fully Athanate wasn't so clear.

What would happen when I did tell her? Mary had said she would have to leave; Adepts don't work with Athanate. I might have to close the business. What would I do then? I couldn't work for anyone else, certainly not until I was sure I had everything Athanate under control. Did that mean I'd have to go and beg a living from House Altau? Diana had said they would welcome me, but I'd never checked what that meant.

In truth, I wasn't even sure about whether I was fully Athanate. Would I feel suddenly different? Would there be a moment when I just knew?

And what about my spirit guide? I'd had a dream vision last night; my Arapaho great-grandmother, Speaks-to-Wolves, had appeared to me. What was it she'd said? '*You are none of the things they will think you are*'. And she introduced me to my wolf spirit guide, Hana, who she said would speak to me '*when your spirits balance*'.

Adepts had spirit guides, not Athanate.

Did that mean I would become Athanate *and* Adept? And welcome in both communities? Or neither?

I rubbed my face, tired and frustrated. An Athanate-Adept, believing dreams and talking to voices in her head. Paranoid and dating a werewolf. At that thought, finally, I had to chuckle. At least my life couldn't possibly get any weirder.

While I was sitting there in the car, I might as well run the blood test. I reached behind the seat and picked up the little unit.

The army hadn't believed in vampires until my team had been wiped out by them in the South American jungles and they got me back more dead than alive. I had healed in five days. My throat had been ripped open and a week later, you couldn't see it. Kinda hard for them to ignore that.

The army had kept it all top secret and put together a medical team called Obs to investigate me. My old commander from Ops 4-10, Colonel Laine, had been put in charge.

They'd kept me in isolation to start with, of course. But they'd developed a test machine to monitor the progress of the infection and when that told them I was stable, they'd let me out. The agreement I'd had to sign was that everything was secret: Ops 4-10, Obs, vampires, everything. If I leaked, I was back in that isolation cell. And if I infected anyone else, then both of us would be in isolation cells.

The unit I strapped on my arm measured the level of a type of prion, a protein string, in the body, that was a marker for what Obs still called vampiric infection. According to the colonel, an active vampire would have an index of 0.8, and I'd confirmed that on Diana when I'd run the test on her. I'd had a reading of 0.5 or so last week. I was guessing I was close to 0.8 now.

It didn't bother me as it would have done once, but still…

There was the eerie sensation of the microsensors finding my vein, the prick of the needle and then the hum of the unit as it went through its routine.

The readout started flashing at me.

Damn. The batteries were probably getting low. I didn't even know where they went in. I unstrapped it and turned it over. This wasn't a consumer product with a handy little battery compartment. I'd need a screwdriver to take the thing apart.

I turned it back right side up and looked more carefully at the flashing message.

"ANOM 0.38" was blinking, and next to it, in steady letters, ": 0.41."

I reset it. That's to say I switched it off, banged it on the steering wheel a couple of times and then started again. It came up with the same result. It had never done that before. It always came up with a reading like 0.45 or something like that, in solid letters.

Time to ask questions.

The colonel didn't answer his cell. That was the first time ever, and I sat there staring thoughtfully as the voicemail message came on for the second time.

I had one other number—for the Obs team at the main laboratory. I didn't want to talk to them, but those flashing numbers were making me nervous.

One of the scientists answered. I recognized his voice, but couldn't bring the name or face to mind.

"Hi, it's Amber Farrell, can I talk to you about the blood test readings please?" I said awkwardly. I probably wasn't supposed to have the test unit.

"Oh, yes, Ms. Farrell. It's time you came in and we did another full review."

"Fine," I lied. "When the colonel arranges it. But today, I just wanted to check a message I've got on the unit."

"Okay, but the messages are very simple. It should be obvious."

"So what does a flashing ANOM mean?"

"You can't have that reading. Look, you'll need to come in and we can do a full test of everything."

I rolled my eyes. This was worse than a computer support line.

"Just tell me what it means when there's a flashing ANOM on the readout."

I could hear him sigh. "The unit could be faulty. It's set up to read vampiric prions, and when it does it will give you the standard index reading between 0 and 1. Any other kind of prion, it'll flash up an anomalous reading." He stopped, and I could hear him change mental gears suddenly. "Hey, you sent us some werewolf stuff a couple of weeks ago, didn't you? You haven't just run the test on a werewolf? Oh my God, you have. Listen, you have to bring them in. This is so important."

My stomach twisted. Werewolf prions.

"Yeah," I said, pretending I wasn't concerned. "Tell Colonel Laine to call and arrange it." Over my dead body. I ended the call.

Shit. I sat there shivering and let it sink in.

This can't be happening to me.

Were and Athanate *can't* cross-infuse. Alex had told me that.

Oh, my God. Alex. What had we done?

I called him. Voicemail, and this wasn't the sort of thing you leave messages about.

Had he called me?

I flicked through my messages. He had. My stomach sank.

I'd run out on him this morning, responding to Jen's call for help. We'd been in mid-session, just about to get naked and horizontal. Our first ever time together, my first guy for more than a couple of years. Oh, and my first ever werewolf. We'd been steaming and he had to have been angry when I'd gone, however well he'd hidden it. Had I screwed this up before we even got started? Or was this a call to ask why he was suddenly getting a different type of fang?

I listened to his voicemail, carefully, a couple of times. He'd had to go out of town and would call me on his return. Probably tomorrow. There was something important that he wanted to explain to me as soon as possible. His voice had a warm edge when he said that and in spite of the turmoil I felt, I grinned as my body responded to his tone. Definitely not a 'thanks and I'll call you' message. No indication he'd had any Athanate-induced problems, either.

One of the reasons I'd avoided dating guys for the last couple of years was the danger of infusing them, as Athanate put it. I'd met Alex at a charity ball last week and the memory of it still set my pulse racing. He was tall, six-two or thereabouts, with broad shoulders and narrow hips. He had the right amount of swagger and he was hot as hell, even before I'd looked into his eyes. When I did that, I was lost. There was something wild behind those eyes that called to me.

It had pissed me off at the time, thinking that all I dared do was flirt with him. But that went right out the window when I found out the reason he looked so untamed. He was a werewolf, and, joy, I'd just been told Athanate and Were don't cross-infuse.

Maybe Athanate and Were *can* cross-infuse. Would I end up not just Athanate and Adept, but Were as well? Was Alex going to turn half Athanate? But there was no hint of that in his message.

But what if we hadn't cross-infused? That would mean I had Were prions for some other reason, before Alex and I started making out this morning.

I couldn't decide if that was even worse, because of the implications for David.

David was my friend, so close I thought of him as the brother I'd never had. I'd saved his life last night. He was an Aspirant, someone in the process of becoming Athanate. His transformation was being handled by House Altau, and was supposed to be a safe and controlled process, unlike mine. Altau had assigned David a Mentor, Pia, to guide him through the crusis.

But something had gone wrong and she'd practically drained him yesterday. When I'd found him, he'd been hypovolemic, his heart thrashing as it tried to pump too little blood around his body. He'd been minutes away from dying. With no time for anything else, I'd made him feed on me, and the Athanate organs in his throat had mainlined my blood into him.

I'd known those Athanate organs would be sending the agents of change back into me at the same time, accelerating the process of becoming Athanate in me. But when faced with a choice of avoiding becoming fully Athanate for a while more or saving David, he'd won, hands down.

Once he was out of danger, I'd paid the price. A change had swept through my body, and I'd stumbled away from his house, weak from blood loss but finally, I thought, Athanate. Alex had come and rescued me, wandering around in the park in the early hours of the morning.

So, if I'd had the Were prions *before* I went to David's? He'd mainlined a mixture of Athanate and Were.

We were already in trouble—he'd broken the confidentiality rules by talking to me while he was an Aspirant and I hadn't yet met House Altau, but I imagined that paled into insignificance if I'd gone and infused him with Were prions.

I'd freak out about myself some other time. I had to check on David now. His house was just the other side of Wash Park. I drove quickly.

I parked outside of his white A-frame house. His car hadn't moved since yesterday. One of the living room windows was open, but I couldn't see anyone moving around.

I ran up the path.

David opened it before I could even knock.

He looked much better than he had yesterday. He hadn't shaved and his thick black hair was still uncombed, but his eyes were clear. His color was good, too, even a bit flushed. I would have thought he was running a fever if he hadn't been Athanate.

He seemed agitated, his wiry body bouncing on his toes.

"You okay, David?"

He nodded jerkily and stood aside for me to come in.

Well, so much for 'thanks for saving my life'. Still, he was probably just embarrassed about it all.

I was wearing the bracelet that had been given to me by Tullah's mother. It was some kind of magic warning system, that tingled when someone close by didn't have my best interests at heart. It hadn't tingled for a while. I had a feeling that, in becoming tuned to me, it was only going to warn me when I wasn't perfectly well aware that there was some danger around.

It tingled now.

I froze and looked around.

"David, someone's here," I whispered. "Is the back door open or something?"

His eyes went to the kitchen door. It was closed; someone could have come in through the back door and be waiting in there while he was distracted by letting me in.

Shit, my gun was in the car. I couldn't go and get it now, but surprise would be almost as good as a gun. I crept towards the kitchen door. David picked up a baseball bat from a corner.

I could smell another Athanate scent in the house. I was expecting Matlal, but strangely it seemed to be more Altau, with a difference. It seemed familiar. Betrayal? Someone at House Altau? I crouched and put my hand quietly on the handle of the kitchen door, tensing up.

At that point, David hit me over the back of the head with the baseball bat.

Chapter 5

I came around feeling sore, uncomfortable and really pissed.

I knew just what had happened; there was no one else in the room when I was hit, no one else it could have been.

I tried to get up. No way. I'd been tied into the chair I was sitting in, very tightly, wrist and ankle. There was even a cord around my waist, holding me against the backrest. I wasn't going anywhere and I was completely defenseless.

Crap. What the hell was going on? Had David betrayed me? Were Matlal or Hoben on their way here? I couldn't believe that. Not David. Surely, not David? I'd trusted him completely.

I jerked the chair around to see if there was anything in reach I could use to free myself.

I wasn't alone.

A naked woman lay on the bed, also tied up. Her skin was Persian olive and a thick curtain of wavy hair flowed over the sheets like black ink spilled across a fresh page. She was Athanate and Altau, and I guessed this was Pia. We were both prisoners; this was looking worse every second.

At the sound of my struggles, her head jerked up. She glared at me.

"What the hell did you think you were doing, you stupid bitch?" she hissed.

"Me?" Oh, that stoked me up. The little demon that lives in my throat let rip. "I saved his life after you nearly bled him dry last night. What've you done to him? What's he doing?"

"What do you mean, what's he doing? Oh, give me strength." She banged her head on the bed in frustration. "He's going rogue. You think you can just bind someone and walk away?"

"I what? I didn't bind him. I saved his life. I gave him my Blood because he was dying. Because you walked away and left him to die."

That hit home. "I was coming back," she said. Her head lowered.

"Not anything like soon enough. And I went away because I *didn't* want to bind him. I'm smart enough to realize I don't understand what to do and how to do it. I'm smart enough to realize I'm in enough trouble with Altau."

"You're lying. You can't—"

She was cut off. David burst in, carrying suitcases that he threw onto the floor. He looked across at me and cringed.

"Amber, I'm sorry," he said, coming and kneeling down beside me. "I had to do it. We've got to get away, and I knew you wouldn't agree to start with. You'll understand when I explain. It's the only option."

"Untie me and explain right now, David." I struggled against the ropes, but he'd done a good job of it.

"While we're driving—"

"No. Right now. You're never going to get me into a car like this."

David knelt in front of me, his hands on my knees and his face pleading for understanding. "You've bound me—"

Oh shit.

"Get him to untie us, Farrell," Pia shouted.

David struck the bed with his fist. "You can't speak to her like that." His face, already flushed, became darker, and I saw that he was keeping control of himself with a tremendous effort. His eyes were glittering and his face was twisting in conflict. In contrast to his earlier flush, his face was going pale.

He was in the critical stage of his transformation to Athanate, the crusis. It had gone wrong. I'd messed it up somehow for him. He was going insane; becoming rogue.

"How? David!" His eyes slowly cleared and came back to me. "David, focus on me. Tell me how I bound you."

"Your Blood. Not just bound. I'm not House Altau anymore. I'm…I'm House Farrell."

What had I done? Athanate are territorial. Denver was House Altau's domain. I was accepted as a subsidiary House, but not if I went around stealing their Aspirants.

"You've bound me with your Blood, taken me from Altau," David said. "That's like treason, Amber. We've got to get away. All of us."

"Oh God! No, no, no." Pia squeezed her eyes shut and tried to hide her face in the sheets.

David's face spasmed with effort, then gradually became calm as he looked at her.

"Pia." He touched her shoulder gently. "You'll understand. You'll see."

She shuddered.

He opened the suitcases and began throwing things from his drawers into them. "We need to go tonight. They'll realize something's happened when she doesn't come back, and we need to be away from Denver by then."

"If he's bound to you, you can control him, Farrell!" Pia said. "Just make him untie us. There's nowhere we can go and he'll drive us rogue as well. We'll all end up crazy. They'll hunt us like rabid dogs. You've got to stop him."

"Don't worry, she'll be all right," David said dreamily, his actions becoming smoother, more relaxed. "We'll all be House Farrell together."

"Farrell!" shouted Pia.

I'd had enough. I needed to get through to David while there was still time. Every word from Pia was distracting him. She wasn't getting us anywhere and I knew instinctively that dreamy look on David's face was bad news. I was going to yell at her, but the old sergeant training took over and when it came, my voice was calm and distant, but authoritative. The sort of tone I'd had to learn to stop people in their tracks and make them listen.

"Shut up, Pia," I said simply.

Damn, and it still worked. Blessed quiet for the moment.

"David, listen to me." I waited until I had his attention. "No matter how far you take me away, I will come back. So let's skip the car trip and stay right where we are."

I spoke quietly, and he had to listen hard to hear me. His movements slowed and I could see his emotions fighting in him again. The dreamy look went away, replaced by a frown of concentration. That's what I wanted.

Think, David. Think it through.

"This isn't your fault, or Pia's, or mine," I said reasonably. "It's just something that has to be dealt with. There's no way I can run an Athanate House on my own, without help and support. I'm not going to try. We depend on Altau. I'm not going to use any compulsion on you. There's no need. You understand what I'm saying and if you think for a minute, you'll agree with it."

He stopped and began to twist the clothes he was holding in his hands, but his eyes lost a bit of the craziness.

"Am I right, bro?"

"Yes," he whispered. "It's just…" his voice faltered.

"It's just nothing," I said calmly. "We made some mistakes, but they weren't intentional. No one is to blame. You need help urgently. If they want to hurt you, they're going to have to go through me first. Untie us."

His face spasmed again for a second, his fists clenching, and my heart skipped a beat. But then the frown eased and he almost smiled. "Spoken like the Mistress of the House, sis." He dropped the clothes from his hands. "It's what I gave you the keys to my house for."

Relief flooded through me. If he was talking like that, he was in control.

He knelt and untied me. He was working slowly, as if making sure he stayed calm, so I matched him. I stood carefully and let him move to untie Pia. When he turned his back, I did cast my eye at the baseball bat he'd tossed on the floor, but I left it there. He was going to get a hell of a kicking next time we sparred, but I wanted him upright and functioning tonight.

I was worried Pia was going to upset him again, but being shut up seemed to have had a positive effect on her. Her clothes were scattered around the room, some of them rather tattered. I gathered them up and got her to dress, replacing her torn shirt with one of David's. It looked better on her than it did on him. She found a clip and unselfconsciously pinned her hair back into a dramatic, midnight waterfall.

I shepherded them out of the bedroom.

The cell in my hand and my heart in my mouth, I paused. I wasn't looking forward to this call. I wasn't even sure it was the right thing to do, despite what I'd said to David. My Blood going strange, not telling them about David, then binding him, and on top of it all, this was the week leading up to an Assembly hosted by Altau that was vital to the Athanate community as a whole. I couldn't have picked a worse time. But I had to do what was best for David, long term. I had to take care of him. I'd given my word. And…it felt like even more than that.

Damn. Couldn't it be easy for once? Or at least not hard.

I hit the speed dial.

"Bian, I have an emergency here."

"Oh, Amber." She sounded exasperated. "This is really not the time."

"I understand and I'm honestly sorry. I'm at David Thaler's house with Pia—"

"What the hell are you doing there?" Her voice was cold. "Do you have any idea—"

"Wait, I'll explain. Listen, Bian. He's had a setback. He needed blood last night, really urgently. I had to let him feed from me. But today he's…he's disturbed. I'm afraid without Diana or someone to treat him, he'll go rogue. I can bring us all in, but—"

"No! Shit! Stay there. You *stay* with him. Do *not* go out." I could hear her hold the cell away and issue a rapid set of instructions in Athanate to someone else before coming back to me. "Do *not* let him out of your sight. Keep it as calm as you can. Someone will come within the hour. Do *not* move from the house."

She couldn't slam the cell phone down, but the abrupt end to the call told me all I needed to know about how serious the situation was. For all of us.

Chapter 6

After about forty minutes, I heard cars stop outside and there was a heavy knocking on the door.

I looked through the window. There were three of them, caught in the porch light, a man facing the door and a man and a woman with their backs turned, all of them bulky with Kevlar vests over black uniforms, topped with coats. The one facing me I recognized from the group of four I'd met down in LoDo a couple of weeks back. I'd nicknamed him Fang 2. All of them were carrying the ugly, compact P90 guns, half-hidden beneath their coats. A prickle of nerves ran through me, an impulse to protect David and Pia.

I swallowed hard. The best way to protect David was to get him help, not stand here second-guessing myself.

I opened the door, partway. Fang 2 tried to surge past, lifting his gun. I refused to move, stopping him in his tracks, and the man behind him turned and raised his weapon. I held firm. If he forced the issue, this was going to get very bad, very quickly.

He didn't. "Please, House Farrell," he said politely. "Operational orders. We have to secure the building." He paused. "We have clearance for lethal force."

I swallowed hard, willing the knot in my gut to go away. I knew the drill from his side of it. I stared into his eyes, keenly aware of the P90 pointed at me and the position of the safety. They had a job to do, and they would do it. They couldn't let anything get in the way of that. A misstep now would be fatal.

Taking a deep breath, I stood aside to let them enter. The other man was Fang 4. He nodded at me respectfully as he passed inside. At least they were being polite.

The woman was Mykayla, looking sheepish. "Hello, Amber," she whispered, then turned on her heel so she had a view from the doorway down to a couple of cars that they had arrived in.

That shocked me. I recognized the type of security procedures they were running here, and to have Mykayla involved told me just how dangerously overstretched they were at House Altau.

I still felt Mykayla was another responsibility of mine. Maybe there was something in that old Chinese saying—save a man's life and he's your responsibility forever. I'd saved her from Tucker's gang last week. Did that mean I'd always feel responsible for her? I'd handed her over to Altau, which was what she wanted. But in that short time, she couldn't possibly have learned how to be part of this kind of team.

My sergeant's training instinct took over. "You're focusing on the cars, Mykayla. Your position here is to be visible to them and scan behind them. Watch the street." I managed a wry smile at myself, even though the sounds of the others moving through the house were making my skin crawl.

David's breathing was becoming labored and I went to stand by him. It seemed to help a little.

Fang 4 reappeared and turned the porch and hall lights off. The house was now in darkness. "Clear," he said into a comms unit before turning to the three of us. "In the living room, please." It wasn't a request. His P90 wasn't pointed at us, but it wasn't far away. We were under arrest, and it was too late for second thoughts.

I took Pia and David into the living room, where Fang 2 was closing the curtains.

Pia and I silently arranged ourselves on either side of David. Other than the panting, he'd been calm, but now he started to shiver and twitch again. His eyes went from staring to glazed and back again, over and over. I was worried about him. How long did we have before the slide into rogue was irreversible? I knew how the Athanate dealt with rogues; Bian's words had been—*a quick and humane death*. I needed to persuade them to help him quickly. Pia's arms went around him and I felt much better about her than I had earlier. We might never be friends, but once she'd stopped being the drama queen, she was all right.

Fang 2 finished closing the curtains and turned the lights on.

Diana swept in, taller than me and swift as nightfall, her long coat floating with her stride. She dropped her hood and nodded to the two Fangs. Her face was serene, framed in tumbling dark hair, and her huge eyes gave nothing away.

Skylur followed her in. Anyone would have difficulty picking him out of a group photo. His face was regular, even unremarkable. But up close, his eyes were a startling blue. And they were icy sharp with anger tonight.

Bian came in last, shedding her cloak to reveal she was dressed in her own silk version of the black combat uniform. A Japanese katana in a matte sheath made an incongruous addition by her side. Her eyes passed over me without expression.

I edged in front of the other two. "House Altau," I said formally to Skylur and bowed my head. My voice sounded loud in the silence. I wasn't sure I had the right protocol, but that was the least of my worries.

Skylur stood staring at me for ages. "House Farrell," he replied eventually.

I cleared my throat. Silence didn't seem like a good option. "Quite an arrival," I said. "I'm sorry to have caused a problem at this late stage before the Assembly."

"We are at war with Basilikos, Amber," Diana said. "Not yet declared, but begun. For the duration, any time Skylur and I move together from now on, we move like this. But yes, you have inconvenienced us, to say the least."

Skylur sat down, elbows on the armrests of the chair, and steepled his fingers. His face was pale and his eyes continued to burn with their icy brilliance.

"Am I to understand you allowed this Aspirant to drink your Blood?" he said, his finger stabbing at David.

"Yes, but—"

"After I put a ban in place," he interrupted. "At your specific request."

"Yes—"

"Sit down."

I opened my mouth to speak, but caught the slightest hint of warning from Diana. I shut up and we sat on the sofa, David between Pia and me. Diana sat in the other chair and Bian leaned against the wall. The Fangs slipped quietly out. They'd be taking positions in front and back of the house, to keep everyone out. Inside, we were in a cocoon; in our own, narrow place, where the concerns and rules of the comfortable world outside had no relevance to us. What governed the course of events in this room was the rule of the Athanate. I had almost no idea how it worked, but entirely too good an idea of how abruptly and finally the Athanate dealt with problems. I had no recourse to advisors, no chance of appeal and two other people depending on the outcome. And David depending on the speed of resolution. I had to focus on that, stop worrying about myself now and work on saving David first. Take it a step at a time.

Skylur didn't give me any chance to start.

"You should by now have realized that becoming Athanate does not just provide you with benefits, it comes with duties and responsibilities to the Athanate community. Our situation is such that these are not negotiable. There are the rules and you follow them or die. You are Athanate, in my mantle, under my absolute authority and it is my duty to the Athanate to ensure that you obey me." He paused. "Do you understand?"

His words were all the more powerful for being spoken quietly. Yes, I understood that the Athanate could only have survived this long by strictly enforcing their rules. And I understood that I had no free pass to behave as I wanted. Whether I wanted it or not, I was part of the community and had to follow the rules. Whatever they were.

"Yes, sir," I replied.

"I have tolerated your actions. Do you understand, I am responsible for you to the Athanate Assembly?"

"Yes, sir."

"You have found out the location of my House. It is within my authority to kill any Athanate not part of my House and not sworn to me who has that knowledge."

He paused again and waited. I nodded. I hadn't actively spied on Altau, it was simply that they had used my car to kidnap me for my first meeting with him, and the car had a modified GPS that I was able to use to trace where they had taken me. That would have been a good legal point in a court of law. This wasn't that kind of court, so I kept quiet.

"I am also within my authority to compel you to do things. Such as telling me where and when you were infused. I have held back from this."

I nodded again. Skylur had said he was respecting my prior agreements with the army which forbade me from revealing anything about what had happened. Another good legal point I wasn't going to raise at the moment.

Beside me, David's breathing was deeper and more ragged. That dreamy look came back to his face, and I saw Diana's eyes flick across and register it. But Skylur wasn't finished.

"Instead, I have given you leeway. Not insisted on an exchange of Blood. In fact, put a ban on your Blood. Elevated you to a House. All of which could be subject to question in the Assembly, as evidence that I have insufficient control of my mantle. Almost as if you'd been put up to this by Basilikos." He paused, as if giving me the opportunity to deny it, before going on. "And now I find you have an undeclared relationship with an Aspirant. Who has drunk your Blood in contravention of my ban." His eyes bored into me. "The penalty for which is death."

No!

"Please," I stuttered. "You don't understand."

"Then explain," he said.

"Can't you do something for David first? I'm worried he's—"

Skylur cut across me. "We're not going to expend the effort if we're then going to execute him for breaking the ban."

I felt the blood draining from my face. He would do it, too. I could see it in his expression. I had to get him to realize it wasn't David's fault. "When I came here last night," I hurried on and stumbled to a halt, realizing myself that the next part might contain an equally fatal ruling for Pia. But I had to do something and there was a certain death one way and an unknown the other. Diana's head tilted questioningly at my hesitation. I swallowed and resumed. "Last night, David was dying. He was hypovolemic, unconscious. He had so little blood in his system his heart was thrashing itself to death. This isn't his fault. I had to do something immediately. There wasn't time to get you and I thought an ambulance was out of the question. I made him bite me. I had to force him to bite me."

No one said anything. David's hoarse breathing was the only sound in the room. Out in the hallway, the floor creaked under the steps of one of the guards.

"Pia?" Bian said, disbelief edging her voice.

Pia's eyes were red and swiveling to and fro across all of us, pleading for understanding. She looked terrified and she said nothing. I must have got her into as much trouble as David.

"Pia?" Diana sat forward in her chair, a puzzled frown on her brow.

What was she doing? Was she too frightened to speak?

Diana crossed the floor and knelt in front of Pia. Her fingertips traced her brow.

"She's under a compulsion," Diana said. Pia nodded and looked at me. Diana reached across and stroked David's brow. His eyes were glazed, and he didn't seem to notice her touch.

"Is there no end to this?" Skylur said. "Now you're compelling members of my House. What are you trying to do? Start a rebellion in Denver?"

"No!" I said. "All I did was tell her to shut up. Surely—"

"Skylur," Diana interjected. She swung around to look at him, her face grave, and his eyes left me for a moment. "These are no longer members of your House," she said.

Skylur came to his feet abruptly. So did I, startled into movement.

He was staring at me as if he'd never really seen me before.

I couldn't get air in my lungs. I felt the cold fingers of his mental powers clamping on my head, sliding icy needles into my brain. Diana had taught me the basics of defending myself. I just needed the fuel for it. I reached into the reservoir of anger in my belly.

And stopped.

I couldn't fight him off. There was no point in resisting.

Was that me, or was that him making me think that? Think, dammit, think! My life depended on it.

I couldn't fight him, physically or mentally. That was me. I knew that. The other option was to submit and hope. I'd done some things wrong. It looked bad. From my feeling of protection towards David, I could barely imagine the strength of those feelings in Skylur, and he'd just found out that I'd stolen David from him.

And Pia? How the hell?

None of it intended. And Skylur wasn't just powerful, he was old, he had gathered wisdom and control. I hoped. Something wailed inside me—*no, no, no.*

I was only delaying them treating David. I braced my legs, which were threatening to collapse, closed my eyes and tilted my head back to offer my throat.

Oh, God, no, please don't.

Had I actually said that aloud? Tears were squeezing out and trailing down my cheeks.

Far away, a voice came. "Skylur."

There was a touch of his breath across my throat like flames, sending tremors down my whole body.

And the pressure in my mind eased off.

I lifted my head back up cautiously.

Skylur now stood a little apart. His face was closed, revealing nothing, but at least he'd backed off. I couldn't stop shivering. He'd been an inch from biting me.

"Skylur." Diana spoke again, stepping slightly in front of me. "David is getting critical."

He made a gesture.

What does that mean? What's his decision?

Diana swung around.

There was a sensation of twisting in my head, as if I'd been turned upside down. The urge to protect David flooded through me like an electric shock.

Without thinking, I blocked Diana's path. Sweat chilled my forehead and my mouth went dry. Like Skylur, Diana was faster and stronger than me. Not by a matter of degree, but overwhelmingly. She could paralyze me with a look. There was no way I could stop her from doing whatever she wanted, but my instincts drove me. I needed to protect David and Pia.

"He's *mine,*" I said, my voice strained and my heart in my mouth.

Diana looked as if I'd slapped her across the face. She came up on the balls of her feet. I sensed Pia leap to my side and Bian flowed off the wall like a dark wraith, the katana suddenly singing in the soft light.

Oh shit, this is it.

"Stop," Skylur said, his voice sharp. We froze.

"Bian," Diana said. The katana slid quietly back into its sheath. Bian resumed her nonchalant position against the wall as if nothing had happened. But she was frowning in concern. Pia stepped back. I took a shaky breath.

Diana half-turned to Skylur, a ghost of a smile crossing her face. "What was it you said to me about her needing training in the duties of a House?"

She rested her hand on my shoulder. "Amber, David needs me to help him now." She looked intently at me and her voice became harder. "If he's too far gone, then indeed, he is yours."

I nodded, my stomach sinking. She meant it would be my responsibility if he needed to be put down like a rabid animal.

She sat by David on the sofa, holding hands like a mismatched pair of first dates. David's trembling eased a little, his eyes half-focusing on her. Her gaze held him and then her hands glided up his arms, past his neck until they held his head. Moving sinuously, she came up on one knee, rising above him and pressing his head back. Pia jerked forward, but Bian was suddenly beside her, one hand holding her. Pia looked to me and I made myself stand still. I had to trust Diana. Pia looked to argue, but she stood back, angry and worried.

Diana dipped her head over David as if she were going to kiss him, but floated down alongside his neck. She sighed, loud in the silence, and her lips touched his neck. Immediately, David's rigid body began to collapse back on the sofa and she followed him down smoothly, fastened to his neck.

"Just pacifics," Bian said, so close to my ear that I jumped. "Agents that will relax him. It's all right."

It wasn't all right yet. David's eyes stared and he moaned and shifted, but Diana's fangs were buried in his throat. Her eyes closed, as if she were concentrating on sifting the flavors of a complex taste. Every twitch resonated through me. Had she started in time or would I have to kill David?

Then Diana raised her head from his neck and a little tremor passed through her. David remained slumped, his eyes closed now, blood oozing from the marks on his throat. She turned to look back at me, her movements slow and sensual, her eyes hooded.

"He will be all right," she said.

Relief coursed through me.

"Bian, he's flooded with envirics and Amber's Blood. Take over, while Amber and Pia explain to us just how this all happened."

Bian took Diana's place. With a practiced ease, she put the katana to one side and straddled David. She bent her face to his neck and he moaned as she bit. I blushed. I found it was intimate and arousing. Something I felt I had the potential to do, might want to do. Dammit, something as House Farrell I was supposed to be doing, instead of making everything worse at every step.

"Well?" Diana said as she and Skylur returned to their chairs. Skylur remained quiet, frowning in thought.

With the sofa occupied, I sat on a stool. Pia stood next to me, her face a mask of conflict. I could imagine some of the things going through her mind. No doubt she'd been content in the comfort of Altau, a powerful House, with the most powerful of Masters, feeling secure. Then somehow—*how?*—she'd become part of a House under an Athanate who didn't even know how to be Athanate. Who wasn't even conscious of taking her in. Not comfortable and definitely not secure. And yet she'd jumped to stand with me in a hopeless confrontation with Diana. Her instincts were directed to me. No wonder she was having difficulty.

A bit like me going from being human to Athanate. Suck it up, girl.

"Pia, sit by me, please," I said.

She folded stiffly, as if her joints needed oiling, kneeling at my side.

I unthinkingly raised my hand to rest it on her and stopped. Maybe later, when we'd all gotten used to it. If there was a later for us.

"Well?" repeated Diana.

Concentrate.

"I've known David since he became an Aspirant, long before I first met you. We've become close, like brother and sister. He talked to me about Athanate in general, without really giving anything away." I cleared my throat. "There didn't seem to be an appropriate time to tell you." It sounded pathetic to me.

"And you think this is an appropriate time?" Diana asked.

"No, of course not, but—"

"This is the worst time possible," she said. "Skylur has calls from the Warders on an hourly basis, all being held at the moment. When we get back, what should he say to them? He's lost control of his mantle?"

I couldn't answer that.

"Go on," Skylur said. He was back to steepling his fingers, but at least his face looked less angry now. If only I could figure out what he was thinking, I might take some reassurance from that. But I'm familiar with the military concept of expendable assets, of course, and that's what I suspected he regarded me as. In which case, he was simply pondering how best to get the maximum return from my sacrifice.

"I worked with David on his physical preparation, and on his telergy. It was while we were experimenting with that, projecting images, we had some mixed signals and, well, we ended up kissing." I blushed and Pia stirred. "That's all that happened, but David said that there was some transfer to him in the kiss. Some of my prions."

I paused to let them ask questions, but they were just watching me like a pair of cats around a mouse hole.

"I guess that changed his marque," I went on. "I understand it started to be more like me than House Altau. He and Pia fought over it. I don't know what happened exactly. When I came in last night, there wasn't any time. I just wanted him to survive. He seemed to recover okay, but I also felt that I had completed the change to Athanate. *Then* I really wanted to bite him, make him House Farrell. That's why I left."

I licked my lips nervously. "Today, he was manic. I had to talk him down. But he was still okay. He listened. I called you." I had to say something more. "I have no intention of setting up a House in opposition. I didn't mean for this to happen. I didn't realize what was happening."

"And now, what went wrong, Pia?" Diana gestured to me. "You'll need to release her, Amber."

Had I really compelled her that strongly? I was going to have to be so careful with this control. How did I turn it off?

"You can speak, Pia," I tried.

"Thank you M…" she stuttered to a halt. "Mistress," she finished in a whisper.

"You acknowledge her?" asked Skylur. Pia nodded, keeping her head down.

Before she could say any more, Bian raised her head from David's throat. She turned with an eerie, inhuman grace, her mouth wide in a snarl, bloodied fangs showing. Her eyes were glittering, and when she breathed out, it hissed in her throat. I could barely recognize her.

Diana was there in an instant, a hand on her shoulder. She'd moved so fast, it was as scary as Bian's transformation.

Bian shuddered at the touch, but her pupils gradually contracted and her eyes lost the glittering edge. Her fangs shrank, became normal canines again. She licked her lips and looked like Bian once more. Unnervingly, her eyes had never left me.

"Awesome, Round-eye," she whispered. "I said you were freaking tasty. Even second hand." Still moving with an oiled precision, she got off David and walked out of the living room like a cat. He lay slumped across the sofa, pale and unmoving.

"She's taken too much," I said.

Diana shook her head. "Bian's drunk deeply, but no, she's good. And it's just the first step."

Bian returned with Mykayla, leading her by the hand. I understood then what the next step would have to be. I would have gotten up, but again, Diana had anticipated me. I hadn't even seen her move and she was beside me, her hand gripping my shoulder like a vise.

"*Not* your responsibility," she said tightly.

I forced myself to keep still. She was right. I had done what I could for Mykayla. Her decisions were hers to make, and she was only going to do something that I'd done. She was trembling as she straddled David, but she wasn't behaving as if she were under duress. With shaking hands she stripped off her Kevlar vest and opened her shirt. Bian's hand rested on her back as she leaned forward and placed her throat against David's mouth. I could tell the exact moment he bit, the memory of the fangs making my neck twitch. Mykayla flinched, but stayed put. Bian knelt on the sofa and spoke softly in her ear.

"She's not ready—" I began.

"Hush, Amber. This is our work."

Fang 4 came in, listening to his comms and scribbling a note which he handed to Skylur.

"If we're finished with the floor show," Skylur said coldly, bringing us back. He folded the note into a pocket after a brief glance. "Pia, your side of it."

Pia tore her eyes away from David and sat straighter. "He wasn't doing well," she said. "He'd finished all the physical tests easily but we had problems with his telergy development. He couldn't sustain a connection, let alone compel someone. I couldn't seem to get through to him."

Pia took a minute. "Then his marque changed, just slightly, and suddenly he was handling connections as if there had never been a problem. I tried to fix it. It was like…wrestling a ghost. It got worse and worse. I felt I couldn't bring him in to Haven. I didn't want to add to everyone else's problems." She closed her eyes.

"Yesterday, he became manic. I could barely calm him. I tried to shock his body back." Tears leaked down her cheeks. "I went too far. I took too much. The hunger…" she was trembling and her mouth moved without speaking for a second. "I can't describe it. For a while, I was afraid I was going rogue. It was so difficult. I thought if I just went away and rested for a bit, I could come back and handle it." She buried her face in her hands, her voice muffled. "I was a good assistant, but I wasn't ready to move up to Mentor. I failed everyone, especially David. I'm so sorry."

There was a silence broken only by Mykayla's sighs.

"So." Skylur turned to me, angry again. "I might accept that you changed David's marque accidentally, but then you thought you'd keep Pia in line by taking her too?"

Before my mouth had time to fall open, Pia's head snapped up.

"No!" she yelped. "You thought…" She twisted to look at Mykayla. "Oh, God, no! She's not Aspirant?"

Everything seemed to lurch into motion at the same time. Pia leaped towards Mykayla. Bian came snarling out of her crouch to intercept her. I tried to get between them. Fang 4 turned and lifted his weapon. We all collided. Pia was ignoring Bian, trying to get past and as for me, I was very conscious of the fact that the cold metal ring pressing against my neck was the muzzle of Fang 4's P90, and a twitch of his finger would blow enough high velocity bullets through my neck to decapitate me.

"Stop!" Diana's voice lashed out, and we all came to an abrupt halt. "Everyone, take a step back."

She slipped in between us. "Pia. What's the matter?"

"David! That girl! The girl is not ready." Pia could barely speak for her urgency, pointing at Mykayla.

Bian was rapidly disentangling Mykayla from David's semi-conscious grasp. Diana turned and swooped low over both of them.

She stood back up and shook her head. "There's nothing, no agent of change. What are you talking about, Pia? David's barely started crusis, his bite can't be active yet."

"No, no! Listen to me. You think Amber bound me. She didn't. I know David's not supposed to have progressed yet, but you've got to believe me. His behavior today was late phase crusis mania and his bite *was* active. *He* bound me to House Farrell."

Chapter 7

No one moved for a long, breathless minute. For the first time that day, Skylur's face registered something other than anger—he was deeply shocked. So were Diana and Bian.

Diana bent her head over Mykayla again. After a while, she came upright and shook her head. "His bite definitely isn't active now. Maybe Bian lowered it below the key level just now." She frowned thoughtfully. "I'll grant you, he did seem like he was in late stage crusis mania. And for that matter, Amber shouldn't have even been able to change his marque in the first place."

"I don't understand," I said. "Are you saying I've passed through crusis?"

"I would have said that you were pre-crusis when we met last week. Your Blood acquires its strength during crusis, and that's what gives you the ability to change a human by bite." She gestured to David. "Or change a marque."

"But I didn't bite him."

"He drank deeply from you. After you had given him some preliminary agent of change in a kiss. Prions, if that's what you want to call them. That might achieve the same thing."

"But it felt like *he* changed *me*," I said. "Before he bit me I was almost struggling against becoming Athanate. By the time he was recovered, I...well, I can only tell you how it felt in my head, but it felt like I could bite him and make him House Farrell. That's when I ran away."

"A resonance between Bloods?" said Bian. She held Mykayla against her.

"No, I don't think so." Diana turned to Skylur. "You realize what this could mean?" Her face stayed calm, but her eyes were starting to gleam with excitement.

"If you're referring to another of Tolly's unverifiable assertions, yes." Skylur made a curt dismissive gesture. "I don't believe any of it."

Diana took pity on me. "Amber, David wasn't due to enter full crusis for at least two months. The fitter you are, the stronger your body's defenses, the longer you will hold it off and the better your chances in the end. That's why our Aspirants are prepared so thoroughly, and why we work up to the full dose of the agent of change. And then, once an Aspirant is in crusis, it might last for two more months. That's why the process is so slow, why we transform so few." She stared intently at me. "Your Blood appears to have reduced his crusis to a few days."

Days instead of months? How?

"This is impossible," Skylur said.

"But *if*. Do you see the importance?" Bian said to me. "The crusis is the choke point, the bottleneck. With such a long period and such uncertainty, a Mentor can only safely handle a few Athanate going through crusis and with the physical and mental training, the whole process takes a year or more. If your Blood truly makes crusis quicker and easier, imagine what that means to the Athanate as a whole."

"If it's easier, then those that fail the Aspirants' tests, those that become our kin instead, they now have a new chance," Diana said.

"But it's not easier. David's reaction—"

She puffed dismissively. "That was worse because we weren't here at the start. It would have been nothing."

"Enough!" Skylur got to his feet. "You're speculating wildly." He grew quiet. "And I understand why, Diana." He crossed to David and made his own inspection before turning back to us.

"Imagine if Basilikos heard so much as a rumor of this. They'd do anything to get hold of Amber and test this theory of yours."

I shivered at a fragmentary memory of the windowless cell in Obs, strapped down, unable to move. They'd been testing their theories too. I got a sudden, vivid recollection. There had been a voice one time. I couldn't see the speaker, but I'd heard him call me 'it', like I was a piece of meat on a slab. And Basilikos would be worse.

"No word of this outside." Skylur glared around at us.

I let a trickle of hope warm me. He'd let Diana save David, and he wouldn't do that just to kill him. They even seemed to accept Pia had made a genuine mistake. And now he seemed to be concerned for me and my wellbeing. At least all the shocks had displaced that cold fury. We might just get out of this in one piece.

There were, of course, a couple of other 'little' matters that hadn't been touched on yet. Maybe I'd get away with it tonight…

Diana came and stood in front of me and my heart sank.

"Amber?" Her voice was soft, slightly puzzled. Her hand slipped over my shoulder and gently pulled me towards her. I felt as if I was falling. She came to rest against my neck. The sigh of her breath rushing in was as loud as the frantic thudding of my heart.

Her head came back up almost immediately.

"What?" Skylur said, registering her shock. "What now?"

This wasn't good.

"Her marque has changed," Diana said.

"She's changed her own marque?" There was something in the way he said that. That was very bad.

"I don't think so," Diana said hurriedly. "But her marque has picked up something of the Were. Amber?"

I cleared my throat. "Everyone said it wasn't possible for Athanate and Were to cross-infuse."

Skylur came over, brusquely pushing my head back as he bent over my neck. I forced myself to stand still for his examination.

"How did you do this?" he asked. His voice was back to its icy worst again.

"I don't know. I don't understand anything about what's going on. I'm not trying to *do* anything." I tried to calm myself. "I met with Alex Deauville, the contact you gave me for the werewolves."

"And?"

"And nothing! A bit of kissing and cuddling. *You* didn't tell me it wasn't safe."

"One thing after another," Skylur snapped, returning to his seat. "Sit."

I went back to the stool, Diana to her chair. Bian perched on the edge of the sofa behind me.

"It should have been safe," Diana said. "Any ideas on how this infusion happened?"

"Yes," I said reluctantly. "A complete guess, but when I left David's, I was passing out from blood loss. Alex came and picked me up. Maybe it happened then, when I was weakened."

"Combination of circumstances?" Skylur looked at Diana.

She shrugged. "It can't be just that. In all the centuries, that must have happened before. I've never heard of it resulting in a mixture like this."

They fell silent, looking at each other.

"Why's it so important?" I asked. Was this some purity issue with them?

"You're full of puzzles and worries for us already," Diana said. "Have you really passed through crusis without help? If you did, how did you have such a low level of the Blood? How was your Blood able to change David's marque? What type of Athanate bit you?" She sighed. "Now, you're adding Were to the mix."

"Your reluctance to discuss how you were bitten leaves us guessing," Skylur said. "I'm not prepared to base the safety of House Altau on a guess, nor can I leave you free in my mantle."

Despite my best efforts, the demon got control of my voice. "You tell me why it's so goddamn important, and maybe I'll tell you what happened."

It went quiet. Skylur's eyes bored into me. "You forget yourself, House Farrell. It would be easy for me to get the answers I need from you. Biting you will not change *my* marque."

I felt a chill spread down through me. If he drank my Blood, his Athanate senses would untangle the puzzle of what made me different. But something in me really didn't want him to do that yet. Something that might be too fragile.

"And we may lose something," Diana cut in, seeming to pick the thought from my head. Skylur snorted and steepled his fingers in front of his face again, but didn't object as Diana went on. "It's important because Panethus and Basilikos are more than just creeds, Amber, they are behavior patterns as well. Humans debate nature versus nurture, and so do we."

More chills ran down my spine.

"Athanate tend to follow the behavior of those that infuse them," she said. "Panethus create Panethus. But someone freshly bitten by Basilikos and kept in a Panethus House would also tend to turn to Panethus behavior."

"But I don't know what type bit me, and I haven't been kept in any House."

"Exactly. All our knowledge says that the most likely outcome for that is rogue. You're not rogue. The second most likely outcome is Basilikos, simply because it's easier to fall into that pattern of behavior."

"So you're sitting there waiting for me to—"

"Amber." Diana's calm tone stopped me.

No one else said anything. There was a coldness in my chest that wasn't going to go away until this was settled, but there wasn't anything they could do for me right now. And they were waiting for me to break the agreements I had made about keeping Ops 4-10 secret.

Crap. And worse, I had a suspicion they weren't going to like the truth. But my links with Ops 4-10 were loosening. I couldn't ever go back to them. I wouldn't even get inside the gate without Obs grabbing me, and once they found out my Blood had changed again, I'd never get out. I'd spend the rest of my life in that cell.

This was another decision between a sure bad result and an uncertain one. I had to commit myself to the Athanate, and let go of my agreement with the army.

I took a breath and jumped.

"I was on a mission in South America when it happened, two years ago." I studied their expressions. They all had their poker faces on, but a tenseness that appeared around Bian's mouth told me that just South America was already bad news. "I don't know what they were. They weren't exactly wearing T-shirts with Basilikos printed on them. Matter of fact, they were dressed in nothing but loincloths. Both sides…" My voice came to a halt. My squad. Every one of them, except me, dead. I shook my head to clear it. "There was one of them left at the end and he got to me. Tore my throat open. Fed on me."

"What did you do?" said Diana.

"I cut his freaking head off," I snapped.

"Oh, my kinda gal," Bian said, and she reached over to squeeze my shoulder.

Fang 4 came back in and held a quiet conversation in Athanate with Skylur. Diana sat still, watching me. What was going on behind those dark eyes?

Skylur finished and turned his attention back to us.

"We don't have time to take this further now." He nodded to Diana. "We will proceed cautiously. South America makes it likely that it was Basilikos. That's one problem. And the infusion of Were is even worse."

What?

"We're not saying that Were are like Basilikos," Diana said to me, "but their pure instinctive behavior is much closer to Basilikos than Panethus. This is something that I will be responsible for investigating. We want you as part of us, Amber, but every part of us affects the whole. We cannot take poison into the association, if that is what you are."

She sat back. "We've all been on edge tonight. Some of that may be due to your marque. Not just the pheromones, the telergic element. We may be picking up subtle emanations of Were from you and reacting badly. We can't have *that* in Haven."

"We could isolate her," Skylur said, shortly.

"Not ideal," Diana said. "Better addressed after the Assembly."

Skylur grunted and sat silently for a minute, his eyes hooded, before he spoke again.

"My responsibility tonight is settling the immediate issue arising." He paused. "House Farrell, House Altau, attend."

I stiffened.

"I imposed a ban on House Farrell Blood, on House Altau and all subsidiaries. The penalty for breaking the ban is death."

Oh, shit!

Skylur waited.

A test. Please, he's just testing me.

I clenched my fists and made myself remain sitting. Our eyes met. Whether I swore allegiance to him or not, he was the Athanate Master in Denver. He had power of life and death over me and over my House. And the actions of my House and repercussions of them were my responsibility. He needed to know I acknowledged that. I'd made my choice for the Athanate. I gritted my teeth and dropped my eyes.

"However, as an Aspirant of House Altau, David Thaler was unaware of the ban on your Blood imposed on House Altau, and unconscious at the time he fed. The penalty of death is put aside."

Stop reacting.

I hadn't even considered the ban when it happened. I realized all over again I needed to understand more about the Athanate and until I did, I was a danger to myself and everyone around me.

Skylur went on, "House Altau acknowledges the Blood debt of David Thaler to House Farrell. House Altau also acknowledges and agrees to the change of marque for Pia Shirazi and David Thaler, from Altau to Farrell. House Farrell accepts responsibility for mentoring errors committed by Pia Shirazi, and for dealing with any outcome arising."

I could handle that. I would have to.

He wasn't finished. "As an allied House, Farrell is required to inform Altau of significant security issues, and the failure to inform Altau of Farrell's prior knowledge of an Aspirant falls under that. In recompense for this breach, the Blood debt is annulled, and House Farrell agrees to provide ten days' work, of an unspecified nature, to House Altau."

Ten days. Half a working month, free. I could handle that, too. I'd have to, somehow. But he still wasn't finished.

"Additionally, Shirazi and Thaler will be assigned back to Altau for a fortnight, barring exceptional circumstances. House Farrell will have access, but if in this time, their marque changes back, Farrell will acknowledge that change without dispute."

No, mine! I wanted to argue that, but I didn't dare.

"Is this agreed?" he pressed me.

I cleared my throat. "Yes, House Altau."

"So recorded," Diana said, and my heart missed a beat.

Skylur spoke to Diana. "The ban on House Farrell Blood remains in place and is extended explicitly to Aspirants as well." She nodded, and he continued. "We need to understand what's happened here before anyone else is involved. Amber's already scheduled to come in to get further briefings on Wednesday. That process needs to be increased as necessary."

Diana nodded. "I'll organize both and free up Bian. I'm not scheduled for anything essential until I leave."

Leave? I preferred Diana to Skylur, and I preferred Skylur when Diana was there to take the edge off him. I hoped she wasn't away long.

"If you find the urge to bite is becoming significant, you will need to be at Haven, Amber," Diana said, standing to go. "It is vital that we only progress on that under control. And on your Blood, swear, no more security problems." Diana smiled a little. "At least until after the Assembly, and then you can show us where we need to tighten up."

"On my Blood, I swear," I answered, the words ringing in my head.

Damn. What about Larry? What about Adepts? Will they be security problems? Can't talk about them now.

"Why not come to Haven now?" Diana asked. "Not in isolation, simply at one end of the house."

That might have been intended as an instruction, just politely put, but I shook my head. "I'll come in on Wednesday," I said. I needed time to let all this settle. I needed something outside of Altau and the Athanate that I could cling to and still be me. And I needed to nail Hoben.

Diana lifted David effortlessly from the sofa. "Then I'll see you on Wednesday." I nodded. "You realize, Amber, your House will have needs of you?"

"Blood? Yeah, I guess so." This was freaky. For all my casual reply, this set my stomach churning in confusion. On one level, I didn't want to need or share Blood, on another my body thrilled at the thought of it.

"Yes, but not just Blood. Leadership, amongst other things. House Farrell is not merely a title. You now have two more concerns."

I bowed my head. That much had been burned into me this evening.

Fang 4 killed all the lights, and Diana passed by me. Even in the dark, I saw her eyes looking at me, weighing me. I reached out to stroke David's brow and silently promised I would come get him soon.

"Mistress." Pia stood in front of me, her face betraying a war of emotion and instinct inside her. She slowly tilted her head, offering her neck in the Athanate way. I kissed her and let her kiss my neck back. It felt strange, a symbol of all the confused emotions we both had about this, and it was going to take a lot of getting used to.

Skylur paused to let Diana and Pia get to the car. Unlike Diana, his copper and cinnamon scent wasn't soothing, but uncompromising. His eyes gleamed at me in the darkness. "Our arrangement is your only viable solution," he said quietly. "And I am starting to have a problem with it. Every step on this path, there is a situation. This is not healthy. Fix it."

He swept out.

Bastard.

Bian was helping Mykayla, who was still dizzy. She brushed close to me, giving my hand a quick squeeze as she passed. Her eyes glared at Skylur's retreating back as he strode to the car.

I stood by the door in the darkened house for an age after they'd left, sagging against the doorframe, weak and reeling from the whole episode.

The house seemed incredibly empty without David and Pia.

Wednesday. The timeline to nail Hoben had become impossibly tight. I didn't even know where he was yet. Jen was at risk already, and I couldn't just let him run around free while I was caught up in the Assembly.

Meanwhile, the question they'd all been asking me, I was now asking myself. What the hell was I?

Chapter 8

I tidied up David's room, putting the bedclothes through the washing machine and tossing the ruined clothes in the trash. I showered and changed, taking the chance to put some of my clothes through the wash as well. Anything to keep moving and avoid thinking.

I had to stop eventually and none of it had gone away.

What did it all mean for me? How likely was I to end up rogue or Basilikos? What would happen to David and Pia if I did? If we were allowed to exchange blood, would they change again to match my marque, and become part Were themselves? Was anything that I was still holding out on, Larry or my spirit guide, going to turn into something significant and get me into even more trouble?

That twisting sensation in my head when I'd stood up to Diana to protect David—something had crystallized inside in that moment, down at the level of my bones, what I was and where I stood. The Athanate suddenly made sense. Last week they'd called me House Farrell, but it had been an empty, meaningless title. Now I felt the connections, like physical ties, to David and Pia, to Skylur and Diana; my House, my obligations. Not the details, but the important things were just *there*; I had acquired hard-wired Athanate instincts. And because of the Were taint in my Blood I might be outcast. I couldn't take Pia and David with me if that happened. I couldn't even get angry at Skylur. He was like a general when some brand-new lieutenant had just made a horrendous error. He'd support me, but not at the expense of the rest of his troops.

Wonderful. I'd achieved enough understanding about the Athanate to agree they might need to sacrifice me.

Sighing, I got out Top's letter and read it through again. Master Sergeant Gabriel Wells had died the week before. He'd been my touchstone, the person I'd felt I could share this sort of thing with, and this was his last letter and advice. It seemed eerily relevant to me now, especially on the personal side. And at least a hint of a way to take this forward came to me as I read and reread his words.

As well as his everyday advice—deal with what you can, when you can.

I was not going to get to sleep for a long time, so I got out my laptop and the police report on animal attacks that Tullah had given me and started to read it. I didn't try to analyze the report; it was just a quick pass through to start. I hoped the brain cells put in some overtime while I was doing other things.

I discounted the report of the wolves that spoke in Russian, and the one about the big green dog in the blue spaceship. I wasn't too sure about one that had a wolf sliding out from under a gravestone. Even with those aside, there were lots of things in the reports that concerned me.

I'd reached the end and was about to shut the computer down when something in the filing system caught my attention.

Most of the reports were simply electronic copies of documents on the Denver PD computer. A couple had been scanned in as images from write-ups that hadn't yet been entered into the system. I'd run across the lines on the image, making out one word in two and wondering how the people whose job it was ever managed to read these to type them in.

I came to a stop on a reference number in a stamp on the side.

What was it about the number? Something buried in my memory.

The reference numbers in Denver PD for external communications with government departments have two codes. The second code is like your checking account number—just whatever reference number the other party sets. I ignored that. The first code is like the routing code on your checks. It identifies the other party. Who was 55734? Something federal—all 55 codes were federal.

The reference code told me that someone in a federal department had requested copies of these files. And by the time the other sheets had been entered into the computer, that fact had been removed. Someone was looking into these kind of attacks, presumably over the whole country, and that someone didn't want people to know.

Maybe there was another scientific team like Obs, hidden in the depths of some federal department, looking for subjects to study. And with the sort of legal powers that meant the subjects just disappeared off the map and into the laboratories. Like I had done at Obs until the colonel got me out. I thought of Alex, strapped down in some windowless cell somewhere with no one to hear him scream. The image was so powerful, I felt sick. I had to find out what was behind this.

I carefully copied the reference code and shut the laptop down.

I cleared my clothes from the dryer. I was done here, just starting to wind down, and I really needed a good night's sleep. A glance at the clock made me reassess that to a good short sleep.

Where? I didn't want to stay at David's house, even though I was sure I would have been welcome to it. There was nothing wrong with the place, but it didn't feel right. It didn't attract me like Alex's or Jen's.

Alex was away, not that a good night's sleep was on the agenda there. That left Jen's.

When she'd walked into my office and hired me a couple of weeks ago, I was straight. Frustrated, because I'd been celibate for two years, unable to expose anyone to the risk of my Athanate prions, but straight. But over that two-week period, I'd changed. Diana had explained to me that, as an Athanate, I would need human blood from four or five people to sustain me. Panethus Athanate called their human partners *kin,* and the relationship was based on love. The fact that Jen was a woman was irrelevant to my Athanate instincts.

What came first, I thought, trying to be completely honest with myself. Was I attracted to her before I wanted to bite her? Had the Athanate need for kin come before my human feelings for her?

Neck and neck. So to speak.

It didn't make me as uncomfortable as it would have a few weeks ago, just…a little uncertain, and very lost.

Jen had made sure I was aware that she was attracted to me. Subtly, at first. I grinned, thinking back through the last couple of weeks. Far too subtle for me, but I'd gotten the idea eventually.

And none of which made the slightest difference to my attraction to Alex.

If I wanted Jen and Alex as kin and partners, did that prove I was Panethus and not Basilikos? Now that was an interesting thought.

Well, I wasn't going to be able to do anything with Jen until I could explain everything to her and let her make an informed decision. That couldn't happen till after the Assembly—I'd just sworn to not breach any security until then, and telling a human about the Athanate certainly fell into that category.

And Alex—where to start? Had I affected him as he'd affected me? If I had, what about his pack—were they going to react to him like Skylur had to me? What were they going to think of me? Damn—what was Skylur going to think of Alex? Could Were be Athanate kin?

And even if everything else was all right, I should really admit to Alex I was looking for kin before we took our relationship any further. That would be the right thing to do, of course. He might not want to be kin.

In the meantime, Jen was close, and in danger from Hoben, even with the security I had arranged. That's where I'd go. She'd made the offer of the luxurious guest suite at Manassah, *my* suite as she was calling it, and I'd take her up on that.

It was about 4:30 a.m. when I arrived at Manassah.

There was only one guard on the gate. I recognized him from the week before.

"Hi, Reynolds. Where are the rest?"

"Just me, ma'am. Ms. Kingslund decided the threat's reduced."

"Shit." I knew she didn't like the level of security I'd imposed, but it was too soon to ease off, and this was too much. "Look, situation's changed again. Can you get someone else out here tonight?"

"Oh, sure. They won't be happy being called at this time." He smiled evilly. "But work is work."

"Do it, please, on my authority. I'll deal with that in the morning. I'm inside now. Keep the gates locked and patrol the grounds. And double up the morning relief as well."

He nodded and let me through.

I drove in and parked by the steps up to the front door.

The house was in darkness, but the graceful Spanish arches welcomed me to the airy porch. In the shadows, her Cereus was blooming, filling the space with a scent of vanilla and apple. I paused with my hand on the door, inhaling the perfume, letting the feel of the place seep in and relax me. Lovely.

I went in quietly and moved through the house without turning on any lights.

Jen was sleeping on the sofa in the living room, half-hidden under a blanket. A laptop and a pile of company reports lay on the floor beside her. Embers smoldered gently in the fireplace, giving the whole room a warm glow. There were bottles of brandy and rum standing out on the sideboard, but the glasses were unused. One for me, one for her. She'd hoped I would show up.

I crept down to the guest suite. It had been laid out for me, with towels and robe. The bed was turned down. A couple of my shirts that must have been in the laundry when I left were hanging in the walk-in closet.

I changed into the bathrobe and carried the pillows and blanket from the bed to lay them on the second sofa next to Jen's. With my Athanate eyesight, I didn't need the lights on, of course, and I made no sound. She didn't stir, even when I knelt beside her.

The light from the embers gave her face a ruddy color, but it was easy to see how beautiful she was. The memory of a dream came to me, where I had watched her sleeping in her room. I hoped it was a dream. It was entirely too creepy to think I'd been sleepwalking in her bedroom.

It was very still.

Our hearts and breathing were in sync: the deep, slow rhythms of sleep. I could see the pulse in her throat, a soft drum calling me in the darkness. So warm, so peaceful. A stray feather of blonde hairs falling across her neck was stirred by my breath.

So damned close! I jerked back upright with a start.

And so much for my Athanate side being able to hypnotize her—just looking at her had mesmerized me. I'd been a finger's width from biting her neck. Or maybe kissing. My jaw didn't ache any more when I thought of biting. Instead, there was a feeling of sensual looseness, as if my whole jaw were relaxing. It was the same sensation I got in my muscles when I was about to start fighting.

Jen stirred in her sleep. I backed off soundlessly and curled up on the other sofa.

I'd have to be careful.

And once I told her and Alex, what then? Why would she want to be kin?

But it was too pleasant for those miserable thoughts. Slowly, they faded as I settled. I knew I'd made the right choice to come here tonight. As I drifted, the heightened sensations of the house soaked into me: our steady breathing and heartbeat, the muted tick of a clock in the hall, the soft whisper of wind against the windows, the fireplace's smoky scent and the occasional rustle of ash and ember.

It all tickled an old, fading memory, an elusive, bittersweet phantom of a feeling, until in a moment of surprised clarity as I fell asleep, I recognized it.

This felt like home.

Chapter 9

TUESDAY

So much for being a super-light sleeper; I woke to the smell of breakfast.

My stomach reminded me that I hadn't eaten last night. I followed the smells to the kitchen, where Jen was making omelets and the coffee was in the percolator. She stood at the oven, still in her bathrobe, surrounded by lakes of glossy granite countertops.

I hesitated, feeling uncertain. I'd sent a message by coming back to Manassah. Jen had every right to have expectations of me. She'd been clear with me that she wanted me. But I couldn't—*mustn't*—respond until she knew the whole story.

And I couldn't tell her yet. It felt like I was betraying her.

Her back was to me and I could see the tension in it. She'd heard me come in and she was wondering how I'd greet her. We had argued last weekend. I'd stormed out. We'd sort of made up outside the Nexus building.

I crossed the kitchen to stand next to her and gave her a one-armed hug, mainly on the practical consideration that she had her hands full with the skillet and spatula. I leaned over and kissed her cheek.

"Morning. That smells good," I said, by way of distraction. "What can I do?"

She relaxed a touch. "Set the table and pour the coffee, honey. We're good to go."

We ate in the kitchen, perched on stools at the breakfast table. Jen's cook, Carmen, normally ran the kitchen, but she had the day off.

Neither of us was quite sure how to patch things up and find our way back to the comfortable friendship of last week. I didn't dare do anything precipitate. I could feel myself acting stiffly and couldn't seem to fix it.

In the end, while we ate, Jen filled me in on the events after I had left yesterday. That felt like safer ground.

The Tucker Beacon company was in free fall. Jen's lawyers were talking to them about a fire sale of the best parts, using the terms of the merger pre-contract between the companies as a lever.

"Frank Hoben's still out there. He won't dare show his face to challenge your claims on his father's company, obviously. But you might want Victor's full security detail back in place," I suggested carefully.

Jen shook her head. "Hell, no. José says he'll be long gone. The whole ZK gang has come apart, and they'll all be running, every man for himself. One guy's more than I ever needed before."

"Jen, Hoben had a team watching the Nexus building. They followed me when I left. Whether Hoben's in Denver or not, he'll have someone around. Please. It's really not safe yet. At least three guys at any time. One here all the time and two with you."

Her pale blue eyes looked coolly at me over her coffee cup. I'd found out she had a temper, quick to blow, and just as quick to go. And she really hated the security.

"Two," she said flatly. "One here, one with me."

Then she lowered her head into her hands. "What the hell am I doing arguing with you? I should be thanking you. You saved my life twice and I get antsy because I don't like the intrusion on my damned privacy."

I reached over and squeezed her arm. "Hey. Two will do, at the moment."

Her hand rested on mine and I was looking at those blue eyes again.

"I'll be around most of this week, as well," I added. "If that's okay."

"Of course." She narrowed her eyes suddenly. "Actually, as you've just said, I need more security because of Hoben."

"Yeah?"

"Amber Farrell, I am hiring you to provide additional security for me personally, and," she waved a hand, "to conduct an investigation to bring Hoben to justice."

"You can't do that."

"Why not?"

"It's just an excuse—"

"No. You've proved you're the best person to protect me. I understand you can't be here all the time, but it's a sensible decision—"

"You're just doing it to—" I stopped. Pay me for being here? How could I say that? Jen was staring at me, anger clouding her face. And beneath that, pain. This was wrong on so many levels, but I couldn't deal with it all now.

"Temporarily," I conceded. "Review next week."

Along with everything else.

She hid her relief by dropping her head, but I felt it, and it made me feel better too.

"What on earth do you think of me?"

"I think you're scary," I said.

"Not the effect I was going for," she muttered.

"I like scary," said my demon before I could stop it. I coughed and quickly asked what else had gone on after I'd left.

She smiled a little and picked up her story.

As José had predicted to us, the FBI were all over this now.

Jen paused, trying as tactfully as possible to give me a chance to explain why the FBI wanted to talk to me.

I snorted. "I haven't done anything wrong, Jen. But when they start asking me questions, there are answers I can't give without clearance and it's going to get complicated. I need to keep out of their way, at least till next week."

And maybe I had to disappear until after the Assembly. That, I had to be free to attend.

Jen looked thoughtful. "Hell, talk to them now. If they arrest you just on a vague suspicion I can spring you in an hour and make it really difficult for them to try it again."

She and Tullah were right. Sooner was better. It felt strange when Jen went on and assumed that it would be up to her to get me out if I got pulled in. I didn't want that obligation on her, but I liked that she felt it. I grimaced. I was getting so convoluted.

Jen wanted to know more of course. Even with the flash of temper, I could see she was controlling her curiosity and hating it that I had so much I couldn't tell her, wondering why that might be. Her eyes looked almost bruised with the hurt behind them.

I got up to clear the plates and began washing.

"Oh! I nearly forgot," Jen said. "Your friend Campbell Carter—"

"I can think of plenty of names for him," I said shortly, drying my hands, "but I didn't have friend on my list." He was threatening me with an unfair lawsuit I really couldn't afford. Jen had persuaded me to let her lawyers handle the case. Another thing I owed her for.

"No, no, listen. He contacted me even before my lawyers got hold of him and asked me to get through to you and apologize. Quote—I've been a fool—end quote. Your missing payment, and half again as an apology, are in your bank today."

I sat down heavily on the stool with my mouth open while she laughed at me.

We were interrupted by the sound of the door opening.

My gun was sitting on the table in the living room. I was about to grab one of Carmen's shiny cooking knives when I heard Tullah's voice.

"Hi. Only me."

We were still officially using Jen's spare study as an office, so she was coming in for work. I let out a breath.

Jen and I wandered out with the coffee to chat.

Tullah was looking tense, and when she'd gone off yesterday, she'd been concerned.

"Just heard, Carter's folded and paid his bill," I said to cheer her up.

"That's great," she replied.

Hmmm.

We drifted into the living room and sat among the discarded blankets and pillows. It looked like the tail end of a sleepover. Tullah's eyes roamed the room, taking it in, probably wondering what on earth was going on.

You and me both, girl. I remembered the feeling of home as I'd fallen asleep last night.

Tullah sat very still, her head slightly bowed and her eyes flicking nervously to look at Jen and me. "Jen, could I stay here for a little while?"

"Of course," Jen said immediately. "What's happened?"

"I've left home. It's time I was independent."

"Whoa! What brought this on?" I asked. I'd thought something wasn't quite right, but this was sudden.

"Some of what we talked about yesterday. I don't want to go into it right now. It'll only be for a few days. I'll get myself a place."

"This is a bit abrupt, Tullah," I said.

"It's my decision," she said defensively.

"Okay, okay," I said. "But I'm going to have to talk to Mary and Liu at some stage. They're going to blame me for this."

"It's got nothing to do with you, Amber. Not directly."

"What does that mean?"

Tullah looked frustrated. "It's like we were talking about last week. At my age, you were already in the army, making your own decisions, running your life."

"But Mary might say the army was running my life back then. Look, I'm not going to argue. As you say, it's your decision."

Ever practical, Jen interrupted us. "Have you got clothes and so on in your car?"

When Tullah nodded, Jen got us organized, emptying both our cars. My rag-tail assortment of clothes went into the guest suite that Jen kept telling me was mine. Jen gave Tullah a lovely room on the other side of the house. There wasn't much of my stuff, so I helped Tullah carry hers in.

Tullah grabbed my arm when we were alone.

"Look, Amber, I'm sorry. I know this puts you on the spot with Ma." She hesitated. "I just wanted to say, I'll try not to get in the way, you know, between you and Jen."

"Hmm. Nothing to get in the way of, thanks." I was blushing.

"Yeah. Right," she said.

"Tullah, you know what I am, what I could do to Jen."

She nodded. "But you control that, don't you?"

"I haven't been taught anything. I don't really know what I can do or not. I've promised not to tell anyone about the Athanate at least until next week. I don't dare risk doing anything with Jen until I've told her. And when I tell her, you think she'll still want me around?"

Tullah smirked at that before going on. "What's the big deal with this week? Something to do with all those high-power Athanate in town that Ma was talking about?"

"I can't say anything else." I changed the subject. "What can you tell me about what's going on at home? It's not about me, is it?"

"It's not just you. It's lots of things."

"Like what? If you don't mind telling me."

"Like, I told Ma about my spirit guide."

Ouch. Traditional Adepts like Mary approved of the known spirit guides: bear, wolf, coyote, raven and so on. Tullah's half-Chinese heritage had manifested itself in a spirit guide that was *not* on the approved list. She'd shown me secretly last week. She had a freaking dragon as a spirit guide.

"How did that go?" I asked.

Tullah snorted. "What do you think? Ma had the entire cow. Sideways. Nearly put a lock on me again. And don't even start to talk about Matt."

I had to bite my lip. It wasn't funny for Tullah just now. Putting a lock on her would prevent her from using her Adept abilities. "I'm sure she'll come around," was all I could come up with. "And about me?"

"Hmm. Are you, y'know, drinking?" She made fangs next to her mouth with her fingers.

"No. Not yet anyway." Dreams, yes. I shivered.

"You've changed your attitude about becoming Athanate," Tullah said. "I can hear it in your voice."

"There's not much *becoming* left. Is this going to be a problem?" I asked. "I know Mary won't trust me anymore."

"It doesn't make any difference to me." Tullah shrugged and turned away slightly. "Just so you know, Ma and I aren't agreeing on a lot of stuff at the moment."

"I don't want to be the cause of trouble in your family," I said. Not least because both her parents scared me.

I tried to think of the practical things she might have overlooked. "What about college?"

"I can move to a modular program. I'll manage. Doesn't matter to me if it takes longer. I can work nights."

"Oh, that'll make Matt happy."

She whacked me on the shoulder, then gave herself a little shake. "I better get into the office and chase my cases."

I smiled. She was trying to look serious and professional, but I could remember the first time I said that. I grabbed her arm. "Feels good, huh? Say it again."

"I'm going to chase my cases." This time she laughed. She paused, looking at me a bit shyly. "I mean it about you being Athanate, Amber. I think it would be totally cool, and it changes nothing for me, whatever Ma says. And I sorta think my dragon likes it, y'know?"

"Thanks."

And what?

Perhaps I had to go talk to Mary and just check why dragons weren't on the approved list. Quietly.

We went back to the living room, and Tullah seemed happier to have gotten it off her chest.

"Jen, has Amber talked to you about Matt?" asked Tullah.

Thanks, Tullah.

"No." Jen looked at me inquiringly.

"Ah. Can I borrow Matt for a couple of jobs this week? Not whole days or anything."

"Of course," Jen said. "Be gentle with him, he's still scared of you. I'll call him. What should I say?"

"I need him to be a cyber-ninja," I said. "I'll email details in a minute."

She laughed and dialed him on her cell as she headed out to work.

I sat down and wrote an email for Matt. I needed him to give me an info-dump on Matlal and Hoben, then I needed him to do an analysis on the cells I'd taken from the ambush at Castle Pines. He'd done a similar job on some ZK cells last week and the police had found it was a mother lode.

After thinking it over, I added the reference code from the police reports, telling him all I wanted was confirmation of which federal department it was.

I ended the email with a warning to be a true ninja and leave no trace of his searches.

"What have you got going on today, Amber?" asked Tullah, as I got ready to leave.

"The Quinns, and I guess the FBI." I wanted to check on why the colonel hadn't responded to my calls and I needed to be at Cheesman Park in the evening to haul Larry in, which in turn needed preparation. I was itching to get going on Hoben, but Larry was my best route, and I'd have to wait until I had him.

So, even with all the things on my mind, it looked as if it was going to be a light day, getting back into the swing of things.

As if.

Chapter 10

Before going to the Quinns', I had an important job. I needed a place to stash Larry, assuming he could get away from Hoben and Matlal this evening. Having Hoben out on the street was making me twitchy, as if I was in crosshairs all the time. I needed to bring Hoben down, and for that I needed Larry's intel to be gold.

If he was on the level, I wanted somewhere safe for him, somewhere Hoben and Matlal wouldn't think to look, and one without an obvious connection to me. And if he wasn't, I didn't want him to have access to anyone I cared about. At this short notice, the list of possibilities came down to two.

The first option I looked at was Mykayla's apartment, just across the interstate from Yale station. She'd moved to Haven after the ZK attack, but the rent was likely paid up and it wouldn't occur to anybody to look for Larry there. I drove around the back of the two-story building, into the dirt parking lot. The rusted pickups were in exactly the same place, but the ZK motorcycles were all gone of course. There had been blood in the dirt when I'd finished, but that was gone too.

The door to the stairs was still broken. It screeched loudly as I pushed it open. I'd last seen the stairs and landing full of ZK bikers, trying to break into Mykayla's apartment and carry out the gang rape they'd threatened when she'd refused to tell them what little she knew about Bian and me. Tullah had barricaded the door and I'd arrived just in time.

The apartment door had been replaced. I guessed the landlord had been around, made the minimum repairs, and was probably trying to rent the place out. Mykayla certainly wasn't coming back. The place didn't feel right anyway; the neighbors were too close and there were limited ways in and out. I headed back out and drove to Aurora.

My next option was a real 'hide in plain sight'. The small house in Aurora had been owned by the truck driver that had headed up the ZK drug smuggling logistics, Guy Windler. He'd escaped when I'd busted the operation, but he'd died here when one of Matlal's lieutenants decided Windler knew too much and tidied up the loose ends. By ripping his chest open and tearing his heart out.

The place still had yellow police tape around it, but they'd finished with it a long time ago. It was risky, but it had more ways in and out than Mykayla's apartment, and no one immediately responsible for it. It'd probably not be looked at for six months or more, and Hoben wouldn't think to come here. And the neighbors weren't the curious kind, on this street.

It still stank of death, but Larry would just have to put up with that.

The Quinns lived on the fifth floor of an apartment building, a couple of blocks east of Cheesman Park. Niall Quinn had been a close friend of my dad, and for his sake, I'd help them any way I could.

I parked and looked up at the sage-colored building. It had a strange ridged front, like the corrugated panel of a shipping container. On the side, each apartment had a wide balcony with iron railings that made me think of prison bars.

I called the number and Niall answered. "Mr. Quinn, hi. It's Amber Farrell."

"Ah. Oh, yes. Hello, Amber."

"Is this a bad time? I'm just across the road, but I can come back."

He dithered. Clearly, this wasn't the best time, but he invited me up anyway and buzzed me through the entrance.

It was a shock to see how he had aged since I'd last seen him, at Dad's funeral. His pale hair had thinned to translucent wisps and his pink face was lined with worries. He had put on a sizeable belly as well, but worst of all was his movement. I remembered him as our softball coach, racing around the field, and now every step was careful, every motion slow and considered.

I refused a drink and managed to embarrass him by helping him into his seat in the living room. A couple of walking sticks rested against the wall nearby.

"Well, Mr. Quinn, how can I help?" I said, after we had the usual old family friend preliminaries out of the way.

"Niall, please," he replied, running a hand over his scalp. "I'm not sure you can. I'm sorry if it turns out I wasted your time. It's a bit of a long shot. I just couldn't think of anything else."

"Tell me about it, Niall. I don't charge for listening." I grinned at him, and was pleased to get an answering smile. At least his physical condition hadn't affected his outlook on life.

"Okay." He rubbed his hands up and down his thighs a couple of times. "About a month ago, we had a burglary."

I looked around the room. It did look a little bare, with no stereo or expensive ornaments. Had they been cleaned out?

He saw me looking and smiled a little. "Oh, we don't have much worth stealing. Them up there, on the top floor." He pointed at the ceiling. "They'd be worth stealing from. Not us."

"What was taken then?"

"Just an old medal and some jewelry," he said quietly.

"Oh my God! Not…"

He nodded and made a big thing out of retrieving a handkerchief from his pocket and blowing his nose loudly.

I'd seen the medal once. It wasn't just a medal any more than Arlington was just a cemetery. Niall's grandfather had earned a posthumous Medal of Honor in the appalling Marine assaults on the Bois de Belleau in the First World War. Niall's father had passed it to him just before he died of throat cancer. Unable to speak, his father had scrawled these words on a note which Niall kept with the medal: 'Keep it safe. This is all I knew of him'. Despite the pride, the medal wasn't displayed, and it was only because my dad had been so close to Niall that I'd had the chance to see it.

I sat there in complete shock. It wasn't a matter of value. It was the Medal of Honor. My first thought was—how could anyone care so little about what it represented as to steal it? But that was stupid. The world was all too full of people who didn't care.

Secondly, it was inscribed and it was illegal to sell it. But I guessed a certain type of collector might ignore that.

Worst of all, it must have been someone who knew of the medal. A friend of the family.

"I thought you might understand," Niall said after a while.

I sat up straighter. "What do you want me to do?" At first glance, this wasn't something straightforward that I could help with.

"There are two things," he said slowly, struggling back to his feet. He made his way over to a bureau where some letters were lying and picked up a couple of pages to hand them to me. "First off, the insurance company are bilking us on the damage." He waved at the doors to the balcony, which were obviously repaired but not yet painted. "And when I complained, they suggested they might not renew coverage."

I frowned. Surely, this was more Kath's line than mine. Whatever problems my younger sister and I had with each other at the moment, she surely wouldn't refuse to help the Quinns on a legal matter. She was a lawyer; this would be easy stuff for her. Then I scanned the letters and suddenly it all made sense.

The insurance company was claiming that the thief couldn't have gotten in by the balcony.

"You remember," I said, laughing despite the seriousness.

I opened the balcony doors and walked out. He joined me as I leaned over the railing and looked down.

"Easy. How do you want to do it? You could get an insurance assessor here, or you could film it."

He considered it. "I don't think they'd send someone. I'd rather just film you and send it to them."

"Okay, do you have a video camera?"

"I'll borrow one this afternoon, if that's okay." He raised an eyebrow at me.

"That's fine, Niall. And I'm not going to charge you for climbing up the side of your building."

I turned to go back in, but he caught my arm.

"Listen, spider-girl, I'm not having you do anything without payment. Just not. Get over it. Your minimum charge is an hour. I know. I asked your secretary."

"An hour's standard rate is a rip off for a couple of minutes climb. And Tullah's my…" Damn, I hadn't gotten around to giving her a title. "…apprentice." That sounded right. It had overtones of being given all the boring jobs.

"An hour. Take it or leave it."

I shrugged and punched him lightly on the shoulder. "I can't believe you remembered what I used to get up to when I was fourteen."

"If I hadn't, Cassie would've reminded me."

"Has she forgiven me?" I'd climbed the side of their house and left frogs in his daughter's bed. Well, she shouldn't have called me a toad. No matter how good a friend she was, she should have known the founder of the Urban Crazy Climbing Club was not a person to be messed with.

"What? Already? It's only been, oh, not even fifteen years."

"Sixteen," I said.

"Yeah. Sixteen. I guess you…" He trailed off. Fifteen years ago, Dad's illness meant the practical jokes and climbing and lots of stuff had just stopped. "Anyway, she said to give you her love, and she'll look you up the next time she comes back."

Yup, and I could expect some payback. She was as bad as me about practical jokes. After the frogs, she'd left anonymous messages for me—'revenge is a dish best eaten cold'—at every opportunity. She knew how to get inside a person's head, even at that age. I blame her for my paranoia.

It all stopped when Dad got sick, of course.

These days, she was a freaking shrink over in New York, like they needed another one there. She would be formidably scary now, if the dish was finally ready. I grinned to myself. It would be good to see her again and see how she was. It'd take more than frogs to put me off.

We went back inside. I looked at the insurance letter again and shook my head. They had really gone overboard on this. They were refusing to pay for the damage to the balcony doors, claiming it would have been impossible to get up to the balcony, which I was going to enjoy disproving. They practically implied that the Quinns had damaged their own doors. For what? Then they insisted that the front door must have been left open, and that constituted negligence, which put the whole claim in doubt.

The really bad news was that the medal wasn't even covered on the insurance, not that you could put a value on it.

"I'm very careful about the door when I do go out, which isn't often, these days." He settled himself back into his chair, and I perched on the arm of the sofa.

"Okay, one step at a time. We prove it's easy to get to your balcony from outside first. You said there were two things?"

I heard the sound of the front door, and got up. Niall's lips moved. I can lip-read and what he mouthed was short and Anglo-Saxon.

His wife, Ruth, bustled in and stopped dead. Her face went chalky pale.

"What's she doing here?" she demanded.

Whoa! Where was 'hello, Amber, we haven't seen you in years?'

"Amber's come here just to try and help with the insurance claim, Ruth," said Niall.

Her face went to the other extreme, red with anger. She struggled before she regained control. What on earth had happened?

"I am sorry, Amber, just barging in and not saying hello. This has been a very trying time for us, and thank you for the offer. I know you mean well, but what could you do that the police can't?"

"I haven't said I would do anything about investigating the crime, Mrs. Quinn," I said. "I've agreed to prove the insurance company got it wrong. You know, saying the burglar couldn't have gotten in from the balcony." I was going to ask again about the second thing Niall had mentioned, but he was making signs for me to shut up.

"But that's a waste of money we don't have," she said.

"I've said I would do it for free," I pointed out. I never was good at shutting up, and why had she gone so overboard when she'd seen me?

"Then you shouldn't waste your time on our behalf either, thank you, Amber. I think we'll manage to get the insurance company to allow our claim on our own."

"Ruth, you know they're not playing ball," said Niall. "They haven't answered the last letter, and the guy won't even speak to me on the phone."

She glared at him for not supporting her, but seemed to reluctantly concede the point. Better late than never, she remembered her manners and offered me coffee. I wanted to get away from here, but I couldn't refuse—it'd get back to Mom as rudeness on my part.

We sat in the kitchen around their table. Mrs. Quinn was one of those people who edge towards whatever it is they want to talk about. When she finished catching up on my mother and feeding me news of Cassie, I could almost hear her creeping up on the subject of Kath.

"We had such a good talk with Kathleen," she said finally. "We heard all about the engagement. Taylor Tyson sounds like a wonderful catch for her." Her eyes slid across to Niall, and they did that silent, longtime married couple communication.

Niall, who'd been sitting back and just listening, shifted forward in his seat and leaned on the table.

"Amber," he said, "we've known you so long. Y'know, when you came back from the army…well, when you came back, it felt like you'd never been away. If only Cassie had been here, we'd have had you come around for dinner."

Despite his quick recovery, I caught the stumble and made the connections in my head. Niall called Kath to get my number. Kath claimed I was never in the army.

My service record in Ops 4-10 was sealed and not even the army pay division had access to it. When I left, Ops 4-10 paid me a retainer, but rather than set it up properly, they'd disguised it as a veteran's disability compensation. A pen-pushing bureaucrat called Lieutenant Krantz had got on my case, certain I was going to lead him to a huge fraud running in the army. When Colonel Laine had hauled him off, he'd tried to get his revenge by telling Kath I couldn't have been in the army because he couldn't see any records for me. That had set off an avalanche of mistaken assumptions in my sister's mind.

"With you and Cassie so close, we feel you're like a daughter to us, Amber," said Mrs. Quinn. "You do feel you could tell us if you were in trouble, don't you?"

What else had Kath told them? In her last drunken rant, she'd accused me of being a whore and a drug addict as well as lying about being in the army.

"It's not that we think you're in trouble," said Niall quickly, shooting looks at his wife. "But..." he paused and ran a hand over his forehead. "Look, your mom always made a big thing about you. Kathleen's always felt she was being measured against you. You understand that, don't you?"

I nodded. Even the demon in my throat had shut up. This was like watching a car crash happening in slow motion and not being able to stop it.

"And now she's such a successful lawyer, doing well in her firm."

"I'm doing fine too, thanks," I managed to say. A little stretch of the truth.

"Of course you are," said Mrs. Quinn. "It's just that it's not quite the same thing."

I would rather have my job than Kath's, but I was never going to persuade the Quinns of that. They had an old-fashioned opinion of what was an acceptable job for a woman. Lawyer was daringly advanced for them. There was a good reason Cassie had chosen to be a psychiatrist in New York rather than Denver. PI came down somewhere with sweeping streets.

"You don't resent her success, do you?" said Niall.

"No! I'm happy she's doing well. I'm happy she's engaged. I—"

"It's just that she said you caused a bit of a problem for her with your behavior at the charity ball last week. With the partners in her firm," interrupted Mrs. Quinn.

"The problem was that she hadn't bothered mentioning she had a sister until I showed up," I pointed out. "That kinda drew attention to me."

"Yes, that was clearly a mistake on her part," Niall said.

"But that wasn't really it, was it, Amber?" Mrs. Quinn wasn't going to let this go. I could see Niall thought Kath resented me and was blowing things out of proportion. Equally, Mrs. Quinn thought there was something in it. It was all a matter of what Kath had actually said to them.

"She told you she was being evaluated for a partnership?" Mrs. Quinn asked.

I nodded.

"And she asked you to be discreet. But I understand you danced with all the international delegation—"

"It was a ball, Ruth," Niall said, holding his hands up as if to slow her down.

Mrs. Quinn stopped, but there was more of the meaningful, silent communication between them.

"Look, Amber," Niall said. "It wasn't really about dancing with the delegates. And there was probably a good reason for the other things Kathleen said. But you must know the partners in that firm of hers are…very traditional. " He licked his lips nervously. "We understand a business like yours takes a long while to get going, and things might be a bit tough for you now. I can really understand how dazzling it must be when someone that rich pays attention to you."

It took a second or two to register. It was almost funny. During the course of the charity ball, I had danced with a whole string of vampires, including Luc Matlal. And I'd danced an enjoyable waltz with a werewolf, Alex. I'd saved Jen from Tucker's attempted assassination as we left.

But the thing that Kath and her firms' partners had noticed was that I'd enjoyed dancing with Jen, too obviously for their conservative tastes.

Before I could say anything, Mrs. Quinn cut in again. "Obviously, we don't know her, but the things you hear about the way these wealthy people live…"

"Drugs, orgies, that sort of thing?" I took my jacket off. "Kath probably said she could see I was taking drugs. Have a look." I stretched my arms out over the table. I was right, they tried to look for needle scars without actually appearing as if they were. "As for Jennifer Kingslund, she hired me as a PI and security consultant, and yeah, we've become friends. Why that should be of any concern to Kath or the partners at her firm, I have no idea."

My cell just had to beep right then and I pulled it out to glance at the caller ID. Oh, gods. Alex. What great timing.

"Look," I said, getting up. "I appreciate that you're concerned for me, and clearly, I've got to talk some sense into Kath, but I've got to go now. It's been great seeing you again. I'll be back here at four this afternoon, Niall."

I tried to appear as calm as possible, but as I trotted down the stairs, I was seething. What the hell did she think she was doing, talking to the Quinns like that? Niall apparently didn't believe it all, but Ruth was another matter. I hoped I'd done enough to prevent Ruth from calling Mom and upsetting her on her vacation.

Kath had overstepped the boundary this time, and I was going to have to tell her that in plain terms. If she couldn't handle that, my sister and I had a problem.

But there was something else back there with the Quinns. The Mrs. Quinn I'd known wouldn't have been so shocked to start with, regardless of what she'd heard about me. The thing that seemed to set her off was the thought that I was investigating the theft of the medal. Her first reaction had been alarm and dismay.

I was very, very interested in the second thing Niall wanted to talk to me about.

Meanwhile, I had a man to call back. A werewolf, to be more precise.

"Alex?"

"Amber, are you around?"

"I can be there in five. Thank God you called. We need—I need to—"

"Door's open for the right person," he interrupted me.

"Oh, it's a magic door, is it?" I said, thrown off my train of thought and warming to his tease. I tossed my jacket into the back and got in the car. "How does it work?"

"Smoke, mirrors and the flexor, extensor and brachioradialis in the forearm and various adductor muscles in the shoulder and upper arm. Mainly."

"God, clinicians are the pits," I groaned.

"Ex-clinicians," he corrected me. "Yeah, but we really understand how bodies work. See you in five." He ended the call.

I wondered if I could make it in three. My body had some understanding it urgently wanted him to do. After I'd cleared up a couple of things, my conscience said. He might not want to do anything for me after he heard what I had to say.

Chapter 11

There was no sign of smoke or mirrors when the door opened. Alex was wearing nothing but shorts and he looked hot enough that there should have been smoke. I checked out his flexor, extensor and adductor muscles, mainly by feeling his arms closing around me as the door slammed shut.

I'm no waif, but I felt insubstantial against his body. I slid my hands over his back, enjoying the feel of his strong muscles under my hands as I hugged him tightly to me. There's nothing so precious as something you might lose. Oh God, what would he say when I started talking about cross-infusion? My head fell back and his mouth closed on mine. I'd let myself have just this one kiss, then I'd have to tell him everything.

His lips were insistent and demanding. I trembled at the depth of response he stirred in me. My legs went way wobbly, but that was fine, he didn't seem about to let me go any time now. My hands continued discovering him, kneading his shoulders, caressing his neck. He was like a living sculpture, so damned beautiful, and the scent of wolf and lust came off his skin like a fine wine.

I had to stop now or I wouldn't be able to. I broke the kiss.

"Wait, Alex." My heart was racing, and it was difficult to get enough breath in my lungs to speak. "We have to talk." My voice came out croaky. I put my hand on his chest to push him away, felt the thunder of his heart beneath my palm and all my remaining strength drained from me.

"Hmm. Yes," he said. He kissed my neck. "Talk is good." The way he said talk meant something else entirely.

"No, really talk—"

I squawked in alarm as he grabbed my butt and lifted. He threw me over his shoulder and walked back into the hall and up the stairs. Of course I struggled. Carefully. He might have dropped me, after all.

"Alex, no! The living room. We need—"

"Uh-huh." He turned sharply down the corridor to the bedrooms, making me clutch at him. The sensuous, rhythmic play of his back muscles under my hands drove me crazy, lighting up fabulously erotic images behind my eyes.

"Put me down," I yelled, and he obeyed, slinging me onto his bed. A part of my mind noted it was a very solid bed, very well made. No distracting rattles or shakes. That was a good thing, because he leaped onto the bed after me.

I glared at him. Just because I had enjoyed it didn't mean I should let him get away with it. What kind of a girl did he think I was?

"Is this what you think—"

He kissed me again, gently this time, as his hands tugged my T-shirt from my jeans. I'd shredded his shirt, the last time we'd made love. More accurately, the last time we'd been about to make love. Was it only yesterday morning? He was more in control than I had been and my shirt survived.

We had to break the kiss to get the shirt over my head. The sports bra went with it.

I had to stop this.

"Alex—"

I gasped. His lips trailed down my neck and my traitorous body arched.

No, no, no. It wasn't fair to him. I had to warn him.

The rest of me had other ideas. My nipples were hard beneath his kiss, almost painfully sensitive to the touch of his tongue. I reached up and sank my fingers into his silky hair, gripping it and pulling his head down against me. All my good intentions were evaporating like water in the desert.

"Oh, save me," I breathed, my words and actions running away from each other.

To hell with fair.

All the crap I'd been through, all the stress of becoming Athanate and now Were as well, the gut-wrenching fear of losing David and Pia, the fraying of family bonds that kept me centered as a human, they'd all built into a thunderhead that burst out and scoured every hesitation right out of my head.

Our hands fumbled and hindered each other as buttons popped and zippers rasped open. His hand was down the back of my jeans, almost levering them off me, and suddenly slow, deliberate, playful. I groaned. His hand slid along the flesh of my butt, down my thigh, prolonging the contact, making it absurdly sensuous. He tossed my jeans off the bed and poised over me, fists sunk into the mattress on either side of my neck, trapping me, damn alpha wolf posturing.

I twisted, catching him by surprise and shoving him back onto the bed. I rested one hand on his chest, my fingers flexing and sinking my nails into his pecs, but not pushing him down. Dominance is not all about strength, wolf. I tore his shorts off and threw them away.

Oh my!

I placed both hands on his chest, very deliberately, slowly. We were panting, watching each other, enjoying the play.

Mine!

He surged up and grappled me onto my back, looming over me.

His body was tense as a mooring cable, tremors running through it. The look of desire in his face made my whole body sing, and an aching need pooled in my breasts and belly and spread down into my groin. I wanted to keep that look, I wanted to hold it in my hands, I wanted to be able to feel it forever.

His eyes held mine as his head lowered over my breasts. It was just a kiss. A kiss. His lips on my nipple. His flesh against mine. I gasped at the sensations. My eyes shut, all the better to feel him, as he traced a lazy path of lust down my quivering stomach.

In moments, I had no thought of anything else. He shouldered my thighs apart and I clutched him as his serpent tongue whispered wickedly against my trembling body.

I gripped his hair and pulled him back, reaching down for him.

His eyes were all wolf now. Golden, scary, wild, as I guided him inside.

I moaned as he filled me and we began to move, matching each other, rocking together in a haze of delight. I held onto him desperately, my arms and legs wrapping around his sweat-slicked body as I abandoned myself to the soaring sensations, burying my face against his neck.

His neck. The dark thrill seared through me like sheet lightning. His blood, hot with desire, was pumping through him not a finger's width away from my mouth, my fangs. *Oh my God, no.* My sight dimmed and I howled with hunger.

But it was too late anyway. The rising tide of pleasure was like an avalanche, lifting us together and hurtling us over the edge. I arched backwards and screamed in release as my climax hammered through me and his frenzied thrusts peaked.

We shuddered to a halt like an ancient, battered locomotive run off the rails. And peace fell. Shocked, wordless, touching, kissing peace. And the knowledge that nothing was ever going to be the same again.

Chapter 12

He'd rolled us around so I was lying on top of him.

I had thought for a minute there that I could make this work, like a normal relationship, boosted by the glow of satisfaction from fantastic sex. Right. I knew too little about my own nature, almost nothing of his and absolutely nothing about what had happened to my marque. This couldn't work. Anyway, he wouldn't want to be kin any more than Jen would. And I'd just made love to him without warning him about what had happened to me. He was going to be pissed.

I hid my face against his neck. Make believe just a little longer.

"You going shy on me, hot stuff?" His words vibrated through my chest.

"Sorry," I muttered. So cool. "Stupid. I was going to bite you just then."

"Yeah, and? Knock yourself out, vamp. If you get a bit carried away, I'll let you know." The amused tenderness in his voice made me look up. Bad idea. The wolf still lingered in his eyes, and my heart missed a beat.

"Alex…"

He caught the tone and looked puzzled.

Crap. Here goes nothing.

"You remember you said Were and Athanate don't cross-infuse?"

"Yeah. That's right, they don't."

"Turns out that's not the case for me."

"Eh?"

I pushed away a little. "I…my marque's changed. Diana said I've picked up a bit of Were. I'm sorry, I should have said."

"Not possible." He frowned.

"Use your damned nose, you stupid wolf," I snapped, angry at myself. I was the one who'd been stupid. And now irresponsible.

He did use his nose, pulling me back tightly against him and pressing his face against my neck. My heart stuttered and I pushed him away again. I didn't trust myself.

His eyes cleared and lit up. "Oh, yes. *Damn.* You have."

"I'm sorry," I muttered again.

His brow creased. I managed to stop myself from stroking it smooth. "What are you sorry about?" he said. "This is awesome. Weird, I'll give you that, but fantastic."

"Alex, think. If you're changing my marque, what am I doing to yours?"

"Shit."

I saw the realization hit him, and braced myself for his anger. But when it came, his response wasn't what I thought he'd say.

"How has this gone down with Altau? What can I do to help?"

"Not well, but I'm okay for the moment, I think. That's not the point, Alex. I'm just a side issue for Altau. You're a full pack member. What's the pack going to do?"

"Hold on, Amber. We don't know that anything's happened to my pack marque. I mean, can you tell?"

"No," I said. "But I've got nothing to check it against."

"Okay, let's think this through. You're new Athanate, I've been Were for a while. Whatever happened, it's so unusual no one's ever heard of it. It'd be double that for it to happen both ways."

He was trying to convince me, but he wasn't sure himself.

"Unless I'm the unusual thing," I said. "You've got to admit, I'm already there."

"Yeah."

He pulled me back in again and I didn't move to get away this time. It was strange. I'd relied on people in the army—it goes with the job, you have to. Then I'd come out and learned to rely on nobody. And suddenly, I was wanting to be able to rely on someone again, to have him on my side.

"You're not mad at me?" I grimaced. I was sounding like a freaking fifteen-year-old.

"What? No."

"But it would be a big deal with the pack?"

He snorted. "If you have the pack marque, you're in, and if you don't, you're not. I've heard of people moving between packs, and your marque has to change when you do that. Being in Denver with a different marque? Yeah, that would be a problem for us."

Us. That little word carried such a lot of thoughts behind it, good and bad. The pack wouldn't like me being partly Were and in their territory. Maybe the same for Alex with Altau. But 'us' also implied we'd face it together.

And together for me involved kin. If Alex became a little bit Athanate, would that make it easier for him to understand kin?

Suddenly uncomfortable, I slithered off him and buried my face in the pillows, trying to think how to put it all into words.

He rolled on top of me, trapping me, and started to kiss my back, working up my shoulders to my neck. All those bright, smart words spilled right out of my head.

His kisses reached my ear and my heart started doing double time. One hand made lazy patterns on my back and the other slid beneath me. I snagged it, dragged it back out.

"Stop," I whispered, mouth and body heading off in different directions again. I kissed the inside of his wrist.

Wasted on a man, Tara said. *Try that on Jen, she'll love it.*

"Shut up," I whispered, but his wolfy hearing was too good.

"Talking to yourself?"

"No," I said, fighting my way out and twisting around to face him. "That would be crazy. No, I'm talking to Tara. She lives in my head."

He grinned and bent his head to plant a single kiss on my neck. "What did she say?"

I took a deep breath. "She says I have to tell you about kin and blood and everything," I blurted out.

"Hmm." He kissed the other side of my neck. "*Everything* will take a long time. This Tara is a smart girl."

"Stop it." I held him away from me desperately. "Look, all this 'us'—what if this is just temporary?" He looked angry at that, but I plowed on. "New Athanate, dizzy with hormones, burning it out with a Were. Right?"

His eyes were gold again, inches from mine, and not happy.

"I'm sorry," I said, and I was. "I didn't mean that like it sounded. It's not you. It's me. I'm the one with the hidden agenda."

"And that is?"

"I'm looking for kin, Alex." *Go on—say it. Say it.* "People to feed off." I tried to hide my face in shame.

"You really don't understand it yet." He was chuckling, like a big diesel truck engine idling, lump, lump, lump. I would have hit him if I could have wriggled out from beneath him. That's probably why he didn't let me.

"You've just paid me the ultimate Athanate compliment," he said. Lump, lump, lump.

I glared at him. "So, I'm Athanate now. What happened to 'vamp?'"

"I only call you vamp to yank your chain." He eased to one side, then the other, letting me get my arms out. I decided against hitting him, for the moment. It was either lie there with my arms flat, like the classroom resuscitation dummy, or put them around him. I put them around him. It felt far too good.

He went back to kissing my neck. "I don't even know if I qualify for kin, but when an Athanate says kin, they don't mean letting off a bit of steam, having just a physical thing."

"Yeah, but..."

"But what?"

"It's not like it's exclusive, Alex. You want something one to one, don't you? Forget about us just for a second. Just theoretically, okay, a couple of weeks ago, maybe you were thinking where's the one girl that's right for me. One guy, one girl. That can't be me."

"Why?"

"Because kin is plural," I said, exasperated.

"Hmm," he said, completely unsurprised. "So, who else are we talking about?"

"Jen," I muttered. "Jennifer Kingslund."

His chuckling paused, but his kisses didn't, damn him. "And what does she think of being kin?" he asked between kisses. "Alongside me?"

"I can't tell her anything till after the...till after the weekend. Mucho Athanate secrets." I huffed. "She'll probably walk anyway."

"Maybe." My head was tilted back, all the better to offer him my neck, damn him again, but I could hear the smile in his voice. "Have you and she..."

"No! I can't even think of it until she knows what she's getting into. Maybe even not then, until I know I can control myself and not turn her. And I could be misreading it all."

My heart skipped another beat at the memory of Jen's kisses on my neck, her voice whispering, *I'm good at this.* No, I hadn't misread it at all.

He laughed. "I don't think so. Kingslund's not one to leave you in the dark about how she feels."

I pulled his head back from my neck and stared at him. There could be one obvious reason he knew her so well.

"Oh no," he said. "Not me. Look." He kissed my forehead. "I understand kin, I understand Athanate, sort of. I don't know if my blood will be what you need. I don't know if I'll be suitable for kin, but you want to bite me, go right ahead. I'm a big strong wolf and we heal even quicker than Athanate." He took a deep breath. "And if we are cross-infusing and I'm becoming part Athanate, then the sooner we learn how that will balance out, the better."

"And to hell with the pack?"

"No, not exactly, but we'll work something out."

"And Altau?"

"Same thing, and I'll be there for you."

"Why are you there for me?" God, I hated the way I sounded sometimes. So damn needy. But I might as well get it out of the way. "Why not the girl in the photo in your living room?"

"Because she's dead and you're not," he snapped. He took a deep breath. "Because you're damn hot. Because I really, really like you when you aren't trying to think your way up your own backside."

Ouch.

I could handle *really like.* And I'm not beautiful, but I could take him calling me *hot.* It said in the constitution that he was entitled to an opinion. And yes, I was thinking about it too much. I felt a little seed of hope start to push its head above the ground.

Lying there, pinned beneath him, my body was trying to convince me everything would be fine. Better than fine.

Hmm. It was probably a bit soon for him, but I was ready to roll again.

"Are there really no other girls in Denver that are hot?" I teased as I trailed my fingers down his flanks.

He snorted. "Yeah, there are plenty of girls in Denver. Some of them are pretty, and some of those might be interested in me, and a few of those might be physically up to it and maybe a couple of those might be willing to risk becoming a werewolf. But they're not hot." He frowned in concentration. "I don't know. Maybe I should get out more. Where would you recommend I go to meet hot, tough, pretty girls?"

"Domina's on 8th Avenue," I said, straight-faced.

"Like I'd have any chance there." We laughed and he squinted at me. "How come you know about Domina's?"

"It's not exactly a state secret, Alex. And no, I've never been. What about girls in your pack?"

"Shit, no! All right for some, but it feels incestuous to me. No thank you." He looked down at me, amusement and exasperation in his face. "So…did I pass?"

I hit him. Gently. And began to lick the side of his neck.

A cell beeped and we both jumped.

"It's not mine this time," I crowed. If it was his turn to get called away, I was going to be as cool as he had been yesterday.

He was getting called away. I could see it as soon as he saw the caller ID. He sat up in a hurry and started talking about problems with deliveries in Salt Lake. From his side of the conversation, I could hear him mentally gearing up to go and fix the problem.

I opened his closet and looked at his work clothes. What would he look good in, apart from anything or nothing? I pulled out some alternatives and laid them on the bed. I picked out some brogues from the shoe rack that would go well. I'd leave him to choose his boxers and socks. I'm not the controlling sort, much.

I wandered into his master bathroom and got in the shower. A minute later, he joined me.

"Here less than a morning and you're telling me what to wear," he complained as I soaped him up with my body.

"Uh-huh." Much more of this and he was going to be delayed. I stretched up for a kiss, but it was disappointingly brief.

"We gotta talk."

"Hmm. Yeah, I know your idea of talk." I smirked and grabbed his butt.

"No, seriously, Amber." His hands stopped roving and just held me. "You're going to think I'm crazy—"

I laughed. "I'm the bag lady who talks to people inside her head and I'm going to think you're crazy? Wow."

"Yes, you are. There's not enough time to explain it now. I'll be back on Thursday and we need you to meet with the pack as soon as possible. There's a file out on the table in the living room. Read it. Call me. It may be just what we need to divert attention from this stuff about changing marques."

"Okay. You have a date. I needed to talk to the alpha anyway."

"Huh? Why?" he asked, shutting the water off.

"It's complicated," I said. "We'll talk while you get dressed."

I wrapped up in his bathrobe and lay on the bed, watching while he toweled down. Yum. It was seriously difficult to concentrate. He was completely unfazed by me watching. Peacock.

"First, let me ask you something." I cleared my throat. He had his pants on, which helped, some. "Are there any Weres living in Denver who aren't part of the pack?"

"No," he said, too quickly. I waited while he made a show of choosing his socks. "Yes," he amended. "There's a group trying to set up. We aren't going to let them. And you're not supposed to know that. Is that what this is about?"

"Maybe. I'm an unofficial consultant for the Denver PD on paranormal stuff—"

"What?" He looked startled. "They don't know—"

"One of them does." I waved it off. "That's an even more complicated story. But for now, take it on trust. I've got a police report compiled from every attack in the area that mentions big dogs or wolves. I need to discuss it with the pack. There's something happening, and I'm afraid it means a rogue."

Alex slipped on his jacket. "This is *not* going to go down well." He checked his watch. "It's going to have to keep until Thursday. I can't just send you to talk to the alpha. Certainly not with that as an introduction. It's going to be bad enough as it is when he smells you."

I shrugged; another person who's going want to tear my throat out. *Take a number*. I'd deal with it when the time came. "Thursday it is."

I followed him down the stairs and he pulled a set of keys off a rack in the kitchen. "These are your keys," he said simply. No conditions, no boundaries.

We wrapped around each other at the front door.

"Got your head straight now?" he asked.

"I think so."

"I'm your kin and you're my pack?"

I nodded. I could work with that.

He kissed my nose. Definitely a wolf thing, that.

"I'm not going to get along well with Kingslund," he warned. "And…"

He stopped.

"Spill it, wolf."

He sighed. "You think you've melted the ice queen…I don't know." He shook his head. That was the end of that part of the conversation.

"We'll work something out," I said, realizing that was actually Jen's phrase. It was starting to be a mantra for me.

His hand was on the door when he turned. "Tara?"

I swallowed. I shouldn't have said anything. I must seem crazy enough to people without adding her into it. "Twin sister. Stillborn."

"And she talks to you?"

I nodded warily.

"Cool," he said, and he was gone.

I strolled back to the kitchen to make myself some coffee.

Skylights flooded the place with light and I sat there, eyes closed and purring to myself, snorting the scent of Alex's Blue Mountain coffee. I had a truckload of problems, but I'd find a way around them, one at a time.

Alex seemed to understand that my needs as an Athanate might be complex. Was that just because he was an all-around good guy, or the effect of Athanate changes working on him already?

And not just Alex, but Jen as well. This morning, everything seemed possible, whatever Alex said about Jen. The Athanate in me stirred in contentment, like a snake dreaming in the hot sun. Yesss.

I gave myself a little shake and took my coffee to the living room.

She was still there, on the one section of the bookshelves that was clear. I'd walked away quickly last time, not wanting to see her, trying to pretend she didn't exist. This time, I did her the courtesy of picking her up and looking at her while I drank my coffee.

There wasn't much I could tell from the photo. She was bronzed and raven-haired, maybe Arapaho, maybe closer to that side than me. I'd dismissed her as pretty last time, but she wasn't; she was beautiful. And it's hard being jealous of a dead woman.

She was dressed for the outdoors, the sun on her face and the Rockies in the background. She was laughing. I knew I would have liked her, if we'd met. And that changed it for me. I touched the photo with my fingertips. I'd learn about her. If she lived a little in my heart, she would not be dead.

Then, having made my peace with her, I got down to Alex's file.

But my thoughts kept returning to kin, to Alex and Jen, and to my new Athanate family, David and Pia. And so to my own human family. As much as I'd kept myself distant from them, for their own safety, they'd always been true family. They'd always been a constant, something I held to when I'd worried about becoming Athanate. When I woke from another nightmare, sweating and shivering, I'd sometimes eased myself back to sleep with memories of Kath and me braiding each other's hair, or brushing it out, singing along to the radio. And all those precious memories were now turning sour. My teeth started to clench.

I managed to finish Alex's file before I went to pay my sister a visit.

Chapter 13

"Really, Ms. Farrell, she's not available except by appointment."

The receptionist was fashionably dressed, like something off the cover of a style magazine. I wondered if they had a spare receptionist in the back office who did all the work to make sure the one at the front desk never mussed her hair or broke a fingernail.

"Well, if she's so busy, maybe she'd prefer I talk to the managing partner instead."

"I'm afraid he's busy too."

"I didn't doubt that for a moment, but I'm a PI. By closing time I can find out where he lives, what clubs he belongs to and which restaurants he goes to. If that's what my sister wants."

I turned and walked away. There was no chance she'd ignore that with the firm evaluating her for a partnership. It was heavy handed, but I didn't have time to mess around.

It was a big lobby, and I hadn't made it halfway to the door when the receptionist called me back.

"She says she can spare you five minutes." Behind her professionally blank face, I knew she was seething. I gave her a big smile and thanked her politely.

A secretary showed me to a gloomy meeting room in the basement. I knew Kath had picked it to keep me away from everyone else at the firm. I didn't care.

I wasn't kept waiting long.

"How dare you come here and harass me," she hissed as she closed the door firmly behind her.

"I'll tell you how I dare. I've been talking to the Quinns this morning."

"So?"

"What do you mean 'so?' You're telling them I'm a drug addict and a whore and I'm supposed to shrug it off? Show me." I pulled off my jacket and held out my arms. "You said you could see the needle marks. Where? And how about you call Jennifer Kingslund and tell her she uses whores. Come on, Kath, what's the problem? Afraid she might sue for slander and win? Ruin your bid to be a partner?"

"I saw needle marks," she said, folding her arms and lifting her chin.

"You saw I'd had a couple of blood tests. You've turned that into drug addiction. You saw me dancing with Kingslund and you think that means I'm a whore. Another client gave me a car in lieu of payment and that's proof positive I'm a whore as far as you're concerned. You're supposed to be a lawyer. Doesn't the word 'proof' mean anything to you? And whatever you think, how could you say things like that to the Quinns?"

"You left the ball with Kingslund."

"Yeah. And I'm staying at her house. Big deal. I'm her freaking security consultant. There was a security problem at the ball."

"No one else had any problems."

"Because they weren't after anyone else. Did you watch the news yesterday? See anything about people being rescued from the Nexus building? Kingslund Group employees and a police captain. Ring any bells? That was me, doing my job for Kingslund."

She turned her back on me, trembling with anger.

Kath and I had been close until I joined the army. The job I did there being what it was, I hadn't been able to come home often and I'd never been able to talk about what I really was. Becoming Athanate had made that immeasurably worse.

I could see that might seem to Kath like I was being distant, but her response was out of all proportion, and worse than hurtful to me.

But I had to try and stop this from escalating. It was my responsibility. I was her big sister. Surely, I could get through to her?

"Look, I understand you might feel—" I started.

"You don't understand anything," she shouted at me, turning back. "Not one thing. Ten years of being told to look up to you. Ten years. Yes, you sent money, like some rich cousin who can't be bothered to visit. I looked after Mom, too. I was there for her when she needed it. Week after week, night after night, when she woke up crying. And then you come back and you can barely bother to talk to me. In two years, how often have we spoken? You're not interested in what I went through or what I'm doing, because it's not exciting enough for you. Not like the army," she said sarcastically, making quote marks in the air. "Then I find out that's all a lie."

"It's not a lie! Lieutenant Krantz is wrong. He can't see my records."

"I called the army. I'm a lawyer, whatever you think. I don't take uncorroborated evidence. I told you. I called them and asked about secret units and special forces. They don't even take women."

"And what exactly made you think they'd talk to you just because you called them? The whole point of secret is that they don't tell anyone, for God's sake."

We stood there glaring at each other.

There wasn't a way forward on that one, and there was an elephant in the room I was going to have to deal with. It'd come out over a family lunch a week ago that I'd paid for Kath's education. Mom had used it to try and reconcile us. Kath had later given me a check while suggesting I use it to go to a drug rehabilitation program, so I guess it didn't work quite that way.

I took her check out of my pocket and put it on the table.

"I didn't do it to get paid back, Kath."

"Fantastic, now you're trying the guilt trip on me. I was wondering when that was going to come." She paused, her arms folding even tighter. "So why did you do it then?"

"Because I promised Dad before he died."

"Perfect! Now we get Dad involved in this too. He asked you to pay my way?"

"No." I turned away from her. This wasn't how this should have come out. "I was sitting with him one afternoon, just before he died. He'd just woken up and told me he'd been having a dream: seeing us graduate from college."

"And what's wrong with this picture?"

"Kath, for God's sake!" I spun around. "Stop treating everything as a chance to bitch. If I'd stayed in school, we'd have lost the house and neither of us would have been able to go on to college. It was the only way; I got out and helped you and Mom."

"And I'm supposed to be grateful."

"No! You weren't supposed to know. And you never would have, if you hadn't gotten Mom so worked up by refusing to help me last week."

My cell went off in my jacket pocket. I snatched it up.

Bian—*Call. Urgent!!*

"Shit. I have to go."

"Typical. Your friends are more important to you than family. And too important for us ever to meet them."

She'd crossed the line too often. Suddenly, it was as if she was far, far away from me.

"Right now, they're more like family to me than you are," I said. Her eyes went wide.

I brushed past her and made for the door.

"Amber," she said. I stopped and looked back over my shoulder. She took a deep breath. "I didn't mean it to be like this, honestly. I'm too stressed and angry. But you need help. You can't go on being in denial. Whatever it was you had to do all that time, that's done now. And I am grateful for what you did. Really I am. You're back in Denver now and we will help, but only if you let us. Come back to the family and start by admitting—"

"No, Kath. You've got it completely wrong. I can't deal with this now. Just don't go speaking to any more of our friends. And leave Mom out of this while she's on vacation."

I walked out. Unfinished business, but I wasn't getting anywhere and I was out of time.

Chapter 14

"Bian, it's me," I said as I walked out of the building, trying to get everything back in perspective. I had to be thinking clearly for this call.

"Round-eye, are you busy?"

Like nothing had happened.

That she was making an effort told me something already.

"I'm okay at the moment. I'll be busy later this afternoon. Is it important?"

"It is. I have a job for you."

"Shoot."

"There's a Diakon, my equivalent for House Romero in New Mexico, who's flying in to DIA in an hour. He needs to be met and escorted here. Securely."

The New Mexico label warned me that this wasn't necessarily an everyday chore. I didn't know what was up, but I gathered Altau's ally down there had become unreliable, maybe was even talking to Basilikos. "Secure as in he won't know where he goes?"

"You got it. This is important. I wouldn't normally ask you without a better briefing, but as I say we're really stretched here."

"Okay already. Name and details?"

"Oscar Jaworski, Frontier Air, landing at noon."

"Will do. I guess he has permission to be here, so I shouldn't kill him?"

Bian snorted. "House Romero is allied to us and he has permission, so play nice, Round-eye. We *think* there may be a problem down there, but there's no confirmation."

"Is this Skylur asking?"

"This is me, Round-eye. I'm in charge of security, this is my call. Screw it up and I'll bite your ass." She ended the call.

So, I wasn't an outcast exactly. In truth, I was glad she'd asked. It gave me something to do for Altau that would show me in a better light. If I didn't screw up. But hey, pick someone up at the airport and drive him to Haven? Walk in the park.

The drive would give me a good chance to think over Alex's file, rather than worrying that I'd caused major problems for him with the pack or grinding my teeth over my family problems.

I found a flat piece of cardboard in a store's recycling bin and borrowed a marker pen from them to write 'Jaworski' on it, then got in the car and drove north.

Alex's file was the result of years of research into the oral traditions of Arapaho and Cheyenne beliefs, covering shape-shifting, totems and spirit guides. The front had the word 'Therianthropy' scrawled across it, and I had had to look that up. Big fancy word for Were. The bulk of the file was to do with bears and werebears. He'd marked up his transcripts with a highlighter, picking out passages which described the first changes and the problems with changing. There was a copy of a monologue from a shaman about a 'bear-speaker', a shaman who'd been able to talk to werebears and 'ease the first steps'. It was a frustrating article; it had been copied from an old academic work, and the monologue was broken up with snarky, disbelieving comments from the academics.

Gripping stuff, but I was unsure what relevance it had to me until I reached the end. The last entries in the file were background on the Arapaho Wolf Clan and a Farrell family tree. One sheet was the scan Alex had made last week of the photo of my great-grandparents, Padraig and Speaks-to-Wolves. If that's where Alex was making a link, I could completely believe Speaks-to-Wolves had been a shaman, and for all I knew, she did actually speak to wolves. But I also absolutely believed that I wasn't and didn't.

The Farrell chart started with Padraig's generation. He was born in 1876, Speaks-to-Wolves in 1889, and they married in 1915. I could only guess the difficulties they went through. Liam was my grandfather, born to them in 1921, the second child and the only one who survived. The same story played out in Liam's marriage. I had to put it aside at that point. Too many children dead.

As to where Alex was coming from on all this, I'd wait till I spoke to him. I'd brought the file with me, and I'd read it again when I had the opportunity.

At DIA, the flight was on time and I guessed the man making his way toward my scribbled sign was my meet. He was neatly turned out: straight black hair combed back, about my height and age, dressed in business casual—gray blazer mixed with slim jeans and loafers. Rolling suitcase and a briefcase. His eyes matched his jacket. Cool.

He was scowling. Not cool.

"Jaworski?"

"Yeah." He pushed the suitcase forwards and held the handle out to me.

It took me a second to register what he was expecting, and something snapped in me.

"Go screw yourself," I said. I couldn't believe it. If he'd said hello and we'd been walking, I might have offered, but expecting me to do it wasn't going to make him by new best friend.

He tried to brazen it out, standing stiffly, his eyes angry. That made it worse. I got my first good scent of his marque and my regret at losing my temper died before it got started.

"You can bring that to the car and I'll take you to where you're going, or you can play statues the rest of the day. Your call." I turned on my heel and started the walk back. After a few seconds I heard the rumble of his suitcase wheels. Oh boy, this was going to be a fun drive.

I opened the trunk and left him to put his luggage in. He slammed the trunk on the suitcase, but kept the briefcase with him and sat in the back. He hadn't managed a second word yet, and I wasn't going to keep him amused with conversation.

"I have a couple of stops to make," I said, my tone intended to tell him I didn't care if that happened to be a problem for him. He just sat there, looking out the window.

Securely. Hmm.

I called Matt.

"'Lo Matt, it's Amber. You got an all-band portable scanner? And a Faraday cage that'd fit in my trunk?"

"Yup and yup."

"Any chance I could pick them up from your office in an hour?"

"You got 'em."

I headed downtown on 6th.

I knew I was going overboard here, but Jaworski had pissed me off and I was concerned about him from a security point of view. I knew that marque. I stopped at the Aurora Plaza and left him in the car. That was safe enough—if he wanted to get to Haven, he needed me. And I kept it short; I could have sat in a café for an hour and let him stew. I was a good girl; straight in, straight out. I bought some men's sweats, a towel and some duct tape. In fifteen minutes we were heading downtown again.

Matt was waiting for me outside the Kingslund Group building. I guessed they must have a side entrance for him to use. His scruffy jeans and black T perfectly complemented his sun-bleached surfer hair and Paul Newman eyes, but I didn't think he'd look good walking through the main lobby. He was beaming, so he must have gotten over being scared of me.

We put the cage in the trunk and he grounded it with croc clips on the frame of the car.

"So long as it's got a good connection to something like the frame of the car, almost zip will be able to get out," he confirmed in answer to a question from me. "And for sure, nothing from a handheld device."

"Good." I put Jaworski's suitcase in the cage.

Matt demonstrated the handheld scanner. It was a trick piece of equipment, just what I needed.

"Thanks, Matt. I'll call later."

"No probs." He looked eager and curious. He peered into the car, where Jaworski had sat, fuming, while we'd loaded up the cage.

I climbed back in and set off.

"No more diversions," said Jaworski.

It might have been a question, it might have been an order. I didn't bother to check. "Just one," I said. One I was going to enjoy.

I took I-25 up to I-70. Jaworski still didn't say anything, but I could see him in the rearview, watching the roads, trying to see where we were going.

Not for much longer.

After ten minutes I pulled off at the Kipling intersection and drove down into the cluster of budget hotels. I parked in some dead space between them and alongside a blank wall which would hide us from casual view.

I got out and jerked his door open. He looked around, confused.

"This isn't it," he said.

"Well spotted." I tossed the sweats at him. "Strip and put those on."

"What the f—"

I had the HK out and pointed at his face before he finished his sentence. For the first time his arrogant veneer cracked and his face went pale.

"Who are you?" he said.

"My name is Amber Farrell. You can call me ma'am or House, I don't mind which. And you should have checked that at the airport. Especially given the tensions just now."

"Are you Basilikos?" he said, his face going even paler. *Point in his favor.*

"No. Are you?"

"I don't understand—"

"I'm House Farrell, allied to Altau. I've been requested to take you securely to House Altau. I'm going to do that. Now, in army speak, I figure Panethus is in Defcon 3, so I'd be taking extra precautions with you anyway. But yesterday, someone from House Romero was working with Matlal to try and capture me."

I stopped and watched his reaction.

"This is madness! We're allied to Altau. We're Panethus."

"Yeah? Well, make sure the rest of your House know that." I was tempted to use Larry's name to see if that got a reaction from Jaworski, but it wasn't good tradecraft. "Anyway, when another Romero turns up and behaves like an asshole, he's going to get the treatment."

"You can't—"

"We're wasting time, Jaworski. Change now."

I punctuated the end of my speech by cocking the HK.

In ten minutes he was in sweats, the towel taped over his head as a blindfold and his hands taped together. He was in the front seat, but laid all the way back. I'd gone through his cases and pockets, turning everything off and tossing it with his clothes into the Faraday cage. There was plenty of electronic stuff, including a smartphone with a GPS. I ran the scanner around the cage. There were no signals getting out of it, and I guessed that meant nothing got in as well. So, even if there were something in there waiting to turn itself back on and transmit its location, firstly, it wouldn't know where it was and secondly, no one would be able to hear it. I had no intention of leading anyone to Haven.

The remaining half-hour of the drive passed quite peacefully for me, and it's a pretty drive along I-70 and the Evergreen Parkway, if you don't have a towel taped over your face.

Chapter 15

At Haven, in contrast to my last visit when I wasn't supposed to know where it was, the two guards greeted me with a polite, murmured 'House Farrell'. I used the security system for the first time, placing my hand on a portable tablet scanner, and presenting my face for the camera to record. Again, I took it as a good sign; I wasn't being treated as an outcast. For all his locked-down rage, Skylur seemed willing to step back and give me a chance to prove myself. Just so long as I hadn't messed it up for Bian.

When he realized we had arrived, Jaworski began to make a fuss.

The guard looked in at him and raised a brow at me. "We have you bringing Diakon Jaworski from DIA," he said. His colleague made no move to free Jaworski, working his way around, checking underneath the car with a mirror and then popping the trunk.

I shrugged. "That's him, according to him. Whoever he is, his marque matches someone who tried to attack me yesterday. I was told to bring him in securely. That's my interpretation, under the circumstances."

The second guard gave a thumbs-up and closed the trunk. They both ignored Jaworski. I guessed that meant I outranked him.

After a call to the house to check, they directed me around the side and down into an underground garage. I parked in a spare slot and got out.

Diana emerged from a door and strode over.

At the sight of her, my heart stuttered. I'd expected Bian. Diana and I exchanged Athanate neck kisses and I wondered if I was in trouble again. And had I just created another one of Skylur's unhealthy situations?

Jeez, bit late for regrets.

Maybe I'd overcompensated in making sure there weren't any security problems. The asshole deserved it, but I might have created all kinds of diplomatic problems.

Apparently not. After giving me a quiet smile, she reached into the car and effortlessly lifted Jaworski out, setting him down on his feet roughly. The tough duct tape snapped under her fingers like stale pasta and she tossed the towel aside.

The bluster died on his lips. "Diana," he stammered.

I had a full view of his face. I would have laid good odds that, for whatever reason, he hadn't expected to see her.

Diana thought so too. Her eyebrows lifted gently. "Surprised, Diakon?" She began to pace around him. He froze into place. I stood back and watched. "Romero declines to attend an Assembly, and sends a Diakon, late, with an instruction to be accommodated in House Altau, and you didn't expect me to get involved?"

"You have to understand, things are very difficult," he stuttered. "There's pressure from Matlal all the time. We feel threatened."

"You feel threatened by Basilikos, and Romero has to be in New Mexico to keep control?"

"Yes, that's it exactly." He was standing straight, trying to appear confident, but he was shifting his weight nervously. I guessed no Diakon would be a dummy, but I'd match Bian against him any day. I could smell the fear coming off him, hear the tripping of his heart.

"Even though this puts the Panethus vote at risk in the Assembly?" Diana said.

"Panethus voting is solid on all the major issues, Diana." He sounded almost as if he'd prepared this little speech. "And I will address the Assembly on behalf of House Romero on any points you wish."

"But you won't vote, because you can't," Diana said flatly. "And outside of the major issues are a host of minor issues that will become major if we don't settle them now. Basilikos are eager to exploit the slightest weakness in Panethus. If Romero doesn't attend, what signal does that send to Teugis or Madrone or Ubbriaco? If Romero is too frightened or too hard pressed to attend, why should they? How many before it's a major issue in itself?"

"But Matlal—"

"The only thing keeping Romero free from Matlal, is that Romero is too small to bother with. Romero has his head locked in the 19th century, thinking he has a border to protect." She whirled on him. "The border is meaningless. Matlal is here, in Denver. And if he wanted, he would be in Albuquerque too."

Diana's voice hadn't risen, but her words were like ice. She paced around him once more before coming up behind him, very close to his ear. "Or is he there already?" she whispered.

"No, Diana. No. I swear it."

"Can you? Tell me, have you come straight from a briefing with Romero? You were in Albuquerque?"

"No, no. I was in Santa Fe. That's my area of responsibility. But we spoke by phone just before I left."

Diana snorted.

A guard came into the garage. She was armed with Altau's standard weapon, the stubby, ugly Herstal P90.

"Put him in a cell. I'll question him later," Diana said.

"I protest—" Jaworski stumbled as he was led away, and the door closed behind them, cutting him off.

Diana strode back to me. "It'll be a waste of time. He doesn't know anything. His ignorance is telling me more about what's going on in New Mexico than he could say himself. Romero has deliberately sent a junior Diakon to us. One who hasn't been briefed, who hasn't seen Romero in months. Who has no scent of Matlal about him."

Diana had no real concept of personal space, or chose to ignore it. I made myself stand still as she rested a hand on my shoulder and bent close to me, her nostrils flaring. She snorted again.

"So, one of the people who tried to ambush you yesterday was House Romero?" She walked around me, the same way she had with Jaworski, but without the menacing edge to it. Or, not as much.

I nodded. "Jaworski was being an asshole as well. Not that it influenced me, of course, but under the circumstances, I thought it was better to be careful."

"I like your careful," murmured Diana.

"How can Jaworski not know about what's going on in House Romero?"

"Romero's is an old structure, a border House. They deliberately set up to cover a lot of territory, with sub-Houses in major towns. It's feasible for Jaworski to be out of contact with Romero himself for a year."

"Would they really go to Basilikos? I mean the whole House—Romero just decides and his House follows him?"

"No. Changing creed tears a House apart. Some will go and some won't. They'll fight." She sighed. "Almost everyone is damaged."

Did that mean Larry could be one of those that was fighting, not following? But if he was, how come he'd been sent to work with Matlal? And how damaged? More questions to ask, if he showed.

When, not if. Stay positive.

I felt a sting of guilt as Diana's eyes swept over me curiously. I should be telling her about Larry, especially now that I'd found out he was Romero. But I'd just gotten back to what felt like level footing with her. What if I said something and created another of Skylur's issues? After all, I didn't *know* Larry was going to show tonight. I decided to keep a lid on it until I could present it neatly gift-wrapped: a solution, not another problem.

"Where's his luggage?" she asked.

I popped the trunk and explained the Faraday cage. She brought out a scanner even more trick than Matt's from her pocket and waved it over the open cage. When it didn't respond to anything, we took Jaworski's luggage and clothes out and dumped them in a carry bin at the side of the garage. Nothing lightweight would be able to beam out a signal underground.

"Good," Diana said. "I knew it would be the right thing to have you look at our security after the Assembly. We get complacent sometimes."

She walked me to back to my car.

"Can I see David and Pia before I go?"

"Not at the moment. But they're fine. I'll make sure they schedule a break tomorrow and you can see them." She caught me off guard by changing tack completely. "Your visit with Alexander went well, then?"

I looked at her nervously. It was stupid of me not to have realized she would be able to tell. Her face showed no hint of what she thought about it. "Is it that obvious?"

"You reek of wolf, Amber." She closed her eyes and put her head back for a moment, looking tired. "We'll discuss it tomorrow. You can explain to me what you think you're achieving. And after that, we'll talk about the complaints Matlal has made about you."

That sounded like one step forward and two leaps back; I'd lost some of the traction I'd gained by bringing Jaworski in. Crap.

I started to ask what complaints, but she overrode me.

"You'd best go now," she said.

Something prompted me to stand my ground. "Because?"

"Because I haven't fed for too long and that fool Jaworski has got my Blood up." She paced behind me, and I twitched as I felt her breath on my neck. "Because, despite the overtone of wolf, you smell more delicious all the time. And Skylur's ban is still in force."

I turned my head to watch. Her movements had become slow, almost languorous. She continued circling. Her face had paled and I could feel the air crackling as her breathing deepened. There was a scent of violence about her, like a thunderstorm threatening to break. A shiver passed through me and I wasn't entirely sure if it was chill or thrill.

I'd made a decision last night on the matters in Top's letter, and I needed to take my first step now. I tried to act calm and keep my heart rate down. I caught her and held her arms, leaned forward slowly and kissed the side of her neck. Then I stood straight again and tilted my head back. I was completely aware of every throb of the pulse in my neck.

I was watching her eyes. They glittered, fixed on my pulse, but her half-smile was back on her lips.

"Testing, Amber?" she said softly, her voice low. My neck felt warm and loose.

"Yes," I said.

"Why?"

"I'll tell you tomorrow."

Her head bent forward. I could feel the warmth of her face near me. My eyes closed. I didn't think Skylur's ban extended to him or Diana. I truly didn't know what to expect, teeth or lips, but I had to know.

Her lips grazed my neck.

"Then I'll see you tomorrow." She strode to the door. "It would be a shame if we can't find a way to encompass you," she said over her shoulder. "As Bian says, you are so much fun."

Chapter 16

Heading back to Denver, I texted Niall that I was running late and then I called the colonel.

Colonel Laine was the last remaining link between me and the army. Thanks to Lieutenant Krantz's investigation, I wasn't even being paid a retainer. So what exactly was the army's hold over me now?

Other than emotional. I'd loved my time in Ops 4-10. What I'd done there had sunk such deep roots in me, it'd left me feeling hollow when it had all been torn out. My brief time with the police had been a pale imitation. Being a PI was better than the police, but nothing on 4-10, so far. Over time, would my job and my new friends and the Athanate start to fill those empty places in me?

I didn't know. But if I was going to talk to the FBI and if they started asking questions about the time I spent in the army, I was going to toss the ball to the colonel.

His voicemail came on again.

Damn.

I'd never had any problem getting through to him before.

I suspected the trouble might revolve around Major Petersen, the guy who made me sign that original bullshit agreement. I'd been warned, he was now angling to take over the whole unit, Ops 4-10 and Obs. And that he had an agenda about vampires. The only place I had in his organization was strapped to a table for examination.

Now I was worried, but I couldn't exactly drop in on 4-10 and resolve it.

With sigh and a feeling that I was making a mistake, going in without backup, I checked the note that Tullah had given me for the FBI, and called the number.

"Griffith," was the terse greeting when the call was answered.

"Farrell," I responded in kind, and waited. Any excuse.

After a moment, he relented. "Agent Griffith, FBI, who is this please?"

"Amber Farrell, PI. You left a message with my assistant that you have something to say to me."

"Oh, yes, Miss Farrell. We need you to come in. We understand you were involved in identifying the criminal operation at Crate & Freight, and that's now under our jurisdiction. It would be most useful for us if you could answer some questions about that and also the events at the Nexus building yesterday."

"You keep saying we and us. Who are we?"

"The Federal Bureau of Investigation, the Drug Enforcement Agency, the Bureau of Alcohol, Tobacco, Firearms and Explosives. And the Department of Homeland Security."

I didn't like the sound of that, and I didn't like the sound of Agent Griffith. Anyone who chanted the names out like that was full of it himself. He was trying to intimidate me. Wasn't going to stop me from being flippant though.

"Nothing from the Coast Guard? Park Service? Those slackers at the CIA? I'm disappointed."

He ignored that. "Where are you, Miss Farrell?"

"It's Ms.," I said, "and I'm assuming you're at the CBI building."

"Yes—"

"I'm on Route 6 and I'll be there in five," I interrupted him. "You've got an hour, so get all your bureaus in line and get all their questions in order." I ended the call.

A couple of minutes later, I came off on Garrison and made my way back to the Kipling cloverleaf. I parked in the shadow of the Colorado Bureau of Investigation's threatening office building.

What if they just chucked me straight into a cell? I felt some of my bravado evaporate.

Man up, Farrell. Always made me smile, that phrase.

Agent Griffith wasn't there to greet me. Big surprise. But security knew who I was and escorted me to an empty interview room.

I turned in the doorway, preventing the guard from closing it and accidentally locking me in.

"I need you to pass a message to Agent Griffith, please. I've given him an hour and that's all he's getting."

The guard looked down his nose at me. I was here in an interview room to talk to an agent, so I was a criminal, naturally. He tried edging closer, invading my personal space, so I would move back and he could close the door.

Sergeants don't have personal space, they have attitude. I leaned against the doorframe and crossed my arms. I did not back up an inch.

"Are you coming on to me?" the little demon in my throat asked.

He retreated in confusion.

I left a chair holding the door open, and checked the room. It was blank and bare. Table, chairs and one wall taken up with a one-way mirror. Not even a wastebasket for trash.

After five minutes of pacing, I sighed and sat, cross-legged, on the table, facing the mirror. I straightened my back, closed my eyes and started visualizing my way through Master Liu's Kung Fu forms.

Tick tock.

Forty-seven minutes later a man came in. I stopped the Praying Mantis visualization and eyed him. He was pasty-faced and jerky in his movements. He clutched a file and a tablet computer in one hand and he was eyeing a text on his smartphone in the other. It looked as if he was trying for the image of a busy guy, but just managing to look like someone who was always late.

"Would you take a seat, Miss Farrell?" He slid sideways onto one of the chairs.

"I've already told you, it's Ms. It doesn't bode well if you can't even remember that. As for the invitation, I'm already seated and comfortable. And you're running out of time. Drop the text and ask your questions."

Griffith had a problem, but no idea how to deal with it. He'd expected my wait to soften me up, make me amenable. He had all sorts of training on how to sit *at* a table and induce a person to talk. Someone sitting *on* a table threw him.

He knew he'd just lost the initiative and that was a mistake. He'd never trained for a situation where he was trying to verbally subdue a person who was sitting on his table.

He tried to get height advantage back by standing up, but that put him in the subordinate position. He realized that too late and thought about sitting right back down again, but couldn't stand to appear indecisive. I almost smiled.

"You don't seem to be taking this seriously—" he started.

"You can't even remember whether it's Miss or Ms., you've apparently forgotten that I said an hour, and you've wasted over fifty minutes of that already. You're the one who's not taking this seriously."

"If you think I haven't got other—"

He'd walked right into my trap. "So, it's not a priority then. I'll let you get back to your *important* work."

"Miss Farrell—"

"It's Ms., and you've wasted the opportunity to talk to me with bad manners and stupid attempts at mind games."

I swiveled my butt off the table and made for the door.

He grabbed my arm. I stopped and glared at him.

Another agent breezed in, as if completely by chance, and I mentally grimaced. This one wasn't an idiot asking to be pushed around. He was tall and silver-haired, carried a bit of a belly, but comfortably. His face was tanned; this guy got out a lot. His bright blue eyes had little laughter lines running back from them and he had a nose that twitched like a fox's.

"Howdy, I'm Hal Ingram," he drawled, Texas slow, and offered his hand. "Is there a problem here?" He made at least two syllables for every one in each word.

I wrenched my arm out of Griffith's grip and shook Agent Ingram's hand.

"I'm not sure," I answered. "Master Griffith seems to think I'm under arrest." I had to fight my demon not to stretch all the words out like Ingram did. I bet I could make four syllables in arrest.

Ingram's eyes smiled, while his face remained solemn. "Absolutely not. Nu-uh. We were just fixing to see if you could come in and shed some light on a couple of incidents. I surely must add that the Denver police made a point to inform me just how valuable your assistance was in those incidents."

"Thanks." The police had only known about the drugs shipment at Crate & Freight because I called them. And they'd still be negotiating at the Nexus building if I hadn't gone in and rescued the hostages, including Captain José Morales. Yeah, my help was invaluable. "That's what I thought I was coming in for, an hour ago. It's a shame I've spent the hour I said I could spare, in this room, without a single question to answer."

"Maybe—" Griffith tried to wrestle the initiative back. He shouldn't have tried it with a sentence starting with 'maybe'. Didn't apply to me, of course.

"Maybe we could rearrange. Pick a date and a place where other important things don't get in the way. Send me a text or an email." I retrieved one of my cards and handed it over to Ingram. If he made a joke about it I was going to punch him. Tullah's choice of my skin tone for the color and the tag line 'reliable—efficient—discreet' made me seem like a hooker. But I'd gotten kind of attached to them.

And now that Tullah was running her own cases, she'd have to have one as well. Ha! See how she liked it.

Agent Ingram exchanged it for one of his, which was a boring business card, but at least gave me a number to bypass the office idiot.

They trailed after me as I made my way back to the reception area, and let me through the scanners.

At the front desk, I handed in my visitor's badge and turned around.

"You have about two minutes left. I guess there might be time for your two most important questions," I said to Ingram. Mistake.

Ingram let Griffith ask the first. "We're having a bit of difficulty tracing you in the period before you returned to Denver—"

"I was in the military. I have to refer any questions regarding that to Colonel Laine." I had prepared for this one and gave Griffith the colonel's name and number on a blank card. "That's his contact information." I turned. "Agent Ingram?"

"Well, I thank you for that, Ms. Farrell. Happens I do have a question, too," Ingram said, as if he were just shooting the breeze. "Y'know, what with all the drugs and guns and gangs and hitmen, you'd think it would be about that. But I kinda like odd questions." He chuckled. "And y'know the craziest thing that's being asked?" His nose twitched and I got a bad feeling. His hand came out of his pocket with a little Dictaphone. He shook his head as if he couldn't believe those good ole boys down there would come up with a question like this. "Homeland Security's question. What's this here language?"

He pressed the 'play' button and my heart sank. Crap. It was Athanate, two or three of them talking over a conference call. Double crap.

"Umm. I can tell you it's not Spanish and it's not Vietnamese," I said, truthfully. "Doesn't sound like Arabic. Beyond that, you really need an expert."

"Well, they are that, Ms. Farrell, over there, I do assure you. They know every documented language in the world. They got guys speak, whadya call it, Klingon and Elvish." He beamed at me. "But they never heard this."

"Wow. Freaky. Why should I know?"

"Well, Ms. Farrell," He scratched his ear. "'Cause folk you speak to on your cell, they speak this a lot."

Ingram didn't wait for me to bluster through any other lies, or ask him whether tapping my cell was being done illegally.

"Anyhow, we'll clear that up next time, over a coffee someplace. And I'm real interested in hearing all about how come you learned Vietnamese, too. I thank you for your time today, Ms. Farrell. Been a pleasure." He stuck his hand out again and we shook.

He wheeled away, gathering Griffith with a friendly arm around his shoulders.

"That was useful, Ray, dontcha think?" he was saying as he guided him back through the security gate.

I fled.

Chapter 17

I parked outside of the Quinns' at 6 p.m. I spent fifteen minutes checking for trackers without finding anything. Not that I didn't trust the FBI, *of course*, but if they were bugging cells, what else where they doing? I'd have to get a warning to Bian. I just couldn't do it until after I'd squared Larry away, one way or the other. If Bian was going to yell at me for holding out, at least it would be for something concrete.

The light was already fading, but the Quinns' job wouldn't take long.

"Niall, sorry I'm late. I'm outside now," I said into the intercom. "Do you want to come out to play?"

Niall tried to shield the phone, but I heard some comments about my punctuality from his wife. Regardless, he said he would be down.

We stood at the base of his building while he tested out his borrowed camera. I showed him how to turn on date and time, zoom in and out, and we were ready.

"On me, Niall, in close." He focused in on me.

"Hi, my name is Amber Farrell, I'm a private investigator in Denver. I'm outside the building where Niall Quinn owns an apartment and I'm about to demonstrate how to get to any balcony on this building, from the outside."

I trotted to the small boundary wall, leaped up and launched myself at the lip of the first balcony. I hadn't done this in ages, but I guess it was like riding a bicycle. You can fall flat on your face anytime. I was already gripping the edge when I thought that a straight lift might not be the best demonstration of how anyone could do this. I changed to a one-armed swing and caught hold of the iron railing and hauled myself up that way. From the first balcony, I balanced on the top of the railing and repeated the process. In two minutes I was outside the Quinns' apartment. Mrs. Quinn was trying to ignore me through the balcony doors, but I wasn't going back inside anyway. I twisted over the railing and made my way back down, which was actually more difficult and dangerous.

At the bottom I signaled Niall to zoom in close again.

"That's taken less than five minutes, up and down. I used no equipment, no one driving past has stopped, no one in the apartments noticed. I'm not a professional climber; it's just a hobby I used to have. Not only is it *not* impossible to reach a balcony this way, it's relatively easy."

I gestured for him to cut and it was done.

"Amber, that's great. Here, hold this for me, will you?" He passed me an envelope while he fiddled with the camera memory card. Like a dummy, I took it and he wouldn't take it back. It was my fee. Arguing that took us back to the door, where he tried to apologize for his wife.

"Look, don't take any notice of Ruth. She's upset at the moment."

I let that pass. "Niall, you said there were two things you wanted to talk to me about."

He fussed and fiddled and didn't meet my eye. "It's not important. You've done us a great favor. I'll pass your contact stuff to Cassie. She'll be coming out this way soon."

He stuck his hand out. I ignored it.

"You know who stole it, don't you?"

"Don't *know* anything."

"You've got a good idea or you'd never have mentioned it. You're convinced, aren't you?"

He grunted, but didn't deny it.

"Spill it, Niall."

"Floyd," he sighed eventually. "Ruth's brother, Floyd Underwood." We leaned on the railing next to the door and Niall spoke quietly.

"He's a collector. Been wanting me to hand over the medal for ages. Kept coming around the apartment, getting me to bring it out. Always calling Ruth." He ran a hand over his head. "Got to saying that money he'd lent us a while back was down payment, stuff like that."

"You can't sell it," I said. "It's illegal to sell a Medal of Honor."

He just shrugged. "Floyd didn't care what it was called, just that it ended up with him. But anyway, all the calls stopped as soon as the burglary happened. I hadn't told him. Ruth says she didn't either, and we haven't heard from him once since it happened. Ruth says it's coincidence. Now what do you think?"

I figured Underwood had 'thief' stamped on his forehead, but I'd need to look into it. I didn't immediately know what I could do, and it was getting late for Cheesman Park.

I got Niall to let me in to change into my running gear in the lobby restroom, then I gave him a hug and trotted off into the evening, tucking my hair under the black ski cap.

Cheesman Park was just a block away and a whole lot less easy.

Chapter 18

A minute later, I was trotting the mile circuit in the park. It was getting dark, and joggers would be thinning out, but this was better than just walking up to the pavilion.

Cheesman is large and ringed with trees, giving the inner park an open country feel despite the roads that came in and the apartment buildings visible over the trees. The acropolis pavilion on the east side has gardens behind it and reflecting pools in front. It's slightly raised with good lines of sight all around. It wasn't the ideal meeting place, but it'd work.

The perimeter circuit passed a few yards from the pavilion, giving me an opportunity to look it over. I couldn't see anyone standing inside. There were lots of reasons for him to not be there, of course: Hoben had sent him somewhere else; he'd gone back to New Mexico; Matlal had killed him. Or simply, he hadn't gotten here yet.

I did another half circuit. There were groups in the park, but nothing suspicious or threatening.

I trotted into the pavilion and started doing stretches, making sure I changed position and checked every angle. The pavilion was open on all sides, just columns and a roof. It did feel vulnerable, but I figured that the last thing Hoben or Matlal wanted was to attract attention to themselves. I guessed that wouldn't stop a sniper. I kept moving randomly. The columns seemed much thinner than I remembered them.

Of course, a second kill option would be up close with a silenced pistol. Okay, I was not going to stand around if someone came in.

What about a capture? I started thinking how I would run a trap for someone in the pavilion without anyone else in the park seeing what really happened. Getting out was easy—a fake ambulance picking up a 'sick' woman or a group with a 'drunken' friend.

How would I keep the target in the pavilion distracted long enough to get my people in?

Send someone in to talk to the target with information they really wanted to hear.

I tried not to fixate on that thought. Give Larry a chance.

I checked the HK in my jogging bag. I would use it only as a last resort. I had a concealed weapon permit, but firing in the park would get me hauled in by the police, and the FBI would be two paces behind.

Next to the HK, I had Matt's scanner. It wasn't intended for this, but it was the best I could do at short notice. I'd set it to hunt short range frequencies. It might, just might, give me a hint if someone was using a tactical comms unit in the area. At the moment it was picking up occasional static, but real trick comms sounded like that to eavesdroppers.

And then, I had Mary's bracelet on my wrist. I didn't want to rely on it because I didn't understand how it worked, but it had warned me before when I was in danger from someone close by.

A panting group trotted by on the circuit behind me, encouraging each other to raise it for one last lap.

Where was he?

I owed it to Larry to wait, but my jogging outfit wouldn't be a good disguise for much longer—once it was full dark, it'd make me stand out. And I was starting to get an itchy feeling about this. Five more minutes and I was gone.

Looking through the gloom made me aware of another step my body had taken towards being Athanate—my good night vision was being helped by sensitivity in the infrared end of the spectrum. Without actually changing the way I saw things, there was an overlay, a slight glow to warm bodies and a hint of air haze around them. Way cool.

With that advantage, I was able to see a man emerge from the darkness under the trees at the northwest corner and start across the park towards the pavilion. Alone, which made him stand out. Moving erratically, as if he were drunk. I guessed that could be a disguise. If this was Larry, his tradecraft sucked. And if it wasn't, I was out of here.

I kept to the shadows and slipped around a pillar as he came in, silently re-entering behind him. It was Larry all right, stinking of cheap bourbon and waving a bottle. My hand caressed the textured grip of the HK. He'd changed his cargo pants and sweatshirt for a wrinkled suit and a shabby coat, but he wore running shoes.

"Out for some fresh air?" I said quietly.

He jumped. "Jesus Christ, Farrell! Don't do that."

He was smart enough to keep his hands in sight.

"Stand in the middle," I said. I paced the pavilion, one eye on him and one on the night. The sounds of laughter drifted in from a group of friends ambling past. The scanner whispered and hissed in my jogging bag. My bracelet didn't tingle. My hackles weren't up, quite.

"You sure you haven't been followed?"

"Yeah. Doubled back and triple checked." He waved his hands for emphasis and the bourbon sloshed on the floor.

"Put the bottle down." He did. "It's not aftershave, you know. You're supposed to drink it, not wear it."

"You wouldn't say that if you tasted it," he replied.

I laughed. I wanted to like him. It had to take balls to get out from under Matlal's nose and then make jokes. Or to come and be bait in a trap. I needed to be sure about him first.

"How come it's so easy for you to get out?"

"It wasn't! That's why I was late."

"If you want out, why haven't you just run?"

"And go where? I need a House to give me sanctuary. And Denver's full of Matlal people."

There was still nothing out of place, but my training was starting to make me nervous about staying put for so long. I needed to make a decision on Larry and either get him squared away, or get myself the hell out of here. I decided to push him.

"Has Romero gone to Basilikos now?"

He twitched at the name, but didn't speak, didn't nod.

"If you're Romero, how come Matlal's trusting you?"

He didn't deny his House.

"He isn't. One of his lieutenants put the—" He stopped, balling his fists in frustration.

"Put a compulsion on you about some things?"

He nodded. "And I was given a Matlal babysitter."

"Where's he?"

"Recovering, for Christ's sake. You gut-shot him, remember? That's one reason why I was able to get out."

"And they think you've gone where?"

"They don't. I'm supposed to be…" he stuttered to a stop, looking sick, but this time I didn't think it was the compulsion. "I'm supposed to be feeding," he finished quietly and shuddered. It took me a second to realize what he meant. Somewhere in this city, Matlal had captives being held to provide blood for his troops. If Larry really was Panethus, no wonder he looked sick at the thought.

He went on. "A new batch of Matlal people came in today—some special team. They're reassigning people. I slipped out in the confusion." He twisted his wrist to look at his watch. "They've probably realized by now."

I could see the thought trickling through his head. *Too late to back out now.*

"Okay, Larry, we need to cut to the chase. What have you got for me? How can I track Hoben down?"

"Like I said, he shifts where he stays. But there's a place near the interstate junction of 25 and 70, this side of the railroad tracks. Used to be a bowling alley or something. He's always going there. And another, up on 64th Avenue in Commerce City, an old auto auction shop."

He hesitated, and wiped his hands down his coat. "I know they're planning something big."

"Like what?"

He shook his head. "The deal was Hoben. I've given you what I can. Get me somewhere safe."

"And then?" I said. "You'll still be under the compulsion."

"And then, we'll have time to get around it. They're like computer programs, you know, you can always find a way." He tapped his watch. "We need to go."

I huffed. He had a good point; it was late. I wasn't going to get any further in my evaluation of him tonight, and everything so far suggested he was on the level.

The scanner chirped in the silence.

"What else are you asking for the rest?"

"Just a place for me and my kin." He spoke very quietly, more uncertain than at any other time tonight. His kin meant a lot to him and I could hear a plea there. Nothing else he had said carried the weight of that plea in the balance of my decision.

"Of course your kin," I said. Bian and Skylur were going to string me up anyway.

I nodded to the back of the pavilion and our route out. We started to walk.

"I'm going to take you to a safe house down in—"

I stopped.

The scanner was still picking up static, but there was suddenly a rhythm of noises emerging that was all too familiar to me from my days in Ops 4-10. I ran back and looked out across the park.

Vague figures shimmered into my heat sense view in the direction where Larry had come from. They were moving purposefully, spread out and spreading wider. Searching. And they were organized enough that they were coordinating with secured comms.

Shit.

Our only advantage was they hadn't spotted me yet and didn't know I'd spotted them. We still had a couple of minutes. I grabbed Larry and shoved him against a pillar, out of sight.

"What the fuck?" he grunted, but to give him his due, he kept it quiet and didn't struggle.

"They followed you, asshole." I'd come to my decision about Larry; he was on the level. But those people out in the park didn't stumble here by accident.

I went through his pockets. I was expecting to find something like a replacement cell phone left switched on, but what came out was an apartment key on a ring with a large blue tag.

The scanner chirped.

"Idiot! There's a tracker in there."

I hurled it away and grabbed him by his lapels.

"If we get split up, 248 Monroe Street in Aurora. Say it back."

"248 Monroe, Aurora. I can't see anyone," hissed Larry, craning his head to look.

"Shut up. Run. Now. That way. Towards 11th Avenue."

I followed, trying to see any pursuit in the dark. The group who'd been tracing his path were still walking. It was our good luck that they hadn't seen us yet.

And that's where our luck ran out.

All that comms traffic had been to coordinate a net around us. We were just barely quick enough that the net hadn't completely closed. More figures were converging on us. With their sudden appearance, Larry instinctively tried to stop. I knew our only hope was to bust out now. I pushed. He tripped.

As I bent to get a grip on him, there was a hissing sound and something whipped past my head to shatter against a pillar. Crap. Tranquillizer dart.

"Larry—" I pulled him. I felt him reach up swiftly and thrust something in my pocket.

"Go!" He hissed as he lurched up, waving his arm. "Not us, you fools," he yelled. "Over there." He sprinted away from me across the gardens, pointing ahead. "She's getting away."

That was smart. Even Athanate eyes would be confused in the darkness. He'd gained us valuable seconds. I bent double and ran straight ahead towards where the dart had come from. Those things take a while to reload.

They were in the trees.

I'd caught them just in time. They weren't in position. The guy with the dart gun came up out of the shadows and I used our combined momentum to drive my forearm into his neck. He fell, choking and clutching at his throat. Matlal Athanate.

A second man was behind me now. I could hear him running after me. I couldn't stop for anything or he'd catch up. I vaulted over the third, hoping he'd tangle up my pursuer, but that just left me with two people chasing, and I was heading for the fourth man. Woman, I corrected.

She was in the open, waiting, balanced on the balls of her feet. *Good stance, but not going to help you, bitch.* I outweighed her. I gritted my teeth, lowered my head. *This is gonna hurt you more than…*

I was flying. Crap! That would teach me. I tucked and spun, slamming the ground with my arm before I hit and converting my momentum into a roll quick enough to spin me right onto my feet again. She was *good,* but her throw had just sent me in the direction I was going anyway. I sprinted for the streetlights of 11th Avenue and vaulted the close-parked cars. *She* was House Matlal, without a doubt, and a whole heap of trouble to boot.

One of the chasers followed, coming between two cars. Big mistake. He couldn't balance, couldn't evade. I stunned him with a punch and slammed his face down into the car's hood. The second man grabbed for me. ZK, not Athanate, I registered as I broke his wrist. As he gasped and stumbled, I high-kicked and sent him reeling into another attacker.

She was already behind me, scary quick. I slipped her headlock and jabbed back with my elbow. I hit, but it did me no good. She was padded up. Not Kevlar, but body punches were a waste of energy. I grabbed and twisted, trying to throw her, but she slipped out like water, landing a punch as she jinked back.

I was in a fix. I outweighed and outreached her. She was quicker than me. I needed to disable her, soon. All she needed to do was slow me down. There would be too many of them here, or another tranquillizer dart would end it.

She took advantage of my hesitation, ghosting in and landing a body punch combination. I wasn't wearing any padding, but she wasn't going to hurt me that quickly and she'd made the mistake of coming within my reach. I went for a grip.

For the second time that night I was flying. This time she wasn't letting go. I could see her planned sequence, like a textbook example. Land me on my back and flip me, or land me on my front. Either way, get my arm behind me and immobilize me. No way.

I balled up and twisted to get my feet beneath me, yanked her sideways. Her punch hammered my jaw. Damn, but she was *real* good. A couple more of her friends sprinted out from the park. Looking bad.

"FREEZE! Federal agents!" came from the other direction.

Oh, hell. Frying pans and fires.

But he was too far away. She lit off, and her buddies went with her, clearing their wounded.

Griffith fired. I dropped to the ground and lay there, hands outstretched. He ran up and fired twice more into the dark, but he was wasting his time and bullets. Worse, he was Endangering The Public in the words of The Manual. At least I hadn't done that. I could almost hear him swallowing painfully as the thought of his post-event report struck him.

I stayed still and swallowed my pride. "Thanks, Agent Griffith. That was very good timing." No harm in a bit of crawling now. I'd stay flat until he put that gun away.

"You…" He knelt beside me and I felt his hand on my wrist. The touch of the slick metal was shocking.

He wasn't going to…

"You have the right to remain silent." The cuffs snapped closed. "You—"

"Now, Ray." A drawl overrode the Miranda. "I'm thinking there's no need for them."

I closed my eyes and gave silent thanks. "Agent Ingram. I didn't think I'd be saying what a pleasure it is."

He chuckled like everyone's favorite uncle at the barbeque. Griffith sulkily unfastened the cuff and let me get back to my feet. The adrenaline burn was easing and my breathing was already back to normal. I shivered, checking out a couple of bruises. That woman had been hardcore.

"You really have to wear your weapon, Ingram," Griffith murmured, trying not to let me hear.

Ingram shrugged it off. "Wouldn't have made a difference here."

"What were you going to arrest me for?" I asked Griffith, rubbing my wrist with one hand and my jaw with the other. He ignored me.

"Would you care to fill us in on what happened, Ms. Farrell?" asked Ingram.

"I just finished jogging in the park. I was heading for my car, when I got jumped by a group. Seven at least. You showed up." That was simple enough; I could remember it. And it wasn't untrue.

Ingram grunted and nodded at Griffith, who called it in to the police. Attempted mugging, FBI on site. No one would come out here.

"We going to do any good in there?" Ingram waved generally at the park.

"I doubt it."

"Then why dontcha come sit in our van over yonder," Ingram said. "We can have some coffee, an' we can spin our wheels for awhile." He took my arm gently and we walked back towards the Quinns', where I'd left my car.

That was fine by me. Some of the ambushers had been ZK, and they might think twice about taking on federal agents, but the Matlal Athanate wouldn't. If they figured out that this hadn't been a smart trap set by me, and there were only two agents here, they'd come back and finish the job.

Their van was parked a couple of spaces down from my car. It was a slab-sided Dodge 8-seater with mirrored windows in the back. The outside was ordinary, but I'd bet money the engine was tricked. The inside was full of tech. The cabin was arranged around a small table and I settled apprehensively into one of the seats.

Ingram pulled a thermos flask from a container and poured the three of us some coffee in small mugs. It was good stuff. We took a moment to savor it.

"Well, y'know, I'm mindful that a rich person, a really rich person, can get to the point that they have so much money that they can't ever get to spend it all." Ingram slumped back in his seat and looked up at the roof of the van. "I wouldn't want to think that there was a point like that with questions." His eyes came back down to look at me and he smiled like an alligator.

I shrugged. "Y'all need to talk to the colonel."

Stop it, demon. Do NOT start talking Texan.

"Ahh," Ingram nodded. "Yup. The colonel. Fact is, I called that number, right after you left."

I shivered. It was cold, even in the van. The colonel hadn't picked up my calls for a couple of days now.

"Mighty interesting," said Ingram.

I refused to rise to the bait. I sat and sipped my coffee.

"Especially after we pulled your police file. And spoke to Lieutenant Krantz," Griffith said.

I was in stealth mode. I was determined I was not going to respond to this sort of probe, but Krantz's name made me twitch.

"Lordy, he's got your goat, hasn't he?" chuckled Ingram. "Thing is, they none of them can agree. Your police file says military, and when they don't say anything else that usually means woo-woo stuff. Now Krantz, he swears blind he has access to everyone's military pay records and you were never there. Says there are no women in any of that kind of unit. Anyhow, I called that number you gave me. I didn't speak to any Colonel Laine. No sir, I spoke to a Captain Baker."

Ingram was watching me like the fox he resembled.

There was no Captain Baker in Ops 4-10 when I was there.

"Don't know him," I said.

"Much what he said 'bout you. I asked about the special forces stuff and he laughed. Boy, oh boy, he laughed. Said that if every person who claimed to be in special forces actually had been, the whole US government would have gone bust trying to pay them."

I just sat and waited him out. It was like having my head pushed through mud, but there was a point to this. Agent Ingram was a man with a point.

"Thing is," he said, "this Baker fellow, he claims that phone number's in army pay administration. Now they aren't woo-woo, so their numbers are up there for me to check, and here's the funny part. It's got the right area code, but it ain't no admin number, and no one called Captain Baker works for army pay. I even asked your friend Krantz."

The number was a blind. It went into some system that rerouted it to the colonel's cell. Or it had before.

"So, where does that leave us?" I asked.

"Still not believing you," muttered Griffith.

Ingram smiled, and I shivered again. This time the chill was more than the temperature or the aftereffects of adrenaline. I desperately needed to talk to the colonel and House Altau, as soon as possible. I couldn't call anyone on my cell with the FBI listening to my calls. I needed to get out of here. Altau at least I could reach. As long as these guys didn't take me in for obstructing an investigation or for my own safety. I couldn't think they'd be able to use any other excuse.

"Tell you what," said Ingram, reaching behind his seat. "I got me a couple of little tests here."

He put a package wrapped in chamois on the table. It was heavy. It clunked. I knew it was a gun.

"Spoke to a friend of mine. He says you should be able to field strip this, sweet as a nut."

I sat up and flicked the chamois back. A smirk tugged at one corner of my mouth. "Almost any grunt would be able to do that," I said. It was an HK Mark 23, the same model as the one in my jogging bag. It was a special forces gun rather than general army issue, but the principles would be the same. "I'll make it more interesting."

I didn't know that this would prove anything, but if Ingram felt it did, I was happy to go along. No skin off my nose. I took the chamois, spun it into a strip and tied it around my head as a blindfold. By touch, I safed the gun, checked the chamber and ejected the magazine.

I stuck my hand out. "Ballpoint," I said. I felt one drop into my hand. I pushed the stiff release pin with it, put the ballpoint down, and felt the familiar components of the gun separating in my hands like a well-worn puzzle. *How many times had I done this?*

I placed the parts in the right order on the table, clapped my hands and re-assembled the gun in five seconds.

"Well, that's mighty impressive, Ms. Farrell, but now, that might just be because you have one." Of course, he would have that on file about me. "Keep the blindfold on, if you would, and try this." There was a much heavier clunk as he pulled something out of the back and laid it on the table in front of me.

I felt the weight and size of the weapon. A rifle. My hands roved over it.

"Special operations combat assault rifle, known as the SCAR. Made by FN for SOCOM," I said as I started disassembly. It was stiff, probably brand new. "This is the heavy, for the 7.62mm NATO cartridge. Long barrel." I placed the last of the pieces on the table. "Taken on officially after I left. I only got to play with it a couple of times."

I put it back together in a dozen seconds and tossed the chamois on top.

Ingram was still smiling, a professional smile that meant nothing. A little worm of doubt punctured my self-satisfied feeling.

Why had he done this? What was going on behind those eyes? Sure, someone with my history would be able to do what I'd done. But so might a spy or a hitman.

Or a terrorist. My heart skipped a beat. Had I just earned myself a stay in a lockup under the Patriot Act? Or worse. My fingerprints were all over those weapons now, and only the two of them witnessing how that happened. Had I been set up for something, or was this a threat to hold over me?

I couldn't figure out what was going through his head, but he'd probably gotten every single thought I'd just had like it had been written on my face.

But he was playing a long game.

"Well that's about it, I guess," he said, finishing his coffee. "For now."

I chewed my cheek to keep my face blank and made to go, but he put his hand up. "Just one last thing, Ms. Farrell," he said. "For tonight, anyhow. That's a mighty fancy car you got there for the amount of money you're clearing."

"It was goods in lieu for a job I did." House Altau had given me the car in exchange for work I had done for them, so I wasn't lying.

Ingram grunted. "Hope you remember it on your tax returns," he said.

"Gods, Ingram. Set Homeland Security on me, but leave the damn IRS out of it, will you?" I opened the panel door.

He laughed, the good ole uncle at the barbeque again.

"We'll need you to come in again, Ms. Farrell," said Griffith. He was bagging the SCAR. Wearing gloves.

"It would be unfortunate if we had to…retrieve you," said Ingram.

Yeah. Very unfortunate for me. 'Wanted in connection with' type of unfortunate. I got out and walked away, furious with everything, myself included.

I drove around the south side of the park, desperate for any sign of Larry. It was futile; if he'd gotten away, he'd still be running. There was a good chance. It'd all happened too quickly, but I had the feeling that every one of Matlal's people was after me, not Larry. That was better than a chance, and Larry was smart enough to take it.

I wanted to head to Monroe right now and wait for Larry. But he could take hours to get there, and there was nothing I could do to help him in the meantime.

Think.

Training kicked in. I had other responsibilities as well.

Refocus on the next objective. Altau telecommunications had been compromised. I had to get that message to them.

But I couldn't drive there in this car. And I couldn't use it to check out Monroe either.

It was no freaking coincidence the FBI van had shown up right next to me. They must have planted a bug on me that I hadn't been able to spot.

I went through how big it might be and where they could have hidden it in the hour I was at the CBI building. It needed power, it needed a transmitter, it probably had GPS or movement detection, it needed to be able to send and receive. There's a limit to how small you can make stuff like that, and where you can plant it, even for the FBI spooks. Trouble was, I didn't know what that limit was. I'd need to ask an expert.

It was dark and I couldn't do it now. I couldn't risk driving the car out to Haven, I couldn't call, and I shouldn't delay telling Altau their phones were being monitored.

I'd have to get unconventional.

Chapter 19

I drove across to Aurora, and parked the car near the main mall.

I changed out of my jogging gear in the back seat and walked down to Colfax Avenue. No one followed me. I made double sure of that. My paranoia was on overdrive.

Late as it was, I got lucky; Rom was still working in his garage.

Rom had helped me maintain my old car for next to nothing, officially renting me out the space and tools, and ignoring all the advice and assistance he gave. And we'd met at raves and parties. We weren't exactly friends, but he'd lent me his motorcycle when my car was up on jacks and I'd needed to go somewhere. That was what I needed from him now.

Rom was cooler about it than I was. I didn't like banking favors, but he laughed it off and handed me the keys and his heavy biking jacket and gloves. Five minutes later, I was on the road, enjoying the rumble of the Harley and weaving sinuously through the nighttime traffic on I-70. I started to feel better and gave the bike its head out on the Parkway. The wind whipped my hair out in a banner behind me. Tears leaked out the corners of my eyes, freezing on my cheeks, and I had a stupid grin on my face listening to the thunder of the engine. I was thankful for the loan of the jacket and gloves.

And it was at about that point my brain got over the FBI and started processing what had happened in the park.

Seven people? More like a dozen. Tracking Larry? Completely uninterested in him once I broke cover. Elite Matlal people taking over. Tactical comms. A trank dart. This wasn't Hoben anymore, this was Matlal. Larry knew. He had known that as soon as he saw the size of the hunt—he'd run off yelling *she's getting away*, not *they're getting away*.

Shit, Matlal was after me and he wanted me alive. Skylur's chilling warning from last night came back to me: if Basilikos heard about my Blood, they'd do *anything* to get hold of me.

I had to pull over and kneel next to the bike, shaking with reaction.

Who told them? Ahead of me waited Haven. Everyone else who knew anything about what had been said at David's house was there. Who was I going to trust?

I flashed back to Ops 4-10 training for covert solo ops.

Red Team. Tied up as an involuntary guest of Blue Team. Caught stupid, sold a pup. Awake for forty hours straight and doused in icy water every ten minutes as punishment. Instructor Ben-Haim screaming in my face, inches away—"Trust no one! Do. You. Understand. Now?"

And whispering in the silence afterwards, his voice sad. "Only people you trust can ever really betray you, Amber."

What would you tell me to do now, Ben-Haim? *Run.*

I could run. With my training I could disappear forever. I'm no instinctive mechanic like Rom, but I could work with engines. I could do fitness training. I could dye my hair, buy a fake ID, trail up and down the coasts. I could almost smell the sea. Always working cash in hand, always moving. Always alone.

And I would have to leave behind Alex, Jen, David, Pia, Tullah and whatever was left from the wreck of my family. No. I wasn't going to do that.

You were wrong, Ben-Haim. I'm a team player. I was always better in 4-10 working in a team. I tried being alone for two years and it sucks. I need a team now.

I had to trust myself, my new instincts and my old ones, and fight my way through this.

If I thought it was cold kneeling next to the Harley, another minute of riding dispelled that. My face and legs were frozen when I got to Haven.

The place was dark, and no one appeared at the gate when I leaned the bike on the kickstand. I could feel them watching. I didn't doubt that a gun or three were pointed my way. Unannounced arrival at night—I huffed. I wasn't making any friends with the security team here.

"House Farrell," I said to the empty night, my mouth feeling slow with the cold. "Urgent communication for the Diakon."

"Run out of carrier pigeons?" said a voice from the gatehouse. A man emerged with the hand scanner. He relaxed a little as it verified me.

"Fresh out. Sorry to arrive like this, at this time of night."

"De nada. Not as if we close down. Nice bike, House." He listened to his earpiece for a second. "She's on her way. Main gates are staying closed—standing orders at the moment."

I shrugged and spent some time rubbing my legs and restoring circulation. How was this going to go?

"Round-eye, what a surprise." Bian came out through the personnel gate. "Shall we walk a little way?" She snagged my arm and we wandered back up the road. I wondered which Bian I would get tonight. The Diakon, or what I was starting to think of as the Leopard, the Bian who threatened to bite me and drag me off to her lair for wild, snarling sex.

"No moonlight tonight. Shame," she said.

I couldn't help but grin in the darkness. "As if that mattered to you, Pussycat. Aren't you concerned about what might be out and about tonight?"

She snorted. "We are the things that go bump in the night, Round-eye. Now, much as I want to believe it, I don't think you rode all the way out here on that pretty motorbike to take me for a walk."

"No." I sighed. Diakon Bian. "I've had a load of fun since I left Jaworski here. And I held something back from you that maybe I shouldn't have." Her hand tightened on my arm but she didn't say anything. "I had to speak to the FBI…"

Bian listened without interrupting as I went through the afternoon: the interest of the federal bureaus, the tapping of phones, the tracking of my car, why I was meeting Larry at the pavilion and the attack.

I slowed, conscious of the grip on my arm, the silence broken only by our footfalls. We were out of sight and hearing of the gatehouse. Why had Bian guided me out here?

She turned us around and we started back.

Trust and Jump. My old watchwords.

I told her my fears about the implications of the attack.

"Calm down, Amber," she said, keeping hold of my arm. "Think it through. There were very few of us that came to the house and know anything about what went on. David, Mykayla and Pia have been isolated from everyone else, and they don't have any means of talking to anyone outside. Besides them, there was Skylur, Diana and my security team involved. How could Matlal have found out?"

"Someone at Haven might be aware that David's passed through crusis. When he was brought in, someone might have noticed his marque's changed, too. Isolating people will cause rumors. People talk, people put two and two together."

We stopped. We'd returned to the gatehouse, and Bian used the intercom system to talk Athanate to someone in the house before rejoining me. She pulled me inside, into the house grounds, and set us off on a circular route around the house.

"Skylur may want to talk to you," she said, when we were out of hearing of the gatehouse. "Right, here's how I see it. It's possible someone put together what happened with David, but it's unlikely. I think you're jumping to conclusions there."

Somehow, that didn't make me feel a whole lot better.

"As for the FBI," she went on, "we're not as clueless as it sounds. We don't use Athanate for phone calls and we don't discuss Athanate business on unsecured phones. Usually. From what they said, they got this recording from putting traces on a phone you called. A phone here. That can only mean my cell has been used by someone else, because for sure, I haven't spoken Athanate on it." She was silent for a while. "It's what was said that's the key. And who said it, of course. Is there any chance you could get a copy of this recording?"

I sighed. "I'll try, Bian, but it's the freaking FBI, okay?"

"I know. And thanks. I'll organize some secure comms for you to pick up tomorrow."

"Okay. I may be a bit late if I have trouble finding how they're tracking my car."

"Just deal with it, Round-eye." We walked in silence for a few yards. "Larry saying they're planning something big…" she shrugged. "I'm not discounting it, but he's under a compulsion. They cause damage. He might have been having an induced psychotic episode. Screwing with someone's head does that a lot."

"Or they really are planning something."

"We can't tell until you get Larry and bring him here."

We were headed back to the gatehouse, and I was glad of it. Bian kept strange hours, but I liked to sleep nights. At least sometimes, anyway.

She was silent again, deep in thought. Then, "I don't understand why you won't just stay here till after the Assembly." She sounded frustrated, almost disappointed—as if it should be something I would *want* to do. Was this Diakon or Leopard talking? Or a real Bian, who might actually be concerned for me personally? She was so damn hard to read. "It's what Skylur will want when he hears about Matlal trying to kidnap you," she added.

Ah. Diakon talking. Purely professional. I didn't know if I was sorry or relieved.

Stay here with David and Pia. Or back in Denver with Alex and Jen. Here with someone I suspected had betrayed me and Altau. Or back in Denver with Hoben and Matlal bent on imprisoning me for the rest of my life. And Larry. I wasn't going to give Larry up. Not just because he was my route to Hoben; he'd slowed up the pursuit at Cheesman. I might owe him my life.

"I can't."

She waited, hoping for elaboration that I didn't give. She gave a frustrated hiss. I sensed her body going taut like an animal about to spring. "I see." The silence lengthened. "Wanting to stay out wouldn't have anything to do with that dreamy wolf, Deauville, would it? Diana says you smelled of wolf this afternoon." Her tone was teasing, but there was an edge to it. Did she have an issue with Alex? She leaned in and inhaled deeply. "Hmm. You still do."

Bian never had much respect for personal space, but this was making me uncomfortable. I moved slightly away.

"Alex is out of town at the moment," I said.

Bian closed the gap again. "Jennifer Kingslund, then?" She slipped an arm around my waist. "Why should blondes have all the fun?" Again there was the edge. Leopard, but not quite. And I felt nervous about digging for the answers to what.

I pushed her away and snorted. "She hasn't had any fun."

Bian's eyes widened. "Amber, honey, you're so slow," she drawled in an excellent imitation of Jen. But the humor was missing from the eyes. It was almost a challenge.

"I'm…" I halted, blushing. Annoyed with both of us. "Why the hell am I talking to you about this?"

She looked at me for a long moment, then shrugged and started walking again, quickly. I had to hurry to catch up. Physically and mentally. Why was she so changeable?

"Because Skylur appointed me to teach you Athanate rules and customs," she said coolly, as if that intensity was all in my head. "Correct little misunderstandings about what's happening to you. Reassure you about things. Make sure you understand what's happening at the Assembly. Useful things like that."

"Huh." Diakon was back, with a vengeance. "Anyway, I promised no security breaches. I can't even talk to Jen until the Assembly is over. And even then, I need to be able to tell her what the risks are and we don't know them yet. I caused an effect in David just with a kiss."

We were nearly at the gatehouse. "We'll see," she said. She was definitely Diakon Bian again. "You want to get back now. Okay, but listen up first, Round-eye. The woman you fought? You're right. She'd be one of Matlal's elite people. Now, I can believe he loans people to Hoben just to keep an eye on him, but not that level of person. He's got some interest in you and the more you frustrate him, the more intent he'll become."

Bian turned at a call from the house.

"Hold on," she said, resting a hand on my arm. A man ran up and they spoke hurriedly in Athanate. Her grip tightened.

"Right," she said, turning back. "Skylur wants to see you now, and I've got another damn emergency."

We went back to the house, my stomach churning again. I did *not* want to talk to Skylur. Especially if he'd been woken just for this. As we reached it, Bian had three people talking at her at once. "Last room on the left, take the elevator down," she said to me, startling me with a swift hug. She wasn't just hard to read, she was downright schizophrenic. "I'll come back when you're done and see you out." She was swept away.

I walked down the hall. The first time I'd been brought here to see Skylur, I'd been blindfolded, but I knew where I was.

I got to the end of the hall. 'Left' she'd said. 'Right' said my movement memory. I went into the right-hand room, and I was correct; it was the one I'd been taken to the first time. Bian must have been distracted.

I walked over to where the elevator platform was hidden—a circular pattern on the carpet. I stood there, feeling stupid. There was no control panel I could see. How did I get it to descend? I was going to look like an idiot wandering around looking for someone to tell me how to operate the elevator.

No need. Curved glass doors whispered out from the column behind me. The floor dropped away and a few seconds later I was in Skylur's creepy dungeon.

How deep was I? Sixty feet? Seventy? Five floors beneath the house? Exactly what did he have hidden down here?

The light was the same as I remembered—deep blue and directionless. Even with my improved Athanate eyesight, I had trouble making out details. And it was cold. I hadn't registered that last time.

Skylur wasn't here. The statues along the wall were.

They looked different to me now. When I'd been down here before, my eyesight hadn't been so developed. I'd had to go over and touch a statue to confirm they were warm; flesh warm. Now, I could see the soft haze rising from them in the cold air.

I found myself in front of Anubis again, looking up at the muzzle, the rippling muscles beneath the sun-dark skin, the fathomless eyes. The skin still felt as unyielding and warm as if Anubis himself had just this minute been turned to stone.

No way this was just a statue.

Unlike the last time I was here, I heard Skylur entering behind me.

I turned and was walking towards his throne at the end as he sat. "Good evening, Amber." His voice was genuinely pleasant when he wanted it to be. It sounded like I wasn't on his shit list today, but I wasn't relaxing yet. I'd believe it when he let me go. At least there was nothing of the controlled fury in him today.

"Hello, Skylur. A little late to wish me a good evening."

Like midnight. I grabbed a chair from the side and sat on it facing him. It was too dark to make out his features.

I strangled the demon in my throat, which was about to say something even more flippant.

Silence.

Shit, was I even supposed to sit in his presence without his permission? He'd specifically ordered me to sit at David's house. I'd probably pissed him off again. If I couldn't get little things like this right, what chance did I have with the bigger things?

But his voice was contemplative when he eventually spoke. "You're an affiliate of House Altau. What do you think that means with regard to my policies and commands?"

Crap. I obviously screwed the pooch again. What was it this time?

I cleared my throat. "I haven't had time for a full briefing, Skylur. I honestly don't know. I apologize if—"

"It would be different if I'd taken you into House Altau, but Diana insisted on affiliation, and I trusted her judgment."

I bowed my head. This was shaping up to be more than a disciplinary hearing. It sounded like he was aiming to make House Farrell the shortest-lived House in the history of the Athanate. There had to be something I could do. I couldn't have him order me into Haven. I had to be out there.

"I don't know what I've done—"

"It's not what you've done," he interrupted. "It's what you're going to do. Tell me your view of what happened at Cheesman Park."

I was more unsettled than if he'd been yelling. I started to stumble through what had happened and he stopped me.

"I know the events. I want your interpretation. What's behind all this?"

I was ready to start gibbering—they were going to grab me and drag me somewhere to…

But he didn't want my knee-jerk gut reaction. He wanted interpretation. It was as if he'd slapped me. My brain crunched painfully into gear.

Shape up! Think!

"There were too many. Too much effort, too much tech. It was almost…"

He leaned forward as I slowed.

"It was almost as if they were using this as a sort of live fire training exercise."

"Not about you at all?"

"No, that's not what I meant. Their training and my capture were both objectives."

If it was, my escape had to have severely pissed them off. Small victory.

He leaned back again in the silence.

"Matlal troops in Denver," he said dismissively. "What could they possibly be preparing for?"

I swallowed. Thinking of it like an abstract military problem, a frightening possibility leaped out at me. But I was taking a huge jump here. Making myself look like an idiot.

"Pre-emptive strike. If Matlal is about to restart the war against Panethus, what better way to start than taking out the leadership of Panethus while they're gathered for the Assembly? Over before it begins."

He snorted, but without being able to see his face, I didn't know what to make of that.

"Basilikos representatives would call that completely ridiculous," he said. "Anyway, the Warders are keeping the delegates separate and moving around. There is no single target to strike against, and the first strike gives the whole game away. Not to mention alerting the human population of Denver. No Basilikos wants that. They are fanatically opposed to humans knowing about the existence of the Athanate."

"Attack here during the Assembly," I said immediately, warming to the theme. "Maximum target concentrated in a remote and secret location."

"He doesn't know where Haven is. Delegates will be brought here 'securely'."

Was securely a joke about Jaworski? Nah. Not Skylur, surely?

"He might know where Haven is now." With security procedures lax enough to let someone use Bian's cell phone, who knows what had slipped out?

"Oh, he might. And I might have defenses he doesn't expect, too." He shifted in the darkness. "But Basilikos have dissenters too, certainly if it came to attacking the Assembly. There would be at least a rumor of it. There's nothing. Nothing about that, anyway."

"So what are the rumors saying?" I said.

"Rumors say that an affiliate of Altau has a Blood with remarkable properties. That Altau is seeking to keep this for itself. That Matlal is determined to get hold of this affiliate. For the greater good of the whole Athanate community, of course. That he is hunting her through the streets of Denver."

That lay like ice in my belly. Just because it's a rumor and wrapped in lies, doesn't mean it doesn't have a kernel of truth. Matlal was after me with his top teams. I'd been spouting garbage about attacks, trying to prove my worth, and all I'd achieved was to sound like an idiot. He'd haul me in now out of embarrassment that he had such a stupid affiliate.

"I doubt you underestimate an opponent when you spar, Amber. Apply that caution here."

I peered into the gloom, trying to make out any clues in his face.

What did he mean? Despite everything, a sliver of excitement tickled me. If I was sparring, I might feint one way and go another.

"The rumors are a feint. He's not after me at all."

"Oh, he wants you as well. Never doubt that. You refused him at the ball, in front of Basilikos representatives. Don't underestimate his pride. And now you've escaped him again."

Skylur stood abruptly, making me jump. "And putting everything else aside, if he catches you, what then?" He stepped down onto the dark granite floor. "Either you have this miracle Blood, in which case he will use it. Or you don't, in which case he says nothing. And for as long as he can say nothing, every Basilikos dissenter will be failing to dissent on any matter in case they lose out on the benefit. And even Panethus dissenters might cross the divide rather than risk not getting access to this miracle Blood. Oh, he wants you all right."

I stood as well. Skylur had moved into the vacant senior military commander slot in my reflexes, and I didn't feel comfortable sitting while he stood. If he noticed, it didn't show.

"You don't believe my Blood's different, do you?" I asked.

"It's different. No doubt about that at all. Is it a miracle that reduces crusis?" He turned and walked slowly to stand in front of me. I could see a frown on his face now. "I'm not sure I want to believe that," he murmured, as if talking to himself.

"You could find out," I said. Shivers went down my spine. He could bite me, and he'd know, somehow. I wasn't ready for that. I didn't know why.

He swayed closer and my eyes closed. This time there was no Diana to stop him. I could feel his stare, focused on my throat. Part of me wanted him to bite, wanted to submit and become part of Altau. It would be safer. So much easier to belong. The rest of me was trying to push him away.

"Would you like me to?" he whispered.

My lips felt numb.

"No," said Tara.

Oh hell! Shut up!

"Not yet," I added hastily.

My eyes stayed closed. I sensed him move away, and unobtrusively sucked in a lungful of the cold air. Something creaked. When I looked, he was seated again.

"For another day, then. You *will* ask me, you know."

"Yes." It seemed the safest thing to say. Short and simple, while I gathered my tumbled wits.

"On Matlal's layers of deception, Amber," he said, as if we hadn't paused. "What would you recommend we should do? Considering that we don't want him to know we know."

"Ahh. Respond to the first layer of his plan." *Crap.* "Hide me away."

"My Diakon has offered you sanctuary, and it seems you don't want it."

"I have things that are important to me that I have to do."

"Hmm. And what if we don't want to take away Matlal's first layer? If we want him to think he doesn't need to change his deception? If we want him distracted? If we want him to underestimate us?"

I sat back down and tried to marshal my thoughts. The only thing I could think of was absurd. There had to be something else. His foot started tapping. I had nothing else.

"I stay out there," I said. "In defiance of orders."

"Yes. That might do it." He shifted his weight, laced his fingers together. "Of course, there is the problem he might catch you."

"So I'm clear, why is it a problem for you? You don't believe my Blood will affect crusis and I'm sure you can counter any unsubstantiated assertions by Matlal." I didn't care for Skylur's dry analysis of my potential, unpleasant fate at Matlal's hands. "I think I just about understand the problem for me," I added.

"You are not a sacrificial pawn, Amber. You are an affiliate of my House, sworn or not. I will not order you to do this. But on the other hand, having Matlal distracted is important for the whole of Panethus, and I think you understand that could mean the whole world too."

I was okay with that, really. The thought that he was just maneuvering me into agreeing to be bait was not worthy.

"How good are you, Amber? Can you keep one step ahead?" he asked.

"Purely on my own, yes." With Ben-Haim's old lectures whispering in my ear, I could vanish from sight. "But there are two things against me. I have to get past Matlal to take out Hoben. That's why I have to be out there."

"Hmm. And the second thing that's against you?"

"If I'm reporting back and there's a spy here."

"What I'm thinking takes that into account." I waited. There were too many possibilities he could be talking about, none of them palatable. *Never operate at the end of a compromised line,* Ben-Haim had said.

He stood again.

"It's fortunate you made the mistake of coming in here, rather than where you were sent. It saved me coming up with a plan to speak privately to you. But we can't use that again. It might be noticed. *If* there's a spy. It's possible we may not be able to speak again before the Assembly, Amber, so your decision now is important. Given what you know, are you willing to be a distraction for Matlal?"

"Yes," I said.

"Then you have my secret permission to ignore my demands for you to come in and stay at Haven, which I will feed through the appropriate channels. No one but Diana and I will know of this. This meeting, the room itself and everything we've said is completely secret. Tell no one. Do you understand?"

"Yes."

"And the difference between an affiliate and a member of my House is in the amount of discretion. As an affiliate, in theory, you could argue against coming in to Haven. But to individual members of my House, you will inevitably appear to be a troublemaker. And at the same time, Matlal and Hoben will become increasingly desperate to catch you the closer to the Assembly we get. I cannot spare any resource from my other preparations to protect you. Are you still willing?"

"Yes, I am."

"Then be careful, and remember, don't discuss this conversation with anyone. Not even Bian, who is waiting to see you out in the elevator room."

I nodded and started to walk back down to the elevator. I was both cold and sweating. I wanted out of this creepy dungeon as quickly as possible and a chance to think through what all of it meant.

"Oh, Amber," he called after me. I turned and went back. What now?

"I just wanted to say, the distressed biker jacket suits you."

He slipped through his door and it closed seamlessly behind him.

Asshole.

"Good night, Skylur," I said, as I returned to the elevator. "Thank you so much for your advice. Hope I didn't keep you up. Do sleep well."

Bian met me and walked me out to the gate.

"Just for your information," she said, "the Warders have raised a concern with us, about you."

I sighed. "Yeah? What have I done now?"

"We're not taking it seriously, Round-eye. Don't look so sour." She took my arm and put on a news presenter voice. "Your presence in Denver is a provocation, needlessly escalating tensions and distracting from the purpose of the Assembly." She was back to playful Bian. That was a relief. I could deal with that.

"Matlal's breaching how many rules and I'm the one classed as a provocation?"

"I said we weren't taking it seriously."

We reached the gate.

"Do I get a goodnight kiss?" she said.

I huffed and kissed her neck, then tried to get back at her for all her teasing with a nip from my teeth. That was so dumb. She returned the favor and it wasn't her ordinary teeth that scratched the skin of my neck. Skylur had put me off limits, so I was probably safe. Probably. Unless Bian had some secret instruction from him to disobey his orders, like I had.

I shivered and slipped through the gate to the sound of her laughter.

∞ ∞ ∞ ∞ ∞

248 Monroe Street was silent, wrapped up in cold and dark and misery. Larry wasn't there.

I could hear Ben-Haim whispering in my ear again. *He's not there. Go! Now! Do not return! He is no longer a safe contact. He may have been taken and revealed its location. You can no longer assume this is a safe house. This is how you live for another day.*

No, Ben-Haim. I wouldn't abandon Larry. But I'd have to be very careful visiting again. I slipped back out, tired and depressed. Where was he?

It'd taken ages to check Monroe, return Rom's Harley and pick up my car. I left the car down in Wash Park and snuck in through the golf course next to Manassah. I was not going to lead the FBI to Jen's door.

At 4 a.m. I tiptoed into my suite and I was asleep as soon as my head touched the pillow.

I can't breathe. Why do I dream of suffocation so often?

I stumble into the living room and a darkness my eyes cannot pierce presses in on me. But my lungs heave and sweet air fills them. Here, I can breathe again.

Shadows gather and stir from every corner; sibilance caresses my ears.

"Welcome." It's as if the whole room speaks, and the word shudders through my chest.

"Who's that?"

"See." A ball of flame, painfully bright blue, emerges from the darkness and floats into the fireplace, setting alight the neat stack of wood waiting there.

The warm glow pushes back the dark. Reflected gleams spring up like a thousand eyes snapping open in the night.

Tullah sits asleep on the sofa.

Around her, filling the space of the whole room with shiny scales and restless movement, stirs her dragon.

"Is Tullah—"

"She is all right, of course. Greetings, Amber Farrell. I am Kaothos."

Her head is huge, resting on the floor next to the sofa, one eye the size of my own head turned to me. The pupil is oval like a cat's.

I sit slowly on a stool. Our eyes are level. The fire warms me. "Greetings, Kaothos."

"Greetings also, to those within you," says Kaothos.

I feel a disturbance in my head. Hana, my spirit wolf, is twisting in consternation. From Tara, only fascination.

"You will speak with Tullah's parents soon. They will warn you of the dangers of dragons, just as they warned you of the dangers of Athanate." The huge orb of the eye staring at me dims as a clear inner lid sweeps briefly over it. The pupil widens, black as space. "Do you think I'm evil, Amber Farrell?"

"I think all creatures have the potential to be evil. I don't know you."

A hissing sound like water splashing over very hot rocks. A dragon's laughter.

"And you have this potential too?" says Kaothos.

"Yes."

"It may be we can help each other in this."

Kaothos wants this. We hear it in her voice. Hana stops to listen.

"We will speak again, Amber Farrell."

The great outer eyelid descends like falling silk and in the fireplace, the flames pop and disappear.

I surged upright. I was on my bed, lying on top of the comforter. The house was completely silent. My skin was warm as if I'd sat next to a fire, but I was shivering. A dream. Just a dream.

Chapter 20

WEDNESDAY

Jen was long gone to work by the time I got up.

I sorted some dirty clothes for Jen's maid to clean. Gods, I was getting used to this lifestyle. Maybe not a good idea. Who knows what tomorrow brings?

Checking pockets, I came out with a scrap of paper. Larry had shoved it into my pocket just before he'd started running at Cheesman. A little superstitious chill lifted my hair. I pushed that aside. One side, it was a jumble of letters, numbers, and what looked like map drawings of river deltas, or maybe stylized ferns. On the other side, a meaningless jumble of lines. I folded it carefully and tucked it away for later. I'd tease him over a beer about what it meant.

In the living room, there were ashes and partly burned wood in the fireplace. I stood looking down thoughtfully for a minute as I worked out the stiffness from the fight last evening. Nothing I could do about the bruises, but it would all heal soon.

Tullah was in the study office.

"Oh, hi," she said. "I didn't see the car. I thought you were gone already."

"I left the car well away from the house. The FBI have some kind of tracker on it." I sat at my desk. "Did you sleep well last night, Tullah?" I asked casually.

"Oh, absolutely fine, thanks." I could see her looking at my bruising, but apart from the usual roll of the eyes, she didn't bother to comment.

I updated her on the events with the FBI and with Hoben and Matlal's attempt to kidnap me at Cheesman Park. We compared notes on our PI cases and I logged Niall's fee. I kept the cash—it was too handy, usefully untraceable. I wasn't going to use a card unless I had to, with the FBI breathing down my neck.

Tullah's case had involved a bit of surveillance and plenty of digging into internet records that I suspected Matt had helped her with. She didn't ask me for advice, and I didn't want to nudge her elbow, so beyond making sure I knew what she was doing, I left her to handle it.

"What about your mother, Tullah?" I asked, with business out the way. "How's she taking your move?"

Tullah winced. "Still not good. I've told my parents it's got nothing to do with you, but they want to talk to you."

"Okay. When?"

"This afternoon?"

I thought about what I had to get through today.

I needed to check Monroe Street again, carefully. There were the two locations that Hoben used which Larry had given me, but Larry himself was still the best source of a clue where to find Hoben, even if he didn't think he was.

I'd texted Matt with a request for information on the locations, and I'd need to drive by. But I was also due back at Haven for a briefing on the Assembly and to talk to the Judicator. I needed to make some progress on the Quinns' case, have a look at Floyd Underwood. All complicated by keeping out of the way of Matlal and the FBI. Sigh.

"Sure," I said to Tullah, "but I'll have to call them later to confirm a place and time."

Tullah frowned and moved uncomfortably on her chair. "You need to be careful around Ma."

"Gods, Tullah, you don't need to tell me that. Mary scares me."

"It's not just that. Ma's downer on the Athanate is normal for Adepts, and she's…quite senior in the community."

"Head witch, hey?" I tried to make light of it, but Tullah didn't respond. More sighs. One more thing to look out for.

"So, what do Adepts do, Tullah?" I asked her. "Besides hate the Athanate, of course." I wasn't expecting a response really, certainly not what I got.

"Save the freaking world by making sure no other Adepts actually use their powers," she snapped. "Prevent anyone from actually realizing their potential." She stopped abruptly, looking disturbed.

Her eyes flicked to me. "I didn't mean that," she said quietly.

"Okay," I said. I didn't want to make a big deal out of it. Shooting off her mouth in that way wasn't her style at all. She seemed upset with herself, and I thought it best to let it go for the moment. Time enough to talk it over later, when worrying about where she was living wasn't such an issue.

Instead, I called Matt on the landline to see how he'd done with his searches and to talk about secure communications. I was getting seriously paranoid, and luckily, he loved this kind of thing.

"Yuh, Amber, forget the burn phone thing unless you have two for every person you want to talk to, one for them and one for you. Otherwise, even using a cell they're not tracking, you get through to someone you call a lot, and they can put a back trace to get a position on you. And you can't use that SIM again. So, you can go out and buy double handful of SIMs and throw them away after every call, but that's expensive and there's a better way."

"Tell me."

"Y'know you can do calls on computers using the internet? I have a trick system I put together to use that. Only drawback is, it'll only work in city limits or near unsecured connections. It can't be backtracked. It'll even disguise your voice. I'll send you the files and a list of stuff to get. Of course, they could be monitoring whoever you're calling, and you still need to be careful what you say, but I guess you'll have plenty of code words and stuff."

"I wish, Matt. I'll keep that problem in mind. The cell is just so damn useful, it really throws me that it's about as secure as shouting across the street. Okay, enough. Did you find any stuff on Matlal and Hoben?"

"Nothing special. Not quite as phantom as some people…" I grinned at that. Matt had looked for any traces of me on the internet, and there weren't any the whole time I was in Ops 4-10. "But anyway, it's in your inbox, in an encrypted file. Tullah's got the password."

"Thanks. You did keep your head down while you pulled this cyber-ninja stuff?"

"Yeah, yeah."

"Okay, last thing. May not be your scene. I've picked up a tracker on my car. I checked and couldn't find it. Do you have anything on the latest tech for trackers? Like how I'd find one?"

"I know a guy has this info. I'll get it on an email in, say, fifteen."

"That's ace, Matt. I'll call later on your spook phone."

"Cool."

We signed off.

"He's so smart," I said to Tullah, looking dreamy, "as well as good-looking. Do you think he's too young for me?"

"Enough of that," she said, grinning, and twisting her computer screen around. "Is this Alex the wolf?"

She'd pulled up an image on her search engine. I guessed it was three or four years old. Alex was at a black tie event. On his arm was his late girlfriend. I reached across Tullah and checked the details. Her name was Hope Gilliam.

"Yeah. That's him."

"Who's the girl?"

"Old girlfriend. She died. He still has a photo of her in his living room."

"Hmm. She's pretty, but he is like so freaking wolfy hot."

I grinned. "Even better in the flesh."

That made her snigger. "I'll bet!" She scribbled a meaningless password down on a piece of paper and passed it to me. "That's for Matt's emails."

I picked up my laptop and keys and started for the door.

"Amber?"

I turned.

"This…" she waved at the screen, the house, everything. "Alex and Jen. This is Athanate behavior, isn't it? You're really there?"

I huffed. "I can't say that becoming Athanate caused all this. I'd have found both of them attractive before, I guess, but I'd never have thought…I don't know. Either I'm Athanate already or I'm something else. Whatever. They're what I want. I think I'm at wherever it is I was going, Tullah." I was making little sense to myself, so I wouldn't have been surprised if I was making no sense to Tullah.

She just nodded. "Ma will know," she said.

"Yeah. That's one of the things I'm worried about." I smiled and headed out.

Instead of walking straight back to where I'd left the car, I diverted to Alameda Avenue. There was an Asian restaurant there with three things going for it—good food, early opening and free internet. I ordered a sweet and spicy chicken with rice and a hot shrimp dish; apart from Jen's breakfast yesterday, I'd only snacked on the run and I was hungry.

I downloaded Matt's files and briefed myself as I waited. I hoped the food was easier to stomach than the Matlal report. There was little hard evidence, but his profile was eerily close to many I'd read. How had this man not come to the attention of whoever allocated tasks to Ops 4-10? If half of what it said was true, he should have had a swift, fatal visit from the team years ago.

Last, the kicker, was the department reference on the police report about animal attacks. Matt had found that department 55734 was an FBI project team called Anthracite. Thursday's meeting with the Weres just clicked up a few notches in importance and I had one more reason to stay away from Ingram.

∞ ∞ ∞ ∞ ∞

Back at the car, parked on a quiet road a couple of blocks from the park, I began a thorough search for the tracker. I was working on the theory that I'd been bugged when I visited the CBI building. Given my car was in plain sight in the parking lot, and I was in there only an hour, that should mean it wouldn't be too deeply hidden. That was a comforting thought. I didn't need the disruption of taking it into a garage and having it taken apart.

There was nothing in plain sight. Matt's scanner that I'd borrowed for Jaworski chirped once as I walked around the car with it, but it gave no indication of where the tracker might be.

Matt's notes on tracker technology suggested it might be much smaller than I was originally expecting. The size of a wristwatch rather than the size of a smartphone. It still had to be big enough for a battery, a GPS receiver and a signal transmitter, and it needed to be fixed securely. It couldn't be completely flat or tiny.

I gave up looking by eye and started to go around the car again by feel.

I found the bastards had glued it behind the license plate on the front grill.

It was about the size of the battery in my cell. Having levered it off the back of the plate with a knife, I prized it apart and found a super-slim battery, which I took out. I tossed it all into the Faraday cage which was still in the trunk.

I left Matt's scanner on just to check that there were no further chirps to indicate something transmitting, and drove off toward the nearest computer store on Virginia Avenue. I bought the equipment Matt listed to turn my laptop into an internet cell phone and the adaptor to run it off the car's cigarette lighter. All for cash.

Then I connected it all together, put the antenna on the dash and clicked on Matt's install file.

An animated octopus tap-danced onto the screen. I rolled my eyes. Geeks. One of the octopus's legs went out at an angle and stilled. Then another, and another till all eight were still. The octopus shrank and became an icon at the bottom of the screen. A message popped up. "I have eight unsecured internet connections in the vicinity. I will warn you if there are less than four at any time. VOIP communications and internet access will be multiplexed through all connections and remote sites." The message faded and another popped up. "Call Matt now?" I clicked on it and Matt's voice came through.

"Hi, Amber." He sounded like he was speaking in a cubicle.

"Matt, this is freaking A. Is it for-sure untraceable?"

"Yeah. The remote sites spoof the addresses. Once they know it's being done, and given federal budgets and resources, it can be reconstructed, theoretically. But I'll know if they start backtracking. And those remote sites are real remote. Yeah, it's untraceable until I tell you otherwise."

"Absolutely awesome. I owe you."

"No problem. I've really wanted to give it a run for ages."

"Hold on, I'm testing it?"

"No, no. I tested it, you're giving it its first run. Uh… gotta go now. Call me later about those two industrial units you were asking about."

I shuddered and signed off. I'd had a lot of experience with cutting edge equipment, not all of it good.

To test it in a different mode, I sent him an email using the system and asking him to do some more digging on the topic of the police reports about animal attacks. It'd be interesting what he could come up with.

I drove away west, doubling back to see if I had a tail and checking the octopus icon from time to time. No tail and some unsecured connections.

I headed towards Monroe Street for a while, then stopped halfway and checked my cell. If they were tracking it, they had a location for me at that moment, but I wasn't going to hang around. Most of the calls listed on it I could ignore. I would talk to Niall and Jen today anyway.

There was a brief message from Agent Griffith. "Ms. Farrell," he said carefully, "I have some notes here mentioning you in connection with a Project Snakebite in the Denver PD. I can't seem to find any other references to this project. Please give me a call."

No, I wouldn't call the FBI this week and talk to them about the Snakebite codename that Captain Morales and Colonel Laine had thought up to cover anything to do with vampires in Denver. I groaned; now I'd have to warn José as well—he had a police team assigned to this, and they'd need to disappear. But at least Agent Griffith was being polite now.

I was nearly at the end of the messages. I got sales calls and wrong numbers like anyone else. My finger touched the button to delete a voicemail that was a woman I didn't know who had obviously accidentally dialed my number.

"…it's not the same river, and you're not the same woman."

I froze. I didn't know the voice. The woman was clearly in the middle of a conversation. That's reasonably unusual, just enough to make me pause. But the words were a rework of the second part of a quotation from the Greek philosopher Heraclitus. The part everyone knows is the first half—'you can't step into the same river twice'. And the only time I could ever recall discussing it with anyone was with Colonel Laine, the week before.

Another voice I didn't know cut in. "But what does the book say about who will help you up?"

I'd skipped school to join the army. I don't read philosophers and Bibles for fun.

I started reading stuff about Heraclitus because of what he said about change. It seemed very relevant for me as I became Athanate.

And the colonel had quoted the Bible to me just once. He'd said it was a happy coincidence that the buddy principle we used in Ops 4-10 was endorsed by the Bible, Ecclesiastes 4:10.

I'd taken those words to heart, and I whispered them now. "For if they fall, the one will lift up his fellow: but woe to him that is alone when he falleth; for he hath not another to help him up."

I shivered. With this, along with 'Captain Baker' on the Colonel's contact number, I now knew that something had gone very wrong at Ops 4-10, and that was a seriously scary thought. A battalion of Ops 4-10's capabilities in the wrong hands? I didn't want to think about the chaos that could cause. And even if there were nothing to worry about on that level, why was I suddenly being denied? What had happened to the colonel? Was the whole paranormal investigation side under new management and being 'cleaned up'?

The voicemail ended abruptly. Just as it would if someone had found they'd accidentally dialed a number.

I turned the cell off and drove on a few blocks before parking on a side street.

Was that last part simply the colonel saying he was out of it and warning me that my cell was being monitored? Or was it a more sinister warning—who could I rely on to pick me up if I fell? Who was my buddy now? I couldn't just put it all aside. Important as my visit to Haven was, I needed to find out what this meant.

The octopus had made some more friends; I used the laptop to call Jen and left a voicemail saying there was a problem with my cell, but I'd be back this evening. I wanted to call José as well. He needed to know that Ingram was asking about Project Snakebite. But if they were tapping my cell and they knew something about Snakebite, what were the odds they were tapping his? It wouldn't help if they couldn't trace my call but recognized my voice. Even if I used Matt's software to disguise my voice, I didn't have an agreed code to warn José and I couldn't just come out and say Snakebite. I guessed a personal visit had to go on my to-do list.

I risked another look at my cell to see if there was any follow up from the Colonel. There was one more message—a sales spiel suggesting I might find the meaning of life if I logged on to a fortunetelling website. That raised a twisted smile. I turned the cell off again, drove a couple more blocks and logged on using the octopus.

If this was the colonel, then he had hidden depths, or he'd found at least one buddy. It was a real fortunetelling site, and when I logged on as a guest and put my birth date in, I got a short screen of fortune cookie style quotes. Standard stuff, except one—'in change we find purpose'. That was another Heraclitus, and aimed at me, I guessed. I clicked on it, and for a second, a number flashed on the screen and the website closed, as if there'd been a fault. I dialed the number on my internet phone.

The call went through to silence.

"Colonel, it's Farrell. I'm on a secure line."

There was a moment more of silence, and then his voice came on, sounding tired. "Hi. Thanks for following the breadcrumbs."

I took a deep breath. "What the hell happened?"

"I wish I knew. I'm still trying to figure it out, but the unit is now a hot zone for both of us. I will find out what happened, but I've got to get Vera out of this."

"They'd involve her? What about the rest of your family?" He was seriously rattled to have used her name in a phone call. Instructor Ben-Haim would have been having apoplexy.

"I always discussed things with her, never with other family. And I found a listening device at home." I could hear the anxiety in his voice.

"Okay. Colonel, bring her to Denver. I can make you two disappear until we straighten it out."

"I appreciate it, Sergeant. Obviously, I hoped you could. I'm sorry to add to your concerns."

"Forget that, just get here."

"How do I contact you?"

"Text my cell something random from the unit and I'll call this number again."

"Done. I'll be there in the next couple of days."

"Make it after the weekend."

"Got a party?" he tried to joke.

"As if. This stuff at the unit…it isn't the people we know, is it?"

"No. The unit is on lockdown while personnel are being merged into another one run by Petersen. It's that other unit that's the problem."

The name Petersen gave me a sick feeling in my stomach. I'd found out his main interest in me was to see me dissected. For the greater good, of course.

"I was told he'd been promoted," I said.

"Yeah." The colonel's voice betrayed what he thought of that.

Good tradecraft should have meant we cut the call off as soon as we'd covered the important things, and we were way past that already. But I knew how isolated and exposed he would be feeling, and we were safe enough. I'd been there. No matter how tough you are, out in a situation like the colonel was, the sound of a friendly voice would be welcome to him.

I cast around for something to say.

"I never did get around to apologizing, Colonel."

"Apologizing? For what?"

"Well, I screwed the pooch, down in South America. Got you demoted," I said.

Got myself bitten. Got my squad killed, too. Colonel Laine had been in charge of Ops 4-10 up to that operation. By the time I had recovered, he was only in charge of the medical team observing me. That had to have been a painful demotion, but he'd never once mentioned it.

"Amber, you got it all wrong," he said. "You did an exceptional job down there."

"I got them all killed!" I said, and bit my lip. Gods, this was still raw. My squad, my responsibility. I should never have opened this conversation.

"Bullshit."

My mouth dropped open. I had never heard him swear before.

"We'll sit down with a drink and talk it through sometime," he said. "But just for your information, I volunteered for that post. If things went wrong at Hacha del Diablo it was *my* responsibility. The least I could do was figure out what happened and how we could avoid it in the future."

"Okay," I said finally. "Okay. That's a date, Colonel."

Time to quit the call, but I didn't want to leave him with Hacha del Diablo on his mind, especially if he felt responsible as well. We hadn't shared many light conversations. I couldn't even remember what sports teams he supported. I tried the one other thing about Ops 4-10 that I'd thought of recently, and ended up opening a whole new can of worms.

"Hey, Colonel, I've just read a report on a drug lord down Mexico way. I can't think how he's still walking. We should've taken him out long ago."

"Name?" He sounded professionally interested.

"Matlal. Luc Matlal," I spelled it out. Again, we shouldn't have been naming names, but he'd asked.

The line was quiet.

"You still there, Colonel?"

"Yeah. Look, I realize you probably have secrecy issues, so you don't need to say anything else about why you're reading up on him. But just to tell you, Matlal's name came up all right. I put it forward three or four times myself. No green light."

"Shit." I didn't like the sound of that. The more I thought about the ways this could link up, the more I didn't like it.

"Yeah. We can't talk about it now. I'll see you next week."

"Okay."

"Oh…and…" he stumbled.

"Yeah?"

"It's safe, isn't it?"

He meant would my Athanate friends bite him and his wife. I'd never heard uncertainty in his voice before. It shook me as much as anything we'd said.

"Nothing's safe at the moment, but no one I'd hide you with would harm you."

We ended the call on that and I drove to Monroe Street. Time was getting shorter. I should have done this in the dark, sneaking in over a fence or something. But Larry wasn't there and neither was anyone else.

All of which left me more frustrated and with three chilling thoughts. Larry had been caught. That was edging towards a sick certainty. And if he had, and he was still alive, he hadn't told them about Monroe Street, yet. But he would. And lastly, there was nothing I could do about it unless we got lucky.

Regardless of the people in Ops 4-10, some of whom I would've still thought of as friends, with it a hot zone, I had some precautions to take before I went to Haven.

I went back into the city, to the storage facility where I kept things I didn't want to see or wasn't supposed to have. I took some time checking the place out before going in, but it was clear. At least one person in Ops 4-10 knew of this place. I wasn't worried about Keith, my former boyfriend from my army days; he wouldn't betray me, even if we were no longer an item. But he'd been able to trace the locker from the old fake ID I'd kept. Anyone else in Ops 4-10 could follow that lead the same way.

I laid the car back seat flat and emptied both storage units. All the weapons and army equipment went in first, in bags, then I put my old army uniforms on top to hide them. When I was sure it all looked innocent enough, I drove out. My fake ID from my Ops 4-10 days, Mrs. Abigail Welchester, disappeared forever, shredded into a dumpster.

I finally got to head for Haven. I had warned Bian I might be late, but this was pushing it. And now I had things to ask for and lots to think about. I'd gone from my comfortable absolutes, the army and Ops 4-10 among them, to a sense of being completely adrift.

House Altau could have been my new certainty, but I found Skylur too difficult to read. That left Diana. I'd started working on that yesterday and I wondered how it would play out.

Chapter 21

The late morning sun was summer-white and haze made Haven insubstantial as a reflection, almost dreamlike.

At the gatehouse, I strolled on the gravel drive while the guards called through for clearance to open the gate. I turned in circles and thought about Ops 4-10, the colonel and Haven's security issues.

Skylur had said an attack here would meet a surprise. What did he mean?

Apart from not being told things like that, the problem was I didn't know what level of security was necessary.

The wall, gatehouse and clear lawns around the house itself were an adequate layout to counter singlehanded assassination attempts, or small teams. I knew the building had a basement area which would probably provide sufficient protection against a medium-scale attack, say with rocket-propelled grenades or similar.

But treating this as a mission plan for an Ops 4-10 attack, I could see the defenders lasting between ten minutes and half an hour depending on whether it was a kill or a capture mission. Taking it the other way and treating it as a defense problem, the best solution was that the house itself had to be a decoy with escape or defense options underground. But that scale of work meant difficult requirements for secrecy and expensive adaptations.

The guards themselves were more than adequate for everyday security. But again, a defense force against a serious attack was a completely different beast. I had plenty of ideas about that, if they were needed.

The guards called me back and opened the gates. I drove in and parked in the underground garage, then walked up into the house, searching for the room they'd given me. The place was cool and silent all around me. Not for the first time, I wondered where everyone was. Underground?

A door onto the corridor opened and Bian slunk out like a cat. "Oh! I thought I smelled something nice," she said.

She was wearing her silky black combat pants, but with a loose white T-shirt advertising a biomedical center for blood donors, showing her leopard skin shoulders and neck. Her feet were bare. Her hair was gathered into a single top knot. Through the door behind her, I could see a couple of people arguing over a complex flowchart on a long board. Yeah, I understood why she wanted out of that.

"Hi, Pussycat," I said. I didn't want to rise to her bait, so maybe that wasn't the right response.

She casually blocked my way, leaning close and sniffing.

"Hmm. No wolf. Are you coming to stay? I'm sure I can find a bed for you."

"Bian, I'm not staying at Haven." A moment's inattention, and my little demon was up and running. "Besides, I'm not sure you have a bed strong enough." I tried to distract her from that and get her on the defensive. "And what about Mykayla?"

Bian's eyes lit up. Not distracted in the slightest. "We can have her along as well if you like. She gets tired so easily one on one. And the floor's plenty strong enough."

I rolled my eyes. She was completely outrageous, and there wasn't any way I was going to win this type of conversation.

I pointed through the door she'd come out of. "Shouldn't you be concentrating on—"

"Oh, I think the security arrangements for catering during the Assembly will go just fine without me," she purred, leaning in again.

I was saved by Diana's arrival. "Bian, you have no excuse not to be in that meeting."

Bian slunk back in, grinning at me over her shoulder. It was impossible not to grin back.

Diana sighed and ushered me down the corridor. "I did warn you that she would get you back for your joke last week."

She opened a door and we walked into a sitting room.

"She can be so fun and irritating at the same time." I sat down on the sofa. "Changes direction like the wind in a storm. Tell me, how long does adolescence last for Athanate?"

Diana laughed. "Forever. Or until they come out of it on their own. Don't be embarrassed, Amber. If Bian can't get a response out of you, you're already dead."

I was more embarrassed that I couldn't ignore it. And whatever I thought I ought to do, I was being nudged off course by my Athanate reactions.

"How do you manage it?"

"The mock-aggressive intimacy? I don't fight it."

"So that stops her? You just stop fighting and she backs off?"

Diana shook her head. "You need to understand, Bian makes no promises, even in fun, that she is not prepared to keep."

Crap. I'd misread the situation between Bian and Diana. "Are you…"

"Lovers? Yes, occasionally," Diana said calmly.

I blushed. "I'm sorry, I didn't realize. Are you mad at me?"

"Why? Am I jealous? No. I love the butterfly. That doesn't make me jealous of the flowers." Diana frowned. "No, perhaps it's not fair to dismiss it like that. Of course, Athanate have all the human emotions, including jealousy. But with our needs, and over time, we're unlikely to get jealous over something like that. Bian and I are not exclusive."

"Why…" I paused. Diana was old. I didn't know how old, but the last time we'd spoken about kin, I knew she'd survived many of them and it had taken its toll. "I'm sorry, I don't know what's not polite to ask. Why do you need any more partners? You have kin. Aren't they your partners?"

"Athanate endure," she responded, her voice dropping and her great eyes going dark. "Athanate endure, when kin do not."

She turned away, and I gave myself a little shake. Talking to Diana was always unsettling.

"This is Bian's way with people she likes," she said eventually. "She hides serious points behind joking."

"What was the point in what she just did?"

"Well, what have you been talking about recently?"

I cleared my throat. "Well, everything that happened yesterday..."

"And…" Diana prompted.

"Kin."

"Ahh. She may feel your needs are changing more quickly than your comfort zone." Diana shrugged. "Perhaps she's trying to make you realize fully that, as an Athanate, you'll experience relationships differently. And as House Farrell, it'll be even more complex. You got a taste of that at David's house on Monday."

I nodded, remembering the feeling.

Despite what she said, I was sure that Bian had layers to her behavior and I had a strong feeling there was at least one layer I wasn't seeing. A feeling that something deep watched me, and that it was neither the sexually playful Bian nor the serious Diakon.

"And she *is* making a serious point," Diana said. "We'll have to talk this through. Maybe we should talk about Athanate politics and the Assembly later this afternoon. We have a lot of important things to cover today. None more important than how you changed your marque, and why your Blood had the effect it did with David, even though I have no plan in place, yet, to investigate that. But first, you have to make time for the Judicator."

"What is he going to do?"

"Some tests, nothing more. Tests that provide a sensory stimulus and measure how your body and brain react."

"What do these tests prove?"

"Well, this is the method the Warders consider the best way to independently determine your Athanate status. It's nothing really, Amber. And the independent Warders' assessment cannot easily be challenged."

I didn't think Diana would actually lie to me, but I didn't like the sound of these tests.

The Warders had a strange position, brought about by the creation of the Assembly. They were effectively a large Athanate House, independent of Panethus and Basilikos, with embassies in most countries and guaranteed free passage throughout the Assembly domains. They were intended to police the Assembly and provide escorts for representatives when they traveled on Assembly business. They provided neutral venues for small meetings between Houses on opposite sides. They prized their neutrality and tended to claim ownership and responsibility for everything that they deemed to be for the common good or advancement of the whole Athanate. I hadn't heard a good word for them yet.

"How does he do these tests?"

On cue, a funny little man pushing a cart full of equipment came into the room. I took one look at the contents of the cart and my skin started to crawl. It was a horror of wires and tubes and that cloying antiseptic smell. Something about it made the Obs tests look like a Sunday stroll.

Chapter 22

Diana's hand rested on my arm as if I might run away. That didn't look like a bad option.

"Welcome, Philippe. Amber, this is Philippe Remy, Judicator of the Warders from their Belgian office. Philippe, Amber Farrell."

"Of course," he said, his voice heavily accented. *"Mesdames, enchanté."* He bowed over our hands. "At your service."

He was a short, fussy man with flat, black hair that looked as if it was starched in position. My nose quickly told me he was kin, not Athanate. His round face would have looked jolly, but the eyes were too sharp.

"I understand, Ms. Farrell, that this appears daunting." He plugged a cord into the wall socket and baleful red LEDs started to glow on parts of the gray equipment as the demons inside it woke up.

"Yeah," I replied. "You could say that."

Diana looked at me as if I was a specimen in a lab. "Fascinating," she said. "You are almost contemptuous of physical danger, but this harmless equipment concerns you."

"Associations," I muttered. Dad, Top, Obs. Nothing good ever came of equipment like this.

Remy noted my concern and fluttered around me, settling me into a chair and bringing a drink of water, all of which had the effect of making me more antsy.

"This will influence the readings. No, no, no. This is not good." He took my wrist pulse and peered at my eyes.

Diana nudged him aside and perched on the armrest.

"Come, Amber." She leaned forward, her eyes pinning me in the chair. "Be at ease."

It was like looking up at a skyscraper with clouds passing behind it. My brain tried to tell me I wasn't falling. What the hell was she doing? The feeling of power that she gave off was staggering.

My body was tense as a blade. She slipped a hand behind my head and pulled me gently against her neck. As an Athanate, it had become more and more difficult to get my heart rate over 120, but now it went skywards and my lungs started to labor. But quickly, quickly, her scent of copper and cinnamon percolated through me. It was so strangely soothing.

"Have you thought of the reason we kiss necks in greeting?" she murmured.

"It's where you—we—bite," I tried. "Sort of a symbolic offering." My eyes closed and my fists unclenched. Her neck was warm against my face. I could feel her pulse, lazy as sea surf, and mine slowed to match it.

"There's that, too," she said. "But the real reason is that our Athanate glands are at the base of the throat. Most of the Athanate scent pheromones are released from there. And the receptors are concentrated in the nose, of course."

I was floating. "The greeting brings them close together," I said. "You get a dose of what the other person is feeling. Or wants you to feel. Clever greeting." I giggled. "Damn. You've just sedated me, haven't you?"

"A little. Come, let Philippe run his tests. I will be back soon."

I slumped in the chair and let Remy stick electrodes all over me. After the electrodes came tubes, one taped to my neck, and a nasal cannula against my upper lip. A set of blank goggles went over my eyes. It felt almost funny. Whatever Diana had dosed me with was good stuff.

But surely, a sedative would distort the readings as much as an overdose of adrenaline?

"No, no, no," said Remy, and I realized I had actually spoken. "It does not affect the test. The oniric state is most conducive to accurate readings. Stressful excitement is not."

At that stage, I didn't care what that meant.

I didn't even care when he took blood from my arm and made me spit in a specimen jar.

Then a set of headphones went over my ears and his machine started its routine.

It was like a peculiar dream, or sequence of dreams and semi-nightmares. I wasn't entirely sure if I remained awake through the whole thing. My body responded to scents from the cannula, lights from the goggles and sounds from the earphones. The electrodes on my head tickled my brain. Sensations and emotions chased each other through my mind. Fragments of memories floated up, to be chased away by bizarre phantoms of things that I was sure had never happened to me.

"I'll feel better tomorrow," Dad says, patting my hand. "We'll go walking in the hills." But he doesn't, and Cassie is crying because the wound in my neck will never heal. "You won't get better," she says. "You can't speak to me." Burnt popcorn. The wolf looks in through the window, its tongue like a pink washcloth hanging down. Fresh cut grass. And Kath gives me her ice cream, even though it's her favorite. "David is taking me to the ball game," she whispers. "Try it again, higher intensity," says a disembodied voice. "The colonel will be here soon. We don't have much time left."

I twitched and cried and laughed and shivered.

I was very glad for Diana's pacifics because it was far, far worse than the tests that Obs used to run on me. The thought that this was a one-time thing helped a little, when nightmares seemed to flicker just outside the limit of my perception.

And, unlike the Obs room, this one had windows and a door. I could tear this stuff off and run away. But then there would be no other way; Skylur would have to bite me to find out what was going on inside my body.

Remy was finally peeling off the electrodes when Diana returned.

"Well?" I said to him when he removed the cannula.

He paused, cocking an eyebrow at me.

"Am I Athanate or not?"

He looked offended. "Madam, I am not a fairground prognosticator. There is a veritable mountain of data to work through before I will venture an opinion."

"Fine, whenever." I pulled the last tubes away from my neck and threw them over his cart.

"When, Philippe?" asked Diana.

"Definitely at the Assembly, of course," he replied and gave an expressive shrug. "Perhaps earlier. One cannot be entirely sure."

"That's unacceptable," Diana said. "We must have the results before the Assembly."

"Madame, science does not move quicker because we wish it so. I will make preliminary results available as soon as I can."

He wheeled his equipment away and Diana closed the doors behind him.

Diana settled into the next chair. "Are you all right?" she asked.

I waved it off. It was done.

"What is it, Amber? This has unsettled you more than it warrants."

"I don't know," I said. "Maybe because it reminds me of Obs."

She raised an eyebrow. My brain got back into gear. She knew nothing of Obs, of course.

"When the army decided that vampires did actually exist, they formed a scientific medical team to investigate me. Called Obs."

"And they did these kind of tests."

I shrugged. "I was suffering some kind of shock; I don't remember the early parts very clearly. There were machines like that. I remember being strapped down in a room with no windows. Probably for my own safety. I think I can remember lashing out or something. It seemed to last…"

What? Weeks? Months? Can't have been. It was all such a blur.

"I thought I would never get out," I whispered, rattled.

Diana frowned and waited, but I'd had enough of stirring those memories. Time to change the subject.

I nodded after Remy. "Do you trust him?"

"I trust him to do exactly what I expect him to do." If I hadn't been so dosed, I would have picked up on that, but she went on smoothly. "I have an idea which will help with the schedule today. Would you drive me to the airport? Then we'll have an extra hour or so."

"Of course."

"Good. We'll take my Jeep. I want you to borrow it while I'm away, and I have an apartment on University Boulevard where you can stay. You're welcome to use it tonight. If you'd rather go elsewhere, at least you won't be tracked, driving my car."

"Thanks." I stopped and chewed my lip. "I don't want to appear ungrateful but—"

"But why am I doing all this for you?" Diana smiled. "Some entirely self-serving reasons. It is important, under the very eyes of the Assembly, that Skylur's mantle is fully under control, that Altau's associate Houses are safe within it. And it's not just the FBI. Matlal will be actively searching for you. The loan of a car and an apartment are nothing in comparison to that. I wish we could do more." She paused. "Then there's our interest in the effect your Blood has had." She got up and started pacing. "Then, as well, my purely personal reasons. You are the key to a path I wish to follow to bring the Athanate Emergence. And lastly, my offer to be your Mentor still stands."

"But I may already be through the crusis. Surely I don't still need a Mentor?"

"A Mentor does more than guide an Aspirant through the crusis. In fact, that part of it, I cannot help with. Your path through the crusis seems to be different from everything we've seen. If you need help there, all I can do is walk beside you." She paused. "But Mentors exist for every step of the path. And again, if I cannot show you the way, I would still walk beside you. The way is dark, and long."

The hairs on my neck stood up. "And if I fall…"

"I will lift you up," she said. She got up and patted my shoulder before turning to the windows overlooking the gardens. "Think on it, Amber."

"I will." I cleared my throat, feeling adrift. "Ahh. There's a problem with that plan on Emergence." The week before, we had discussed starting a process with Colonel Laine, recruiting senior army commanders into a group, one at a time, and introducing them to Diana, until we had a path of trusted people all the way to the president. "Colonel Laine isn't in the army anymore."

Diana looked at me questioningly. I explained and requested asylum for Colonel Laine and Vera.

Diana was quiet for a while, looking out at the gardens. "This may still work. Your Colonel wasn't always in this secret unit?"

"No." I stopped and got up to join Diana at the window. I wasn't supposed to discuss Ops 4-10 with anybody. Even if the agreement they'd made me sign wasn't enforceable, the whole project was under Special Access Program levels of secrecy. But I was starting to have doubts about it all now. Who really commanded the unit? What the colonel had hinted at had unnerved me—a unit like 4-10 effectively being told not to go after some drug lords? I had a lot of questions to ask him when he got here.

"He moved from a different branch of the Special Forces to take over the unit."

"It may still work," Diana repeated. "From what you and everyone else *can't* tell me," she said, "I know this military unit is self-contained, sealed off. Your Colonel would have had to use his contacts outside to make any progress. Maybe, he can still do that." She closed her eyes and sighed. "And if he cannot, what else can he do for us?"

I had been thinking through this.

"If you're about to fight a war, you need an army. A secret one. He's the best operational commanding officer you could possibly have for that."

Diana looked at me for a long time. "A position like that is key," she said, slowly. "That means he would have to be Athanate or kin." She watched the effect of those words on me. Damn. What would the colonel think? I would need to explain that all very carefully.

"Come, Amber, it's time we discussed kin."

I retrieved the glass of water Remy had brought me. Bian and Diana seemed to effortlessly keep me off balance. I didn't think Diana was doing it to needle me.

"In lots of ways, I feel Athanate." I took a sip. "The physical side: feeling stronger; being healthier; seeing in the dark. I love all of that. And I get the structural thing." I frowned. There didn't seem to be quite the right words to describe it. "The connections, the obligations between me and David and Pia. Different connections to you and Skylur and Bian. I get all that, sort of."

"How do you mean 'sort of?'"

I'd known she wouldn't let that go by.

"Well, I'm Athanate, or part Athanate, but I'm also an American, and part old world and part new world, Celtic and Arapaho, and I'm proud of all of that. I'll swear oaths to Skylur, but I swore oaths before, to this country, and I won't let them go. I just don't know what happens when they come into conflict."

"We didn't think you would just let your human side go, Skylur and I. His approach is that we must all be more like you. At least all of us in America." She frowned. "There will be conflict. It may be a terrible price that you pay while you are in transition. But, Amber, however much you try and rule over them, your Athanate instincts will become stronger. All of us will try and find this new balance. Some of us may fail, and we do not know what will happen then."

A chill seemed to sweep through the room.

She turned away. Beside the window sat an old world globe, the colors faded by sunlight. Diana edged it around and traced the contours of the US thoughtfully.

"We were talking about kin," she said.

"I don't understand kin. You said last week that I would need four or five kin to sustain me, that it would be a bond of love. And that doesn't feel right to me, that number. I know I'm changing. Is it just I haven't finished changing, or am I…"

"A deviant Athanate?" Diana smiled. "I don't know. I need more time with you, precious time that we do not have, thanks to Basilikos. Maybe you will change some more. Maybe you are where you need to be." She closed the gap between us, giving me a little spike of adrenaline. But all she did was cup her hands around mine on the glass, and tilt it so she could sip as well.

I cleared my throat nervously. "Yeah, change. Last month, hell, a couple of weeks ago, I said I was straight and I was telling the truth."

"And now?"

"I'm still monogamous," I blurted. Maybe it was the little demon in my throat.

Diana arched her eyebrows in surprise.

"Well, for definitions of monogamous that mean I can have one of each."

She laughed. "From the scent, I can take it that Alexander Deauville is the man. And your lady friend? Jennifer Kingslund?"

I nodded.

"Ah! I see one of the problems. You're worried about what might happen to her and you've promised us to say nothing to anyone, so she is puzzled by your behavior."

"I've promised to say nothing until after the Assembly." I stared at Diana, waiting for her to challenge that. She ignored it. "But yes, I think she's wondering what's going on."

"Don't wait to talk to her, just take her," Diana said casually. "She is suitable. Naturally, not all kin must come from the Aspirants. You can be sure, she won't complain. Once she's bound to you, you can tell her everything."

"No!"

"You'll risk everything to give her the chance to say no? You'd be doing her a favor to take her now."

"No, I won't." I wanted to pull away, but Diana's hands still covered mine on the glass and her grip was simply unbreakable. I'd have to shatter the glass to get away. Water splashed over my hands. "I can't be like that."

"Calm, Amber," she said. "Be calm. Your answer is exactly why we value you." She released my hands and took the glass from me, a small smile passing her lips. "As you test me, so I test you. Come, let's walk."

How could she unsettle me so easily and so often?

She led me outdoors and we started to stroll around the gardens.

I wanted to move past the tests. I had a request to make to Diana and a letter in my pocket. I was struggling to think how to introduce it when she started talking again.

"Enough of Jennifer for the moment. Tell me about Alexander. I understand he's extremely attractive."

"He's gorgeous. Hot as…hot as hell. And he does seem to understand a lot about Athanate."

"He's the liaison with the Denver werewolves. Bian's equivalent, if you like. She would have briefed him quite thoroughly about us to ensure there are no misunderstandings."

I felt a spike of irrational jealousy. The dreamy wolf, Bian called him. Thorough briefings, Diana said. Did that mean what I was afraid it did? There would be a lot of teasing if I tried getting that information from Bian, and Diana didn't seem about to tell me either.

"Is it unusual?" I asked. "Alex and me—Athanate and Were?"

"For entertainment, no, it's quite common. For a relationship, yes, it is unusual. And for kin, you need to understand, his Blood will not fully sustain you."

Alex had said as much.

Diana turned her face up to the sun and stood for a moment with her eyes closed.

"As for relationships…" she said. "Understand, I am not warning or advising you, Amber." Her eyes opened and she turned back to me. "Traditionally, we find the bad boy attractive. It's a thrill. It's a challenge. We think we can control him. Silly, really. If we control him, it's no longer a thrill, is it?"

"Never analyzed it myself," I said. It wasn't just a bad-boy thrill. There was something about him.

As if she read my mind again, Diana took my arm. "But the thrill. You seek it out in every part of your life, and I can see you looking for it here."

I shrugged. I found Alex exciting. I couldn't argue with that. "Okay, so?"

"Werewolves can't be controlled. Violence is part of what makes them werewolves. They can be managed, after a fashion, and that's what the pack does for its members. That's what the alpha provides. Take a werewolf out of the pack and it will almost certainly end up as a rogue."

What if Alex were kicked out of the pack? For that matter, what if I were kicked out of the Athanate? The thought of the two of us being together, somewhere else, without all the fear and worry was tempting, until the image of the pair of us going rogue surfaced.

"But what about the alpha?" I said. "How is their violence controlled?"

Diana laughed. "Clever question. I have no clever answer. Alphas are different."

We passed some shrubs thick enough to provide cover and I distracted myself enough to make a mental note for my security review.

"The advice I have is to settle these issues in your mind before the Assembly. You'll take the oath there, and that will make us associated. But how we proceed after that will depend on the risks, and there are risks in being so close to a werewolf. It's not as if it's contagious, but werewolves are disinhibited when the wolf is in the ascendant. And that profile is closer to Basilikos than Panethus."

What if Alex and I ended up as half and half, but he was Basilikos and I was Panethus? The more I thought about what was happening, the more apprehensive and unsettled I became.

Diana was silent for a long while after that. We strolled into a hot conservatory and her hands automatically reached out to caress flowers or carefully remove dead blooms.

"Regardless, we must proceed extremely carefully with you," she said, almost to herself. "But I have an idea. Yes." She paused and absentmindedly picked a dramatic spray of lilies of the valley to weave it into my hair. "There," she said, smiling. "That's for sweetness, you know, in the language of flowers. So pretty, people forget the danger. They're poisonous."

I huffed. I did *not* wear flowers in my hair, but I could hardly tear them out in front of her.

"Please, Amber, no biting or being bitten at the moment. Nothing with Jennifer, blood or sex, for her own safety. I suppose whatever has happened with Alexander has already happened. If Alexander behaves strangely, call…" she stopped. "Well, no. There's no one available this week." She sighed. "This is such an awkward time until we get the Assembly out of the way. Perhaps you should avoid Alexander."

I felt my heels digging in like a donkey's hooves, but I said nothing.

"The project I have in mind will tell us why your Blood had such an effect on David," she went on. "I will find a volunteer and we'll see what happens when you try to change them."

What? What if I succeeded? Would they become House Farrell? Was I going to have responsibility for some random person? If I didn't like them, would my Athanate instincts override that?

Diana didn't give me time to ask all those questions. She went on so quickly, I almost lost the next thing.

"Next week, bring your colonel and his wife to Haven if you wish, securely, of course. It will be up to Skylur whether they can stay and whether the colonel will help us. And whatever conditions he may impose. I make no promises."

"Thanks." What if Skylur said the colonel had to become kin? Eww. Not to mention what the colonel might think of that. But again, Diana didn't give me a chance to dwell.

"None of that has me as concerned as the changes that you and Alexander brought about in your marque. Without the benefit of all of Remy's equipment, I feel the Athanate is in the ascendant. The trouble is, I'm not sure which way around is less dangerous."

"The other way around, surely? That's the dangerous way, from what you're saying, if the wolf becomes stronger."

"I don't know, Amber. Athanate influenced by wolf might go to Basilikos, wolf influenced by Athanate might go rogue. The only positive thing, as I mentioned, my Athanate senses still approve of your marque. My instincts are still saying sharing would be a benefit." She smiled. "Meaning, I still want to bite you. More, if anything."

I snorted. "It seemed to have that kind of effect at the ball as well, before I met Alex."

"Don't put it all down to your marque."

I folded my arms.

"Even Skylur likes it," Diana said.

"You're joking! He's so damn…superior, when he isn't pissed at me. He sure as hell doesn't let on, anyway."

"No, he doesn't." She smiled and brushed the topic away. "Don't overemphasize the changes the Athanate brings in you. Imperatives is too strong a word. Being Athanate does not so much make you do anything, or be anything, as it might urge, it might suggest, it might enhance…"

"It makes me drink blood." I stopped and corrected that. "It will make me drink blood."

She nodded. "Granted. That it will."

"Is it different for others? Does it affect Bian? I mean the way she…"

Diana turned her huge, dark eyes on me. "No. There is a reason Bian behaves the way she does, believe me, and it's nothing to do with the Athanate." She closed her eyes again, let out a long breath. "One day, she will tell you her story."

We left the conservatory for the gardens again.

"You realize that you are making Bian's job even more difficult? Although you haven't taken your oath, she accepts you as an affiliate. That means, as Diakon, she is responsible for your safety in our mantle. And at the moment, she cannot protect you from Matlal outside of Haven. This is a responsibility you must bear. You must be extra vigilant."

Diana paused at an ornamental pond, looking down at the fish swimming beneath the surface.

It would all make more sense if they told Bian what they were doing, but I couldn't get a feel for whether Diana approved of Skylur's plans or not, and really it all revolved around what Skylur wanted.

"Skylur doesn't really like me, does he?" I asked. "He doesn't believe there's anything in the rumors. He just thinks I'm trouble."

She shook her head. "You don't do him justice. And not only in this. A younger House would not tolerate your behavior."

I raised my eyebrows in a question.

"They would have seen the way you act as a challenge and responded. And deadly as you are, Amber, you aren't ready for that."

"So, he's 'older'. Just how old is Skylur?" I asked.

"Get him in a good mood and ask him yourself."

I should have known it wouldn't be that easy getting an answer.

We had come around the other side of the house, next to the entrance to the underground garages. That reminded me.

"I should mention, there are some weapons and equipment in the back of my car."

Diana nodded. "I would be surprised if there were not. Do you need to get them out?"

"A couple. I was going to ask to leave the rest here in a storeroom, but my car will do fine if I'm using yours. But it's not just a couple of handguns. I have shotguns, a machine gun, grenades and ammunition as well as surveillance equipment, a parachute, Kevlar vests and so on."

"Whatever are you planning on doing?"

I started to laugh and it cut off. The premonition I'd had earlier in the week returned.

"What?" Diana said.

I shrugged. "I don't know. It's just that all the people I think of as friends or allies, all the institutions that I used to trust, everything, everyone, has different agendas. Their aims are just too wide. Some things aren't what I thought they were. I can't be on everyone's side, and I'm just me. I'm more expendable than someone's principles, if those principles are really important. Someone is going to betray me soon. Or I'll betray them. It's inevitable."

Diana went pale and quiet. The air seemed suddenly much colder.

"One of your…no, you and Skylur remind me, I must say 'our', we must be American now. One of our great American city's founders once said to me: 'only trust thyself, and another shall not betray thee'."

Chapter 23

I got to see David and Pia briefly while I waited to drive Diana to DIA.

I was so wrapped up with what being House Farrell might mean to me personally, I'd forgotten what it meant to them. Or for that matter, what it meant to us. This was scary; a commitment that had just happened, with needs and boundaries and limitations I didn't fully understand. Not only that, it worked at a deep level on all of us—they came in and we simply and wordlessly met in a three way hug, however awkward I felt about it.

They looked tired, which was fine; I probably did too. David had his optimistic good humor back, but Pia was unsettled. Very slowly she calmed, and as she did, that tranquility lapped out gently over all three of us.

"They're keeping you busy," I said.

"Yeah. Can't talk about it," David said. "Specific orders." His eyes flickered to where Diana was talking to an aide. "Brought you some fruit, sis." He held up a bag. "Bet you haven't had lunch."

I chuckled. "You know me too well, bro." I bit into the apple, and put the rest in Diana's car.

"Mistress—" Pia began.

I winced. "Ah, Pia. House rules. I'm Amber."

She gave me a weak smile. I could only guess at how distressing it had been for her to have her hardwired loyalties to Altau suddenly transferred to me and then have to come back and work here.

What would Top have done? I gave her another job. "Pia, I know you're stretched already, but I need something from you."

She looked up at me, if not exactly eager, at least focused on something else.

"A charter; I think that's the word," I said. "At least a draft. What you and David should expect from House Farrell, and me. And what I should expect in return. Athanate obligations and traditions. Can you do that?"

"Oh. Of course." She actually looked pleased.

"Temporary rules: Diana doesn't want me to bite or be bitten until we figure out what happened. Are you two going to be okay with that?" Gods, what a calm, organized Athanate I was, talking about them needing to bite me.

"We'll manage," David said and changed the subject. "Hey, really cool flower arrangement."

We laughed and untangled the lilies and transferred them to Pia. They did better against her striking mane of wavy, black hair than against my auburn.

Too soon, Diana was ready and it was time to go. It was frustrating. We'd have to have security with us and there was no privacy, no time for my request of her.

I drove her hard body Jeep Wrangler up the ramp and stopped outside the front door to wait for the guards who would be joining us.

"Why not stay with David and Pia tonight?" suggested Diana. "It doesn't need to involve anything other than your presence. It will be beneficial for both of them."

"Not tonight, maybe tomorrow," I said. "Aren't you supposed to have another car of guards following us?"

"Yes, but I've elected to do this quietly. We're just having one team come with us."

The guards came out the door.

"Hey! It's the Fang team again." I smirked. The four of them had unsuccessfully jumped me down in LoDo in the first attempt at trying to get me to come in and meet Skylur.

Diana introduced them to me, and I explained my system of pet names. They enjoyed that.

One of them was missing. I found out his name was Marlon Pruitt and he was missing because he'd broken his leg when I'd tossed him down a flight of stairs. He was the leader of their little team. In his absence, Tom Sherman, the one I'd met later on guard duty, took over.

He was the one I'd nicknamed Fang 3. The complete ban on information I'd had last week was lifted and he confirmed he'd been a marine. I'd guessed that, when I'd promised him a sparring rematch. He'd seen service in Vietnam and I judged him to be about seventy. He looked no older than me, of course.

Fang 2 was Jason Newberry and Fang 4 was Paul Samuels. They were also ex-military, and younger, Athanate-wise, than Tom. I liked them immediately. They shared Tom's sunny outlook and completely ignored the fact that we'd been fighting when we first met. And they'd lost. Heh.

Tom took over the driving and I sat with Diana and Jason in the back, where she started to brief me more fully on Athanate politics. Before I faced the Assembly and Matlal, and committed myself irrevocably to Skylur and Altau, I needed to know what I was getting into.

"The basic view which I gave you before is there are two creeds, Panethus and Basilikos. Skylur is the leader of the Panethus and president of the Assembly. Matlal is his equivalent in Basilikos…"

If only it were that simple. Both creeds apparently embraced a variety of subgroups. Panethus' major subgroup maintained the status quo—no fighting among Athanate, no open contact with humanity. Basilikos' major subgroup were represented by Matlal—hard line domination of humanity, with the inevitable megalomaniac goal of ruling the world. But the Basilikos subgroup represented by Arvinder Singh was large and powerful, which was why Skylur and Diana had been so pleased when it turned out that he was behind the secret communication that I had collected at the charity ball. Arvinder's group's opinion was that Athanate formed an elite and humanity's appropriate position was to worship them. Not a view I agreed with, but more palatable than Matlal's.

To complicate matters, there were three independent Athanate bodies, who supported the Assembly's existence, but refused to accept any government from it. They had no creed on behavior, allowing each individual House within their domains to adopt the style that suited it, within reason. They monitored the Assembly and made their opinions known. Even if they didn't actually vote, they carried plenty of weight.

Oldest amongst them was the Domain of Carpathia. I did grin at that. Among a secretive people, they were the most secretive and least communicative. They refused to name their leaders or define their boundaries. They were the cradle of the Athanate people and extended at least through Romania, Moldova, parts of Ukraine, Hungary, Bulgaria and Turkey. Anywhere around the western Black Sea, other Athanate approached with care.

Next oldest, and the largest of the independents, was the Empire of Heaven. This was based in China and included the Domains of Japan, Korea and Vietnam.

Last was the Midnight Empire. I burst out laughing at that name.

Diana smiled. "The British Athanate sense of humor. It was an insult that the Empire of Heaven used when the international press started to write that the sun was finally setting on the British Empire. The British Empire approximately defined the territory of the British Athanate Domain. They adopted the name, and they've used it ever since."

"But India used to be part of the British Empire. Arvinder is Basilikos."

"Yes, the Athanate of the Indian subcontinent moved to leave the British Domain and became joined with Basilikos. If we can now get them to leave Basilikos for us, then Panethus will be, outright, the most powerful Athanate group. We'll get even better links with the Midnight Empire as well. But we'll need to be careful not to push the Empire of Heaven towards Basilikos."

Diana sketched a map.

"Panethus covers much of the western world: USA, Europe, Scandinavia. We've also gained from the Midnight Empire over time: Australia and New Zealand. Basilikos covers Russia, most of the Middle East, the 'Stans, South and Central America, Indonesia and the Philippines. The Midnight Empire and Basilikos contend over Africa. The independents don't always agree with us, but they understand well enough why another war must be averted."

"Because humanity would discover us if there was fighting."

"And see us at our worst."

"But we're going to be discovered anyway. The FBI tapping phones is the tip of the iceberg. And it's not just law enforcement," I said. "What about the IRS? How do you file your taxes? How do you get passports, licenses, open bank accounts?"

"You don't need to persuade me, Amber. There are ways to achieve all of those, but every step moves us further from the mainstream until it is not possible to return. We do *not* want to emerge as a band of criminals. And yet, many of us are survivors of previous attempts to be open with humanity." She looked gloomily out the window and murmured quietly, "They didn't go well."

"Okay," I said. "I get the big picture. What about the Assembly? Who's on our side?"

"The Assembly is made up of forty-two representatives, the heads of Houses. Twenty from Basilikos and nominally twenty-two from Panethus. But, we now know, Romero has either gone over to Basilikos or is under some kind of coercion. Others are giving excuses not to attend. Some will attempt to be there by internet or conference phone, but that may be challenged." I noticed we passed the I-25 intersection. Halfway to the airport and I still seemed to have too little information. Could Matlal have enough votes to take over the Assembly? Or, as I'd suggested to Skylur, was he planning to do it the old-fashioned way, by assassination?

"The really major decisions need a two-thirds majority, but there's a host of smaller issues that Basilikos just keeps digging away at, undermining everything," Diana went on. "They may get a number of them through this time, even with Skylur controlling the agenda." She shook herself. "Anyway, your section of it will not be so long or difficult." She handed a paper to me. "This is the oath. Matlal has challenged in advance on your Athanate status and will challenge again at the Assembly. He may have an opportunity to enlarge on the challenge at the Assembly. Bian will have to guide you through it."

Oh fun! We get to make it up as we go along.

After a glance, I put the oath away to study later.

"Along with the representatives, there will be Adepts in attendance."

Crap! Would they be able to see Hana? Would they say anything?

"What for?" I said. "And surely they keep away from you?"

Diana's smile went a little cool. "So the Adepts have spoken to you. I wondered. I'm sure it's not a flattering portrait they've painted. Nor is it accurate. Anyway, the Adepts at the Assembly are there to monitor Skylur and anyone other than the representatives and Warders attending the Assembly. You and Bian for instance. They are Truth Sensors."

"Why do you need them, if you can tell lies from someone's heart rate and the smell of their blood chemistry?" And dammit, could Mary tell if I lied to her? Scary thought.

"Not in a crowded room, and there are ways to disguise those. But not from the Sensors."

"What about the representatives and the Warders?"

"Oh, they can lie their heads off. But the Sensors are the reason that Skylur does not know where I'm going and does not know that I've spoken to you on Emergence. He must be able to say so in front of the Sensors."

"I understand. I think. And I'll have to rely on Bian." *And hope whatever is making her act so crazy doesn't get worse.* "Okay. But what about your role?"

"I'm a simple advisor to Skylur. I don't have a formal role."

There was no reason for her to lie to me, but simple advisor didn't seem to cover it. Every question I asked seemed to uncover two more. But it was too late. The distinctive peaked roofs of DIA were rising up right in front of us.

At the drop-off area, I got out with Diana.

"Tom," she said, "drive around the circuit. Amber and I are not quite done here."

His eyes flickered to the crowds, but he nodded and drove off, leaving us alone.

Diana led me into the main hall. People flowed around us. That letter was burning a hole in my pocket and I wanted to talk to her, but this wasn't the place or the time.

"Come, Amber. You've had something on your mind all day to discuss with me."

"I can't…it's wrong, it's too public," I muttered.

"We are never more alone," she whispered. Her hand rested on my shoulder.

I closed my eyes for a second and took a deep breath. She was right. The sounds of the hall faded away to a meaningless murmur of noise, no more than the wind in the trees. When I opened my eyes, people were still there, but like flickers of color at the edges of my sight. We were the tranquility at the center of the river. And holding me fast were her eyes, the half-smile on her lips, and the gentle hand on my shoulder.

I fumbled Top's letter out of my pocket. It was a little battered. I'd read my half of it over and over. I handed the sealed second half to Diana.

"What's this?"

"It's a letter for you from my senior sergeant in Ops 4-10, Gabriel Wells. Think of him as my Mentor in the army. Or a second father. He died last weekend." I took a couple of deep breaths and lost myself looking into her eyes again. "I told him everything that was happening to me just before he died. Everything."

Diana's face was a mask. She turned the letter over. "It's not addressed to me," she noted.

"He wasn't able to choose who it should go to in the time he had. He suggested I give it to the person I trust above all others for the task."

"Not Alexander or Jennifer?"

"Not for this."

Her hand left my shoulder and I swayed, but the sensation of seclusion remained. She opened the envelope and read the letter. It wasn't long.

"Amber, do you have any idea what this says?"

I nodded.

"Tell me."

I was committed now, past doubts and questions. "It asks you to kill me if I slide into becoming Basilikos."

"Why, Amber?"

Even in the cool of the airy hall, I felt a prickle of sweat start.

"My personal nightmare," I said, "is to become insane, but to be unable to notice it."

"Basilikos—"

"Basilikos are not insane, by *their* definition," I interrupted. "They don't think they're evil either. But they're both by mine, by what I believe *now*. And my nightmare is that I could become insane and evil with them, step by step, without realizing. I need someone who I know will never become like them. Someone who will accept this duty. Someone who I can trust absolutely to carry it out."

"It asks me to swear," Diana said quietly, looking down at the letter.

"Will you?"

"Will you accept me as your Mentor if I do?"

"Yes," I whispered.

She gathered my hands and held them, the letter crinkling between our fingers. "Then attend, Amber Farrell, House Farrell. On my Blood, I, Diana Ionache, swear, I will abide by the terms of this letter."

"It is done." That was a phrase I'd spotted at the end of the oath I would take with Altau at the Assembly.

"It is done," echoed Diana. "I wish I'd met Gabriel. And I wish you'd left the lilies in your hair. To remind me—sweet and deadly." She looked pale and somehow vulnerable all of a sudden; a woman, tall and powerful and beautiful, but alone in the midst of this flow of noisy, unknowing humanity. Everyone depended on her, and she had nowhere to turn. I felt ashamed that I had added to her responsibilities.

Then she smiled, as if everything I thought was an open book to her.

Her eyes flicked past me. "Tom is back and you must go." She shook her head and said something in Athanate. Then: "We will meet again next week and you will understand." We kissed necks and then she turned and left, pulling her little travel case after her.

Chapter 24

Tom didn't let me back in the car. He handed me a cell phone.

"One of our secure ones. Only for talking to those numbers on the speed dial."

I glanced at it. The top one was Skylur.

"Skylur wants you to call him now," Tom said.

I made to get in, intending to call as we drove, but Tom stopped me again.

"Confidential call, your ears only."

He seemed completely at ease with his instructions. I looked around. There were people being dropped off, busy in their own worlds. This would be okay. No one would notice me, no one would overhear more than a word or two.

"He specified the timing?" I asked.

Tom nodded. "He said as soon as we dropped Diana off." He got back into the Jeep.

I was concerned as I walked along the drop-off area. Why did Skylur want to talk with me only after Diana had left? I hit the number and listened to it ring once before he answered it.

"Hello, Amber."

"Afternoon, Skylur." Diana's comments about provoking Skylur were still fresh in my ears, but I couldn't resist. "Not another unhealthy situation I hope?"

He snorted. "The whole situation is unhealthy. I have a request for you that under almost any other circumstances, I would have refused or advised you to refuse."

More dangerous than waving me in front of Matlal like a matador's cape? Oh, great. "What do I have to do now?"

"You don't have to, Amber, if you don't want to. Or if you feel it's too dangerous." I almost smiled at the way he let the hook dangle. "Arvinder Singh has requested a meeting with you."

Everything just got worse.

"Nice guy, and maybe, secretly, on our side, but he's still Basilikos. How smart would it be to meet him?"

"He's aware that it's a concern. He said you can make all the arrangements. But you can't meet at Haven and I can't let you have any security assistance." He sighed. "As I said, anyone else I would have refused, but—"

"But he's a potential ally and it would be a coup to move his group out of Basilikos, so it would be nice to show some trust."

"Precisely. But not at the expense of risking you."

"Why, thanks. Okay, give me the contact information and I'll figure something out."

He gave me a number to call.

"Not on this cell phone, remember." He paused. "It's getting dangerous out there, Amber," he said.

I could almost feel him changing his mind about keeping me out in Denver. I had to head that off. "I'll be careful and I'll be in on Friday. Do you think Arvinder wants to talk about the rumors?"

"It's the obvious thing."

"Do you trust him?"

"As much as I trust any House in Panethus. After all, that's what he may be, soon."

"You have this way of making me feel so much better, boss," my demon said.

Skylur didn't take offense.

"I'm so pleased. Very well, Amber. Use this cell to talk to me if there is an emergency. Do try not to have any emergencies. And talk to no one, except me and Bian, about Arvinder. No one."

"You got it."

"If I genuinely need you to stop running this deception, I'll call or message on this cell. Understood?"

"Yup."

"And when you drop the rest of them off here, walk around with Marlon and give him your opinion on how someone would attack Haven."

"Okay. Is this another half-day off my fine?"

He laughed and ended the call.

I joined Tom up front for the drive back.

I wanted to sit back and puzzle my way through everything. They didn't let me. Without Diana in the car, the Fang team were a lot more chatty.

"Tom says he has a date with you," Paul said.

"Ha! He's got a date to get his ass kicked is what he's got," I shot back.

"Strictly speaking, I have only a promise of a date," Tom said, his mouth turned down sadly.

"Can we have some of that?" Jason asked.

"You want to get your ass kicked too? Is Marlon the only sensible one in this team?" I said.

"Yeah, he is. We check our brains in with him every morning—"

"On account of it wouldn't do us any good to be thinking too much."

"So can we?"

"Sure, team. You can all come," I said. Unfortunate choice of words. Made them laugh, and get a whole lot ruder. I didn't mind. Ten years of the army does that to you, and I gave as good as I got. It was stupid and it was fun. It made the trip back seem too short.

I left the Jeep outside and we walked through the personnel gate. I waited there for Marlon. As they started moving away, I called after them.

"Hey, team—ass kicking—next Tuesday?"

"Deal." They grinned and gave me the thumbs-up. "But promise, no bad jokes this time."

"No way! Part of my offensive armory." I chuckled. "Oh, one other thing, Tom. You speak Athanate?"

He nodded, strolled a little way back.

"What does this mean?" I gave him the words Diana had said as we parted, as best I could remember. It was probably good enough.

He scrunched his face up. Hmm. Maybe my recall wasn't quite good enough.

"The first part I can't tell. Something about binding. The last part is probably an Athanate saying. 'Strong indeed is the wisdom of innocence'. That helpful?"

"Like an ashtray on a motorcycle. Thanks, Tom, and the rest of you guys. Later."

Marlon came out with a cast and crutches. Okay, no ass-kicking for him next Tuesday. Athanate heal quickly, but I guessed there were different rates for different injuries. My scrapes and bruises seemed to go in a day, but Marlon looked as if the leg was still giving him pain.

"Sorry about that," I said, nodding at his leg and shaking his hand. "Are you okay to walk around the house?"

He shrugged and winced as we started off.

"Bian's responsible for security generally," he said, without preamble. "I'm in charge of Haven's defenses. Skylur wants you to brief me on how you'd go about attacking." He fiddled with a remote microphone on his lapel. "Bian's listening in for the moment. She'll join us when she can."

"Hi, Pussycat," I said to the lapel and then went straight into Ops 4-10 mode. "How I'd go about attacking depends on what my mission objective is and what parameters there are—collateral damage, alerting third parties and so on. I'll give you a worst case scenario—no concern about collateral, minimal concern about third parties and no restriction on weaponry or casualties. The mission is, let's say, to evacuate some of the Assembly and kill most of the rest." I squinted at him and he nodded. Fair assumptions. I turned on my heel and pointed back at the gatehouse. "Start with those. Impressive little forts, and completely useless. I'd allocate two small teams, no more than six people with a couple of laser-guided anti-tank missiles. Less than a minute to set up. No survivors. Regardless of which way I was really attacking, I'd do it anyway as a diversion. Big, bright explosion, lots of people looking the wrong way."

Marlon looked as if he was about to argue the point, but I know the weapons. If it can take out a T-90 tank, a brick building with a nice open slot in the front would be a joke.

"I say the wrong way because I would *not* use the front as the main route to attack."

"Why not?" asked Marlon.

"Because it's the obvious way. And you've probably got the drive mined."

Marlon looked startled. *Bullseye.*

I sketched a couple more diversions as we walked slowly down the side of the house. At the back, I pointed down into the valley below.

"That's where I'd come up. Plenty of cover, even inside the grounds. Second most obvious way, of course, that's why I'd have diversions at the front and sides."

I looked at the stretch of gardens, the rise of the ground and thought it through. "Ten minutes, less than five percent casualties in the attacking force."

"Ten minutes to what?" he said.

"Ten minutes from the first diversion until all the above-ground part of the house is in my hands."

"But…"

"I'm telling you how long it'd take my old army unit to get in there against anyone who didn't have the equivalent training and weapons. Guaranteed."

We stared at each other for a minute. Marlon didn't like it, but he granted me some knowledge on the matter. He'd been almost dismissive at first, but he was starting to get engaged by this.

"Well, what are they going to do then?" he came back with. "You say minimal concerns about third parties but you've had explosions and gunfire going on for ten minutes. Now you're stuck—how are you going to get into the underground section? It'd take hours and by then there'd be police SWAT teams here."

I laughed. "It'd take minutes, and everyone who's leaving would be taken out by helicopter. Half an hour, start to finish."

"You can't possibly fight your way down—"

"I'm not talking about much fighting, once the house is breached, Marlon. You're thinking of defenses like house-to-house, slow work and high attrition. You're stuck in that thinking. It doesn't happen like that anymore in these types of situations."

"So what do you do?"

"Blow freaking great holes through the roof of every level underground." I saw Bian come out of the house and walk towards us. "You've heard of shaped charges? Bunker busters?"

"Yes, but—"

"The same helicopters that are going to lift the evacuees and attack team out, fly the charges in. Those charges can blow holes through yards of armored steel, so your underground building structures aren't going to hold them. And no one in the next level down is going to be in much of a state to fight when whole ceilings start to disintegrate above them."

Bian joined us and tugged out the earphone she'd been using to listen in. "What about casualties in the Basilikos that you're trying to evacuate?"

I shrugged. "It's a risky business. Those that are in the know might gather at the north end of the room, and the attackers concentrate on attacking through the south end. Shaped charges don't spread."

"So how do you defend against this?" asked Marlon.

"Having the Warders do their job to start with." I was just being flippant, but Marlon didn't like it.

"The Warders have a complex job to remain neutral and keep the tensions from escalating. I have a high regard—"

His cell interrupted him.

"He's the primary contact with the Warders," whispered Bian while he was distracted. "Gets a bit defensive."

He was looking pale and sweaty rather than argumentative when he turned back to us.

"I've got to handle this call in the office," he said. "This has been…interesting, House Farrell. Thanks."

He went off on his crutches back up to the house. Bian frowned at his retreating back.

"Okay?" I said.

"He's not healing quickly," she said. "He seems unsettled. He gets even more upset than normal by the comments that everyone's making about the Warders."

"It could be just the stress of the Assembly coming up."

"Hmm." She sat down on a bench and crossed her legs. "He backs a plan to make the government of the Athanate a fixed, unaligned body based on the Warders. He has some good arguments, but it would never be strong enough. He doesn't see that. He believes in the innate goodness of Athanate emerging if given the chance." She made quote signs in the air.

I laughed, which was unkind.

"He's a good man, Round-eye," said Bian sharply.

I sat beside her on the bench. I wasn't going to argue it. He was a bit dour, but he was okay. For all their joking, his team respected him and that was a strong argument for me.

She sighed. "Your attack analysis is pretty bleak. What's your advice on defense?"

"Knowing what's coming can help. I'm assuming the attackers will be well trained for this type of operation. Much better than you've been trained to defend. So, if you can't defend the perimeter and the house, don't try. Have people hiding out in the woods with the right equipment to take down any helicopters that come in. And sufficient numbers to cut off the retreat of the lightly armed attackers. There's no way the attackers will be able to carry enough shaped charges up that hill, so any attack that gets in the house is then in a trap. No way in, no way out."

"You make it sound so straightforward."

"The planning always is. But no plan—"

"Survives contact with the enemy. Yeah, I can quote Clausewitz too."

I nodded. "Altau needs specialists to deal with this sort of thing. No offense, but you've kinda fallen asleep while the Assembly has kept the peace."

"Agreed and agreed. I need to get back. Thank you, Amber."

She walked off, distracted, and there was no teasing. Not even a kiss on the neck. Or was that teasing in itself? I really didn't know with her.

Outside, I spun the Jeep around and headed back. Talking tactics had given me a renewed sense of the space in me that the army had once filled.

I didn't have the comfort of my old army unit around me, and heading back for Denver, it felt like I was going into an operational hot zone. I wanted them at my back.

Despite that, as soon as the octopus got some connections, I called Alex.

"Hi, you good to talk?"

"Er… Not really as fully as I would like, under the circumstances."

"You're in someone's office, aren't you? And they can hear you."

"Yes."

I chuckled and told him what I would like to be doing to him at that very minute. In detail. I enjoyed it.

"Yes, I see. I look forward to that," he said. His voice sounded a little strained.

"What time should I call you later?" I said sweetly. "I need to arrange where I get to meet the alpha."

"Speak again at seven."

"You got it." I signed off, grinning.

Mary and Liu were next on my list. That wasn't so much fun. At least I got through to Liu rather than Mary. I said I would be at the Kwan by 6 p.m.

I left a message for Jen. I would be back after 7 p.m.

That left me the remainder of this afternoon to check whether the old bowling alley was a Hoben hideout. It would just be a drive-by today. I had transferred some of my armory from the Audi, but I wasn't set up for any frontal assault.

I was cutting it close, because I also had to go past José's place in Lowry on the chance that he was still recovering from the gut wound he'd picked up on Monday. I needed to warn him that the FBI were onto Project Snakebite.

And just one last check on Monroe Street. Sorry, Ben-Haim.

José's car was outside his house, and there was no one obviously watching his place. I cruised past a couple of times and went around the block. I knew I shouldn't be cutting corners like this but I felt I was running just to stand still. I couldn't afford the time to sneak over his fence at midnight.

There was a mall on Quebec Street, a couple of blocks away from his house. I picked up envelopes and paper and wrote some notes, then played mailwoman.

Luckily, it was José who came to the door.

I held up the note that said: *FBI tapping my phone—okay to talk?*

"The Lord may be watching you, brother, even now," I said. "Can I interest you in attending a meeting?"

He grinned and came out, pulling the door almost closed behind him.

I'd never seen him in anything but a suit. He was in shorts and a hoody, with sandals on his feet. Comfortable, just a regular guy at home. He was favoring his side where he was wounded, but he looked relaxed for the first time I could remember. I hated bringing him this kind of news.

"I did warn you about the feds," he said quietly.

"Yeah, you did. Look, José, they've gotten hold of something. I got a message on my voicemail asking if I knew anything about a project called Snakebite."

"Damn. Hold it right there." He fished a cell from his pocket and dialed.

"Wally? José. The game's off, obviously… Yeah. Maybe next time."

He ended the call.

I raised my brows. "Wow! Just like that? All prearranged? So I'm not the only paranoid one around?"

"Yeah. That was Edmunds. Game's off is code. Snakebite just disappeared."

"Hope it's not too late." I sighed. "Good to see you up and about, José, but I'm going to be out of sight for a few days. I'll call you when I get back."

He grinned, lopsidedly. "Good to see you too. And I don't want to know any details."

"Thanks." We shook.

"Take care," he called after me.

Like that was ever an option.

It had been a warehouse at one time. Then a garage. Then a theme bar and finally a bowling alley. Lucky's Lanes said the plastic signage, the loopy italic letters in faded red. Now it was derelict and boarded up, surrounded by heavy fencing and warning signs. A decaying monument to the spirit of misguided enterprise and poor naming choices.

Railroad tracks ran along the back, and a cement contractor owned the two adjacent sites. Tucker had bought the place as an investment, knowing one or the other of the new businesses sited around would want to buy eventually. They might, but too late for him.

Matt had hacked the power utility's servers and found out the place was being used for something. The car auction depot was not. Exactly what was happening here was a question for me.

I was only scouting this time. I drove past, seeing the weeping of rust from nails making dark, sad trails down the boards, the flapping pieces of corrugated tin repairing holes in the roof, peeling signs, the whole air of dank desolation.

And the brand new lock and chain on the gate. Crushed weeds on the lot. Tire tracks in the dirt.

It was too light now, too many people around. I'd be back later.

The house on Monroe Street was cold and empty, and the afternoon seemed a whole lot bleaker all of a sudden.

Chapter 25

The Kwan was open for business, as it was every evening. Liu's assistant was teaching a class. He nodded at me and tilted his head at the back office. I wanted to join in, but obviously this wasn't the time. I bowed to the group and made my way around them.

Liu and Mary were sitting, waiting for me. There were mugs of plain green tea in front of them on the table, and a large pot. I sat opposite them and Liu handed me a mug, pouring me tea without a word. I wouldn't have put it past them to be using the silence to try to unnerve me, but sergeants don't get rattled that easily.

I eyed them as I sipped, gave them the benefit of the doubt—it wasn't a ploy. Liu didn't go much for ceremony with his tea, but he liked to savor it quietly before getting down to business. Mary had adopted his Chinese habits. I wondered, as I had before, how they'd met and overcome their very different backgrounds.

Mary was Arapaho, and a senior Adept, if Tullah was right. Liu's family had arrived from China to build railroads and stayed to build a quiet, insular community. In addition to being my Shi Fu, my martial arts teacher, he'd often been the most reliable source of calming perspective on my life since I left the army. All without my saying so much as a word about the Athanate changes that had been taking place in me. I tried to look at him with fresh eyes. Was he an Adept too? It would sure connect some loose ends.

"Yes, Amber," he said. "I am an Adept."

Okay, so silence hadn't spooked me, but reading my mind was a whole different ball game.

"No paranormal ability was required to know what you were thinking." He smiled slightly. "I've come to know you well in the time you've practiced here."

We sipped our tea. Mary sat expressionless while Liu and I exchanged a few comments about the Kwan.

Mary placed her mug down on the table with a decisive click, and Liu and I turned to her.

"My daughter doesn't have the ability to cope with what she's attempting," she said. Mary was never someone who'd creep up on a subject.

"You were the one who was asking me what I was doing when I was nineteen, Mary. I don't know what she's attempting, but is it more dangerous than what I did at that age?"

"Very possibly." Mary settled back in her chair, her eyes hooded. "This isn't just about a mother's ordinary concerns for her daughter."

"It's because she works with an evil, corrupting Athanate?"

"Stop trying to pick a fight, Amber." Mary poured herself some more tea. "What do you know about her spirit guide?" she asked, looking up shrewdly at me.

I snorted. "About as much as I know about mine." Mary waited, so I went on. "She has a dragon. And that's not on the approved list." I was not going to tell her that Kaothos and I were on speaking terms. Or maybe, that I had begun dreaming that I was speaking to Tullah's dragon.

"Do you know why it's not on the 'approved' list?" asked Mary. The stress she put on the word told me she didn't like the description.

"No," I said, and helped myself to some more tea as well.

"In China, a dragon would not just be on the approved list, but a cause for celebration," Liu said. "Unfortunately, not here."

"Why there and not here?"

"Because they are rare," Liu said. "And extremely powerful. And very dangerous." He paused. "In China, communities are formed around Adepts with dragon guides."

I frowned. Surely…

"There are no other communities with dragon guides in America, Amber," Mary said. "And, unlike the Athanate, we have no connections across the world."

"Well, make them," I said, exasperated.

"There will not be time," Liu said with absolute finality.

I shook my head. "You've lost me," I said.

"All spirit guides begin as incomplete, unsure," Mary said. "Full of potential, but lacking direction and focus." She stopped to squint at me, reached across and touched my forehead. "Your spirit guide has appeared to you?"

"As a wolf cub," I said. "This week."

Mary sighed and her head dropped. "More problems," she muttered.

Liu rested his hand on hers in support and she looked up again at me. "All Adepts who wish to use their spirit guides enter communities. These communities have other Adepts with spirit guides, either the same or related. The communities across America span all the common types and tap deep into the history of this land, the oral traditions, the ceremonies, the knowledge that nurtures the fledgling spirit guide."

"What you're saying is the guide needs a guide?" I said.

"Not in accessing the energy. In developing it. And in the correct use of the energy."

"Correct use? Some kind of moral guidance?"

"Yes. But not just that, also awareness of the limitations of the channel, the human host," Mary said.

"So you think Tullah's dragon might make her evil and burn her out somehow?" I laughed; surely not Tullah.

Mary's eyes flicked to Liu. "Yes."

Shit!

"But how? Not Tullah. I mean, she's as far as—"

"It does not need a person to be evil to start with, Amber. It is power, and untrained, unrestrained power will create evil of itself."

"Has it—"

"No, it has not started yet," said Mary, and I felt a tiny spark of relief. Maybe there was still time. There must be something. "And it would be most subtle at first," she went on. "We know the way of this."

"And what about me then? I can't be accepted into your community. What about my spirit guide making me evil and burning me out?"

"The wolf is not as powerful as the dragon," Liu said. "No other spirit guide is. It's unlikely the wolf will burn you out. But," he sighed, "forgive me, with the presence of the Athanate, the powers of the Athanate and no supporting community…"

"I'll turn out bad. Mom always warned me."

"This is not a joke, Amber."

"Yeah, sorry."

It's gotten to be kinda laugh or cry, guys. I already have Were and Athanate duking it out in my head and making it likely I'll go rogue. Now I find out that Hana can achieve that all on her own. Think.

Tullah's case was more urgent. "So, why can't the two of you provide a community for Tullah?"

Mary and Liu exchanged a look. Liu took up the question. "We tried, as soon as we found out. But the dragon rejected us. She has developed this far in secrecy and isolation. She will not accept advice from us."

"We think this…this arrogance has spilled over into Tullah," Mary said. "It is the first warning sign. Rejection of community."

Hmmm. Tullah had seemed on edge this week, but not exactly arrogant. And I thought Kaothos wasn't rejecting community itself, maybe just theirs.

"Not accepting Matt as a boyfriend didn't help there," I said.

Liu looked embarrassed. "More my fault than Mary's."

Yeah, dads and daughters. Nice that even the inscrutable martial arts master and Adept fell prey to the simplest of human reactions. And a weak ray of hope that the both of them might be overreacting here because it was their daughter.

"Okay. Given you don't have any links to Chinese Adept communities and there are no dragon guides around, how certain are you about all this?"

"Tullah's argument exactly. All we have is tradition from China that we have kept in our family," Liu said.

"Which warns of what?"

"The last unrestrained spirit dragon swept whole empires away," said Mary, "from China to the gates of Byzantium. Whole peoples were wiped out."

Liu fixed me with his stare. "It is very difficult to kill people with swords on this…industrial scale," he said. "Imagine what can be done with more modern technology today."

I could imagine it indeed. I had seen it, far too close.

"So what do you want with me? I won't fight her and I'm not going to spy on her."

Mary ducked her head. Liu answered, "Be there for her, keep talking to us. I don't mean behind her back. We want you to tell her you're talking to us, and what you say. We need her to know we're always here." He paused. "Then, also, the dragon may listen to you," he said quietly. "There is a little hope."

"But you believe I'm going to become evil. Why do you want me influencing your daughter's spirit guide?"

"You're not there yet, Amber, and…"

The pair of them exchanged looks again.

"There's something you want to tell me?" I prompted.

Liu cleared his throat. "If Athanate are truly evil or not…we disagree on this in the Adept community. But there is hope. If you can form a link to her and we can form a link to you. There is hope. Maybe for both."

I rubbed my face in my hands. At some stage, I'd have to stop holding out on everyone, but it didn't feel right telling them everything yet. I wanted to get out and let this percolate along with everything else that was happening. See if something smart might occur to me. But I had one question I wanted answered.

"I know there are Athanate who are evil, but the Athanate in Denver don't seem evil to me. What argument have you got that they are?"

I waited. Liu looked uncomfortable.

"I know the way you were brought up." Mary leaned forward. "I've met your mother, Stacy. She taught you that everything has a cost, doesn't it?"

I nodded.

"So what price do Athanate pay for their powers? Or does someone else do the paying?" asked Mary.

I didn't have an answer to her question. "What about Adepts?" I countered.

"We pay, Amber. Our own life force. Adepts who use their powers often, they live shorter lives. Yet within the Athanate kin, Adepts and humans live longer. Why? How?"

"Dammit, I don't know. Some effect of the Athanate blood. It's clear you don't know either, but you're just assuming it's evil."

Mary went quiet, as sure in her own viewpoint as I was in mine. Time to go. I got up.

"Liu, Mary," I said. "Tullah's like a sister to me and I'll do what I can to keep her safe, short of trying to change her completely. I don't think I'm evil. I don't think all Athanate are evil. I've stopped fighting becoming Athanate."

Liu followed me out the door. "You say you're not fighting it, Amber," he said quietly, his voice masked from the class by the noise they were making, "but you're no more Athanate to my eyes than you've always been."

"I get fangs, Liu. My senses have gone crazy. My heart rate won't go over 120. I'm looking for kin. I'm there."

Liu smiled and shrugged. "Your description is similar to changes the Were go through as well, you know."

Damn, I hadn't fooled him. He could see what was going on.

"Trust me, Amber," he said. "I have known you longer than the Athanate, longer than the Were. There is a tremendous strength in you. I can help, if you let me. Athanate, Were or not. Keep up your training sessions here, and we will talk."

His face became more serious. "That anger," he tapped my chest and belly, "trapped in there. That is not good. Not for the human. Not for the Adept. Not for the Were. But especially, not for the Athanate."

Chapter 26

"Ronit Chopra," the voice said. I checked the number Skylur had given me. This was it.

"Amber Farrell," I replied. "Can I speak to Arvinder?"

"Ms. Farrell, I am so very pleased you called. I am the Diakon for House Singh. Arvinder has asked me to set up a meeting with you urgently."

"Ronit, I've had attempts to kill or capture me in the last week. You realize it's all sorts of crazy for me to be risking a meeting." I eyed the octopus on the computer and hoped he was doing his job hiding where I was as I drove slowly northwards.

"Ms. Farrell, we absolutely guarantee your safety."

"That's nice, but it might be difficult to make a claim against that guarantee." I huffed. "If he really wants to meet, it'll be tomorrow. I'll make a call and ask him to show up alone somewhere. If I get any feeling that it isn't safe, your fault or not, I'm out of there."

"We understand, Ms. Farrell, and thank you."

I ended the call. Whether I actually managed the meeting or not, at least I'd shown I was willing. His eagerness to set the meeting had my antennae twitching, but if he thought he could manage something with the security I was going to put in place, he had another think coming.

It was getting late, and I'd promised to be back at 7 p.m., at Jen's house, Manassah. Only, that wasn't what I was calling it in my mind. I was calling it home.

I called Alex.

"Wolfy, can you talk now?" I said when he answered.

"You are a—"

"Bitch?" I suggested. "Yeah, I can do that. I'll be your bitch and you can be mine. Didn't you enjoy my last call?"

He laughed. "Not as much as you did."

"Well, it sounds as if you can get me back now."

"Hmm. I'm more physical than verbal."

That was an opening for me. Not one I'd been waiting for particularly. I'd have much rather done this face to face.

"About that, can I ask a tough question?"

"Not got doubts again already?"

"No." I smiled. "Just asking." I was painfully aware of how little I knew about Weres, how much Alex would be happy to talk about. The question had formed in my mind from other people's descriptions about them. I wasn't even sure what answer I wanted to hear.

That untamed look in his eyes, the wildness, it was scary. It spoke of danger, the potential for animal violence. But I *liked* scary; it turned me on. And I was no powder puff. I guessed I just wanted to know how much of a leash there was. Trouble was, how to put that into words?

"Well?" he prompted me.

"Er…when we were in bed yesterday, y'know, afterwards, when we were talking."

"I like this part." There was almost a growl behind his words.

"Just before your cell called you away and ruined it." I tried throwing a bit of cold water on him. "You said not every girl was physically up to it." I swallowed, hearing a deep silence on the line. Oh crap! Why couldn't I just shut up?

"Yeah, we can get rough, dominant, and believe me, even in human form, we enjoy biting as well." He paused. "I wish you were here," he said, very quietly, very simply.

I'd pulled over and parked. That was a good thing because driving wouldn't have gotten my attention at that moment. I'd wandered into difficult ground in a new relationship, a very important relationship for me, and all the nonverbal communication stuff was out.

"I wish you were here, too," I replied.

"You're in your car."

"Doesn't matter where we are."

He chuckled. It was a deep, rich sound and it told me we were okay. "I didn't come looking for someone to be submissive all the time, hot stuff, and I won't promise I'll always be gentle, but I am not a complete animal. Not even when I am."

I laughed. I could handle that. "When do I get to see the complete animal? I'm guessing the full moon is just Hollywood."

"Hey, full moons are good. Much better light to go running in the woods." There were some background noises. "Hold on a second."

I could hear him speaking to someone, promising to be out in a couple of minutes. Then he came back on.

"I gotta go. The client is back on board. I just want to be sure they're going to stay that way. I'm back in Denver tomorrow, and I've set up a meeting with the alpha in the morning."

He gave me the address of a ranch off the Deer Creek road, out near the national parks, southwest of the city.

"Amber, this is a very bad time," he warned.

"It's never a good time."

"Just give the alpha some leeway, okay? His name's Felix Larimer."

"Alex, I'm not accusing Felix of anything—"

"You are, whether you mean to or not."

"What's the big deal?"

"The big deal is the Athanate poking their noses into our business when it suits them and freezing us out when it doesn't. Athanate making decisions on behalf of the whole paranormal community without consulting anyone else, and then demanding accountability from us. Taking and never giving. The world doesn't revolve around the Athanate concerns, Amber."

"Ouch. Sorry. I'll be nice. And I'm not there as a rep for the Athanate."

"No, I'm sorry. I shouldn't have gone off on you. It will help if you make it clear you're just there personally. Look, gotta go."

"Are you coming with me?"

"I'll be there. See you tomorrow."

We signed off and I sat thinking it through.

Hmm. 'Be there' rather than 'come with'.

There was some justification in what he said about Athanate, at least in the way I'd be perceived. Maybe he had a point that Athanate tended to think the world revolved around them. Diana hadn't made any mention of Were or Adepts in her plans to talk to the government.

I didn't want to make trouble for Alex with his pack.

There was a text message on my cell, ordering me back to Haven. It was from Tom, who quoted it as coming from Skylur. Well, the decoy was running. I deleted the message.

I wasn't as late as I feared. I got there just as Jen's driver, Kingston, was emptying some bags from the trunk of her car. She'd been shopping and I saw she'd even had Tullah in tow.

"Another new car, honey?" Jen asked.

"It's just on loan for a couple of days. Am I late?" I said.

"You're early," Jen said as we kissed cheeks. "Hell, early enough we can decide where to go for dinner."

Tullah was quiet. She must have known where I'd been, and I guessed that was the reason. I would have to talk to her privately later.

"Why not eat in?" I said as we walked in.

"My treat."

Now Jen and I would have to talk. It wasn't that she couldn't afford it. She had to be one of the richest people in Denver. It was all about my pride, and the sting when my sister had accused me of being dependent on Jen. Also, if I argued it and paid, it'd have to be on my card and I didn't doubt the FBI would be tracking that if they were bugging my cells.

"You can't just keep taking me out for meals. And I haven't got anything to wear," I said.

Tullah suddenly moved off down the hall. "I'll go change," she called over her shoulder.

Kingston came back from the other way. "All done, Ms. Kingslund."

"Thanks, Kingston. That's it for today. See you tomorrow, usual time."

He slipped out the front door, and Jen took my hand and pulled me, protesting, along to the guest suite.

I realized why Tullah had run off. Jen hadn't been shopping for herself.

"No, Jen. You can't keep doing this." I wasn't really angry. Not really. I understood it wasn't her fault. The total cost of all the clothes she had bought me probably meant as much to her financially as it would for me to buy Tullah a coffee. She just didn't see that there was a difference. "Can't you see the problem?"

"No, honey, all I could see was you don't have any clothes left." Now she was angry with me. There was more than a lack of understanding there. I could see a frustration boiling underneath. It wasn't the cost, but this meant so much to her, and I needed to puzzle it out, quickly. The air felt dry as tinder, as if a spark might set it off.

"What do you want me to do?" she snapped. "How can I make it better if you won't let me?" Her blue eyes seemed lit from within. She was seconds from blowing up.

I ran out of smart words, and I did the thing I knew I really shouldn't do, because, despite that, it was what I wanted to do. I slipped my arms around her. Her body was stiff.

"I don't need you to do anything, Jen. It doesn't need making better."

The breath left her and with it, all the tension from her body. Her hands slid over my back, and I closed my eyes.

"Sorry," she whispered against my neck, lips like butterflies on my skin.

I smiled.

"What?" She pinched me gently.

"Just something totally inappropriate and cheesy I nearly said."

"You can't do that, honey. Tell me," she said, "or the dinner's off." Hidden in a joke, she was asking if it was all right to go out, and I guess, having retreated from arguing about the clothes, I might as well capitulate on everything.

"Okay, we'll go, but I choose where."

"Done. That doesn't get you out of telling me what you were thinking, sneaky."

"Just how lovely you look when you're angry. I did warn you it was cheesy."

She giggled. "Really?"

"Yeah. Take it from me, that is really cheesy, I promise you." She hit me. Luckily, it's difficult to punch someone you're hugging.

"You going to try some of the clothes on, honey?"

I could imagine getting my clothes off, but I was having difficulty imagining getting others back on in a hurry. And she hadn't said anything that made me think she'd wait outside.

"Shy?" Her face looked so innocent.

I laughed. "After ten years in the army? No, Jen, not body shy. But actually, I do need you to do something for me." I ran my fingers up into her hair, enjoying the feel of it. Little shivers ran down my body. If I didn't stop this soon, I wasn't going to be able to. I kissed her forehead. "I need you to wait until after the weekend, and I can explain everything about me, before we take it any further."

She looked up at me, flushed but resigned. "Okay, honey." I guess she'd gotten used to me being strange, and asking strange things. Her hands sank to hold my hips and rested there. Her teeth nervously worried at her bottom lip.

She took a steadying breath. "I'm not going to change my mind. I know we're not in Kansas anymore, Toto."

I tilted my head and looked at her, wondering. She knew about werewolves; part of her case had involved Alex's pack. And I guess, like many things, once you've opened your mind, all kinds of other thoughts present themselves. Had she figured out what I was? At least approximately.

"So," she said carefully, "do I miss you on nights with a full moon?"

I giggled. "I'm not playing twenty questions, but moonlighting is strictly Hollywood." Before I could shut my mouth, my little demon made me say, "You might get me to howl, though."

She looked up at me, big blue eyes blinking. "Why, honey, whatever do you mean?" Butter wouldn't melt, etcetera.

I persuaded her to go off and change into something more casual while I picked out an outfit from the clothes she had bought me. She'd nailed it on the size and her taste was excellent. Not a single price tag was left on the clothes, but I could imagine. At the end of it, though, I was still in jeans and a shirt, just way upscale.

I was out before Jen, and Tullah was waiting in the sitting room. She smiled a little at the clothes. "That went way better than it might have, then," she said.

She was still subdued.

"What's up?" I asked, sitting beside her. I assumed she was expecting me to launch into a lecture from her parents.

I could see her check that Jen wasn't around yet. She took a deep breath. "How well do you know Alex?"

A little chill settled in my stomach. "Not well at all. Not really. Why?"

"I shouldn't have gotten involved, Amber." She rubbed her face. "But when you said that Alex's old girlfriend had died, I had to check. I couldn't help myself."

"Check what?"

"There's no death certificate," said Tullah. "She's officially listed as missing."

I struggled to stay calm. "Hope was a Were too, I'm pretty sure. There are many reasons that it might not be a good idea for a human coroner to see her."

"Yeah. It's probably nothing, and I know you can take care of yourself. I had to tell you though. I'm sorry."

"You did right, kiddo." I wasn't going to worry about this tonight. I would ask Alex tomorrow and he'd explain to me. Fine.

I gave her a hug just as Jen came in. Thankfully, my problems didn't suddenly increase. Jen had figured out my relationship with Tullah, and all I got was a whisper in my ear when Tullah was on the phone making the reservation.

"Is everything okay?"

"Yeah, it was nothing really."

Tullah was booking us in to Lario's. My choice and the steaks were to die for.

"Is that your hand on my butt?" I murmured.

She sighed. "Just checking the fit, honey. Did I get it right?"

"Feels good," said my demon. "The fit, I mean."

She chuckled wickedly and then behaved herself as we piled into the Jeep. After making sure cell numbers were up to date, I let the guards stay at Manassah.

Lario made a fuss of me. I hadn't been in for a month. Well, I couldn't afford to eat there regularly, even with the discount I got. With kisses on cheeks all around, he ushered us to a corner table and let the wait staff loose on us. I doubt Lario noticed it was Jen; he wasn't interested in much outside of his restaurant, but the staff knew who she was and the service zinged.

The steak and the wine did the job of unwinding us all. So much that I ended up agreeing to go out with Jen the following evening, not to a restaurant, but to the site of her new Quarter Horse race track. It was out towards Golden, on the west side of Denver. Although the stands and facilities would be a long time coming, the Quarter Horse Association wanted to run some inaugural races to celebrate. Jen had to attend the planning for a media ceremony formally signing over the site. I groaned inwardly; I had just agreed to go to a business meeting.

On a completely different topic, the meal turned out to be a gold mine for me. Jen mentioned in passing that she was considering buying some art from a gallery owned by one Floyd Underwood.

Tullah had read my update on the Quinns' case, including the strong suspicion that Underwood had been responsible for the theft of the medal. Without so much as a glance in my direction, Tullah became fascinated by Underwood's gallery and the range of his collections. The wine worked on Jen as well, and she chatted, happily and indiscreetly. I felt several twinges of guilt, but hey, it wasn't me asking the questions.

"…and you wouldn't believe the private military collection he keeps in his office."

"Military? Like medals and so on?"

"Yeah. He showed me a couple. Not my thing, but he has pretty much every medal type ever awarded."

Tullah, you just earned yourself a stripe.

I simply knew that the medal would be in his private collection, in his office, at the Keynes building in Capitol Hill.

Back at Manassah, Tullah headed off to bed while Jen poured herself a brandy nightcap.

"Not for you, honey?" She held up my favorite rum.

I shook my head.

"Heading out again?" Her voice was flatter. Not so happy.

"I have to go check out something on a case," I said. Another late night, but it made sense for creeping around the old bowling alley. I changed the topic. "You know, it's not secure enough here." I tested that the patio doors were locked. Through them I could see the larch border stirring in the wind and the distant lights of the Country Club twinkling. "Maybe you should get one more of Victor's guys back to patrol the grounds?"

"Enough guards. But all the more reason for you to be here." She sipped her brandy. "That's when I feel secure."

I didn't rise to the bait. Yes, I had saved her life twice, and yes, she was safer if I was around. I just couldn't be all the time.

"Also, I have a shotgun in my room," she said. "I used to shoot clay pigeons."

A shotgun that might or might not be loaded, that might have been fired ages ago by someone who used to use it to shoot at practice targets. Not going to be good enough if I had my way.

Jen finished her drink.

She paused and I could see her think through a dozen things to say, but in the end she chose to keep it simple.

"Be careful. Please."

I gave her a hug and waited till she'd closed her door before going to my suite.

I rummaged through my walk-in closet and found a dark sweatshirt. I changed into my work boots and took out my gloves, black ski cap and a stockman's coat. I'd liberated the coat when I'd busted Tucker's drug smuggling operation, and one of Jen's staff had patched, cleaned and weatherproofed it. The night had turned wet, and I would be glad of it. It would also make me look twice as big and, even better, it would hide things.

From the trunk of the car I picked a couple of things for it to hide. I was already wearing the HK in a shoulder holster. I added the silencer. I took a shorty pump action shotgun for use as a last resort when silencers wouldn't be any good. And my old entrenching tool. Personally, I'd never entrenched since boot camp. Sure, we used the tool in Ops 4-10. We called it our portable toilet. I wouldn't want that tonight, but it had a lot to recommend it for breaking into old buildings.

I checked my messages on the octopus. Matt had sent me an update—*Power use at the bowling alley fell off a cliff this afternoon. Car auction place still cold, has been for a week.*

Crap. I tried to kid myself that it could just be they'd decided to move somewhere more pleasant to hide out. I still had to go; the bowling alley was my only trace on Hoben. I was tired of shadow boxing. I growled. I needed to hit something. And I might get lucky and find a clue to where they'd moved to, or maybe where they'd keep Larry.

But realistically, moving out today? No coincidences. They had spotted me drive by.

Or in the worst case—*the most likely,* whispered Ben-Haim—they'd gotten Larry and he'd talked. They had found out he'd told me about the bowling alley and the car auction site.

Either way, I was going to walk into a trap.

Chapter 27

The night made the old bowling alley look very sinister.

I left the car half a mile away, in the parking lot of a hotel tucked up against the intersection of I-25 and I-70. It was quiet; I'd seen few other people as I walked here, my collar turned up against the rain, and none of them had been walking.

The adjacent cement manufacturing businesses were closed and their security lights just made the shadows darker where they gathered. A couple of old cars were parked on the street in front of one of them, but there was no sign of their owners.

I went up and over the fence with no more noise than it made anyway, rattling in the wind. Even that was lost against the clatter of trains passing on the railroad tracks behind the building.

Inside the perimeter, rain had blurred the edges of the tire tracks in the dirt, but it was still all churned up. Several large vans had been here recently. I slipped into the shadows around the building. Nothing else stirred on the site.

I couldn't hear anything from inside the building. I couldn't smell anything other than rust and old oil, and cement from the neighboring businesses. There was no sensation of warmth in the walls. The jury-rigged repairs to the roof screeched and banged in the wind.

I did a circuit of the building, not being a fan of places with only one way in or out. Rotting wooden shipping pallets and rusted forty-gallon drums were littered around the back. Weeds had forced their way through the concrete slabs ringing the building and taken over the space between the building and the fence separating it from the tracks.

The main doors at the front were sealed behind a metal grill bolted to the building. There were old emergency doors halfway down the side, but they were heavily boarded up. The only obvious way in was a small side door, and that was the last way I wanted to try.

I climbed the metal grill on the front doors, then up over the Lucky's Lanes sign to reach a ledge just wide enough to stand on. From there I could stretch and peer in through slot windows too narrow and high to have been worth boarding up. They were caked in cement dust.

It was almost completely dark inside. Except where a lone guard sat next to a caged work light, smoking a cigarette and fiddling with a pistol. He sat on one of the old row seats where bowlers had waited their turn. The plastic covers were ripped and a plank of wood evened the legs. On the left was an old office structure, just about the only thing in the building that remained enclosed. Even the ceiling tiles had been taken, leaving the interior like a metal skeleton draped with trailing light cables. The old alley borders were there, and a sad pile of rental shoes in one corner. The flooring and the racking mechanisms had been too valuable to leave; they had been torn out, leaving gaping holes in the internal wall at the back.

I was almost insulted. This was Hoben's old hideout and it was screaming 'trap' at me, but why leave a single man inside it? One so dumb he sat there with a light on, ruining his night vision. Of course, the internal wall might hide more of them. Or the office.

I was ready to climb back down when the guard moved.

He checked his watch and got up, flicking ash off his jacket. Then he walked to the office and shone a flashlight through the glass panel in the door. Apparently satisfied, he took a cell phone from his pocket and dialed. Amateur hour. He was calling in. What was he reporting on in the office? Larry?

Why set up a trap and leave Larry here? As bait? Easier to believe if I could see him. What if it wasn't a trap, and they hadn't found anywhere to store him safely yet? Or it was something or someone else being held in that office? Blood slaves?

Trap or not, I was going in—the problem Hoben and Matlal would find with traps is they don't always work the way you think. The guard had to know something, and that was more than I had any other way at the moment. He might be my only lead on Hoben, and the clock was running down.

The question was, how? *Not* through the obvious side door.

I got down and walked around the building again, getting impatient and knowing that could be fatal. I had no one to call on. House Altau were too stretched and the Snakebite police team had been disbanded. This was a solo job. I had to do it right.

In the back, there were holes in the brickwork where the venting systems had come out. The valuable metal had been ripped out in a hurry, leaving large irregular gaps. They were about twenty-five feet off the ground, high enough that they hadn't been completely boarded over like ground floor windows. They looked like the only alternative way in, with a bit of work. And one that would be at least partly shielded from the guard by the internal wall.

A couple of old rusted drums allowed me to get a handhold on a ledge. Using the entrenching tool like an ice pick, I hauled myself up until eventually I got a foothold in the damaged wall. Then I got the tool's blade in behind the boards and levered them off little by little, the noise masked by passing trains. In reasonably short order, I had a new way in, and possibly a way out.

Beneath the exit vent holes there was the skeleton of a raised floor which had presumably been used for maintenance access to the racking systems. I slithered in the hole and lowered myself carefully onto the frame and from there to the ground.

The scene inside the main hall hadn't changed. The guard lit a cigarette from the stub of his last. His back was to me and the way I'd come in was shielded from him by the tattered remains of the internal wall.

I could smell his cigarette now, so there would be movements in the air if he paid any attention to that. But I could also smell chemical toilets and wet cement, masking other odors.

From this angle, I could see some wired-up devices rigged over the small door at the side that I was supposed to have come in.

Nice little surprise.

The advantage was all with me. The guard was in a bad position, and even if his brain hadn't caught up, his body knew it—I could smell his fear.

And through the spectrum of other smells assaulting my nose, there were traces of Matlal. And blood. My gut tightened.

The guard started his check and report-in routine. That made it once every fifteen minutes or so. Plenty of time, hopefully.

The wind was rattling and banging the jury-rigged roof repairs outside, and I couldn't hear him talking to his contact, so it wasn't a surprise he didn't hear me. He'd sat back down and put his pistol on the seat beside him while he called.

He ended the call and I reached over and took his pistol away.

He fell over, scrabbling for something in his jacket.

I vaulted the seating.

"Should have gotten it before," I said as I paralyzed his arm with a blow and shoved him face down on the floor. He'd been going for a dart gun, little brother to the one they had used in Cheesman. Only accurate to about ten yards, just about good enough for me coming through the door.

I lifted him up and slammed him against the bare brick wall, holding his own pistol underneath his chin. Dust drifted over us in a cloud. Cement dust. That did nothing for my temper.

"Please, I had nothing to do with him," he shouted. His eyes were wide with panic and he stank of fear and sweat and cigarettes, enough to make my nose try to close down.

"Who?" I said.

"Him. In there. It's the fucking vamps, I tell you. I said not to get involved. The boss wouldn't listen."

The chill that had hung over me settled in my stomach.

I dragged him to the office. The small window I'd seen him looking through was almost opaque with dust. So thick, I could barely make out Larry slumped in a chair. The ropes binding him seemed to be holding him up. He didn't move.

The guard hadn't gone in. That thought stopped me. What would they expect me to do? Rush in.

"There's another trap, isn't there?" Two traps. Two chances to get me. It's what I'd have done.

"N-no," he stammered. He was lying. How stupid did he think I was?

I used his body to break the door open, shoving him through and then snatching him back. Sure enough, a spring-loaded net whipped down. If I'd gone through I'd be trussed up like a turkey now.

I used him to force it out the way and get to Larry.

Who didn't stir. And would never stir again. He sat there with his chest torn open, his heart and lungs ripped out. His face was stretched in his final agony.

I'd been far too late for him.

I closed my eyes for a moment, feeling a cloud of despair and hate build over me. But I couldn't let blind fury take over. There was only one thing now that would make his death mean something—getting his killers brought to justice.

I couldn't linger. I hauled the guard out and shoved him back against the wall.

"Who did that?"

"Matlal's bunch," he stammered.

"Where?"

He looked blank.

"Not. Enough. Blood." I kept slamming him against the wall for punctuation. "He was killed somewhere else and brought here. Where? Where was he killed?"

"Don't know. It's the truth," he whimpered. "I don't know."

"Where's Hoben, then?"

He started to cry, shaking his head from side to side.

Even if I face a certain, painful death one day, I hope I face it better than that. I wasn't going to kill him, and even though he didn't know it, that made his cowardice worse for me.

My anger started feeding on itself. My hand gripped his throat and he choked. His eyes bugged out. Why not kill him? The waves of fear coming from him seemed to flood my brain. With a shudder, I realized my Athanate could learn to feed off that.

"What were you guarding here?" I asked him, easing off the pressure. "What was your assignment?"

He hesitated, his eyes darting back and forth. I tightened my grip slightly. No escape. "C-capture you," he stuttered. "For Hoben."

Damn. There were no clues here—he was nothing but bait. Except…why nets *and* trank darts? Why risk a live guard at all?

"I wasn't gonna hurt you, I swear," he continued, his voice pleading. *No, just turn me over to his sick, sadistic boss. Touching, all this concern for me.*

Hold on. *Turn me over to his boss.*

"You were supposed to deliver me to Hoben, once I was unconscious, weren't you?" His eyes widened in fear. I gave him a little shake. "Where?"

He moaned. "I can't tell you that! You saw what they did to him." His eyes flicked toward the office. "Hoben will get one of those vamps to rip my heart out."

"Hoben's not here," I said. "I am."

My own rules. I wouldn't kill him now, but he didn't know that. I pulled the hammer back on his pistol and stuck it in his groin. He held up his hands as if to ward me off and started babbling incoherently.

The clock was ticking, and he was annoying me. I jabbed him with the pistol. "Dammit, where?"

His eyes shifted to the watch on his wrist. The babbling stopped as suddenly as a radio in a power outage. He met my eyes, cold as ice.

"Here." The corner of his mouth twisted. "Got you, bitch."

Outside, the compound gates smashed open. As in, someone drove a pickup through them at full speed.

He punched and caught me in the side. No weak, half-hearted jab, either. A powerful blow. But, in his arrogance, he'd given me a warning, and I'd turned slightly. He busted his knuckles on the shotgun hidden under my coat.

I swore and hit him with his pistol, hard, thrusting it deep into his solar plexus. I jumped back out of his reach as he doubled over and flick-kicked him in the face. He staggered, blinded. I grabbed his lapels, swung him around, and threw him onto the trap that had been set up for me coming through the side door.

The net snapped down and spun him around, tangling him like a fly in a web. Just as they got to the door, I jammed the seat he'd used against it. As they tried to force the door open, I ran.

In Ops 4-10, we never left any of our team behind. I couldn't manage that tonight. I was shaken by flashes of Larry. Smelling of bourbon and acting like a drunk. Joking about it. The way his voice changed when he spoke of his kin. Him kneeling on the road at Castle Pines. I'd thought he was a coward then, and he wasn't. Next, I'd been afraid he was trying to trap me, and he wasn't that either. He was brave and he was dead, and I had to leave him here.

I was clambering up towards my emergency exit in the back when they rammed the pickup into the door, making the whole building shudder. Cement dust billowed off every surface and formed a choking cloud, quickly shot through with powerful flashlight beams as they fought their way in through the twisted wreck of the seats and the body of the guard.

The skeleton of rotten supports groaned and started to buckle beneath me. I leaped upwards as it fell, desperately scrabbling, just catching the edge of the vent holes. As I heaved myself upwards, I heard more pickups follow into the yard, engines snarling and tires squealing.

I fell out of the building, twisting around, catching my foot on a rusty drum which buckled at the blow. Luckily there was no one out back yet.

I ran flat out for the fence. A pickup came racing around the side and skidded to a stop in the back, then revved again as it roared across the lot towards me. No freaking amateurs, these. There was shouting behind me. I'd been seen. Reach, grip, lift and…flip. Up and over. A pull from the razor wire on the coat. It was going to need repairs again, but I hadn't lost my skills getting over obstacles.

Someone fired. The chilling *wheep* of a bullet going by my head told me I wasn't clear yet. Apparently the orders to take me alive didn't apply if I was going to escape.

More shouting and firing behind me, cut off abruptly by the scream of the train as I ran across the tracks right in front of it. Close enough that it flicked my coat tail as it passed. Then there was an unending clatter of railroad cars passing behind, with them on the other side and a long wait to chase me, courtesy of Union Pacific.

Except, of course, they could start vaulting fences and jumping onto rolling stock.

I sprinted back to the hotel, tossed the coat in the trunk and was merged with the interstate traffic before they'd gotten the first pickup on my side of the tracks.

I hammered my hand on the wheel in frustration.

I'd gotten nothing from that. Nothing. I had failed Larry and he was dead because of it. Hoben was surrounded by Matlal now. The guard hadn't been ZK, he'd been Matlal's elite team. They'd read me to perfection. He'd hidden his marque behind cigarette smoke and something that faked the smell of fear. He'd made me react to him, dismiss him as a threat, ignore the subtle hints of Matlal. He'd played me.

And he'd so nearly delayed me long enough. If I hadn't had the escape route, I'd be in their hands now.

As for Hoben, even if I could find another clue to where he was, maybe the next trap would be better, or they'd get lucky. They only needed to get lucky once.

I was wrong about there being only one thing to make Larry's death worth something. There were two. I'd accepted responsibility for him. He was dead, but his kin weren't, as far as I knew. I felt in my pocket and retrieved the scrap of paper he'd given me when we started running at Cheesman. He hadn't expected to get away. Underneath the grief, I felt a pull as deep and strong as the ocean tide. This was some coded message to find his kin, and I would. They'd become my responsibility, part of my Athanate House.

On my Blood, Larry, I so swear.

I left the Jeep at Diana's apartment in her underground garage and walked back to Manassah. I was tired, but too pumped up to sleep, so after a shower, I went back through Matt's reports and his fresh updates, forcing myself to concentrate.

Matlal first. On the surface, he was as Bian had described him: glossy. His main company, and the source of his fortune, was Bioteca Eztlian, a biotech company based in Mexico City. To this, he added a thriving cattle business, based on ranches all over Mexico, and strangely, companies growing and selling flowers. He supported urban renewal projects, zoos and orphanages. By the evidence of the photos and media releases Matt had cropped, the man had to be on first-name terms with every politician in Central America and half of them in South America. His actual politics didn't seem strongly defined, though a couple of Nahuatl groups claimed his support. 'Wannabe Aztecs', their opponents called them dismissively.

Matt hadn't been as lucky in finding out Matlal's history. The story of barrio to boardroom on the official websites seemed way too slick. It was so unbelievable, it almost felt true.

Similarly, substantiated criminal connections were thin on the ground. *Unsubstantiated* rumors had him the puppet master of the whole drug trade from Columbia to Mexico. *El Jefe Sombra.*

Equally difficult to pin down was anything outside of the official scope of his biotech company, which rumor said included bio-warfare and illegal genetic experiments.

There was nothing that was going to help me particularly over the next few days, but I like to know my enemy, and I didn't consider it a waste of time reading the report.

Matt's additional report on the animal attacks and the correspondence surrounding them were gold dust for the meeting with the Weres the next day. My gut feeling had some backup now. He'd even found some more references to the FBI Project Anthracite, and some exchanges with police consultants that hadn't made it into the police reports.

In the end, too many things still sat uncomfortably in my mind, and I'd hardly exercised this week, other than some running in the park. I changed and crept downstairs into the gym.

An hour later, I finally lay down on the practice mats to catch my breath and chill the sweat. The uncomfortable, itchy feeling wouldn't leave me, but I closed my eyes for a minute.

I walk upstairs. I need no lights, but the darkness in the living room is absolute until she spits brilliant blue flames into the fireplace.

Tullah sits asleep on the sofa again; the room is cat's-cradle-full of twisting dragon.

"Kaothos," I say, folding myself down cross-legged on the floor.

"Amber Farrell," she says. "You spoke to Tullah's parents and they warned you?"

"That you will be evil and exceed Tullah's ability to channel energy. Yes." I see no point in disguising what I've been told.

"And your feelings about this?"

"I'd still prefer to make up my own mind on the first."

Kaothos ripples, reflections shimmering along her scaled flanks. She seems pleased. "I would like to propose a community," she says.

"Of two?"

"Of many. What is a House but a community? You have advantages for me that Adepts do not have. And I am sure I have advantages for Hana that other wolf spirits would not. Those would be advantages to both of you, too. And Tullah needs your help and guidance to realize her potential."

"What are these advantages?"

"That will come in the process of learning for both of us."

"Well, while it's all so vague, so's my answer."

Sizzling noises of dragon laughter.

"Cautious…maybe that suits our little community, surrounded by enemies. Do not speak of this, Amber. Amber."

"Amber? Amber?" Tullah shook me awake. "What are you doing sleeping on the floor?"

I was in the living room. There was a fire in the hearth.

Chapter 28

THURSDAY

I came off Deer Creek and after a couple of wrong turns down twisty roads, managed to find the way to the ranch.

I stopped outside the entrance. The sound of my door closing was as loud as a shot in the still morning. I leaned against the car and looked the place over. I was about to meet a pack of werewolves and my stomach was churning. How would they react to Athanate mixed with Were? Depending on how things turned out, was this my pack?

A rambling house was tucked away to the right, half-hidden by a waving screen of maple and cottonwood trees. Behind the house, dark green pine stretched up the hill and I could almost feel the cool air leaking out from the shadows, all the way down to the gates. A yard with farm buildings and equipment dominated the middle ground. A solitary man sat tinkering with an engine in front of one of the sheds. To the left, in an overgrown meadow, a huge, ancient wooden barn leaned drunkenly over some antique harrows that were disappearing beneath the grasses. In the fall sunlight, the whole place was as bright and shiny as the opening scene in a horror movie.

If the Weres were here, I was certain there would be someone watching me. The guy by the engine hadn't so much as lifted his head. That could be either good or bad. Only slightly more terrified than when I'd stopped, I got back in and drove up to the farm buildings.

The guy at the sheds was Leatherface, I decided, in keeping with the horror movie scenario, though I'd happily change it if he introduced himself. He didn't. His nostrils flared and he went very still. I tensed, but all he did was point with one oily finger over at the old barn.

I thanked him and walked into the meadow, my backpack slung over my shoulder. I could feel his eyes burning a hole in my back.

The grasses were tall and dry, rustling as I passed. I wasn't sure about wolves, but I could have hidden a platoon of snipers in the grass, and from the itchy feeling, others were definitely watching me now.

The barn door opened smoothly, mocking the dilapidated look of the place, and I stepped inside.

It was stiflingly hot and humid.

Bright sun sliced through gaps in the walls and roof, illuminating nothing and making most of it seem even darker. Across one bright bar, a freaking huge wolf padded, left to right, golden eyes staring at me. Then it was still. I looked towards the dark parts, willing my eyes to adjust quicker.

The place was full of wolves. I could smell them, long before I could see them. Wolves don't have a strong smell, but a hint multiplied enough times would get through to anyone, and my Athanate-enhanced nose was sharp. Mixed with wolf was the smell of hot hay bales.

When my eyes adjusted and I did see them, I wished I hadn't. I knew a werewolf could be four feet tall; I'd seen them on security camera footage. But it's one thing to know that, and another to be surrounded by a pack of them, the size of small ponies. They were panting. I hoped it was the heat.

I made out Alex in the gloom. Fall colors and pale ruff. Beautiful. Yes, and deadly. I'd never seen him in wolf form before, but my nose confirmed it was him as I knelt down. I knew next to nothing about Were, certainly nothing about the way they reacted when they were in wolf form. I reached out, very slowly, and gave him a very gentle hug.

A low rumble, not threatening, came from him, and I stood up, reassured. But I wasn't here to see him. I had no idea why everyone was in wolf form, but I guessed this might be some kind of test. I noticed there was more space around Alex than most of the others. And I got a feeling that he wasn't happy about it.

"Felix Larimer?" I said to the darkness.

"Here," a voice said from the back of the barn. "Watching you with your pet, Athanate."

"And there was me thinking wolves don't make pets," said my demon. "Or are you just the manager of this pet shop?"

A wave passed through the wolves like the wind through the grass—a subliminal growl. Not smart, demon. I had to keep up the face, so I walked to where the voice had come from, in the deepest dark.

"Are you stupid or suicidal?" he said.

"Neither. But I am so pissed off with the macho games that you and Altau play."

"Then why are you playing Altau's games for him?"

"I'm not here on his business. I'm not even here with his approval."

The pressure of the growl lessened fractionally.

"Interesting. You might even be telling the truth."

I didn't reply. I was staring at the place his voice came from and willing my eyes to resolve his face from the shapeless blur I could make out.

"I don't need them to tell me you're frightened," he added. There was a hiss of fabrics moving against each other as he shifted. He was sitting in a canvas chair. "I like that. It's appropriate."

Fair enough.

"Great. If we've gotten that part out of the way, should we talk about why I'm here?"

The growl was back, like fangs pressing on my neck. I held up my hands; I got the message. He was the one who introduced topics.

"What are you exactly, Amber Farrell?"

"I'm exactly tired of being asked that. What do you think?"

The ghostly shape changed as he got up and walked towards me, resolving into a man, taller than Alex, with peaked black hair and deep-set eyes, bright with that untamed wolf look. His mouth was hard and thin. He wore a cream linen jacket over a white shirt and dark jeans. He carried himself with a tenseness, like a boxer in the ring. His forehead was gleaming with sweat.

"What do I think?" he repeated. "Athanate, partly. Aspirant?" He sniffed and frowned. Instead of pacing to and fro, he abruptly stepped forward right in front of me. I steadied my reaction down to a twitch, and fought to stop my weight from coming forward onto the balls of my feet, consciously loosening my fists and trying to breathe evenly. He was staring down at me. Wolf dominance games, or something else? I raised my head to look him in the eye, then thought better of it.

But I sensed from him that raising my chin was good. Just as it had been with Skylur. Expose the neck. Did these bastards have any idea how similar they were?

I could feel a change around me as I tilted my head back. A softening of the press of hostility.

My heart stuttered again as I caught movement above me. There were more of them in the rafters. Nothing I could do about it now. I closed my eyes and willed my heart rate down.

Larimer bent over my neck and snuffled. I held my tongue. Literally, between my teeth. I didn't need the demon running off with it and making comments about sniffing my butt. Heart rate edged down. Breathe in. Breathe out. Flow like the river. He wasn't going to bite.

"Well," growled Larimer, and I took that as permission to bring my head back to the normal position. He'd retreated into the half shadows and resumed pacing.

"Well," he said again. "I could believe an Athanate plan to seek some advantage from stealing Were by infusing them somehow." He turned and turned, staring at me from the dark. "But infusing an Athanate with Were? Not something Altau would do intentionally."

The pressure dropped a fraction again.

"This was nothing to do with Altau," I said quietly.

He grunted. "And how has it gone down with that stiff-necked bloodsucker?"

"If you mean Skylur, not well. They're concerned." I didn't want to go into the details, but Larimer pounced on my vagueness.

"Why?"

"The mix is unpredictable." I stopped, but he wasn't going to take that.

Trust and Jump, Farrell.

"They're afraid that the addition of Were might lead to instability," I said. "Either Basilikos or rogue."

He growled, but not directly at me.

"So, not quite Altau. How does that work?"

"I'm a separate House, allied to Altau."

"I see. Oh, very clever. Close but not too close. Certainly close enough to fix in an emergency."

I was puzzled and he read it.

"Not taking you into Altau until he can be sure of controlling things. Not letting you disappear elsewhere, and let others make trouble with you. Expecting me to keep the Were sane, while he controls the Athanate side."

"But," I protested, open-mouthed, "he hasn't said anything like that. He hasn't asked me to come and see you. He hasn't—"

"Did he forbid you to meet with us?"

"No, but—"

"Could an intelligent person have assumed that even if you didn't come to us, we would come to you?"

I shut up. It was like standing on sand, feeling the sea eat it away beneath me. But *Diana* had suggested I become House Farrell. *Before* Alex infused me.

"He hasn't told me anything like this," I said.

"Altau never does," snarled Larimer. "What he says and what he wants are two different things. He's only happy when you think you're doing what you want, but you're actually doing what he wants. He leaves you guessing. And if you guess wrong, the consequences can be fatal."

He stepped back in front of me again and glared down. "Here," he rumbled, "we say what we mean."

Crap. He was wrong about Altau. Surely, he was seeing layers that weren't there. And equally, Altau were wrong to leave him festering like this. He wasn't someone to be treated like that. I wasn't going to play the two of them off against each other, but in the short term, I needed to keep my neck whole, and that meant going along with it, with both of them.

I ducked my head. Good girl. "I understand."

He wheeled back into the shadows, doing a circuit. Sensing the reaction of the pack for all I knew. I hoped I felt an easing towards me and hopefully, that meant towards Alex as well.

"You realize," he said, "that Alexander's marque is now at odds with the pack?"

"I wasn't sure," I replied. "It seemed possible, but I had nothing to check against."

"Check it now."

I went back to Alex. Now, concentrating on it, with the pack to compare it with, the difference was obvious. There was a hint of the exotic, sharp fragrance that made David and Pia different from Altau.

"Different," I said humbly, returning to my place. I couldn't see where Larimer was.

His voice came from the side. "Neither of you have the pack marque. Neither of you is pack. And how do you expect me to deal with this?"

I cleared my throat. "Like Altau. A separate affiliate?"

"In my territory?" Larimer was suddenly in my face, making my heart jump. But long hours of being intimidated by hardcore instructors in the army let me deal with it inside. I'd even fallen into a parade rest.

"Yes," I said, focusing my eyes about the level of his collarbone.

His hand lifted my head till I was looking directly into his eyes.

"We're not like Athanate. We don't have charters. We don't do paperwork. We don't do oaths." He measured my reaction before going on. "A temporary arrangement, while we investigate you," he said. "You show up, where I say, when I say, at least weekly. You do exactly what I tell you."

"I can't give that last promise." My voice sounded weak, but there was no point agreeing, only to be told to do something like betray the Altau. "I'll try and do what you say, just as I'll try and do what Skylur says."

He was looking at my throat, and his nostrils flared.

"You should be very glad you didn't lie to me," he murmured. Then he twisted and stalked away. "I expect you to comply with the rest."

There was a long pause. Larimer's boots clicked on the wooden boards. There was a scrabble of claws and whispers of hay as wolves eased their positions around me.

"If not for Altau's business, why are you here?" he said, eventually.

"Because we have a problem."

"'We'? Oh, I like that, I think. At least more than 'you'." He waited, then went on. "Tell me about 'our' problem."

"There's a rogue werewolf killing humans in Denver."

The tension soared in the barn again. Larimer swayed back into one of the slanting beams of light. His eyes disappeared into shadow pools.

"We have learned discretion. We do not kill humans. Usually."

In between all the threats and posturing, I knew he wasn't stupid. I hadn't expected the alpha of the Denver pack to be. There was an element of playing to the crowd going on here, and that helped me relax a fraction.

"Show me." He waved at my backpack, making the correct assumption that I hadn't just shown up empty-handed to start spouting allegations.

I unfastened the flap and retrieved my first exhibit, some plaster casts of werewolf paw prints.

"I took these up at Bitter Hooks. They're your pack, I believe." I knelt and placed them in a row on the ground, in size order, with a ruler next to them.

"Olivia, some light," Larimer said.

There was a creaking and banging in the rafters as a woman, in human form, threw open a skylight shutter, suddenly flooding the center of the barn with light. I blinked. Mercifully cool air stirred.

Larimer came and stood just behind me, looking over my shoulder. I took a deep breath and tried to ignore him, but I had to admit, he had a presence; I could sense him there.

Next, I laid some photographs and sketches down alongside the casts.

"These are from police reports. Some of them, the older ones, are from non-fatal attacks reported as large dogs."

"And the others? The more recent ones?"

"Murder investigations, where the coroner concluded that unidentified animals had disturbed the body post mortem."

There was a silence in the barn; even the panting had stopped. Far away, birds called in the trees. Outside, the wind rustled the grasses and Leatherface dropped a tool onto metal with a curse.

"Ricky," called Larimer.

At the edge of my vision, there was movement, a distortion like looking at a heat mirage. Out of it stepped Ricky, a blond Viking type, unshaven, six feet six at least and completely naked. He didn't seem concerned. He stood behind my other shoulder. Very close.

"Big," he said. His voice was quiet. I had to bite my tongue again. Yes, you could say that.

"Yeah," I said, when I had my humor under control. "Way too big for a dog. As big as the biggest of the casts I took." I cleared my throat. "One or two, I could overlook. I'd take that as coincidence, errors in measurement, whatever. Half a dozen, no way. A dozen makes it a serious problem."

"You haven't got a dozen reports there," said Ricky.

I stood up. I'm not body-conscious, but it was difficult to concentrate with the Nordic god looming over my shoulder like that.

"Those were what the police gave me. There were some where no casts were taken. Anyway, I did some checking, and I found something that isn't in the main police files, yet."

I pulled out the printout and tossed it alongside the rest.

"Those are from consultants brought in by the police and experts the consultants talked to. Some of them are in Spanish, and I'm a little hazy on the science." I paused, wiped some of the sweat from my face. "The first was a zoologist brought in by the coroner to check some bite marks on some femurs and cervical vertebrae in a couple of the recent cases. The zoologist pointed out that the femurs had actually been snapped by bites, not by blows. So they brought in a consultant and asked him what kind of dog can do that."

Maybe I should have been a lecturer; I had the most attentive audience ever. They knew all about bite force, of course, but I needed to build the logic.

"Turns out an average dog can't. Their bite force is around 750 psi. A specialist dog might be higher. An average wolf would be about 1500. The consultant said it had to have been an escaped hyena, because it was over double that."

Fresh air whispered past my face, chilling the sweat.

"The police dropped it at that point. It was costing money and they thought it was going nowhere. They thought the data had problems. But the consultant had gotten curious, and he sent the findings to an expert he'd met at a conference. A professor in Spain, whose area is hyenas."

I stepped around the big square patch of sun and tried to pierce the darkness at the corners of the barn.

"The professor said the data must be wrong too. Either it isn't a hyena and the force calculations are wrong, he said, or it is a hyena and the teeth patterns are wrong. End of story, except he got drunk that night and wrote another email as a joke. In that one, he speculated that it had to be a wolf from the pattern, and attempted to figure out how big the wolf would have to be to generate that force."

Larimer watched me, his face unreadable. Ricky stood listening with a deep frown twisting his pale face, looking down at the casts.

"Answer is about double the mass of a normal wolf. Now mass doesn't increase directly in proportion to height, so he did the math. Came out with a wolf that stood four feet at the shoulder."

I looked around. At least half of them would have qualified.

Larimer stirred. "When?" He waved at the casts and reports.

"Oldest attack, a year ago. Newest, last month," I replied.

"Why have you brought this to us?"

"You're the resident pack. Are you telling me there are other werewolves in Denver?" I asked.

Larimer really didn't like that. Neither did Ricky. Of course, Alex had told me there was a problem, but now I knew it officially. The Denver pack were under some kind of attack.

"So, there's another pack in Denver? Unwelcome?"

Larimer nodded curtly.

"How long?"

There was a snarl from the shadows, but Ricky snarled back and a whine of apology was offered. It got quieter, but there was still the subliminal growl shivering through me, and the sound of wolves creeping closer in the dark, crowding me.

"Three months or so," said Larimer. "They won't be here for much longer."

"So nothing to do with these." I touched the older reports with a toe, trying to ignore the pressure of eyes on me. "Is this the same sort of thing they're doing?"

Larimer grunted noncommittally.

"There's something else," he said, and waited. "You haven't finished, have you?"

"Yes. I don't know what it means, but these files are being copied to the FBI. Whatever is going on needs to stop and it needs to stop soon. None of us want the FBI poking around in Denver."

There was a shocked silence that Larimer pretended to shrug off.

"Ahhh. So that's it. The Athanate don't want the FBI here."

"You can make up whatever damned reason you like, Larimer," I snapped. "I haven't had time to talk to Altau about this. I brought it to you because it's your concern."

He backed off a yard or two, becoming a pale floating shape in the darkness again. I could feel him watching me still.

A half-dozen other Were changed with the eye-hurting distortion, and came forward to look at the reports. A couple of women as well as men. I gave them space. None of them looked at me as if I was doing them a favor, but at least none were actively hostile.

Ricky and one of his friends were frowning at my casts, but Larimer was still intent on me. He strolled back into the light. The look on his face was more wary and evaluating now, rather than outright intimidating.

"Is there more I can do to help with this?" I asked him.

"We don't need help from Athanate," snarled Ricky's friend, looking up from the casts. I just smiled at him and he was smart enough to understand how stupid he'd just been. He didn't like that. He flushed with anger and growled, a sound too tight and light with his human throat, but full of threat.

An answering growl came from behind me, deeper, vibrating through my chest. Alex.

Everyone froze.

Ricky's hand clamped on his friend's arm and his human face made a good impression of a wolf's bared fangs, but too late. The group around him seemed to swirl, coalescing into the pack against the outsider. I twisted the backpack in my hand. I could have the HK out in a tenth of a second. And after the magazine emptied I could use it as a club while they tore me to pieces.

Ricky hurled a couple aside, but it was Larimer who ended it, lashing out at the forming group, breaking the dynamic and snarling at the aggressors. He was sweating freshly for all that he tried to look unconcerned at the challenges.

The pack fell quiet. Alex didn't. Larimer's eyes weighed me, weighed Alex. He saw the way I held the backpack, and I didn't doubt his nose had told him what was in there. He looked past me at Alex.

"My apologies, Alexander," he said formally. "I have mistrusted you on the evidence of something I did not understand. But this is not a matter for challenges." He glared around him.

The noise from Alex lowered without quite ceasing to be a growl. Larimer cautiously came closer to me.

"And my apologies to you too, Ms. Farrell. You appear to be sincere, and if you've caused problems for us, they are less than what you've brought to our attention." His mouth twisted as his eyes flicked to the backpack. "Your willingness to come here freely, and your willingness to die alongside Alexander speaks well of you. Perhaps some good will come of this."

Alex went quiet behind me and the pressure in the barn collapsed like an old tire.

"Honestly," I said to Larimer. "I thought relations were better than this." I cleared my throat. "New Athanate and Were, you know…"

"Oh, that was fine. It worked well."

"Worked? As in used to work? It's stopped?"

Larimer raised a brow at me, surprised I didn't know. "It has."

"Why?"

"Ask the Altau, Farrell," Ricky said. "They haven't told us anything." He'd dragged his friend forward to stand between him and Larimer. The boy stuttered an apology and fled when I shrugged it off. I guess it's difficult for a guy to stand stark naked in front of a clothed woman and apologize for being an ass, Were or not.

"It's not for me to say, Larimer, but I'm sure you and Altau can sort this out next week."

He snorted. "Yes, next week, not this week, not with Denver stinking of Athanate."

I ignored that. "My offer stands, if there's anything I can do. And my gut feeling says that Altau will be on your side if there's a problem."

"That would be a first." Larimer snorted.

"There's something else that Alex wanted me here for." I didn't want to introduce the topic since the alpha seemed so twitchy about protocol, but Alex could hardly do it. "Maybe…" I was going to suggest Alex joined us on two legs, but one glance from the alpha shut me up.

"It's better for the pack if he stays wolf for the moment," he said without explanation. "Anyway, I know what it's about." He returned to his canvas seat and sat back down with a sigh.

"Alexander is entirely too taken in by the local stories. He thinks your great-grandmother was an Adept involved in the transition of new Were, and we should investigate."

I shifted my weight. I didn't really believe it either, but he was dismissing it out of hand. I wanted to be convinced one way or another on evidence. Alex wouldn't have arranged this if he couldn't make a good argument for it.

"And you're having some…issues there." I skirted the problem word, but I wanted to see his reaction. Larimer himself gave nothing away. But he'd used the reaction from the pack to threaten me, and now it worked against him. I could feel their reaction in the dark corners of the barn. There was a problem. And as I came to that conclusion, the same question I'd asked about Athanate came to the surface. Where were all the werewolves? This couldn't be the whole pack, surely? My sense of smell had been getting sharper over the last couple of years as I became more Athanate, and I'd never smelled a hint of Were in Denver until I'd met Alex.

Larimer was watching me shrewdly, trying to guess the thoughts going through my head.

"The thing is," he said, "even if, as the stories say, you were firstborn *and* received the token, *and* it actually worked, you've obviously lost the knowledge that goes with it."

Ask questions and say nothing.

I jumped. Tara spoke to me at the oddest times, but I always listened. Something had just happened here.

"What token?" I said to cover my surprise.

"A fetish." He waved his hand in exasperation. "Some mumbo-jumbo ritual thing that gets passed down. Who knows, a cup? A carving? Adepts are always into that sort of crap. And they'd love to claim it was their role, to help the Were. That the Were need Adepts."

"Who would know the rituals? Adepts? You said the knowledge is lost. Do you mean completely?"

He shrugged. "*If* it exists, the Adepts might know."

"You don't get along well with them either?"

"I prefer thinking of it," he bared his teeth in what he might have described as a smile, "as no one gets along well with us."

Okay.

"So my great-grandmother may have been an Adept."

Larimer sat forward. "She almost certainly was." He pointed at my belly. "I can sense there are echoes in there, Ms. Farrell. That doesn't mean she had any role with the Were. And you want to be very careful with Adepts. They don't like people who aren't Adepts experimenting with powers."

A creak above made me glance up. Olivia was lying on a cross beam like a leopard, staring hungrily at me. She hadn't been in wolf form when I'd come in and still wasn't. Maybe she was one of the problems. I hoped that was the cause of the hungry look, not that there was a tasty Athanate trapped in a barn in the middle of nowhere.

Get out. Now.

"Well, I've said my piece." I indicated the casts and photos. "The one police officer who knows that I'm looking at this will hold off a while, but at some stage he's going to want to talk to me. We need to talk again before then. What the FBI are doing, and what they might make of this, I don't claim to know."

Larimer nodded.

I twisted around. "Alex?"

"You will leave him alone for a while," Larimer said. "It's what he needs."

"Forgive me, alpha, but I'll let him tell me that."

Larimer growled. "Don't call me alpha and then refuse my command."

Alex lay down where he was. He wasn't coming with me, but something told me he wasn't going to stay away either.

I went.

Leatherface didn't look up as I passed. If he had, I might have told him he had the cam on his distributor upside down.

Chapter 29

There were no connections for the octopus to make until I was back in the city limits. That was fine—it gave me time to recover from meeting the pack.

I got Tullah to reserve an interview room for the rest of the day at the Keynes building, and to generate me some fake business cards to be delivered there. Then I primed Arvinder's Diakon that I would arrange a pickup for Arvinder and confirmed he would be alone. Finally I called Victor.

"Vic, you good?"

"I'm great. What crazy bitch scheme you trying to sell me this time?"

"I'm hurt, big man."

"Don't bother." He chuckled. "I can hear it in your voice. What you want, girl?"

"That security system we used last year, will it still work? Say, in the Keynes building?"

He went quiet. "No guarantee. Never was. Look, I'm not gonna tell you not to, but you sure?"

"I appreciate it, Vic, but I've got no time, I gotta do it this way."

"Okay. You there?"

"I got a meeting room there. And I need a guy collected and delivered to me, clean of trackers and followers. It'll be a last minute confirmation. And one of your micro cameras."

We haggled on the costs, but his prices were good for the quality I needed, and most of it I was going to pass right on to Skylur. It wasn't my idea to meet Arvinder. The rest of it, I'd take on rather than pass it on to Niall. Not good business sense, but something I had to do.

I deleted another message on my cell about turning up at Haven, this one from Jason.

And that done, it left me with no way to avoid thinking of what had happened at the wolf meeting.

The shocks and threats, well, I kind of got them; I understood in my gut how the pack worked, how it responded to outsiders and handled insiders. I could have done without the threats, but I knew it was necessary for the wolf side to do these things. Maybe it was exaggerated, but it was only society with big teeth. I shook my head at that thought–when had I become such a werewolf expert?

At least Alex and I had half an understanding with them. I got that it was a problem that needed to be resolved, not parked, and there was a time limit on it.

Strangely, that wasn't concerning me half so much as the trigger that upset Tara.

There was something about a gift passed down to the eldest, an elusive tickle of a memory. Eldest. My hands gripped the steering wheel as a thought emerged. I hadn't been firstborn. Tara had been.

I remembered; there was something in my mother's souvenir box that hadn't been given to me. My father saying it wasn't his to give, because he hadn't been eldest either. Something that was waiting to be passed on to the firstborn of the next generation. A chill went through me as I visualized Alex's chart of the Farrells.

It couldn't be.

I dug his file out of my backpack. One hand on the wheel, I flicked it open. Papers spilled from it onto the floor.

Damn. I pulled over and gathered the sheets up, picking out the chart.

I was right. It wasn't just that children had died. *All* the eldest had been stillborn or died as infants, even among the cousins. And the gift in the box passed unclaimed.

I shuddered and put the thoughts aside. It was ridiculous. I was not going to start believing in multi-generational curses or magically deadly gifts. It was only three generations. It was a coincidence. I'd just ask Mom what was in the box when she got back from vacation. Just for interest.

And how did Mom know all those Arapaho children's stories? Speaks-to-Wolves was Dad's grandmother, not Mom's. Like many things that I'd learned as a child, I'd never questioned it. And when the time came to think about it, it grew deeply uncomfortable.

By the time I'd reached the Keynes building, I'd passed by Manassah and I was dressed in the upscale suit that Jen had bought me. It pissed me off that what she'd bought me was so damn useful. And necessary. I'd try and be angry at her again this evening, maybe.

I got in the elevator and looked at myself in the full-length mirror. Turned, checked my butt. Straightened the skirt a touch.

Gods, Amber, you cleaned up okay. Should've put some makeup on as well. Nice suit. I'll forgive you, Jen.

Victor was already there, setting up the system, letting it sink its electronic fangs into the building. He waved at me briefly, did a double take and then grinned at my outfit. I glared, daring him to make a comment. He wisely went back to frowning at the screen.

I made the coffee and rustled up some doughnuts. While I waited, I found Tullah's fake business cards had arrived and I had a neat pocket in my new jacket for them.

"Nearly there," he muttered through a mouthful of doughnut, and clicked his way through a couple more screens of settings. He shook his head.

"Too easy, this security system," he said. "Remember last time?"

"Yeah, we had a fight to get in."

"Done." He brushed his hands together. "This is just sitting here in passive mode, demonstratin' its capabilities, understand. You gonna be on your own with that thing, girl, so whatever you do, don't hit that button there or it goes active. You understand?"

I nodded. That button. Yup.

"Now, your 'colleague' you want delivered. He okay to ride on a motorcycle?"

"Yeah, he's fit and healthy." A motorcycle would be a good way to do it. Arvinder could decline if he didn't like the idea, and I could stand back and say I'd done everything I could within reason. And I'd still hit Skylur up for the check.

"Good. I'll have a couple of outriders as sweepers behind. It likely to get hot?"

He meant firearms. I shook my head. "Still put them in Kevlar though."

He brought out a sketchpad and a street map and we spent fifteen minutes making sure we had a good plan for the pickup and the right route to get Arvinder here without anyone else knowing. Halfway along, they'd shake him down for trackers. I wondered if Arvinder was going to feel that a chat with me was worth it after all that.

Victor handed over the rest of the equipment and left, sparing a worried glance at the system.

I came up against the first minor problem with my plan. The octopus couldn't find any unsecured internet connections in the building.

I locked the meeting room, made the managers aware that I was just stepping out for a short time, and walked out with my laptop under my arm and the antenna sticking out of my pocket.

A block away and the octopus made a couple of connections. I clipped on my headset and made the first call, a test call to Niall. I told him to disconnect his phone after we finished and not reconnect until late afternoon.

He chuckled. "This sounds fun," he said. "But I suspect I really don't want to know. And before I forget, Cassie said she'll be coming home in a couple of weeks. Will you be around?"

"I'll do my best." I always did, but I wasn't entirely sure that was going to be enough this time around. I could just as easily be locked away. "Tell her I have problems with my cell, but a text message usually gets through, eventually."

I reminded him again about disconnecting and we ended the call. Tests over.

I called Underwood.

"Mr. Underwood? Thank you for taking my call. I'm calling on behalf of the insurers of your sister and brother-in-law, Mr. and Mrs. Quinn."

"Oh, yes." Underwood sounded surprised. "How can I help?"

"You're aware they had a burglary recently?" I rushed on. "Because of the rarity of some of the items, I'm required by our new procedures to confirm a few things. I'm only a block away, can I stop in and take just five minutes of your time, please? Or would it be possible for you to take time to meet my boss later?"

"I don't see quite how…"

Being involved was the last thing he wanted, but I'd got the drop on him and he couldn't come up with an excuse quickly enough.

"It's simply that you are about the only other person likely to have seen some of the items recently. Only five minutes." Five minutes would be easy, and then he could put it out of his mind.

"Oh, all right."

"Thank you so much. I'll be there soon."

I ended the call and headed back to the Keynes building.

Underwood's small office suite was pleasant, even luxurious. His secretary guarded the door and her domain included a table where she was preparing a promotional campaign for an event at one of his galleries. There was no one else in the suite. I'd learned that from listening to Jen last night. Underwood didn't need this office. He would be better and more inexpensively accommodated in one of his galleries, but he liked the impression a separate business office made.

While he made me wait, I found out his secretary, Mrs. Ellis, commuted to work by car. Good. I was going to use that later.

When he came out to meet me, the man himself was skinny and bug-eyed, with lank, gray hair brushed straight back. He frowned a lot and fidgeted, touching lapels, cleaning his glasses, joggling his tie in a constant cycle.

His office was lined with mahogany display cabinets. I showed interest and got the two-minute tour of his private collection. By the end of the tour, he and I were being filmed by a tiny bug I'd planted, hidden against the side of one of the cabinets. It was to cover one of the weak points in my plan. I needed confirmation that the medal was here and, just as important, where it was. I couldn't come in and tear cabinets up or blow safes apart.

Underwood settled down behind the gleaming shield of his bare desk and offered me a drink. I turned it down.

"Well, Ms.…." he glanced surreptitiously down at my fake card, "Johnson, how can I help?"

I handed over a picture of the medal. "This is the item we're particularly concerned with, Mr. Underwood. Can you confirm you recognize it and are you aware of what it is?"

He placed the photo carefully on his desk and bent his head over it.

"Oh, indeed, I am. This is their Congressional Medal of Honor, earned by Captain Quinn in the First World War. This was stolen?" He looked up at me over the rims of his glasses. Mistake. He was trying to overdo the innocence.

"You didn't know?" I asked.

"No. I knew they'd been burgled, but that was all."

Liar.

"That's strange, isn't it?" I did wrinkly-forehead puzzlement on steroids. "Surely, this is the most valuable piece. I'd have thought they'd have said."

"Can't be sold, Ms. Johnson, by law. And it's inscribed, so value is notional."

"Yes, of course. I meant most valuable to them."

He'd started sweating. "I don't think Ruth told me. Maybe she told my wife and she must have forgotten to pass it on."

Liar, again.

"It doesn't matter." I brushed it off. "But obviously, you can confirm they had it and you've seen it recently."

"Oh, yes, fairly recently." He smiled. He knew he was past the difficult part and that I would be out of his life soon. Just a couple more minutes. "They know I have an interest in these things."

"And you can confirm you saw it only at their apartment?"

"Yes."

"Never anywhere else? It hasn't been, oh, here in this office for example?"

"No."

I could almost hear the jolt of panic in him; I could smell his lies. My instinct was right. He had it, and he had it here.

"And there's no possibility that it's a fake, a copy for instance? We've had some recently."

"No. I assure you, I would know."

"The fakes we found fooled half the experts," I said as an aside and stood. "Thank you so much for your time. You've been very helpful." I leaned over and offered my hand to shake. Immediately wished I hadn't. His palm was sweaty.

Back in my meeting room, a couple of floors down, I stood at the window, urging my anger to subside. Underwood wasn't a hardened criminal, and there was nothing profitable in what he'd done. I suspected whoever he'd gotten to do his theft had taken the jewels as payment. No one got hurt and, of course, the insurance would pay for everything, he thought. A victimless crime. He was just a little boy, never grown up, who couldn't stand that he didn't have what he wanted in his collections. He had no concept of the distress he'd caused the Quinns, let alone my outrage. Well, he'd messed with the wrong people.

Victor's system was recording the output from the bug. I scanned back through it. As soon as he'd been sure I was out the door, Underwood had unlocked the bottom drawer in his desk and taken out a simple box. He took a medal from the box and examined it with a jeweler's loupe, almost stroking it. There was no way I could tell if it was the Quinns', but every instinct told me I'd hit the jackpot.

Having put part one of the plan into action, I 'accidentally' hit that button on Victor's system. The security manager here was no longer in control of his system, even though it'd look to him as if he was. I could override him at any point. And if Underwood left the building, I'd know.

I rubbed my face. Time to get on with the other plan. I walked back down the block and called Chopra on the octopus. He took my detailed instructions without a protest. Arvinder had to text a cell phone, then walk down 15th towards Union Station and make a call to one of Victor's phones. He'd be picked up as he walked, code word Siddhartha.

"He will be there, Ms. Farrell, in about..." He checked. "...thirty minutes."

"Just so he's aware, he'll be checked for bugs and tails."

"Indeed. Most prudent under the circumstances. Thank you again, Ms. Farrell."

He ended the call. I smiled crookedly; he was so polite it was tiring.

I called Victor and gave him the green light.

There would be a little while before things would start to happen back at the Keynes building. I bought a fruit salad for lunch and strolled down towards the center. Once I'd put a couple more blocks between me and the office, I turned my old cell back on to see what might be waiting for me. Every time I did this now, I imagined Ingram's eyes flicking to a screen and watching a little icon labeled Farrell pop up on a map.

A missed call from Mom came up.

I turned the cell back off and called her on the octopus.

"Hi Mom! It's me. How's Florida?"

"Fine." She seemed to struggle for a second, which said 'not fine' to me. "How are you, Amber?"

"I'm okay. Mom, what's up? You sound worried."

"Amber," she said, then paused. "I trust you. I trust your judgment. I depended on you for so long. We both did, Kathleen and I, and you never got the recognition you deserve for that."

"Jeez, Mom, you make it sound so serious."

I regretted the flippancy as soon as I said it. The little sob that she nearly stifled cut me deeply. "Mom, what is it?"

"I hate it when you two don't get along. I've told you that before." She paused, then went on in a rush. "You would tell me if something was really wrong, Amber? You would, wouldn't you? Anything?"

I groaned. "Oh no! What did Kath say this time?"

"I don't want to go into it now. I don't want to ruin John's vacation. You know we haven't ever really been away. Promise me, swear to me, Amber, nothing's wrong."

"Mom, things happen, I deal with them. There's nothing that you should be worried about." The Keynes building loomed up above me, and the octopus was flashing warnings that it was down to its last connection. I cast around desperately for something I could say to reassure her. "Nothing, on my Blood, I so swear," was what came out. Not entirely the best thing.

There was a tearful chuckle on the line. "What a phrase, but thank you, Amber," she said. "We'll be back on Sunday. Please come and see us. We've got to settle this with Kathleen."

"We do, Mom. I can't keep letting her walk all over me like this. Saying things to you, to our friends. Hurting you like this."

"Oh God, I don't want to get into this now. But please, Amber, she has some issues, let's listen to them before going to war."

Well, I had issues too. And Kath's issues were likely around things I couldn't talk about or couldn't prove, but Mom deserved peace on her vacation.

"Okay, Mom. I'll hold fire." I looked up. Arvinder had just arrived at the entrance to the Keynes building on the back of a motorcycle.

"Mom, look, I've got a meeting, I gotta go soon, but one quick thing. You remember in your old souvenir box, you had some kind of heirloom?"

"Oh, of course dear, that old Arapaho necklace of your great-grandma's."

Yes! As soon as she said it, an old memory of a beaded blue band came back.

"Do you still have it?"

There was a little pause, and my heart fell. It got worse.

"No. I gave it to Kathleen for a fancy dress party, oh, two or three years ago. I think she still must have it. Is it important?"

Damn!

"It is, Mom, it's…ah…a sort of Arapaho Wolf Clan history group that I'm part of. It'll keep."

"Oh, that's interesting. You kept that quiet, dear. Maybe I can meet them."

The octopus was blinking and Arvinder was waiting.

Ask. Tara nudged me.

"Yeah, sure. Um. You'll think I'm crazy, but when they were asking me, I realized for the first time, of course, she was Dad's grandma. But you always told us about the bedtime stories she'd tell you."

"But yes. Oh, gosh, I must have told you this, Amber. It was always a joke that it was an arranged marriage because Blane and I knew each other from the age of five. We were always staying over. We always joked that Speaks-to-Wolves had chosen me for Blane."

Gods! She very possibly did. What was the reason?

"We'll talk when you come back, Mom. I'm sure the history group will want to hear all those stories as well."

"But it's all just children's tales."

"He's got all this stuff in files and files, I'm sure the stories will be valuable."

"Oh, *he*? Well, yes, of course, dear, I'd be happy to talk to him."

I squeezed my eyes tight. *Sorry, Alex.* Adept Truth Sensors? Nothing on Mom.

"I hardly know what to think," she said. "But if," she hesitated, then plunged onwards, "if you need to make personal choices that aren't what you think I would approve of, Amber, remember, they're your choices to make."

Thanks, Kath. Mom knew about Jen. Yes, this was going to be an interesting family evening when she got back. But I couldn't get into it now.

"I love you, Mom."

"I love you too. I love you *both*, Amber. Bye."

I ended the call just as the octopus gave up.

Could it get worse?

My damned sister. Not content with calling me a whore and a drug addict to my face, she told the Quinns. Then Mom. Who the hell did Kath think she was?

Then it turns out she has the necklace. Oh, freaking perfect!

But I'd promised to leave it for the moment, and I had to concentrate now.

Arvinder was standing in the reception area, smart in a gray Nehru suit, looking a little ruffled, but calm.

If the casting director of a Bollywood spectacular had been here, he'd have jumped at Arvinder. He was handsome, not with the generic pleasantness of the Bollywood heroes, but with the dark, cruel look of a raptor. He'd be just the right casting for the pirate captain, or the chief of the hill bandits. Then his hawk eyes turned to me as I approached and he beamed with pleasure.

Much nicer.

He'd been charming at the charity ball. I'd had to trust him there, and he had to trust me here.

I reminded myself that he was Basilikos. He was still in the enemy camp. Maybe he was looking to come over, but at the moment, I needed to be wary.

Chapter 30

Arvinder settled himself into a chair at the meeting table. It could have been any everyday meeting between a couple of businesspeople, instead of one between an Athanate group leader and a…whatever.

I had coffee ready, and there were some cookies. Arvinder took one for show. He didn't really seem like a cookie person.

"Were the security procedures okay?" I asked.

"A most creditable arrangement. Your colleagues are extremely efficient." He tossed his head, flicking the wave of black hair off his forehead. "I would like to offer you just one item of advice, however."

"I'm always learning, Arvinder."

He smiled briefly. "Your colleagues are not kin."

"They're secure. They know nothing about the Athanate, and I'm positive they will not discuss this operation today with any third parties."

He held his hand up. "I am sure you have the greatest confidence in them, and I have confidence in you. That is not my point." He shifted slightly. "Kin have status amongst Athanate. Harm done to kin is taken as harm done to Athanate. No Athanate would harm your kin short of an all-out declaration of feud." He frowned, considering. "Or war. My point is this; do not lightly use unaligned humans to deal with Athanate. By our laws, we can do what we like to them without legal offense, unless we harm or expose the Athanate."

"Then that's a situation I will work to change," I said. I clamped down on my temper. "Thanks for the advice." I must have sounded like an idiot to him. I'd barely become Athanate and here I was, going to force them to change the systems they'd had in place for centuries.

Arvinder regarded me steadily over the rim of his cup. "I am most certain you will try," he said and took a sip. "If you get the chance. I wish you luck."

He sat back in his chair and crossed his legs. "I regret I can't stay long, for both our sakes. Not only will the Warders be upset with me, but if my absence is noted, my associates will speculate and it is a very few steps before such speculations are in the hearing of Matlal."

I nodded at the security system. "I can't help with the speculations, but for more immediate danger, I'm watching. I should get plenty of warning if someone figures out we're in here." I gestured. "But it's your meeting, Arvinder, you drive it."

"Thank you." His brow creased slightly. "Before I come to my main request, I have one small diversion first. What has been done to disguise your marque? It's almost…lupine."

I shrugged. "Wolf? Yes, I have dealings with the local pack."

"Ahh. Then I have a small gift of information for you. Matlal is sponsoring a rival wolf pack in Denver." He stopped me as I leaned forward. "I know nothing else."

I sat back. "Well, my thanks. The meeting is worth it for that."

He smiled, and I smiled back.

Basilikos, I reminded myself. Maybe not in Matlal's corner, but still, Basilikos.

"Enough delay," he said, and clasped his hands in front of him. "Amber, I most seriously wish you to consider an alliance with House Singh in preference to House Altau."

I nearly choked on my coffee; that approach I really hadn't expected. He was silent, waiting.

"I'm flattered you should make all this effort." I cleared my throat. "And I appreciate what you've told me today, but I can imagine that some of the things I will say, you will find offensive. It's not personal."

He nodded. "Please, go on."

"I don't know if Altau are typical of Athanate Houses," I said, eyes on my hands. "I think they're not, but they're here and they've helped me and Skylur's the leader of the Panethus. Not to mention president of the Assembly. I agree with the Panethus creed. What I know of Basilikos…" I looked up and met his eyes, "revolts me. Why wouldn't I ally myself with Skylur?"

Arvinder snorted. "It takes time to understand Athanate politics. That is time you haven't had. You are aware there are fundamental differences between House Singh and House Matlal, though?" I nodded and he continued. "And, in time, you would have wondered how such diverse creeds became joined in Basilikos. Well, allow me to answer that, quite simply. Basilikos means every creed that has a principle that isn't in complete conformity with Panethus. Basilikos wouldn't exist as a group if Panethus hadn't made it. The independents are those that don't have a defining creed."

"And by creed you mean how you relate to kin?"

He waved a finger at me. "Kin is a Panethus term, and a creed is more than that. But to keep it simple, yes."

"Then what do you call your human…" I struggled for a word, "partners?"

"Devotees. And Amber, our Theokos creed is the oldest Athanate creed. Something Panethus find convenient to forget."

"Being old doesn't mean it's right," I said. He wasn't making any headway with me. Devotees sounded like a cult.

"Ignore the wisdom of long experience at your peril." He dismissed my comment. "I am not asking you to become part of anything fundamentally wrong and ultimately self-destructive like Matlal's group. The Theokos group are only part of Basilikos because Skylur made us that."

"Well, not that I know squat about it, but don't you vote together with Matlal at the Assembly?"

Arvinder had the grace to look uncomfortable. "Skylur delights in maneuvering us to do this." When I looked puzzled, he explained. "Panethus is an equally broad organization, and Skylur's best strategy to keep them together in the Assembly is to have an easily identified enemy—everybody else."

"If you're not on my side, you're against me?"

Arvinder nodded and finished his coffee. I took the last cookie. All that fruit for lunch, I had to balance it somehow.

"So, you're not as evil as you could be," I said, with a smile to take some of the sting out. "Why does this mean I have to leave my home and go live in India?"

He chuckled. "That's not what I said. I am most aware that you would not countenance this." He shrugged. "Where would you wish to set up our associate House in America? You like the Rockies; what about Boise or Cheyenne? For that matter, Aspen or Boulder?"

I snorted. "Boulder? Home of the snappy, sassy blonde? I can't afford a shack in Denver, so places like Boulder and Aspen are way out of range of my pocket."

"Not if you were allied to House Singh. A house, large and elegant, appropriate to your valued status and our requirements would be found. A team for you to make your own, an office, staff and, of course, devotees. House Farrell would be protected by our association, but independent. You will be House Farrell in truth then, not just in name."

"What?" He was joking, of course, he couldn't really mean this. It was outrageous. How could I possibly be worth that sort of investment? "You don't mean it."

He pressed on.

"We most certainly mean it." He leaned forward and tapped counterpoint on the table as he went on. "And we would not stop there. Our far eastern businesses require a suitable headquarters in America, and we are minded that the best option for us is a local partnership. We are most impressed by Ms. Kingslund. With her business acumen and our resources, which you would manage, our mutual enterprises would flourish." He stopped abruptly and sat back, his dark brown eyes watching me closely. "And you would meet her then as an equal."

Oh, smart, smart man, to see that and sink that barb into me. I could feel the hook bury itself in my gut.

So not joking then. My head was reeling and I could hardly take in all of what he was saying, which was not a good point to start trying to make sense of it, or evaluate it. I started at the easy end.

"Why? How could I possibly be worth this kind of effort to you?"

He smiled. "To us, and not to Skylur? Why, if you're so valuable, does he leave you to wander the city and talk to the likes of me?"

"Stop digging at Skylur, and just tell me why I'm worth this."

"You represent what was lost." His eyes gleamed. "Lost when the Athanate strayed from the true way and became obsessed with Houses and secrecy. Shrouded in the Hidden Path, our innocence escaped and the burden of crusis was taken up instead. Houses became divided. Your Blood bears some part of that gift back to us."

Chills ran down my spine. Would Skylur have agreed to this meeting if he'd known that?

"Why doesn't Skylur believe it?"

"He suspects, but can't quite make himself believe. Maybe, he doesn't want to believe it. And he doesn't have the resources we've been able to focus on it. We believe, Amber. We believe."

I went and stood by the window, folding my arms to stop shivering.

"How would you use this 'gift'?"

"A very astute question. Basilikos and Panethus cannot see beyond their struggle for power, and Theokos tries not to get trampled in the fight. What could we do? If we tried to increase our numbers to match them, they might even combine to defeat us. But, what if we do not threaten, what if we maintain a dignity, prove our case and offer to welcome those that come in peace? Neither Matlal nor Altau would be able to force their associates to attack us for fear that either they would be repulsed and excluded, or they might injure you."

I could drive a tank through some of the holes in his argument, if he'd been talking about human groups. Increasingly, I could comprehend that Athanate didn't always respond in the same way.

It was all creeping me out, but I might as well find out as much as I could.

"Still too vague, Arvinder. Do you think it works just by me being bitten, and not biting like other Athanate? How many? Who controls it?"

"My research suggests an exchange of Blood is required." He bowed his head. "More research is clearly required. As to numbers and control, we would sit together to arrive at a comfortable solution for both of us."

Yeah, I believed that.

He was going out of his way to present this in a handsome package, and I couldn't bite his head off for that. But at the end, it was a prospect of a wearying life as the goose laying golden eggs, one after the other, forever. No way they'd trust the goose outside of the beautiful nest they'd build. And no way my wishes would hold sway, not in the long term.

Would Altau be any better? Once he believed?

Better than Matlal, who wouldn't bother with the nest. And I trusted Skylur to defend me robustly a lot more than Arvinder's clever finesse.

I sighed.

"Skylur's going to be more than just pissed that you did this. You're trying to make a deal with him, right? How do you expect he'd react if I showed up tucked under your wing at the Assembly?"

Arvinder swiveled his chair to face me. "He is a pragmatist. Getting Theokos into Panethus would suddenly be his one overwhelming priority, overriding everything else. He wouldn't dare risk that by being openly angry at either of us. And he'd be realistic enough to see that it was a massive error on his part to leave you out where Matlal might have gotten you.

"You do understand that Matlal himself is looking for you now. He's risking retaliation from Altau and censure from the Warders by bringing his people to Denver to catch you. Do not underestimate how unpleasant it would be if he does so. Death would be a mercy you would not be granted. I am amazed that Skylur is risking it." He frowned and shrugged. "It's as if Denver is empty of Altau. Matlal can do as he wishes. This is not a safe situation. Not for anyone."

"How do you mean?"

"The way Matlal works, so like Skylur by the way, is to hide reasons within reasons. We think we know he's bringing his people here to capture you."

Arvinder looked at me, his expression bland while he waited.

"But really," I said, "he's bringing them in to attack the Panethus leadership at the Assembly."

Arvinder smiled. "I didn't think you would have missed that possibility, but it would have been wrong for me not to mention it. I assume the reason that there appear to be so few Altau in Denver is part of the trap? Skylur has them hidden away, ready to pounce on Matlal?"

I wanted to know the answer to that too, but I wasn't going to speculate in front of Arvinder, prospective ally or not. And how much did what he was doing reveal his attitude towards an alliance? "Do you trust Skylur?" I asked.

"I trust him to behave in certain ways. Not the same thing, I know. Why?"

"What I meant is, you communicate to Skylur warnings about Matlal and information about what you think I am. At the same time, you're trying to lure me away to Theokos. How do you expect him to react?"

"Ahh. You come to the heart of it. I don't know. Skylur is the most secretive and canny of us all. It wouldn't be beyond him to be trying to trap me into this very move," he gestured to indicate our meeting, "for reasons I can't fathom. But at the end, I believe Theokos would have a better chance with you in our group than trusting to whatever Skylur might want. That's why I'm making the offer. I also believe it is better for you."

"Why?"

"Because the only strategies I can see Skylur preparing are to do with Emergence—making humanity aware of us. Your part in that could only be to force others to support him or forego access to your Blood. Or to suddenly, massively, expand his closest allies, using your Blood." He stood up abruptly and half turned away. "Forgive me, I speak bluntly, but that is what I believe. Even with the best of intentions, your part in this would render you comatose, supplying your Blood like a…like a machine to hurry more Aspirants through to their Athanate status, more quickly and surely."

"Why would I agree to that?"

"Why do you think you would have any option? You've read the oath of allegiance?"

He joined me at the window, looking pensive now. In silence, we watched the people moving on the street below. People. What did he see? Potential devotees?

When he spoke again, it was quieter.

"They have no idea. They rush around thinking of their work, their friends, the latest movie, the next ball game. And meanwhile, the Athanate gather to argue what the next step is for all of us. Emergence is the strategy that convinced me to move Theokos to join Panethus, long before news of you reached us. This is the most dangerous issue ever to face the Athanate people. And humanity. I must be part of what directs it." He shook his head. "There, I have laid bare my strategy to you, Amber, out of trust."

For your own reasons, and within your own limits. Basilikos.

"You talk a good talk. But I'm sure I would say the same to Skylur if he were standing here making his case."

"But he isn't, and that must tell you something."

I hummed. He could read that whichever way he liked. Skylur was busy.

"And so to the other part of this—becoming part of the Theokos group. I warn you, I'm still human enough that I don't like the sound of other humans worshiping Athanate."

He raised his hands as if warding off what I said. "We all are. We all come from humans. We never lose the human perspective. Not even Matlal. For him, it's not a source of revulsion, it's how he derives his pleasure." Arvinder turned and stared somberly out the window again. "He's not even the worst of them."

"I can't…" I struggled to put it into words. "People worshiping me..." My skin crawled.

"The word you chose is not correct. You will have found this talking to Altau as well—there are words in Athanate which carry just the right weight, when the English word does not. You said 'worship'. Think instead of 'adore'. Panethus focus on love of kin, Theokos, on adoration. It's not so far." He paused. "Forgive me, again, I intrude. If I said Ms. Kingslund adored you, would it sound so wrong? Do not focus on the worship of some blank-faced mass of people, focus instead on individuals."

Gods, he was good at this. Basilikos. Basilikos. The warning I shouted inside seemed to have less and less force every time. *Dammit, he's sounding so damned reasonable and I know he's wrong, I just can't seem to form the arguments.*

He checked his watch. "I must go. We must not endanger everything."

"I'll walk you down," I said. "Thank you for everything today."

We walked to the elevator.

"Will you consider what I proposed?" he said.

"I have. Attractive as it sounds, I feel that Panethus is my home. If my Blood has advantages for crusis and you want a part of that, I think Theokos would be better off joining Panethus, and the sooner the better."

"Within Panethus, those advantages would be within Skylur's gift," he said. "To hold or dispense as he believes fit. Don't be too hasty. Think on it."

As we emerged from the elevator, he handed me a card.

"Use this number to contact me at any time before the Assembly, or Ronit's number if I'm already in the Assembly. Once you walk into the Assembly, the die is cast and it falls where it will."

He signed himself out at the front desk.

"I understand Diana has not rushed off to New Mexico," he said. "That's a wise move. Please tell her to use extreme caution if she visits."

I opened my mouth to contradict him and then changed my mind. "I thought you were the one who gave her the message about problems there?"

"I am. At no point did I suggest she go there. Ronit said she would anyway. It appears he's wrong."

How the hell would you know that? Just how compromised was Altau?

But then another thought struck me. I hadn't seen her get on a plane. I'd just left her at the airport. And I knew, for whatever reasons, she was doing things deliberately without letting Skylur know. Had I been blindsided?

Arvinder and I shook hands.

"If you just want to know more about Theokos," he said, "ask Diana."

"Why her particularly?"

"Ask her that as well." He smiled at some inner joke, passed through the door and strode down the street.

Chapter 31

Skylur didn't answer on the secure phone Tom had given me and I had to stop thinking about the conversation with Arvinder—I had another job to do here and it needed my full attention. Whatever way things went, the Assembly was a turning point and I couldn't afford to not be around. Like being in prison for the illegal acts I was about to do.

I hit the street with my laptop and a half-prepared script in my mind. The octopus was set up with a voice disguise, making me sound like an old man.

"Is that Mr. Underwood?" I said when his secretary reluctantly put me through.

"Yes, it is. I don't believe we've met. Mr. Soule, is it?"

"Soule, Michael Soule. I don't want to waste your time, Mr. Underwood, or mine. I'm clearing out my house and I came across some old photos. Y'know, the black and white stuff that goes brown. Egg white for fixer and all that crap." I could image Underwood's ears pricking up. That clue had dated the photos.

"I see, Mr. Soule. Well, old photos can be of interest to collectors. Can I suggest you bring them in?"

"You can suggest it, sir, and I can call the next number on my list. I'm clearing out my house and then I'm clearing out."

I didn't want to appear too eager, and this was another weak point in my plan. I needed him out of the office and this was the least intrusive way. After a couple of seconds, Underwood cleared his throat. Collectors collect, it's what they do. He wanted to see the photos. Just in case.

"Well, if they were of interest to me, maybe I could make time today. What are the photographs of?"

"Some family shots and portraits of people, weddings and funerals. Let's see, businesses, y'know, store owners and bankers. I guess these'd be the ones people didn't pay for, so maybe not the best shots. Have to say, they look good enough to me. Some gold mining, too. Now, they got labeled; they say Breckenridge and Russell Gulch. Some of dead people lying on the ground, looks like they'd been in some fighting. That's got a date, says 1862. You interested or not?"

Underwood was. I'd baited it with the names and the date and he had to see them. A collection like Grabill's or O'Sullivan's would make his name. Everyone knew there had to be some out there, but what had survived, undamaged, would be extremely rare. He took the address I gave him, and it would take him over an hour to get there and back. About five minutes later, I logged into Victor's system to see that he'd left the office.

Weak points started multiplying. He couldn't trace my call, but I'd had to give him a cell number, and he might try calling it on the way. If he couldn't get through, he might turn back. I'd need to be quick.

The next task was to get the secretary out of the office.

I gave it as long as I dared and then set the octopus up for a female voice.

"Mrs. Ellis? This is State Patrol. There's been an accident out on I-25. First, I want to say that Mr. Underwood is fine. He's going to the hospital purely as a precaution, but he was very concerned about some old photographs in his car. I can stay here another half hour, say…"

In five minutes, Underwood's secretary was out the door and chasing wild geese on I-25.

I was back in the building. As I watched her car come out of the parking garage on the security cameras, I turned off the electricity and security systems in Underwood's office. Then I got the security cameras for that floor to replay video from that morning. There would be nothing to alert the security guard and no video record of my being there.

Still, I walked out of the elevator with my heart in my mouth. Yes, I'd been on the wrong side of the law as soon as I turned on Victor's security override system, but this was where it came down to outright criminal behavior. When I went into Underwood's office, I was breaking and entering. The judge might take into consideration all sorts of mitigating evidence, but I couldn't get into that, I had to be at the Assembly.

Get a grip! Just don't get caught, I said to myself.

There were other offices on the floor. Someone came out of one of them and headed for the elevator. I pretended to be making a call on my cell and walked slowly down the corridor until I heard the elevator doors shut.

The double doors to Underwood's office suite were locked of course, but the left panel was held by a simple flush bolt at the bottom. My laptop bag held a car tire iron with a good spade end. I slipped it under the door, pressing the carpet down. This was the worst time. There was no disguising what I was doing if someone came out of one of the other offices. I felt a prickle of sweat on my brow. It seemed to take forever before the bolt lifted out.

I pulled the door open and slipped inside, resetting the bolt. The base of the door was visibly damaged; I had to get out of here before that was noticed. I jammed it closed temporarily with a door wedge.

The suite was dark, but I didn't need lights and Underwood's office wasn't locked. His desk drawers were. I had expected that. It was a nice desk, too. Shame. My lever shattered the lock.

The crack as it broke made me freeze, but there was no one to hear it but me.

I took the box out and opened it.

Just a medal. It was a strange feeling as I held it. I'd expected anger against Underwood to return, but it was more like pity. I turned it over and ran my fingers over the inscription.

"Above and beyond the call of duty." Hairs stood up on my arms. Captain Quinn's medal was going home to his grandson.

The telephone rang and went to voicemail. Underwood, trying to get in touch with his secretary and check if there had been any calls from Mr. Soule. I retrieved the camera bug.

As I walked to the door, voices passed in the corridor outside. My stomach clenched, but they didn't notice the damage.

Enough of this. Past time for me to remove Victor's security system and leave.

At Niall's, I called him on his door intercom and told him I was outside, with the medal. I wasn't surprised when he told me to wait rather than buzzing me in. He walked out slowly, leaning on his cane, five minutes later.

"Oh God, Amber! How…" he stopped, looking at it in its presentation box. "I better not know, eh?"

I just nodded, my hands behind my back so he couldn't give me anything to hold. He was carrying a suspicious folder tucked under his arm.

"Look, can you drive me somewhere?" he asked.

I blinked. "Sure. Whereabouts?"

He held out a card. I looked carefully, but it was just a business card, so I took it. A museum down in the city.

"I've decided I can't keep it," he explained quietly, as we drove off. "It's not just Ruth and this whole problem. You see, when I really thought about it, I realized it's not mine. I'm just holding it. It's time to pass it on to the right place. These guys have the setup that'll allow them to display it for everyone, to show it in context. They're creating a whole new section on the First World War. That's where the captain would have wanted it to be, in among the story of what happened and why."

"I think maybe he would," I said quietly.

I left him there. The curator knew what he was getting and immediately saw how Niall felt about it. He ushered him in to give him a special viewing and promised he would drop him back afterwards.

The sneaky bastard had left me an envelope with payment tucked in beside the passenger seat.

As I drove away, I called Skylur on the secure cell again. A short recording told me to leave a message. I disconnected the call to think about it.

I didn't know how secure this phone was. The connection might be untraceable and the message encrypted, but who had the physical device at the other end? Someone had gotten hold of Bian's cell phone at some point. Might the same person have access to Skylur's cell phone? I wasn't going to discuss Arvinder unless I was sure that it was Skylur talking to me, but I needed to get the outline of the meeting back to him. In the end I called again and left a message, speaking of 'our friend' and keeping it to the bare bones.

Then I turned the cell back off. Regardless of how secure the communication, all cell phones used the same infrastructure. If security was completely breached, someone had a fix on my position. The smart thing was to leave the cell off and drive away quickly through some side streets, but the continual suspicion was wearing on me. I wanted to see what happened.

I pulled over and eased the Jeep into a parking space off the main drag where it couldn't be seen. Down near the intersection, there was a café with window seats. I ordered a burger meal and sat there half-hidden by posters, looking out at the traffic.

What did I expect to see? A car with Mexican plates, full of guys in suits and dark glasses? How many of them would have moustaches as well? Team Matlal jerseys?

I ate the burger, laughing at myself.

She didn't have a moustache and luckily she was too distracted to see me. The woman I'd fought at Cheesman Park trotted past outside. Silver hair, tightly tied back, shone in the sun and she was wearing a loose jacket. Ten to one there was a gun hidden under that. Fifty yards down the street, a big SUV pulled up and she climbed in. The SUV made a U-turn and picked someone up from the other side of the street before driving slowly the way I'd been going. A second SUV pulled out behind it.

I ate the last of the burger, more to give me some time to think than from appetite.

They weren't gone, I didn't buy that at all. The reason for her to be trotting along the road was to check the side streets. The Jeep couldn't be seen from the main drag, but anyone going a dozen yards down the side street would see it. She'd spotted the Jeep. Once they'd realized I wasn't inside, they'd cleared the area, trying to not spook me. The Jeep would have a tracker now and they'd be waiting to close in on me somewhere less public. I'd seen two cars, and I'd bet there was a call going out for a couple more.

Checking the Jeep, I found their tracker wasn't as neat as the FBI's. It was a standard electronic store gizmo, and with Matt's scanner I found it magnetically clamped to the frame in less than a minute.

The most sensible choice would be to ditch the Jeep. Second would be to toss the tracker and get out of here.

I grinned and pocketed it, swung the Jeep out and burned rubber, heading east on Colfax Avenue.

There was no sign of them behind me, of course. They'd be sitting half a mile back, watching a blinking arrow on a laptop screen. If they were organized, there'd be outriders pacing me a block to either side and probably one in front somewhere.

Enough to give me second thoughts on one of my clear thinking days.

The streets thinned out. The outriders would have to join the party behind me and they all had to have dropped back to keep out of sight. But they'd be happy, watching that little arrow heading for the prairies and thinking of all the options to jump me out there. In Ops 4-10, we'd called it the tech tunnel—when technology leads you down the rabbit hole, but you just keep believing it.

As Colfax merged with I-70, I pulled alongside an 18-wheeler, reached out and stuck the tracker on it, just shy of the big interchange with the toll road. Then I drove the Jeep off the road and straight up the crossover embankment. The big beast barely noticed it wasn't on tarmac.

With the Jeep parked where it was invisible from below, I knelt and watched the traffic stream out across the prairies towards Kansas. I'd almost started to wonder if they were coming when I recognized the SUVs passing below. They were being extra cautious and hanging a long way back—too far, really. There were another three of four cars that were close enough that they might have been with them. That could mean something like fifteen to twenty of Matlal's people were chasing me. I was flattered. I watched them until they were out of sight, laughing.

Well, that would keep them busy for a while, but I'd have to stop driving the Jeep. I was running out of options for cars. Rom's Harley wouldn't be practical and I wouldn't want to get him involved anyway, but I couldn't walk everywhere.

And was that all the Matlal teams chasing my electronic ghost out into the wheat fields?

Back in Denver, I headed for Diana's apartment on University Boulevard. Her parking space was out of sight and I could leave the Jeep there safely. That was assuming that her apartment was still a secret from whoever was spying in Altau.

Arvinder had said she hadn't gone to New Mexico. Maybe she was at the apartment. Maybe I was supposed to figure that out and find her. But why? Why would she let everyone think she was heading for New Mexico and then stay in Denver?

I parked in her space. Trying to puzzle everything out made me stupidly careless; I left everything in the Jeep and went upstairs into the neat foyer. Outside her apartment door, I could smell the calming Altau marque welcoming me, lulling me.

I went in with a sigh, pushing the door closed behind me, and walked into the living room. It was cool and dim and quiet. And there was someone inside. I leaped forward, tucking into a ball and clearing the sofa, coming down behind it, frantically reaching for the gun that wasn't there.

Chapter 32

She clapped slowly.

"Very good, Round-eye."

I peered over the top of the sofa, feeling dumb.

"Unfortunately," Bian went on, folding her arms, "you're now trapped. You do realize it's Matlal's *best* people looking for you?"

"And why the hell aren't the Warders doing anything about it?" I snapped back as I straightened my skirt. "Do they want Matlal to catch me?"

"You could always come back to Haven with me."

"That's why you're here, isn't it?"

Bian didn't answer, which told me I was right. She pulled away from the wall, flicked on the lights and sauntered over to the sofa. She had her hair pulled up into a tie on top and then falling over her shoulders like black horsetail. She was wearing skinny indigo jeans that could have been painted on, a light college sweater with a hood to hide her tattoos and luminescent green running shoes. Restrained, for her.

"Pretty, pretty suit." She smirked, kneeling on the sofa and looking at me over the top. "Are you coming out?"

"Is it safe?" I wasn't sure this was Leopard Bian.

She just smiled. That looked like the Leopard, but even though the actions were there, there was a brittleness about her, as if she were a wire stretched too tautly.

I cleared my throat. "Well, is there coffee at least?"

"I'm going to have tea, but I'll make you coffee. Come on."

We walked over to the open plan kitchen. Neat, functional and looking barely used. Bian made me coffee and an orange oriental tea for herself. She concentrated on working in neat, precise movements.

We sat back on the sofa and I looked around the apartment.

"How did you know I'd come here?" I asked.

"I didn't, but Diana said she would tell you about our place and I thought I'd leave a message here just in case. Then you turned up and played gymnast."

"You and Diana share this place?"

"Yeah. It's restful, not like Haven." She sighed and looked around, keeping her face blank. "It won't be used much now with Basilikos itching to restart the war. Not secure enough. Still, we want to keep it our secret, you understand."

"I won't tell anyone."

Behind the long, low sofa, there were mirrored picture windows looking out toward the Country Club. The sofa and matching chairs in cream leather stood around a walnut coffee table. There were small, subdued spotlights playing over artwork on the walls: tall, abstract paintings and carved Polynesian masks. The main lighting was beautiful, all golden glows bouncing off the ceiling and walls.

We sipped in silence for a minute. Which Bian was I going to have to deal with now?

"You've been a very bad girl," said Bian. "The Warders blame you for causing an escalation in tensions." She got a printout from a pocket and read from it. "'The situation in Denver has become increasingly tense. All parties are urged to desist from provocation and show the utmost restraint in the period leading up to the Assembly'."

"Is that a joke?"

"No. They've put in a formal request for you to be held at Haven till the Assembly." She blew on her tea and peered down into it. "They've asked me to bring you in."

I ground my jaw in frustration. I couldn't fight Bian, and Skylur had specifically excluded her from the list of people I could tell about our plan for distracting Matlal. It had been derailed by the Warders and his own security constraints.

But I really didn't want to be herded in, especially not at the request of the group who should have been keeping Matlal off me. And I had a date with Jen, even if it was a business meeting. And it was unfair. And…

"I'm not the one doing the escalating," I said. "I'm being chased by Matlal."

"And if he turns around and says you're chasing his associate, so he's only responding?"

"With twenty Athanate all the way from Mexico? And what's that about associates? He's claiming Hoben is kin, or whatever it is he calls his slaves?"

"*Marai* is the Basilikos name for humans," Bian said, idly passing her fingers through the steam from her tea. "It means unclaimed cattle. *Toru* if they're claimed by a Basilikos House." She took another sip of tea. "Round-eye, I'm on your side, but we both need to be aware of what they will use to argue their point." She swiveled around, folding her legs underneath her on the sofa and leaning forwards. "Now, did you get to meet Arvinder?"

The Diakon had come out, and somehow seemed just as brittle as the Leopard to me.

"Yeah. I've got Basilikos all wrong. Theokos is just sweet and Arvinder would like me to be his best friend."

Bian snorted. She ran her fingers tiredly through her horsetail hair.

"Offered me a house and staff and devotees, too," I said.

Bian raised an eyebrow. "Are you feeling unappreciated?"

She seemed unsurprised by Arvinder's offer, as if she and Skylur had known he would be making an offer of some kind. But there was something challenging in her tone…had they not quite trusted me to turn it down? Was that why she'd been pushing at me lately, trying to find out how I felt about her and Diana, Alex and Jen? Testing my strongest motivators—loyalty and friendship, or money and self-interest? Was it all a setup between them to see what I'd do? Thinking like this was making my head spin.

"I'm not complaining. But Arvinder knows how to make his offer appealing, especially when he added in some business deals for Jen." I shook my head. "I'm not that tempted. But he wasn't doing this just to pull one over on Skylur for fun. He's after my Blood, just like Matlal."

Bian didn't appear to have heard that—she was staring into the distance, lost in thought. Abruptly she put her cup aside, frowning. "Why don't you want to come into Haven?" she said. "What's the real reason?"

I sighed. "Bian, we've been through this."

"No, we haven't," she said. "You just say you won't. You haven't said why."

She moved like a cat to straddle my legs and sit on my thighs. She stared intently at me. "I could just tie you up and bring you in," she said. Her tongue touched her upper lip. "Actually, I think I'd like you tied up."

Shit. Was this teasing, or the real thing? How could I tell? And how could I bail out?

"Scared?" she said.

I kept my breathing slow and easy, concentrating on being calm.

"Hmm," she said. "Clever, Round-eye. So calm."

I checked her out. Her eyes. They didn't have that hard, glittering look that meant a hungry Athanate. The pupils were wide enough, but she was staring at my lips rather than my throat. Definitely not Diakon Bian and not playing. This was for real. But I guessed I was safe enough as long as I could keep my panties on, and I'd had a lot of practice at that over the last couple of years. Admittedly, not quite like this.

I wished I knew where Diana was. Right here would be handy, to keep Bian in check.

She leaned forward, putting an arm on either side of my head and resting her hands on the back of the sofa. That brought her face just inches from mine. I smelled her copper and spice scent and felt the warmth of her skin like winter sun.

She came closer, until our noses almost touched. "It doesn't make you nervous when I get in your face?"

I laughed, a little abruptly. "I was a sergeant in the army, Bian. I got in peoples' faces for a living."

"Interesting job," she said. "How come I can't smell fear, Sergeant Amber?"

"I'm not scared of you. I respect you for what you are. You would scare me, if you weren't just trying to shock me."

"That's nice. That you're not scared, I mean." She smiled lazily. "And why is your heart beating so fast, Sergeant Amber?"

She took my right hand and studied it with a little smile playing on her lips.

"Do you like me?" she said, looking up at me. Still no fangs.

"Despite the fact that you're well on the way to being the most irritating person in the world, yeah, I like you." I pushed her back a little. "But not like that."

"Oh?" She crossed her hands, grabbed the hem of her sweatshirt and stretched her arms above her head, lifting it off in one silky smooth movement. She wasn't wearing a bra. I'd wondered how far the leopard spots went. Faded out about where her breasts started to rise.

She leaned forward again. Unsure quite where to push, I didn't do anything in time. She settled her face into the crook of my neck with a sigh.

I slipped my arms around her while my heart and brain raced frantically. I needed to do something quickly because I could feel my own Athanate and wolf responses starting to run. My jaw relaxed. All it needed was for me to brush her hair aside and kiss her neck. My Athanate would know what to do next. I could feel my fangs ready to manifest. Her lips pressed their own hot message against my throat.

"Stop, please. We can't," I managed to whisper.

"It's all right, I won't bite," she murmured.

"Bian, no."

She raised her head, her face puzzled. "I'm mainlining your pheromones, Amber. Don't try and tell me you don't want it."

"I won't try to lie to you Bian." I swallowed. "My body does. My heart doesn't, and that means I don't."

"I don't believe you." She angled her face in to kiss.

I got up in a hurry. I managed to twist, so Bian landed on the sofa rather than on the floor, but her look couldn't have been any more outraged. And this was definitely not Leopard or Diakon now.

"What the hell is wrong with you?" she yelled.

"What do you mean, what's wrong with me? I said no. I mean no."

"Do you? Your body says different. I mean what I say, body and soul."

"And you've never thought about how you say it? You've gone crazy on me. I can't tell whether you're teasing or serious. I can't tell who you are from one minute to the next."

She jumped off the sofa and jabbed me in the chest. "I'm hard to read? You're the one who changed."

"You mean I've gotten wary? Couldn't be anything to do with there being a spy at Haven, could it? The spy that everyone says is my imagination?"

"You were the one who said it could be just someone putting two and two together!"

"That was before I heard that Basilikos have enough information to do research on my Blood. That's got to be details that people wouldn't just happen to overhear. Where did they get that sort of detail from? Skylur? Diana? Your team?" My anger was blotting out my reason. "You?"

Bian looked as if I'd slapped her. And I wasn't finished. I jabbed her right back in the chest.

"I made a call to Skylur's secure cell this afternoon, left a message. I might as well have shouted out my position using a bullhorn. Matlal's team were there six minutes later. Tell me, who has access to Skylur's cell and yours?"

Bian grabbed my hands. She was quicker and stronger than me. The realization that I might have just told the spy I was on to her was like a bucket of cold water over my anger. But it was pain and not rage that shouted at me.

"It's not me!" she protested. "If there is a spy and not even Skylur can tell who it is, how am I supposed to?"

She pushed me hard against the wall.

"And he starts issuing orders for you to come into Haven, passing them through my team, but not backing it up when you ignore them," she hissed. "Do you think I'm stupid? Don't try that affiliate independence shit on me either. You have no idea what leeway it gives you. You're running a smokescreen for him. Fine. Where does that leave me? What if I do something that exposes it?"

The unthinking emotion was back. Her eyes got that dreamy look that had scared me about David. She was panting and I could see her fangs manifest and disappear repeatedly in her mouth. All the tension in her seemed to be ready to explode into something—violence or biting. I had to stop her, not just for my sake. I knew Skylur would have to impose the death sentence for breaking his ban. There would be no excuses for Bian.

"I'm Altau head of security, we have a problem and everyone can see that Skylur doesn't trust me." Her voice dropped, but stayed sharp as a blade. "How the hell do you think I feel?"

Her body was shivering like a plucked bowstring. Somewhere inside, she knew she had to stop. She was fighting herself. But there was no way I could fight her. If anything, it would make it worse. I had to work with her. I had to cool this down.

"Bad." I spoke quietly. "If he loses trust in you, Bian, what does that mean for you personally?" I could see her brain working. That's what stopped David. While she was thinking, her Athanate hunger wasn't driving her actions. I needed her to think. For both our sakes.

"For me?" A frown creased her brow. "Who cares what it means for me?"

"I do."

Her eyes flared again, but her grip relaxed a fraction.

She blinked and her breathing slowed. "Even if he believes I betrayed him; even if he locks me away, kills me, he is the only one who can stop us going to war. He's the only one who can prevent the worst possible thing that could happen to the Athanate." She let out a slow breath. "And he is the only leader who can deliver Emergence. Against that, what happens to me is nothing."

I felt the shock of that down into my belly. This wasn't an Athanate reaction. This was Bian's stone-hard rational assessment.

"It's not nothing, Bian. What does Diana say?"

She let my hands go. "She hasn't called. I can't reach her. I don't even know where she is."

I understood. I didn't like the sound of that either. In fact, pretty much everything today was ratcheting up the feeling that we were all sliding into a train crash. I needed to keep her thinking.

"Why, Pussycat?" My voice sounded rusty. Very carefully, I put my arms around her. I held her gaze with mine. I mustn't let her start focusing on my neck. "Why is Emergence so important?"

"Such a question." She snorted and it almost sounded as if the Leopard was back. "Because I want to come out of the closet."

I spluttered. "You're so far out of the freaking closet that—"

"Not that closet, Round-eye. I never got in that closet. I want to come out as Athanate. I want people to know it and accept me for what I am. I want to be able to get close to someone—like this—and when their heart speeds up, I want it to be because they're excited, not because they're scared. Even though they know I'm Athanate. Even though they know I drink blood."

From beneath the armored shell of her sexuality, a different Bian peeped out at me. It was as if we'd been sparring and she'd dropped her guard. Something precious had been handed to me.

It was up to me not to stamp on it. I was good at robust refusals, but this was new.

I didn't get the chance.

"Who do you trust completely?" she said, abruptly in my face again, lips almost touching mine, body pressed hard against me.

"Diana," I answered automatically. *With my life. Literally.*

She nodded, her eyes locked on me. The pressure came off as she stood back, but she didn't let go.

"There's a key in the kitchen to an old Ford downstairs. Leave the Jeep and take it. No one but Diana and I know about it. And come to Haven tomorrow." Her face was still angry, belying the calm in her words.

"Thank—" I started.

"Trust me," she said, jerking me off balance. "Trust me. Less than Diana, maybe, but trust me. And keep your freaking gun on you." She flung me back against the wall and by the time I picked myself up, she had taken her sweatshirt and gone.

Chapter 33

I walked shakily to Manassah, along the side of the golf course. I was early and it was a good way to get my adrenaline overload damped down. But it meant I went in through the patio doors, and didn't see the car outside.

They'd seen me, so there was no point in trying to sneak off and come back.

"Agent Ingram, what a surprise," I said.

"Hey there, honey." Jen got up and kissed me on the cheek. "My, what a lovely suit."

I tried to glare at her, but clearly I hadn't been practicing enough recently and it didn't work.

"So glad to have caught you, Ms. Farrell. I understand you're mighty busy at the moment."

I let the sarcasm slide off, while my little demon reveled in the Texas drawl. Jen brought me a rum, and we settled on the sofa, facing Ingram. Jen looked reasonably relaxed, so I guessed he hadn't been giving her the third degree.

"I assume you've come to see me, rather than Jen?"

Agent Ingram nodded. "Yup. Dropped by on the chance you'd be here. Just a few small points."

I hid my sigh behind a sip of the rum, and let it work its magic on me. At least he hadn't come in brandishing cuffs and dragging Griffith along.

"Where's your partner?" I asked.

Ingram looked uncomfortable. "We had to split up. He's checking some stuff on the other side of town."

Yeah, for sure. Suddenly, this was a whole lot more interesting. Ingram wanted to talk to me without witnesses. At least, without FBI witnesses.

I raised my brows. "Jen okay to stay?" I saw her twitch with irritation out of the corner of my eye, but I wanted to see what he'd say.

He nodded and struggled to settle on his chair.

"Ah, dammit all," he said. "Ray's on a wild goose chase. He is…unimaginative. And not cleared for certain projects."

"Uh-huh," I replied. Anthracite, for example.

He's trying to set me up for a sucker punch.

He finally relaxed and tilted his head to one side. "Y'know, Ms. Farrell, there's more…'scuse me, more horse shit talked about you than a whole roomful of politicians."

I just shrugged.

"An' my interest must be like a red, red rose. Feed it horse shit and it jes' keeps on growing. Lemme give y'all an example," he said. He pulled out some notes and perched a ridiculous little set of reading glasses on his twitchy nose.

"Emily Schumacher." He stopped me before I could say anything. "I haven't bothered the family. Just past the anniversary, isn't it?" He didn't wait for an answer; he knew the date perfectly well. "Let's see. Three men, no known motive. There was a firefight, two police officers killed, little Emily taken hostage, yadda, yadda. You misplaced your partner in all the excitement, tracked them down, called in the SWAT team and it all ended well." He peered at me over the glasses. "Y'see, horse shit, premium grade."

No, it didn't happen like that. But I wasn't about to explain. At the moment, I was more intrigued by how he'd reached his conclusion than worried about where he was going afterwards. I had a feel for the way he worked. He'd explain the first part to me, to soften me up for the next part.

"Y'know, we live in a terrible age," he said. "Ruled by bean counters. And bean counters got their claws into the police like nothing else. So after I got this here report, I looked at the bean counters' stuff. The police do an audit on every SWAT operation. Every one. Can you imagine? Jeez, and every time a gun is fired too."

Yeah, not the way they do it in Texas, Agent Ingram. There wouldn't be enough paper.

"So important, this stuff, so important. And y'know what?" he said, peering at me over his glasses.

Okay, here it comes.

"Not one of the SWAT team fired a weapon that day. Not one."

Oh, crap.

"You, on the other hand, Ms. Farrell, you were lugging around that there cannon of yours and the bean report says you fired it dry."

Ingram leaned back in his chair and tossed the report aside. He took off his glasses and chewed the end thoughtfully for a minute.

"Twelve round magazine. Three men. Only two of them with .45 bullet wounds. I've seen your shooting scores, Ms. Farrell. Care to comment?"

"It was dark."

"More horse shit," he said cheerfully. "No offense."

Athanate can move faster than humans, an ability that develops slowly over time. I was fortunate that the three rogues I'd killed weren't old, in Athanate years, and I'd had a chance against them, even if it'd taken nine shots to nail the second. But I couldn't tell him any of that.

"Four other policemen tried earlier on. Two died and two wounded. You went in alone, ahead of the SWAT team, shot two of them and, uh, defenestrated the third."

Seven syllables said my demon gleefully, *seven syllables. Dee-yuh-fen-es-trah-ay-ted.*

"Oh, and this." He held up a single sheet of paper between thumb and forefinger like it was dirty. "This claims to be the complete forensics and coroner's reports on the three bodies. John Doe, one, two, three. Bullet wounds and massive trauma and…nothing. No blood tests, no DNA, no fingerprints, no scans, no documentation, no photos, nothing at all. Not even details of the disposal of the bodies. And no signatures."

The bodies had disappeared into the Obs laboratories for the scientists to study. Of course no one would sign that document.

"And your little problem at Cheesman Park on Tuesday," he said, and Jen's head twitched around. I hadn't told her anything, of course. Ingram spotted that, too. "Glad to see those bruises cleared up so quickly, by the way. Now, you didn't have a gun on you then. You took two of them out and were having a damn good set-to with the third. They weren't just muggers strolling in the park, were they, Ms. Farrell?"

I pursed my lips and shrugged again.

"And I've seen some fancy fighting in my time. FBI Taekwondo champion in my youth. You wouldn't believe it now." He chuckled. "Seen some moves, but I never seen them like that."

"Dentou-tekidenai," I muttered. "No style." Competition is about points and styles. Fighting is about winning. My opponent that night had certainly understood.

"And when they ran away, flat-out sprint, a couple of them carrying injured men like they weighed nothing. Some muggers, Ms. Farrell. Anyhow. The army feeds me horse shit. The police sure rate you highly, but behind your back, they think you're some kinda woo-woo army experiment gone wrong. More horse shit. Now Captain Morales knows something, but he won't say squat. And it all boils down to this: you were out there doing something for ten years that no one who knows will talk to me about. And now you're doing something else that someone else really doesn't want you to do, and no one who knows wants to talk to me about that either."

I wondered how high in the agency Ingram could reach. If Colonel Laine wasn't able to use his contacts, then what about Agent Ingram? He was on the trail and with his resources he could stumble across the Athanate at any time. Hell, he already knew something about them from the phone tapping. Maybe it would be better to try and get him on our side. If it turned out he couldn't work with us on Diana's project, I was sure Skylur would require him to have a memory lapse.

We'd fallen silent and Ingram was watching me closely. It was a small mercy he didn't have Athanate senses as well.

"Ms. Farrell, I've got no doubts you were in the army, and you did good things there, and I suspect your reluctance to talk to me comes from some agreement you had to make with them."

Gods, he'd gotten so close on so little.

"Still," he went on. "Anything that secret, it's a problem. 'Cause if it's so dammed secret, how do you know it's doing what it should? And when I say secret, I mean the FBI National Security Director doesn't know. I'm a-wondering if the Director of National Intelligence himself doesn't know. Y'understand my point?"

Only too well. He'd put his finger on a problem I'd been having with Ops 4-10 ever since I had heard Colonel Laine's news. Who was running the show now and who did they report to? I'd never had doubts when Laine had been running it. Now? I wasn't sure any more. *Really* not sure.

How high in the FBI ranks was Agent Ingram?

"You speak to those guys?" I asked.

"I'd get a nosebleed from the altitude," he replied, which wasn't confirmation or denial. He could play that game as well as I could.

I steadied myself, took some deep breaths, flicked an imaginary piece of fluff off my skirt. Ingram had just unknowingly signed up for a meeting with Diana and the colonel, if I could swing it. But he wasn't finished yet.

"So's anyway, I got to thinking," Ingram continued. "If there's one, maybe there's more, and Lieutenant Krantz has been a most cooperative fella. And, y'know, it's like there's one of them blind spots you get in your eye." He held up his pen in front of his face and moved it backwards and forwards near his eye. "But not in my eyes, in the military records. Guys and girls just disappear off the books and then maybe reappear a while later in a different unit, maybe with a different rank and pay grade. Not many folk, taking into account the whole military. Maybe a kinda short battalion, say five or six hundred."

Again, close.

"And every request for clarification gets kicked up the chain of command. It'll take time, but I guess we've got to find someone who knows what's going on?"

He made it a question. He could see decisions being reached in my face.

"When Krantz was chasing me, I fed back through Colonel Laine. He spoke to someone and that someone had Krantz hauled off the case. Go ask Krantz who that was. It had to be someone in his chain of command that spoke to him. Maybe that'll get you somewhere quicker."

Ingram pursed his lips and nodded.

"You'll make sure and tell Krantz that he's done me a favor and I will repay it."

Ingram smiled and nodded again, still waiting.

I laced my fingers together to still my nervous hands.

"You're looking at two completely separate things. Give me till next week," I said. "By then, you might have some idea who knows what in the army. And I hope I'll be in a position to set up a meeting for the part that isn't the army."

"Yes, Agent Ingram," Jen came in. "Hell, all I've heard is that Amber's been doing good things and can't talk because of some restrictions that aren't her fault. I think some leeway would be in order."

Ingram scratched his chin thoughtfully while he looked from one of us to the other, taking his time reaching a decision. I noted he didn't say anything about needing to talk to a boss. That added to my impression he was far more senior than I first thought.

"I thank you, Ms. Kingslund, for your hospitality," Ingram said, getting suddenly to his feet. "And I will hold you to that, Ms. Farrell. Keep in mind, I won't stop looking in the meantime. And I won't restrict my investigation."

"Yeah. Fair enough." I stood up, and in a moment of inspiration, I took a complete flyer. "Y'know that recording you played me? It'd be a great help if I had a copy."

Ingram's nose twitched and his eyes got all beady. The Taekwondo champion thought it would give him an advantage to have me in his debt. Maybe he was right. He took a tiny recording disk out of his Dictaphone and handed it over with a smile.

"Thanks," I said. He nodded cordially back.

Jen saw him out, and I collapsed back on the sofa.

"He's gone. You okay, honey?" Jen leaned against the doorframe.

"Yeah," I sighed, rubbing my face.

"Just one more," she said enigmatically, and went back out.

Tullah came in alone.

"Hey."

"Hey yourself. What's up?"

She sat stiffly on the sofa beside me.

"Ma was sort of right, I guess."

"What, you've just realized I'm an evil Athanate?" I grinned at her.

"No! You're not evil."

"Good to hear. Okay, so what was she sort of right about?"

"My dragon," Tullah said. "She's not…safe."

"Okay," I said slowly. "But you sort of knew that already, though."

Tullah looked as frustrated as I felt.

"It's different. It's as if she wants things and they start to seep through into my head."

"Like what?"

"I can't talk about it yet. I have to get my head straight." She hunched her shoulders. "I'll keep working on my cases, but I need to steer clear of you and Ma for a while."

"Look, Tullah, that doesn't fly. You can't tell me you're being distracted and then say you're okay to work."

"I'm not distracted when I work. I'm distracted when you're around." Tullah pressed her hands down on her thighs, digging her fingers in. "She wants something from you."

"And.."

"I can't agree until I understand what it is. The Adept must incorporate the guide, not the other way around."

"Sounds like a bit of good rote-learned wisdom," I said. Which was not to say it wasn't valid. But Tullah and Kaothos probably couldn't manage to besiege Byzantium for another couple of days. "Okay, take off till Monday. Then we talk and settle this." *Maybe with Mary and Liu.*

She nodded agreement. I dug in my pack for my last set of cheap burn phones. "Keep this on you," I said, handing one to her. "For emergencies, use this phone. I mean all kinds of emergencies, dragon included." She nodded again, a brief smile flickering into view. "I'll check my usual cell as well, but with people tracking it, I won't keep it on."

She took the phone and looked uncertain. The implications of going off and doing it on her own were sinking in. Suddenly, all the pressure was on her to get things right.

"I think it's a good idea," I said. "With everyone out there so damned interested in me, all of us would be better off someplace else for a while. In fact, I'm just about to tell Jen that."

That raised a smile. "Good luck," she said. Her eyes flicked up at me and then quickly back down to her hands, clasped on her lap. "Was it like this for you, with the Athanate stuff?"

"I don't know, Tullah. Like what? I don't know what's going on in your head, but if you're asking if I was confused and angry and upset at times, yes, it was like that. *Is* like that."

"You don't show it. You're always, like, so in control."

I snorted and shoved her gently towards the door. "Get out of here."

She got, and Jen came back.

"Are we ready to go to this horse thing?" I asked.

"After what Agent Ingram was talking about, I'm not sure how to take that." She smiled. "Anyway, we're not. I have my new cowboy boots from Werner, and we both have to be in style."

"As in?"

"Why, surely, country and western, honey."

She'd left the right clothes out on my bed. Curly-brim Stetson, blue jeans and jacket, plaid shirt like a freaking tablecloth and a leather belt with a monster horsey buckle that I'd never have worn otherwise. Sigh. I decided to go along with it. I'd pick my battles.

At least the denim jacket fit neatly over the shoulder holster. I wasn't going anywhere, even a business meeting, without my HK.

Chapter 34

I picked my battle and I won it. By the time we drove off in her pink Mercedes, dressed like line dancers, Jen had agreed to stay at least a couple of nights at a hotel. The guards were closing Manassah and would meet us at the hotel later.

In retaliation, she insisted we get in the mood with a C&W CD karaoke session. We arrived at the race track giggling.

That was the last entertainment I had for a while. There was a rocky start to the meeting when Jen found out that the woman who was supposed to be signing the property over to Jen's consortium hadn't been able to make it. Her replacement was an arrogant easterner, Anthony Vance, with a horribly fussy way of talking. He just about managed not to correct Jen, but his own staff weren't so lucky. Worst off was the gofer, a guy just out of high school who'd had the misfortune to be from Alabama. I thought he was cute and I like southern accents, but Vance gave him a hard time every time he spoke.

There was nothing I could say really, and Vance obviously didn't expect me to speak, so I just sat there with my arms folded. As much fun as a visit to the dentist. Thinking that made me feel better. Athanate health benefits meant no more dental visits for me. Another check in the plus column. And at least Jen wasn't enjoying it any more than I was. Although no one else seemed to notice, I could feel the level of irritation in her climbing like one of those ominous cut scenes in a movie where the boiler meter edges toward the red.

"Well." Jen wrapped it up and stood. "That's everything except the catering for the inaugural meeting. I think we'll close now and I'll leave that to an expert."

Oh my God, why was I suddenly leaning forward?

"Amber?" Jen said quizzically.

"I don't figure you should leave this to others. This inaugural meeting is a special occasion and I'd be all choked up if the food wasn't in keeping with the event."

Except that wasn't the way I said it. The demon had control of my throat and what came out was the illegitimate offspring of Agent Ingram and Alabama gofer, brung up in the trailer park. Just broader. Five syllables for inaugural.

"Yes, of course, thanks," Jen said, straight-faced, and turned back to the table. "I want it done exactly as my colleague suggests." She walked away quickly, ostensibly to retrieve our Stetsons, and leaving me to it.

At Vance's increasingly panicked look of blank incomprehension, I turned to Alabama.

"You understand me, don't you, sonny?"

"Yes, ma'am."

"Big ole steaks on grills, size of a cow and thick as a saddle. Sauce fit to make your eyes pop. Potatoes in their skins with gobs of real butter. Beer colder than a well digger's. An' all the fixins."

"Yes, ma'am."

At Vance's prompting he translated.

"What if someone doesn't eat meat?" Vance said plaintively.

"If'n they don't like meat, they can always eat hamburger," I replied and we left before Alabama had time to translate.

Jen drove us, only slightly erratically, off into the night.

We took the scenic route back. So much for being a bodyguard. Long days and late nights were catching up and my head was definitely lolling when we stopped.

I looked up. We'd only been going ten minutes.

"Did we run out of gas?"

"Honey, would I try a line like that on you?"

"You never know. Might be worth a try," said my demon before I could catch it.

"No. Plenty of gas. It's just worth a look, since we're out here."

We were somewhere up on Lookout, with the lights of Denver below us. We got out and leaned against the front of the car.

Three million people down there and Jen had to pick the one with a paranormal problem she couldn't talk about yet. Sigh.

Somehow, Jen had slipped inside my arm and her hand snuck around me to rest on my hip. Her head lay on my shoulder.

"View's out that way." I nodded down at Denver.

"Hmm. That's one opinion," she said. "Ah, you're blushing."

"It's dark, how can you tell?"

She chuckled. "Just a lucky guess, honey."

I laughed and couldn't stop myself pulling her into a hug. We fit together, perfectly, like one of those puzzles. I had to stop this, or I'd start thinking about how warm the hood would be beneath us, if we lay down on it. My jaw definitely didn't ache now. Instead, there was a soft feeling of anticipation in my canines. They felt warm, comfortable. There was a promise of pleasure, a lazy wickedness that I knew would come from biting.

I closed my eyes. I could feel Jen's every movement, sense her whole body. I could hear her heart, sweetly thumping in time with mine. I could feel the rush of air in her lungs and the push of blood through her veins. I could taste her desire and I could even feel how carefully she held herself in check. It was good that one of us was in control.

I'd never been so aware of another person, so absorbed, so sensitive to every nuance. I started to imagine I could feel the breeze against her cheek. The feeling of my back under her hands. My warmth against her. The sensations of both bodies merged in my head. To my closed eyes, we were naked, transparent as deep sea creatures but wreathed in light, full of murmuring…

She stirred against me, and our oversized belt buckles clinked together. Jen gave a huff of amusement, her breath soft on my neck. My eyes opened. We were clothed and cold and shivering up on a windy hillside. My breath came out in a shaky sigh.

"Hell, honey, I never met anyone like you," she whispered.

"No, you probably haven't, lucky you." I gave a short laugh. "You know I've never lied to you?"

She nodded against me. "Just a bit choosy about what you answer." But I could hear she was smiling.

"I swear," I said, "after this weekend, I'll never refuse to answer anything ever again."

"That sounds like a long time."

Neither of us said anything to that. Her heart rate had stepped up and mine followed.

"Would you tell me everything now, if I asked?" she murmured, teasing.

I swallowed. My throat was suddenly, painfully dry. But there was only one answer I could truthfully give. "Yes," I said.

She looked up and her hands were suddenly on my cheeks.

"Oh my God, Amber, I wouldn't. I was just teasing. I'm sorry. I'm sorry." She clumsily wiped away the tears.

"No, I'm sorry. Being stupid."

"It's not stupid at all. Thank you, honey." She cleared her throat. "Now, let's go check in at the hotel. You need to get to bed. Alone. For the moment."

Chapter 35

FRIDAY

I was at Victor's office early enough for breakfast, so I brought takeout.

"What about my gut, woman?" Victor complained as we unpacked the waffles, doughnuts and coffee onto his desk.

I eyed his middle. Yup. The belt was still fastened at the same hole, but the pants and the shirt were pulling in opposite directions.

"Get out more," I said complacently, crossing my legs and sticking my boots on his desk. I patted my belly. He shook his head. Didn't stop him taking his share. Just to be sure they were safe from him, I balanced my waffles and doughnuts on my lap.

I'd brought all his security gear back and payments to cover it. I took a bite from a waffle and licked the syrup carefully off my fingers before handing the two checks across the desk.

"I dated one the end of the month. Hope that's okay?" There was just barely enough in the account to cover the rental of the equipment and Vic's delivery of Arvinder. I wanted Tullah to have some reserve while payments were coming in for her cases.

Skylur might pick up the tab for some of it. Might.

Victor grunted and swept the checks into a drawer without looking. He took a long swig of his coffee.

"Anythin' you want to share?" he said. He kept his deep Georgia voice casual, but I heard the undercurrents.

"What would there be, Vic?"

He snorted. "Why people lookin' for you, girl? An' I don' mean puttin' an ad in the papers, that type of lookin'. I mean banging on doors, roughhouse, kicking over tables type of lookin'."

"They came around here?"

He nodded, took a huge bite out of a doughnut and chewed it thoughtfully, still watching me. "Told them to Foxtrot Romeo Oscar," he mumbled.

I smiled. I was putting all my friends in danger, but Victor was capable of handling it at this level.

"Thanks, big man. Can't talk about it. Should be over soon."

He just raised a brow skeptically. I knew what he was thinking. That kind of effort was for something that wasn't just going to go away. But I couldn't tell him any more than I could tell Jen. Not now and maybe never.

"Well," he said when I stayed quiet, "I already told Tullah thanks for the business she passed to me, but I'll say it again to you. And I sent her back some surveillance and internet jobs. She's smart with that stuff; made us look good for a client this week." He finished off his doughnut. "Helpin' out seems to be doin' us both good."

"Thanks. I'll catch up with Tullah next week, see if we can make it even better."

If I'm around.

Something of that thought got through and Victor's brow went up again. I kicked myself mentally and concentrated on the doughnut.

"If…" Victor paused and thought about it a bit. "If you get tired of runnin' the business and want to get out more, there's always room for you and Tullah here. Y'all got the skills, girl."

He was offering me a kind of safety, and I loved him for it. Business was tough enough for solo PIs, and training Tullah was going to make it even tougher in the short term. Victor had a steady business and I'd earn an income instead of feast and famine. I'd be able to put aside regular savings for clothes and a house and…no. Not me. Not just too proud. I simply wasn't that kind of woman, deep down. Never really had been, for all the care I'd managed my money with when I'd been supporting Mom and Kath. And what Victor didn't understand was that, if the situation with Matlal and Basilikos wasn't fixed at this Assembly, then his levels of physical safety weren't going to be nearly enough anyway.

"Thanks again, Vic, but I'm not ready to pack up shop." I drained the coffee and sighed. "And I got errands to run today, gotta go run them."

Away from his office, I pulled over and turned on my cell to check my messages.

Nothing from Alex. Nothing from the colonel, either.

The colonel's silence didn't bother me. He was smart. He would make his way here eventually and we'd fix things for him if they could be fixed.

Alex's silence really bothered me.

Okay, so I would make my way toward Haven. Just a telephone call first. Shouldn't take long.

Chapter 36

The octopus wasn't disguising my voice when I called Alex's office number, and somehow his secretary knew who it was, right away.

"Ms. Farrell, I'm sorry, but I expect Mr. Deauville will be in meetings all day. It's just not a good time. Can I take a message?"

I slowed down. I sure as hell wasn't giving some secretary a message about Matlal sponsoring the rival pack.

Worse than that, something wasn't right here. Pure instinct told me this wasn't Alex putting me off, which meant this would have to be a pack thing. I didn't like it one bit.

"Ms. Farrell?"

I'd ignored my instinct before and regretted it. I don't like regrets. And if I had some bad news coming up, I didn't like not knowing. I *really* didn't like not knowing before I gave my oath at the ceremony. Even Diana had said I needed to know where I stood when I gave that oath.

I was going to deliver the message about Matlal, and get answers to my questions as well.

So much for the calming drive out to Haven.

"Ms. Farrell? You still there?"

"Yes. And I have a message. You can tell him to make the time to see me. I'm on my way in."

"Ms. F—"

I cut her off and brought the Ford around in a U-turn, tires smoking, upsetting a couple of cars who were yards away from me, and in no real danger.

Alex had given me his business card at the dance, and I knew where his office was. I wasn't going to take busy signals from him now. If there was something I could do, I'd do it. If he didn't want me, he could tell me himself.

And if he said that? My guts twisted. Must have had too much coffee and doughnut.

His business was called Tallbarn Transportation and the premises was made up of a frame warehouse two stories high with a neat brick office on the side.

I guessed the secretary hadn't taken me seriously enough to post a guard and there was no front desk as such. Someone called out from the warehouse as I walked up the open plan stairs, but I must have looked as if I belonged. They watched, but no one chased me.

The landing had just the two doors. To the left was a meeting room. It was empty. So much for the all-day meetings. Straight ahead had to be the boss's office. Or rather, the secretary's office, guarding her boss.

She jumped up from behind her desk, and I recognized her immediately. Olivia, from the rafters at the Weres' barn meeting.

"What a surprise," I said.

"You can't go in—"

"Yeah, you told me. He's in a meeting." I ignored her, marching past.

"You don't understand. It's not safe—"

My hand closed on the handle as she reached me.

"Then he can tell me himself, or I'll find out." I opened the door.

Alex sat in darkness behind the broad mahogany arc of his executive desk. He was alone, his desk clear except for phones and pens and pads. His head was in his hands and he raised it slowly. His face looked tired and puffy, there were shadows under his eyes and his hands weren't steady. But a tiny smile flickered in welcome and it was enough.

I turned in the doorway, blocking Olivia.

She tried to call over my shoulder. "I'm sorry, Mr. Deauville—"

"Olivia," I said, calm and quiet, gripping her jacket and getting in her face. I was a hand span bigger than her and sergeants can do intimidating in their sleep. She wasn't even going to get to finish a sentence while I was here.

Her mouth shut with a snap and she looked scared.

"Olivia, I'm going to be talking to Mr. Deauville for a good while, and I'd be pissed if we were disturbed. You said it's not safe in here. Well, it just got a whole lot worse."

"It's all right, Olivia," Alex said quietly.

She looked as if she had one more argument left in her and took a steadying breath. Brave girl.

I hadn't come here with a plan or any idea of what I'd find. I was working on gut instinct—dangerous, but useful sometimes. My gut instinct had told me Olivia was one of the Weres having problems with changing, and it also told me that I might be part of some solution to that. Whether it suited my purpose or not, I couldn't let that pass.

"You can't change, can you?"

She stopped what she'd been about to say. A flush spread up her cheeks, her eyes dropped and her head followed. Wolf behavior.

"No," she whispered. I'd seen the hunger in her eyes at the barn, and now I knew.

I let go of her jacket and tilted her face up until she had to look at me.

"If I can, I will help you. On my Blood, I so swear."

She stood, shocked speechless, her mouth open and that look of hunger bubbling up in her. Alex's breath hissed in the gloom behind me.

"Go take a coffee break," I said and gave her a little push as I closed the door.

I stood resting my forehead against the door. I'd taken on another commitment—I was fine with that—but I'd taken her trust as well, and that wasn't a burden I took lightly. Was I justified to make that call on a gut feeling?

The office was now nearly silent behind me. The solid door cut off the noise from the warehouse. There was no computer running, no air conditioning. I reached out with every sense and drank it all in: the scent of Alex, the hush of his breath, the thud of his heart. The wolf was very strong, very menacing. I knew this was stupidly dangerous, but I didn't want to stop. Even with the violence threatening in this room, I didn't want to leave. What the hell had they been doing to him? If I walked out now, the pack won.

"He's making me change every night," Alex said, answering my unasked question. His voice was hoarse. It raised goose bumps down my spine.

"Why?" I said, still facing the door.

"To drive out the demons." He laughed. It had an ugly sound, like a madman's laugh. "And he calls me superstitious."

"What?" I turned.

Alex sat back in his seat, the leather and springs creaking. "Changing every night is supposed to reinforce the pack marque and loyalty. Get rid of the Athanate demon. It brings the wolf close to the surface."

"Yeah? Well, you look like shit," I said. If Felix thought he could 'cure' Alex, what might he have in store for me? What if he succeeded and Alex's marque went back to the pack, leaving me as the sole odd one out? At least he hadn't rejected Alex.

But if Alex was part Athanate, getting the wolf close to the surface made me worry about him turning rogue.

I inhaled his scent again. "And it's only a couple of nights, I guess, but I can still smell the difference between you and the rest of the pack."

Another tired smile chased across his face like the sun playing with the clouds. My stomach twisted, and it definitely wasn't coffee and doughnuts this time.

"No. And it won't change. I can feel it."

"So why keep it up?"

"Because I'm pack and Felix is the alpha."

"Why's it that way around? Is Felix stronger?"

Alex didn't like the question. His lips curled briefly in a snarl before he got it under control. "Felix wants the job and he's good at it. The pack is stable under him. The last thing we need now is a split pack."

"Oh, yeah. The other pack muscling in." I felt too warm. I made myself stroll casually to the desk, slipped my jacket and shoulder holster off and draped them over the back of the guest chair. I sat down, just the width of the desk between us and the tension building in the air. "That's one reason I had to see you."

"Gods, Amber, how many reasons are there?" A glimpse of the real Alex showed through and a little thrill startled me into a shiver.

"Three. It's traditional." I leaned back and carefully crossed my legs, the rasp of jeans loud in the quiet. Alex shifted uncomfortably, his breath coming slower and deeper. The wolf rippled beneath the surface of his face.

"Don't tease me," he said.

I deliberately misunderstood him. "Okay. I've found the other pack *does* have an Athanate connection."

He sat upright abruptly, making my heart lurch. "What?"

"One of the other Athanate in town is the leader of a faction of Athanate opposed to—"

"We know about Basilikos and Panethus, for God's sake. We're not stupid. You're saying this is Basilikos?"

"Yeah. Matlal's the name of the Athanate who's doing this."

"The same one who's looking for you?"

"How—"

"The pack's spread throughout Denver. We hear things, and your name gets our attention." He sat back again, thoughtful. "Makes sense. We heard the other pack was doing some of that looking for you."

I rolled my eyes. "Oh, joy. Athanate *and* Were chasing my tail. *And* the FBI."

He chuckled. The tension eased.

Well, that won't last.

"Message received," he said. "Why are you here, really?"

"You wouldn't answer the phone. I didn't know Olivia was your secretary, and even then, I wouldn't be happy leaving that message with her." I stopped and the silence pressed in on me. Big breath. "And I have to know where we stand, Alex, before the…before this weekend." All the smart ways to put it, and I was left with words tumbling out, clumsy as a child's building blocks.

It was important, and I couldn't quite put it into words even for myself, but where I stood with the rest of the Athanate somehow depended on who stood with me. And I wanted him to be standing with me, whether that was in body or in spirit. I needed it.

He didn't say anything. He got up and brought a jug and glasses from a side table, poured us water and handed one to me.

Our fingers brushed.

I could taste the desire in him. My Athanate was feeding on it. And Alex would know exactly how my body was responding. His wolf would be reading me: every page, every word, every letter, laid out before him. I might as well be writhing naked under a spotlight.

Was that reason two, or reason three for me to be here?

Down, girl. Reason three.

He sat back in his chair, gripping the armrests. His eyes wandered over me, lingering.

Oooh. I like.

"Olivia was right, it's not safe for you to be here."

"Why?" I asked.

"Because I'm not safe," he snapped. "The more I go to the wolf, the more he bleeds back into me. He's not changing my scent, but he's changing how I behave." His eyes looked up at me, full of hunger. I shivered again. "I can't…you can't ask a wolf to be restrained." He twisted in his chair, trying to look away. "Now go."

"No," I said. "I told you there were three reasons. I guess you found the first one worthwhile?"

His temper flared, but he kept it under control, barely.

There were two ways I could do this from here. I chose the sergeant's route. Frontal assault.

"Reason number two I've got to talk to you is Hope Gilliam."

Alex nearly lunged over the desk. He caught himself, grabbing the edge for support, or to restrain himself, and snarled wordlessly at me. His bone structure hadn't changed but I could see the wolf in his face, and it wasn't pleased.

I could face down Olivia, but Alex in this state was another matter. Not that I wanted to. The wolf was frightening. But the fear and desire were pooling in my belly, mixing into a heady cocktail of lust and my Athanate was *loving* it. I stood, Athanate smooth and slinky. Maybe reason three had to go in front of reason two. The woman before the sergeant. Time for a tactical change of plan.

How close to the edge can I go?

"Alex..."

"Get out," he said hoarsely. "It's not safe."

I didn't meet his eyes. Instinct kept my head down as I edged around the desktop. I made no wolf challenges to him. Athanate or Were, whichever was feeding me suggestions, kept it coming.

He was panting, his chest laboring as if he'd just run a mile. I slunk closer, eyes down, my own breathing raggedly matching his. My hands were desperate to hold his body, my eyes eager to look into his, my whole body aching for him.

Slowly. Slowly. I kept my eyes down.

"Not safe," he repeated, almost a note of panic in his voice.

I slid one hand under his jacket, flat against the crisp cotton of his shirt. He was burning beneath my palm.

"Olivia's here," I whispered. "Isn't she in danger too?"

He was trembling now. I laid my head gently against his chest, caressed it with my cheek as I eased his jacket back.

"Pack," he muttered. "Pack's safe."

"Hmmm." I nuzzled against him, thinking wolf thoughts, breathing in his scents. I nipped at the flesh of his neck as his jacket fell off, and tilted my head back to offer him my throat. "I'm pack too, remember."

This wasn't any fairy tale, and I wasn't ever going to tame this wolf. Certainly not now. He reeked of violence and I was coaxing him to unleash it, because that was what he needed. And because he needed it, I wanted it too. Just so long as I could ride the storm, I would be safe. Falling off would be fatal.

Despite his warnings, the man was still restraining the wolf. His hands hung loosely, and I knew I could turn away and walk out, if I wanted to. I didn't want to.

I'd have to goad him into releasing himself. He'd shown me how to do it, but gods above, I was going to have to rebuild bridges afterwards.

I pulled his head down until I felt his mouth on my neck. His jaw gaped reflexively, wolf instinct, and his teeth were suddenly gripping my throat. I flinched, awful images from that night in South America threatening to leap out from where I kept them. Then I took a shaky breath and relaxed.

I'm in your power, wolf. I'm submitting to you completely.

"Was Hope here, like this?" I asked, the words coming out as a croak from the awkward position.

His groan echoed in my chest and I nearly lost my nerve, but my Athanate could sense him slipping and whipped me on.

"Show me," I hissed.

He growled and shoved me back against the desk. His fingers tore at my belt and jeans, snapping the stud and breaking the zipper. As he ripped the clothes from my hips, his dark desire billowed out of him like a thundercloud.

Yes, yes, my Athanate was crying, drinking it in. I knew exactly what Alex wanted, how he wanted it, so clearly I could almost taste it. I was in his head. *His* lust was searing through *my* veins.

I reached for him.

But this wasn't the considerate man who'd teased me in his bed. He spun me around. The glasses, the jug of water and the writing pads went flying off the sides and I grabbed hold of the desk.

There was no touch, no warning other than the short, ugly rasp of his zipper before he thrust himself into me. Every sensation was overwhelmed by the fierce spike of passion that shot through both of us.

"Yes," I gasped, my face smeared against the unyielding wood, wet with the cold water spreading over it.

I'd never been so powerless making love; I was trapped against the desk by the battering of his lust. And I'd never felt so powerful, with an intoxicating sense of controlling this tornado of desire, discharging it through my body.

"Amber…" he groaned and I felt his teeth against the back of my neck, wolfish, biting, breaking skin. I reached and grabbed his hair, dragging him down closer to my face. Through the staccato panting of our lovemaking I told him how fantastic it felt.

His body convulsed; I could feel the surge of his orgasm lifting both of us, binding us together. His frantic thrusts blurred into one endless burning. I arched up and cried out as it took us. His matching call was strangled through vocal chords no longer fully human.

Our cries blended and died away and we slumped down onto the desk. "Alex," I whispered as we slid off and collapsed on the floor.

Chapter 37

It's undignified having your jeans around your ankles, even more than lying half naked and glowing from sex on the floor of the office, so I pulled my boots off and shucked my jeans and T. I hoped Olivia took her guard duty more seriously now than she had earlier. We stripped him, and I stretched my body over his, purring, sinking my claws into him.

Mine, mine, mine, yammered my Athanate triumphantly.

He snorted and was about to say something, so I pinned him back against the carpet with a kiss.

"Hmmm?" I asked, when I let him get his breath.

"That was stupid," he said.

"Yup." I rubbed against his chest.

"Hasn't changed anything."

"Uh-huh." It had, but I'd let him realize that in his own time.

"Why are you asking me about Hope?"

"Two reasons." I pressed two fingers against his chin.

"Do you have a numbered list for everything?" he complained.

I smiled. The wolf was still there, but deep in the shadows. I wondered if it ever went away. They say for every time you see the wolf, it has watched you one thousand times. I shivered.

"Of course I never spoke to my great-grandmother, when she was alive, but one of the wise phrases that was passed down was this: no one ever really dies as long as someone keeps them in their heart." He shifted beneath me, but stilled again. I kissed his chest, left side, fourth rib down. "You hold her. Let me share the burden."

He was silent for a long time. "What's the second?"

"Part of the first. I need to know how she died."

He tensed, and his scent roiled with conflict, but the wolf stayed hidden. I'd be able to deal with this using words.

"Why?" he said.

"To know her. And to make sure my heart and my head stay in line."

He snorted again, and the tension scent changed, became darker.

"She and I were both infused at the same time," he said. "I could change. She couldn't."

Ahhh.

"Then I'll say it again," I whispered, "for Olivia and for Hope, if I can help, I will."

But I'd pushed him onto a course and he wasn't listening this time. "It kills eventually," he muttered. "The body tries to force a change. It's agonizing. Some parts work, some don't." The stark horror of it oozed out of his voice. "I kept praying she could do it. Just hold off another minute, another minute. She was screaming for me to kill her."

I held him, my words useless for this pain.

"I don't know if I did, in the end, or if she just died. The pack…" he stopped for several breaths. "We were at Bitter Hooks with the pack. They gather for it. For support. They helped me bury her up there. The body…the thing that was left. It's there."

I will remember you, Hope. You will live in me and we will ease this pain together.

His breath sighed out in a long stream. "I'm sorry," he said.

"What for?"

"I was rough. Worse than that."

I lifted my head and stared at him. "I was asking for it. Not some male bullshit like 'walking down the street in the wrong type of clothes' asking for it. I wanted it, because I could feel you needing it. If I hadn't, believe me, you would have known about it, wolf. Understood?"

"Understood," he whispered.

"Good."

I laid my head back down on him, my hands flexing with the pleasure of feeling his body and the drifting sense of still being connected to him. *Mine.*

We lay listening to the beat of our hearts for a long time.

"I'm going to be in trouble with the pack for this," he murmured, lips against my hair. "So's Olivia. I'm supposed to stay away from you. She's supposed to help."

I chuckled. "Well, you said it; you can't be expected to restrain your wolf. If Felix wants you to make logical decisions, it's less wolf you need, not more."

"Huh? I thought your sister was the lawyer."

"Yeah, but she never beat me in an argument."

Gods, Kath. I'd heard her reaction to Jen. What the hell would she think of this?

He craned his head around to look at the back of my neck.

"You're bleeding," he said.

I kissed his shoulder, then bit it playfully. He wriggled around a little and began licking the back of my neck gently. I didn't know if it was like Athanate healing, but hell, it felt good.

In a little while, he stirred against me. "There's another thing you need to know about werewolves," he said, slyly. His hands began to knead my back.

I chuckled. "Stamina, eh?"

He wasn't much more restrained the second time around, and even my ordinary teeth nicked him. I tasted his blood and I worried that would set off some bloodlust reaction, but my Athanate was laughing at me.

Plenty of time for that later.

"Only one of us needs to walk out," I said and shoved him back towards his desk. "You get back to the work you haven't been doing."

"But, it'll be—"

"Yeah, embarrassing. No one ever died of that."

I had to shove him back a few more times before I made it out the door.

My jeans were ruined. Thank God for my belt, because there wasn't anything else keeping them on, and there was nothing left underneath. I was going to have a black eye from bouncing on the desk. My hair looked like my fright wig.

If that wasn't enough, we'd howled. Neither of us was the quiet type.

Olivia couldn't help but know, and that I didn't mind so much. But the way an office works, I doubted there was anyone on the whole site who didn't know their boss had just had his wicked way with his loose woman. And she'd liked it. Loudly.

Olivia had her head down.

I stopped in front of her. She wasn't giggling. She didn't look up. I was afraid she might be crying.

A stray curl had slipped from her hair tie, and I reached over to tuck it gently behind her ear. She pressed her cheek against my hand. Pack behavior. *I am weaker, protect me,* it said.

I pulled her chin up as I had before. "I meant it, Olivia. I don't know what I can do yet, but whatever I can, as soon as I can."

Her eyes looked up at me, faith and trust in them. Then she blushed and kissed my wrist. *Whoops.* Not the reaction I'd been aiming for. I had to stop broadcasting Athanate sex appeal and alpha Were domination.

Still, she looked a bit happier than she had. I smiled confidently at her and walked out.

I could sense the watchers.

The whole warehouse was looking across at the stairs the moment I hit the top step. My Athanate loved it. My head went up and I started to catwalk. Applause and wolf whistles—*if only you knew*—followed me out the door, and then I was striding across to the Ford.

Far from being embarrassed, it made me float away, practically intoxicated by the lust beamed at me from the warehouse.

Head in the clouds. That's the reason I walked straight into the site of Matlal's ambush.

Chapter 38

I couldn't haul my sorry ass to Haven looking like I'd done three rounds with a mountain lion.

I didn't want to go back to Manassah, because that would be the first place Matlal's teams would be looking. But Matlal might not know about David's house.

Craft is craft. No one knew that I was driving the Ford, and I wanted it to stay that way, so I parked two blocks away and walked, just another bag lady down on her luck, accidentally strayed into Wash Park.

But there's a difference between going through the motions and being focused. I was still floating.

I'd already opened the door and walked in before my nose got my attention and instincts took over. I lunged to the side and ended up crouched in a corner, with the HK swinging to and fro across the silent hall.

No one gave me the slow hand clap this time. No heads popped out from behind chairs. No tingles from my bracelet. The clock ticked on the wall. The breeze pushed the door against the stack of mail on the floor. I inched up to stand and began to search, leading with the HK.

The place smelled of Matlal *and* Altau, but it was empty.

On my second pass, I looked at it like a crime scene, even though I didn't have my kit. Who had been here? Where were they while they were here? What were they doing?

I could see from indentations on the carpet that a stool had been put beside the window. Someone had sat there watching the front. There was a cushion on the sofa where someone would have used it for a pillow if they'd been lying down. A team of two, taking turns to look out?

I checked the trash. Long stakeouts require food and drink. The trash cans were empty, but there was a lingering smell of oily fast food and coffee.

Why had they gone? And why bother to clean up afterwards?

The smell from the sofa was a mix of House Matlal and wolf. Was this the rival pack that Alex had said were looking for me?

The most confusing clue was when I cleared the litter of mail from near the door. Matlal's wolf had been injured here. He'd bled on the carpet, and on some of the mail. The scent of Altau was strong.

I couldn't stay here, not even long enough for a shower. I didn't know what had happened, but there were just too many scenarios that involved Matlal's team coming back here. I got out.

This time, I was doing the bag lady shuffle convincingly as I made my way up the road. I'd freaked my hair out even more.

Good thing.

I didn't turn as the SUV passed me. I didn't go slower or quicker. My hand was already inside my jacket as if I were cold, wrapped around the HK's grip.

I heard them stop and the doors opened, slammed shut again. All four doors. Four people at least. I came to the crossroads and snuck a look back as I turned left. The SUV was outside David's house, but whoever had come in it was out of my sight already. Two more limping steps to be certain I was out of their sight and then I took off.

Ten minutes later I pulled over and turned on the octopus.

Bian answered the call neutrally. The caller ID would be withheld.

"Bian, I need a secure number to call you on, now."

"Time to come in, Amber."

"Give me the number now. I have the recording. I'll come in soon." Sheer donkey stubbornness kept me resisting; there was no sensible reason for me to hold off now. She gave me a number and I called it right back. The disk that Ingram had given me was in the reader and I'd found the audio file. When she answered, I clicked play.

"Shit," she said, almost as soon as it played. "Shit. Shit. Shit. Amber, listen to me, nothing is safe out there. Get back here now." Fury and worry twisted her voice. I could tell she was regretting not hauling me in yesterday.

"Soon. Look, that's not all. I just came from David's. Something's screwed up there—maybe an ambush taken out. Matlal and Altau marques all mixed up. What's going on? I don't know how safe *anywhere* is at the moment."

"Hold on." I could hear her talking Athanate to someone. From the sound of it, she wasn't getting the answers she wanted.

I turned on my other cells while I waited. Skylur's secure cell was blank. On my personal cell, there was nothing from the colonel. Just a single, simple text message.

Mike 6 call Bravo 5.

Keith had used that message to get me to call him last week. He'd come with news that my old master sergeant, Top, was dead. He'd brought a parting gift of my Ops 4-10 equipment. He'd warned me that things were changing in 4-10, and gave me the first hint that Colonel Laine had a problem. Keith and I had a history, but he was married now, and with the situation at 4-10, he shouldn't be contacting me unless it was really important. What did he want? The first stirring of nervousness began. I noted the number and turned the cell off.

Bian was getting increasingly tense with whatever answers she was getting.

She came back on the line. "Amber, are you sure about the marques? Matlal *and* Altau?"

"Positive. There was a stakeout there and a fight. The place was empty when I arrived but as soon as I left, a car pulled up and at least four people went in. Didn't stop to check who they were. Cleanup crew? New stakeout?"

She was silent for a while.

"I don't know anything about this," she said. "My team don't know anything about this."

"How bad is that?"

Bian was Diakon of House Altau. Officially, a Diakon was the person who controlled the connection between the Athanate House and the rest of the world. In practice, that made her number three in House Altau. Number two if you accepted Diana's description of her role as being advisory. And Bian was head of security. There weren't a huge number of Altau from what I could see, so how on earth could there be Altau out here without Bian knowing about it?

"I don't know. Amber, I've just put my team under quarantine until I clear this up with Skylur. Don't tell anyone and come straight in."

She ended the call.

I filled up with gas and drove out towards City Park to get away from any tracking on my personal cell. I'd forgotten Skylur's cell and reached over to turn it off. There was a text message from him.

Situation escalated. Deception over. Come in now.

I turned it off.

Bian and Skylur had now both given me a direct order to get out to Haven. But my inner donkey had all my paranoia and my curiosity lending it strength.

Just the one quick call.

The octopus made its connections and I got through.

"Keith, it's me."

"Amber, thank God." It was Keith, talking from a busy street somewhere and sounding…different.

"Can you meet me?" he said.

"Kinda difficult today." I really didn't like the sound of this. What the hell was going on?

"It's about JL. Can't talk on the cell."

JL was the colonel. This got worse and worse. I needed time to think.

"Gonna have to be patient. Are you staying on this number?"

"No. Can I call you?"

"No." I didn't know how you could call into the octopus, and if I had I wouldn't give that away, ex-boyfriend or not. Who might be listening to Keith's cell?

He spouted a stream of gibberish. Embedded in the gibberish were numbers in Vietnamese, a language we shared working knowledge of.

"Okay," I said, and he would know I had the cell number he wanted me to call next. "You here privately, or for the firm?"

"Privately."

I ended the call.

I could turn Keith down and head for Haven. That was the most sensible thing to do, by a long shot.

I could call that number and show up somewhere we agreed. That felt like the dumbest option, and realizing that made me feel ill. Not Keith, surely? Why would he betray me? But I plain didn't believe him. The way he'd spoken and what he'd said just didn't feel like Keith. I couldn't believe he had a private reason for seeing me that involved the colonel.

First decision: I had to check it out. I owed it to Colonel Laine. Second decision: how? I needed some kind of fallback if it did go wrong. There wasn't time to set up a safe meeting using Victor. Not that I had the money to hire Victor's team for another afternoon's work. Of course, I could ask Jen to loan me the money, and I knew she'd say yes.

While I thought it through, I stopped on Colfax to get something to eat. No knowing when I'd next get the chance.

"Uh, ma'am, your change." The kid was holding it out to me at arm's length and not meeting my eyes. Okay, I still looked a fright, but I didn't smell, did I? Or rather, not a smell that he could detect.

His supervisor came over and passed me a large safety pin with a smile.

Ahh. Yes.

"Thanks. I guess I better find somewhere to change, huh?"

She laughed. "Seen worse. 'Specially at night."

I juggled the coffee and fruit, got the safety pin through my jeans without stabbing myself and headed back for the car, dignity personified.

I'd reached my decision.

You have to trust someone. I trusted Diana. I trusted Bian. I trusted the colonel.

I needed to know what was going on. I had to trust some more people.

As little as I wanted to, I set up the octopus and I called the number I knew I had to.

Chapter 39

I knew I'd been betrayed. I just wasn't sure who and how many times.

I didn't know how many Athanate knew about David's house and how close I was to him. Skylur, Diana, Bian, Pia, David himself, the Fang team, Mykayla and whoever had been driving the van they came in; they had all been there on Monday night. Then there was whoever they talked to.

But what if someone had been tracking my cell back then? I wanted to believe that, but Bian's response to the recording wasn't comforting.

And forget about me for a moment, what about the rest of Altau? There was a traitor in the House. What did that mean for Panethus?

Why wasn't Skylur talking to Bian, and who were the Altau in Denver? Bian had to know more than she was telling me.

Now this.

I leaned against the wall, half-hidden by the curtain, and looked down on the little patch of grass outside the convention center far below.

If Skylur didn't pick up the tab for Victor, I was now a long way overdrawn. Downtown hotel rooms don't come cheap even if all you want is to look out the window. And the new burn phone, camera and binoculars in my hand were bought on credit that I couldn't cover. I guessed I could sell the Audi, but then how would I work? Even the HK had value, but I might as well start donating organs if I went that route.

Maybe Victor's offer was the way out financially. He'd make a good boss.

Maybe Arvinder. No money problems in House Singh.

But that was the next issue, after I settled this one.

I raised the binoculars. The army had ruined me for cheap equipment. I'd bought the top of the line German optics. They brought him in so close I felt I could reach out and touch his cheek. He looked so familiar: the sandy hair, light enough to be ruffled by the breeze, the slightly rounded shoulders that came from him sticking his hands deep in his jacket pockets, the long legs. He looked as handsome as he had when we were both in Ops 4-10. When we were an item and my name on his lips had made me feel good. I just felt a cold lump in my stomach now.

Maybe I was wrong. Maybe.

Matt's octopus complained about the single hotel wireless system, but he'd told me it would be secure for a couple of short calls.

I watched as Keith took the cell from his pocket.

"Hello?"

"Keith, I'm running late."

"No problem. How late?" In the binoculars I could see his face screw up in frustration, but his voice stayed calm and reasonable. My gut feeling got worse. His left hand remained in his jacket pocket.

Come on, come on, come on. Time was ticking away and I had to make my judgment call on this.

"Say what? I'm picking up a bit of background noise."

His left hand came out and shielded the cell. "That better? I just asked how late?"

My heart sank. "Better, thanks. Difficult to say. Need to be sure I don't have a tail. I'll call you in ten."

I ended the call and tried to stop the tears. It didn't mean anything, really. It wasn't as if we were still an item. He was just doing his job, just following orders. But Keith, for God's sake.

The ring wasn't on his finger; Ops 4-10 standard operating procedures—no jewelry on a mission. Keith wasn't here for a private meeting. He was here to take me in. As I watched, he hit a speed dial and spoke with someone. That would be his team, probably in the sports club's parking garage across the road, or in the convention center, maybe even in the lobby of the hotel. Updating them. *She's late, she's still coming, next update ten minutes.*

I dialed the next number.

"Since even my best equipment can't trace the call, I'm guessing this is you, Ms. Farrell," he drawled. "Now I'm truly praying you do have something for me, 'cause y'know, a little agent like me has got to expend a whole lot of career credit to put an operation this size together on a promise."

Little agent, my ass. Ingram had clearance on this from the National Security Director with one phone call. Everyone in the FBI had their tails up to find out what the hell was going on under their noses.

For me, I'd had enough. I'd been loyal to Ops 4-10, but it wasn't loyalty that'd cover getting put back in that cell for the scientists to experiment on. It wasn't loyalty that'd cover getting kidnapped off the street. It wasn't loyalty that had been repaid.

And Agent Ingram had hit me hard with his comment at Manassah. If the goddamn National Security Director didn't know about Ops 4-10, just who the hell did? I'd sweated this afternoon, reviewing every operation I'd ever been on. There wasn't one that felt wrong, and I'd been happier when I'd come to that conclusion. But what had Ops 4-10 done since then? What about Keith's comments last week about the way command problems were expected to be handled on the base. Who had oversight of this?

Well, it was time to take the covers off.

"Ms. Farrell? You there?"

"Sorry. Yeah, Agent Ingram, we are good to go. The hammer is on the junction of 14th and Welton, right in front of the convention center. I'm transmitting a photo to you now. This is…" the breath caught in my throat, "this is Sergeant Keith Alverson, of a covert special operations battalion called Ops 4-10." I stopped, staring blankly at nothing, realization coursing through me.

Shit. I'd just breached it. I'd pulled off the covers.

"Ms. Farrell?"

"Sorry. The anvil, well, I told you, these guys are good, I haven't got any confirmed spots, but there are three or four locations where I'd put a team."

"Yup. I'm looking at a map. 'Cross the street, in the center, the café and hotel. Hold on."

I could hear him moving teams around. "Green," someone called out. "Green on teams one, two and four. Red on three. Nine minutes."

"Nine minutes and counting, Ms. Farrell. We'll move in."

"I'll run a distraction," I said. The misery clenched in my stomach. Keith. For God's sake, Keith.

"Yeah, a phone call will be good."

"I'm going down there."

"No—"

I cut the connection and slung everything into the backpack.

Coming up to nine minutes, I was walking towards him. He saw me and turned, his hair ruffling. I couldn't read the expression on his face. I wondered what he saw on mine.

"You never did tell me who the ring was for, Keith," I called out by way of a greeting.

He looked startled. "Yeah, I guess not. Julie. Remember her?"

I did. She was all right, Julie. He could have done much worse. "I do. Does she know where you are?"

"I'm not here to break up my marriage." He started to sound edgy. "What's the problem, Amber?"

"So she doesn't know where you are."

"What's the problem?" he said again.

The gap closed. This was stupid. I'd said I would run a distraction, not land myself in the middle of an FBI operation. Ingram would chew me out for this, and I'd deserve it. But I couldn't stop myself.

"This is nothing to do with the colonel, is it? Julie doesn't know where you are because you're under SOP. She doesn't know what you're doing, but if she did, do you think she would agree with it?"

"What are you talking about, Amber?" He hadn't lied, because he hadn't answered, but there was guilt written all over his face, laced through his scent and in the speeding of his heart.

"You can't lie to me, you never could and you sure as hell can't now. Who's calling the shots on this op, Keith? Who sanctioned it? Do you know who you're really working for today?"

A couple of trucks moved down the road. One slowed and turned to block the line of sight from the parking garage, the other pulled up in front of the café.

Keith knew. We'd run ops together, he was trained as well as I was—maybe he was better now, since he was current. His eyes darted left and right. I'd have been running already, but then again, I'd never done an op on American soil. The rules would change.

"Don't run," I whispered. I didn't know what their rules of engagement were, but the FBI were hot for this.

"What the—"

"FBI. If you're legit, you've got nothing to worry about." I turned before he could see I was crying. "Goodbye, Keith," I said.

"Amber! Amber," he called out. Armed agents in Kevlar vests were sprinting towards us. I half-turned. His hands were held out at his side. He wasn't going to be stupid. The look on his face…I might have thought there was relief, but I just didn't believe in him anymore.

"Amber," he said again, and I did turn, I had to. That's how I am. An agent jostled me as he passed. I barely noticed it. Keith's face was twisted, as if in pain. They'd wrestled him down on the ground. "What did they do to you?" he called out, as the agents started the process of cuffing and searching.

Nothing. I turned and started to walk away. More agents jostled me till I felt like I was in a pinball machine. I looked back once more, but he was hidden behind the dark jackets. Nothing.

They did nothing to me. I started to trot, bouncing off people. Someone was calling me, far away. I broke into a sprint. Across the road. Car horns blaring at me. They did nothing. Nothing. Nothing. Nothing.

Chapter 40

I don't know how many bars there were laid out that way in Denver, but I found too many.

The room was deep enough to be difficult to see in and there was a mirror on the far wall behind the bar, so I could sit with my back to the door and keep one eye open, on the remote chance that whoever was following me found me by accident.

I was pleased that I was so responsible, because I was also drunk.

It had been at least ten minutes since the last drink, and I was thirsty and running short of cash, so I got a couple of Blue Moons. The bartender tried the joke with the slice of orange on the glass and I growled at him. He retreated to the other end where his regulars sat, far away from the bag lady with the crazy eyes and the bruises.

I hadn't gotten drunk like this since '05. We'd lost six of the platoon in a night ambush. One of them was the lieutenant we were supposed to be looking after. I was a corporal at the time, and went drinking with the other three squad leaders. Including Keith.

Keith had been here, in Denver, only a week ago, warning me about changes in the unit. He'd said that none of the people I knew in 4-10 would take a mission to come after me, and yet he'd been there this afternoon. What had changed in a week?

Was I missing something? Did I deserve to be back in that isolation cell? What had so upset me this afternoon that I'd gone on a bender? Every time I thought back to my reaction to Keith's last words, it flowed away, as if I was trying to grab smoke.

Booze is okay for questions, but I've never found it's good for answers. And I couldn't afford to drink any more. I certainly didn't need to drink any more.

I looked in the mirror. One drunk, scruffy, five-ten, sharp-nosed, auburn-haired mix of Irish and Arapaho looked back. I didn't look evil. At least I could see myself in the mirror. Vampires aren't supposed to be visible in mirrors. How would that work? I laughed.

"It works because vampires don't exist, so that's why you can't see them in the mirror. Perfectly logical," I muttered.

The bartender looked at me laughing and shifted uncomfortably. He might be working up to refusing me another, if I was asking. I wasn't.

I drained the last beer and he edged over. I stared at him.

Go on, tell me I've had enough, punk.

"You want me to call a cab?" he said.

I shook my head, feeling a bit ashamed. "I'll walk it off."

Jeez. All the way to Haven. Not likely. Maybe I'd need to call for a lift. I could see that going down almost as well as my failure to get to Haven as soon as possible.

"Not a good idea to be wandering around at this time of night," he mumbled.

I thanked him and swiveled on the seat. He was right, and he'd done his job. I'd clear my head first and then take it from there.

It'd gotten cold outside. At least I had the jacket, and my pack kept my back warm. I was still wearing drafty jeans held together with a safety pin, though. I shook my head again and started walking. I had a long way to go to get back to the car and yeah, I needed to get there for the octopus, so I could make a call, so I could get taken to Haven and get chewed out by Skylur. Better that than either Jen or Alex seeing me in this state.

Dumb.

I took a short cut. Even dumber.

I was still wrapped up in a cheerful, oblivious haze, wondering why the bracelet felt a bit itchy, when the first hiss of warning came out of the night.

"Hey, *chica*. Hey, hey, over here." Someone made kissing noises and they laughed. At least a dozen of them by the sound of it.

I stopped and turned around. A couple of them strolled from the shadows, followed by others.

"Shit. Not so little, eh? *Mamacita, aqui, aqui.* Come here. I'll look after you. I'll make you so-o-o happy." Big mouth.

They were part of the street gangs that come and go. All taken in with the drag-ass jeans and silly hand sign glamor. Tattoos and testosterone. One of them had half his head shaved. For all their Mexican slang, they were as random a mix as these streets could throw up. And they were plenty old enough for this to get ugly.

If I'd have been sober, I would have come up with a comment and kept walking. The alley wasn't that long.

There were a dozen of them. Some would be armed. I was alone and drunk. The HK was in the pack and sudden moves to reach for it would be like blowing a starting whistle.

I took a head-clearing breath and looked at the darkness where they'd stepped from. My Athanate eyes saw clearly, now I was looking. There was another one there, seated, watching. *El Jefé,* the boss man, the one with the agenda to own a patch of turf, to get respect on the back of his crew. He wanted them blooded, outside of society and bound to him. The weak parallel with the Athanate made me snort, even as I realized there wasn't a way out of this.

"Hey!" Half-head sneered when I just stood there as they got closer. *"Marimacha! Es' chavala tiene cojones."*

"Why should she run away when she's found what she wants?"

"Eh-ya, *la putita con buen culito.* I liked it better when she was looking the other way," Big-mouth said.

"Shit, y'always do, nigga."

The gang laughed and jostled each other as they crowded in. Oh, that was so funny.

The lookout at the far end started walking in, wanting to be part of it too. Mistake.

I stopped listening. My street Spanish wasn't that good anyway. It was good enough to hear 'little girl' and 'hot babe' give way to 'butch' and 'whore' quickly. Hard on the heels came the gang insider jokes about anal rape. I hadn't even said anything back to them, but they didn't care about that. They didn't want to think of me as a person; they wanted me to be a mindless thing, in their power, terrified and in pain.

And the boss watched from the shadows. The code was blood in, blood out—murder to get into the gang and execution if you tried to get out. Rape would do as a trigger for blood in. Once you've done it, you gotta kill the whore, don't you? You owe it to your homies.

This was the side of humanity that fueled Basilikos. I would do well to remember that.

But I learned something else as I stood there. The elethesine hormone that fires up an Athanate boils off alcohol like spit in a furnace.

Half-head leaned and pointed. "Lookit the cute pin. She been pricked already, hey?"

Suddenly sober or not, my head was fresh out of words and what came out of my throat was a growl.

"Shit!" One of the gang with his tattoos still scabbed took a couple of steps back. "What the fuck?" A couple of them looked nervous.

"Ha!" Big-mouth spat. "Cut's growling, must be hungry." He grabbed his crotch. "Shame. Not your—"

Down where I'd turned in to walk up the alley, a man came around the corner. He interrupted Big-mouth, running up the alley and shouting. I loved him for it, but Agent Ingram really should have been waving his gun to come steaming in against these odds.

"Shut that motherfucker up," Big-mouth said, shoving a couple of the others.

He turned back, wiped his mouth. Half-head reached out for my safety pin, teasingly slow.

I grabbed his wrist.

"Eh?" he looked bewildered. I was supposed to be cringing or trying to run away. This wasn't how it had gone before. What had he done wrong?

He'd picked on one angry Athanate.

I slammed the heel of my hand up into his nose, breaking it. When he reeled back, I twisted and threw his body, face down, onto the ground. Then I pinned his arm with my boot and broke his elbow like a rotten branch. He screamed.

Big-mouth should have grabbed me; he had time. He went for his knife instead.

I don't like knives. There's the old joke that the winner in the knife fight is the one who gets to go to the hospital, and it has some justification. I got in close, gripping his wrist. My other hand thudded into his groin, got a good crushing hold and I lifted him up and tossed him, squealing like a captured rat, into an open dumpster.

The fight seemed to have gone from the remainder. Ingram was down, but safe enough.

I leaped into the recess where *el Jefé* had watched his crew come apart and caught him as he was desperately trying to find a way to escape into the house backing onto his turf. Too slow.

I dragged him out into the alley by his throat. His hands were frantically scrabbling, trying to ease my grip on him. His eyes were bugged out as he realized he had seconds to live. I lifted him, flicked his feet back and planted him down on his knees. Hard. I could hear the cracks.

My fingers hooked deeper. In a second I would rip and tear and his blood would splatter down onto the dirt of the alley. I wouldn't deign to feed from filth like this, but the wolf in me wanted to hear his last sucking breaths as he drowned in his own blood.

"Sergeant Farrell! Sergeant! Stop. Let him go!"

I spun where I stood, dragging the gang leader around, and snarled at Ingram.

"It's over. It's over," he said. "You don't need to do that. Put him down."

Ingram. FBI. Everything flooded back, dispersing the animal rage. I opened my hand and *el Jefé* pitched forward and stirred feebly in the dirt.

The rest of the gang were gone and the three that were still here weren't going anywhere in a hurry.

I squatted down beside Ingram, trembling.

"You okay?" I said. My voice was hoarse.

"Yeah. Thanks." He tried to regain a little composure. I offered him a hand up, the left one without all the blood, and pulled him back to his feet.

"Yeah, I am," he repeated. "Thanks to you."

"You wouldn't have been out here if it wasn't for me, so I guess it's my responsibility, in a way," I said. "You were chasing after me, weren't you?"

"I prefer 'shadowing'," he said.

"Have it your way." I held up my right hand and looked at it. Normal hand, no claws. I wiped the blood off on my jeans. "Ahh, were there any casualties this afternoon?"

He shook his head.

Thank goodness. Even if they were trying to trap me.

"They're not talking and no one has popped out of the woodwork and claimed them yet, either. But they will, they will."

I snorted. "Why'd you call me Sergeant back there?" I said. Stupid thing to ask.

"I called you a whole lot of things, Ms. Farrell. That was just what got through, it seems. What in hell was all that?" He made a vague gesture at everything that had gone on.

Another figure arrived at the mouth of the alley. Never got Tweedledum without Tweedledee, I guessed.

"I'm outa here," I said, turning to walk the way I'd been going. It *was* a short cut.

Griffith called after me, but I ignored it. Ingram hushed him and I heard them calling an ambulance for the gangbangers.

What was all that, indeed? The feelings that had run through me like electricity hadn't been what I was expecting from the Athanate side. My hand hadn't just clawed at *el Jefé's* throat, the nails had gone hard and sharp like daggers. I'd known that I could rip his throat out. I'd known it, not at an intellectual level, at a physical level. My body knew it could do that. I'd part-changed into a wolf.

Having Were and Athanate mixing in me felt dangerous. Were blood lust, if that's what it had been, had seemed to be as close to Athanate rogue as I'd been warned. Maybe they would feed from one another, if I let them.

Just as I needed help from Altau on my Athanate side, I was going to need help from the pack on my Were side. As Liu had said, that anger deep down inside wasn't good for anyone. It needed better management. And having the Were come through while I was still learning the Athanate stuff made it all feel insanely volatile.

How would Top have put it? *Use a flamethrower to shed a little light on what you got in the ammo store, why dontcha?*

I was finished being dumb tonight. I reached the car and got in with a sigh. What if that'd been Matlal's crew I ran into in the alley? Being so smart and picking bars with mirrors was pathetic. They could have just waited outside.

Instead of three injured gangbangers and Griffith hyperventilating about me walking off, I could have been delivered up to Matlal by now. Whatever he wanted would have been worse than the gang.

I slapped the visor down and slid the cover off the little vanity mirror.

"All the mirrors, in all the bars, in all of Denver, and now she wants to talk," Tara said.

"Sorry, sis. Plain dumb, huh?"

"You said it."

"You know anything about what happened when Keith…"

"Can't see what you can't see, sis. Get your ass to Haven, now."

I got.

Chapter 41

Reception at the gatehouse was cool, formal. I guessed the appearance of unhappiness from Skylur had filtered down and everyone believed I was not the flavor of the month. The deception might be over, but the truth hadn't been made available. Either that, or by not coming in immediately when he texted, I was genuinely back on the shit list.

Following directions, I made my way through the silent house to the room that David and Pia had been allocated. Late as it was, they were still out working. The room was large and luxurious, with a bed the size of a small swimming pool. Nice to know they were being looked after.

Bian arrived, throwing open the door and startling me. I had a glimpse of an escort in the corridor and steeled myself. She saw where my eyes went and kicked the door closed.

I wondered nervously which Bian I had tonight.

It was the Diakon, maybe.

"My escort, not yours, Round-eye."

"In Haven?" I couldn't quite keep the incredulity out of my voice.

She just looked at me.

What the hell was going on?

I retrieved the SD with the recording from my laptop and handed it over.

She stared at it lying in the palm of her hand like it was a scorpion.

"This is that bad?" I asked.

Her fingers closed around the disk. "This is not good for me, personally. Or for Altau," she said.

The door opened again.

Skylur. An angry Skylur.

He closed the door behind him with exaggerated care and motioned me to a seat in front of the window. Bian sat on the edge of the bed.

He folded himself into the seat opposite me and laid his linked hands in his lap. His eyes were hooded, the brilliant blue gleaming from the depths of shadow. He looked tired.

"You got my message," he said quietly.

It wasn't a question, but I nodded.

"And you've turned up here in the middle of the night. Twelve hours later." He ran his eyes up and down me. "You've been in a fight. Matlal?"

"No." The bruises and torn jeans were from Alex, but I wasn't about to tell him that. "A gang jumped me as I was making my way to the car to come here."

"What were you doing wandering around Denver?"

I was in the wrong, but I wasn't going to sit and listen to this for too long.

"Look, Matlal didn't get me. The closest he got was when I used your secure phone and they were tracking it."

It got so quiet I could hear them talking in the corridor. I shouldn't have stayed out there, but my argument was sort of valid. The most dangerous thing happening was that Altau had a spy feeding Matlal information.

I wanted Bian to say I had a good point, like Diana would have, but she didn't. In fact, Skylur was the one to admit it, even if it was with the curtest of nods.

"I grant you that. You provided us with the proof and you evaded the Matlal teams yesterday."

I thought that was better, but he went on.

"Which was a fraction of the number of Athanate and Were searching for you as soon as they found out you'd tricked them. Over two hundred, Amber. Not just their elite squads. In fact, most of House Matlal."

He let that sink in. I'd thought a couple of dozen at worst.

"And they knew enough about you to track you down at any of your usual places. I've had to change long-running plans and use assets that I held in reserve to cover you, flush the ambushes. The ramifications are still running. I keep things secret for a purpose," he said, his voice going colder. "I do *not* like my purposes crossed."

"There are so many Basilikos in the city that even the Warders have had to admit they've noticed it and make complaints to Matlal," said Bian. "And everyone, *everyone,* now knows that you're being hunted by Matlal, and most of them think they know why. And Panethus are demanding to know why there appear to be no Altau in the city."

"Hold on, I'm not responsible for leaking information," I snapped back. "I'm not responsible for the numbers of Altau, which you won't even explain to me. And the rest of what I was doing out there was important. If it crossed your purposes, you should've briefed me better."

Skylur sat forward, frustration coloring his voice. "Perspective, Amber! Matlal was distracted. You achieved that. You provided us with the evidence on the spy. Everything else was just more risk. Unjustifiable risk."

Well, some of it had been risky and not agreed to with Skylur, like working with the FBI. But Diana had specifically said I must not discuss Emergence with Skylur—he had to have plausible deniability in front of the Assembly. Which gave me another problem. How was it going to look if I said that I needed to speak to Bian privately about that, if she was under some suspicion herself? Better to keep this until I could talk to Diana. The same about the colonel as well.

But it was becoming clearer to me that although Skylur might be angry at me, there was something else he was even angrier about. Okay. He was taking it out on me because I happened to be in the way. Not so okay, but I could handle that.

"Well, now that we're talking about it, what else have I done wrong?"

"You've represented us to the werewolves without authority," said Bian quietly.

"I talked to them, on a matter for them. When it became apparent there's been a breakdown in communications with Altau—"

"Stop. I understand, Amber," Skylur cut across me. "I am much less concerned with that anyway. Simply inform me in future."

I seethed, but quietly. What part of 'a matter for them' didn't he understand? But the wording of the oath I was scheduled to take the next day came back to me. That didn't give me leeway. I was being herded into something I didn't fully buy into by the lack of alternatives. And I saw the contradictions in my thinking. If I said there were matters that were just for the pack, then I had to accept there were matters that were just for the Athanate. Both increasingly felt wrong, but they weren't something to fix tonight.

What would Top have done? Play the hand he was dealt.

I took a deep breath. "Okay. My apologies. I can't say I won't get it wrong again, but I'll try not to." I paused. "What's my situation now?"

"Unchanged," said Skylur. "This is not a prison, but you have to stay here while Basilikos remain in Denver, other than in exceptional circumstances."

Everyone was calmer. I'd done what I could out there. Alex and the pack were at least aware of what was going on. Jen was staying anonymously in hotels with guards. Tullah was out of the way, and I suspected it would be an unwise Athanate that went up against Kaothos. With them off my mind temporarily, I could handle the Assembly.

"You need to understand." Skylur leaned forward again, resting his elbows on his knees. "I cannot let you—"

One of his staff opened the door and said something. Some of the team outside looked pale with shock.

Skylur's face went stiff, and he rose.

"Ten minutes, meeting room 6," he said to Bian curtly and strode away without a glance.

I glared after him.

"Cut him some slack," Bian said.

"I am."

"Not enough, Amber." She checked that the door was closed and bent close to me, making my heart stutter. "Listen, it's not all your fault, but you don't understand the position you put Skylur in."

"Then explain it to me!"

"This is Basilikos' perfect storm. If Matlal starts a war, Panethus and the independents would unite against Basilikos. But if Skylur were to start a war, not only would Panethus split, but the independents would stand aside, except the Midnight Empire."

"Okay, I understand that. But Skylur isn't—"

"Panethus need a strong leader," Bian went on, talking over me. "They expect a strong leader. They think they know what your Blood will do. Some of them would have expected him, *required* him to go to war if you had been taken by Basilikos today, simply on the threat that might pose. And they would have split if he had not, in which case Basilikos would strike anyway. Think on that hanging over his head this last couple of days. Now you're safe and he should move to the next concern—keeping Panethus together in the Assembly. And now..." she shook her head. "Well, have some appreciation for his position."

One of her escort put her head around the door and spoke briefly in Athanate, while listening to something on an earplug. Bian went to the door and paused with it held shut. "This has been a frightening buildup to the Assembly, and you've had your part in that, Round-eye. Some of it's your doing and some of it's not. We may be on the brink of a war, which cannot be won, and will be a complete disaster for the whole Athanate. It's a real worry that he hasn't been talking to me, but..." she glanced at me over her shoulder, "I still trust him. He's the only one who can get us through this." She bowed her head and closed her eyes for a minute as if gathering her strength, then squared her shoulders and went out. I was alone again.

Damn. Some of it *was* my fault. Not the war, even though I might have been a trigger to start it. But I had caused problems when they should have been concentrated on the volatile situation. I'd been stupidly angry with Skylur, reacting rather than thinking things through. I wasn't going to waste time second-guessing my decisions from today, but I did have to grant them they had reason to be unhappy with me. And I'd been rattled enough by what'd happened today I wasn't thinking clearly. My mind skittered away from it all. Now, there was whatever had just happened in Haven that had shocked everyone, which no one wanted to explain to me.

I gave up guessing and took a shower, then collapsed on the bed, wrapped up in Pia's bathrobe. I was too tired to deal with things like finding new clothes to wear. I made sure Tullah's emergency cell was at the bedside, and everything else was off.

The next thing I knew, Pia was bending over me. I struggled to get up, but she pushed me back.

"Just rest, I'll get the bedclothes straightened out."

We tugged the sheets around until they covered me and then she left me to go take a shower. I drifted off again. A few minutes later and she slipped in beside me, warm and smelling of lavender soap. And buck naked.

I woke up in a hurry. I was Mistress of an Athanate House. I had duties. I swallowed nervously. Blood was out; Skylur's ban was still in place. That left sex, I guessed. Crap. I surged up. I did not want—

Pia seemed to understand. She giggled. "Relax."

She slipped out of bed and came back in what I guessed was David's bathrobe.

We sat on the bed a little awkwardly.

"I've made progress on the charter you asked for," she said. "But Skylur's been keeping us very busy."

"I'm looking forward to the charter. What have you guys—"

Pia held up a hand. "Mustn't say," she said. "Direct orders from Skylur. Talk to no one."

"Did that mean me?"

She looked thoughtful. "Possibly not. I suppose we could assume—"

"No." I stopped her and saw relief in her expression. "No. I've been too close to the edge with Skylur this week. I'm not going to push it." I narrowed my eyes. How far did this House bond go? "Just for interest—"

"Yes, Mistress," she murmured, lowering her eyes. "I would answer if you asked."

I wouldn't. I wouldn't put her in that position. That would definitely be a misuse of my authority. The feeling of Athanate connections came back to me. Confusing, powerful. Even a little scary.

"I told you, Pia, it's Amber. Definitely not Mistress," I said, mock angry.

She smiled a little. "That's in public." She looked down again. "In private, I need the Mistress of my House. Calling you that helps me feel the connection with you."

"What's it like?" I asked, curious.

"The connection? A little of everything. My spouse, my boss, my priest, my team captain, my big sister, my friend."

I chuckled uneasily. "Damn! I hope I can manage all that."

"You will," she said, and this time her smile was stronger.

"Can I ask about when you were in House Altau?" I was worried that might be taboo for Athanate.

"Of course!"

"Was the connection like that with Skylur?"

She shook her head. "It was a very safe feeling, being part of Altau. And we're affiliate, so I can sort of keep that." She tilted her head. "But it was never so…" she frowned and shrugged, "companionable, I guess. Skylur was always too busy for me. Diana's too scary and Bian's too, well, Bian for me." She paused.

"I'd never get to sit on the bed with Skylur and just talk about things." I could feel her contentment, almost smugness. "And you've made me exotic and popular. Our marque is attractive. I can't tell you what a boost that's been. Even tucked away and working my butt off, I've never had so many proposals before."

"As in you're getting proposals for sharing blood?"

"They're not allowed to have the real thing," she looked shyly at me, "so they try for the next best. But Skylur says no Blood for the moment, and besides, I don't want to dilute it in any way. I really want to be House Farrell, Mistress."

My Athanate purred.

"And as for the other proposals," she gave a contented little growl, "I have David. Or at least, I do when we have time. Been a bit busy this week."

I laughed and leaned back against the headboard. This wasn't so bad.

David stumbled in at that point, hollow-eyed with fatigue.

He came and sat on the edge of the bed and Pia twisted around and gave him a hug. He spared a smile for me.

"Done?" Pia asked.

"Yes, finally finished."

"Go shower and come to bed," said Pia, giving him a gentle shove in the right direction and watching him as he dragged himself into the bathroom, shedding clothes.

She was facing away from me and her beautiful hair cascaded down her back, black waves making a startling contrast with the white bathrobe.

I picked up a stray lock and let it run through my fingers like a piece of silky midnight.

Kath had always had beautiful hair too. We'd sat just like this countless times.

Pia sighed and stretched, shaking her head and making the whole dark waterfall shiver.

I combed it back with my fingers.

"That's nice, Mistress," she murmured. "Why so sad?"

I hesitated, then went on combing. "I was thinking of my sister, how we used to do this. Now she hates me."

"We are sisters, now," she whispered.

David's shower stopped. It was very quiet.

"There were a lot of other roles for me," I said.

"You're doing well, believe me."

She leaned back a little, so I could run my fingers the whole length of her hair. I could feel her willing my dark thoughts away. "You get ten Mistress points right now," she said.

"For combing your hair?"

"With your fingers. In bed. And you only get one for the combing. The other nine are for enjoying it." She sighed. "I can feel that. It feeds me and it feeds the bonds between us."

"Oh." That wasn't so difficult. "Good."

David came to bed. At least he had a pair of boxers on.

My uncomfortable feeling returned, but in seconds they arranged themselves on either side of me like brackets. David was asleep as soon as he lay down, his face against my shoulder.

Pia switched the light off and settled down on her pillow. The earlier tension was back. It was wrong. I did have a duty and it was for nothing more than we'd felt while I combed her hair.

Moving tentatively, I reached out and pulled her closer. She wriggled up against me until her head rested on my pillow and she let a last small sigh escape.

I was tired. A profound sense of Athanate family stole over me. I would do everything to be worthy of the trust that they were placing in me. Some mysterious Athanate response kicked off in me and Pia breathed deeply and purred as she fell asleep. David shifted closer without waking.

Haven wasn't home, by a long shot, but this was my Athanate family. I was putting out something soothing in my marque and they were unconsciously reacting in the same way. It felt like I was being stroked to sleep.

I slept very well. All the more shattering when I was woken early by Tullah's call.

"Amber, Jen's been kidnapped."

Chapter 42

SATURDAY

"Exceptional circumstances, Bian," I said on the cell, gunning the Ford out of the underground garage. "That's what Skylur said."

"You don't even know where she is," replied Bian. "And this is just one woman against the future of the Athanate. This Assembly—"

"This Assembly is a farce and you know it. Basilikos are already moving against us. They're only interested in keeping the appearance of the Assembly going to weaken support for action in the Panethus party." I took deep, calming breaths. "And for me, it's not just one woman. It's Jen…and she's family. She's kin."

Bian was silent. I turned onto the driveway and headed for the gates. They were still closed and the guards were coming out now, weapons in hand. My heart thudded painfully in my chest. I had to get out, but I couldn't fight these people. They were family too.

I could hear sounds in the background as someone asked Bian a question and she replied. They spoke in Athanate, so I didn't know what had been said. It sounded angry.

"I understand, Amber," Bian said to me and the gates started to open. I blinked, relief flooding through me. Bian's voice sounded strained. "Good hunting. If you find her, call me, and I'll push for help."

"Thank you, Bian," I whispered and ended the call. The guards moved aside and waved us through.

David's hand came from the back seat and squeezed my shoulder. "We'll find her," he said.

David and Pia were dressed in black combats and carrying their P90s and Kevlar vests in a sports bag. The ugly little P90 machine gun was Altau's standard issue and they'd be useful.

I was in yesterday's damaged clothing, but I'd brought all my operational equipment from my Audi. I was as well armed as I could be, heading into the unknown. And if this wasn't the most experienced team I could have as backup, it was still immensely comforting to have them there.

At Manassah, Tullah was standing outside and I skidded to a halt next to her.

"Stay in the car, guys," I said to David and Pia. "I don't want the police to see you in that gear."

Tullah was white-faced and trembling, deeply shocked. I hugged her and coaxed her through what had happened.

When we had moved the office here, Tullah had linked the alarm system into her cell and it had sent her a message when it went off. She'd arrived first, followed by Victor's quick response team and the police. She'd managed to get in and out before them.

"The patio doors were forced open." She swallowed. "Reynolds…he's dead, Amber. The other guard too. I think they were wounded first. Then…" she angrily wiped tears from her cheeks and looked away. "Then they were shot in the head as they lay there."

After a moment she continued. "The guards fought back. I think Jen fired a shotgun. There were five other bodies in the house." She took a breath. "No messages left."

This was all my fault. I hadn't found Hoben. I hadn't warned Jen and Victor how serious the problem was.

"I need to know who did this," I said and made to move past her.

She held me. "It wasn't Athanate, if that's what you're looking for."

I looked at her. "This is some Adept thing? You know this for sure?"

She nodded jerkily.

"Were?"

"No. They were human. A dozen of them, I'd guess."

The only person it could be was Frank Hoben. But why Jen? It was me he was after. Unless he was using Jen to get to me. Why the hell had she come back here?

I had to put that aside. The police would take note of us if we hung around. Tullah had stopped me from making a big mistake walking in there. I could not have the police looking at my personal armory in the trunk, or asking me questions for hours.

"Tullah, you've done what you can, thanks. This is up to me now."

"I can help, Amber."

"I'm in enough trouble with your mother already." I didn't give her any chance to argue. I got back in the car and hit the gas.

David's place was out. That left Alex's.

On the short drive, I couldn't think of anything but the worst case scenarios. I was already angry, now I added guilt and frustration to the mix.

"Please, Amber," Pia said quietly. I looked into my mirror. Her eyes were wide and unsettled. I realized both of them would be reading the emotions off me and picking them up themselves. Pia was my early warning system. She was very sensitive to the emotional signals around her. It had probably been what made her good with Aspirants, even though she'd made mistakes as a Mentor. But I wasn't an Aspirant, I was her Athanate Mistress, and she would be unable to block out my emotions. I was having to learn this role as I did it.

"I'm sorry," I said and forced my mind onto useful, logical paths about what we could do when—not *if*—*when* we discovered where Jen was being held.

Alex's house was jarringly bright and cheerful in the morning sunshine. And empty. Maybe Alex was catching up on his work. Or maybe he was being a wolf, out in the mountains. I sent David to the kitchen to make coffee while I paced in the living room and tried to force myself to think constructively.

Pia stopped me and cocked her head. "Car pulled up outside," she said and ran to the front door with her P90. I grabbed the HK.

"Amber, it's Tullah," she called. "She must have followed us here. She's alone."

I felt a spike of anger at myself for not noticing that she had followed us. I was head down and reacting, behaving as if I'd never had training, blinded by my personal involvement. I had to change that. The only way to get Jen back was for me to be operating at my best, for me to be cool and calm, however difficult that was.

I met Tullah at the door. She was carrying her laptop and glared defiantly at me as she tried to force her way past.

"Tullah, I won't stop you. But I have Athanate here with me; are you sure you want to come in?"

She nodded nervously, and I stood aside. She slipped past, keeping as far away from Pia and David as she could without making it obvious. She went straight to the coffee table in the living room and set up her laptop, with a patchwork of odd cables and hubs attached.

"Your old cell, Amber," she said, holding her hand out.

Puzzled, I handed it over. "What's that?"

"They weren't after Jen," she said. "They wanted you. They'll use her to get to you." She connected my cell to her laptop with one of the cables and fired up a message recording app.

"They took Jen's cell," she said, "so I'm betting that's the way they'll contact you."

She put her cell phone on another connector.

David held his hand across the table. "I'm David, by the way, and this is Pia."

After a tiny pause, Tullah shook their hands carefully. I wondered if they could tell she was an Adept. Her tension eased a bit as she fiddled with her laptop.

"Can you track an incoming call with that setup?" asked David.

"This isn't some TV show," replied Tullah. "But I've got someone who may be able to help." She picked another app off her toolbar and spoke. "You still there, Matt?"

"Yo." His image came up in a window. He was surrounded by racks of equipment.

"Amber and some friends are here. You want to tell them what you told me about tracking?"

Matt's voice, replayed through the laptop's speakers, was wary. "Hey, the short answer is, I don't know how successful it'll be. I'm trying to access the repeater tower traffic. As long as the cell's turned on, it's in contact with the nearest towers. Even without, like, cracking the GPS data, I would be able to get a reasonable fix..."

"But?" I prompted him when he slowed.

"Well, back here in the real world, I might not get in quickly enough and I could get thrown out of the connection by their security systems. Then, even if I do manage to get in and get a fix, you know, the bad guys watch TV too. That phone and Ms. Kingslund could be on different sides of Denver."

My cell rang and everyone froze.

I grabbed it and read the ID. I closed my eyes.

I shook my head to the others and turned away slightly. "Alex, hello."

"Amber, my security system says—"

"Hold up a second," I cut across him. "There's a problem. Jen's been kidnapped and I think they'll use this number to call. I'm sorry, I'm in your house with my team. I didn't know where else to go."

"Forget that, you're good. I'll call on my landline."

He called right back.

"Amber, I'm sorry," he said. "Is this something to do with Tucker? Is there anything I can do?"

"Don't know yet, Alex. Hold one second." I turned to Tullah. "Did Matt track Alex's call to my cell?"

She shook her head. "Too quick," Matt said.

Tullah fiddled with another cable to Alex's landline base.

Alex's voice came from the laptop speakers. "You still there?"

"Yeah, we just rigged you into a laptop, like a conference call hookup, so we can all hear you and you should be able to hear us."

"Hi everybody," Alex said. "Amber, can you tell me what happened?"

Between Tullah and me, we gave him the outline of what had gone on. Talking about it was strange. It moved it away from the personal, a little. It helped me to be much calmer when my cell rang again, this time with Jen's ID.

I grabbed it, and everyone else went silent.

"Who is this?" I said.

"Tell me, was it you killed my old man?" I recognized his hoarse voice.

"Don't try that shit on me, Hoben. He killed himself, and if he hadn't, he was going to kill you over the money you wasted on the hitman."

"Was he?" Hoben snorted. "Asshole. Now, shut the fuck up and listen, or I end the call."

There was a gasp of pain, and Jen's voice: "Amber, don't—"

There was the sound of a blow and a cry from Jen.

"Jen!" I called.

"What your bitch is trying to say, is don't be stupid, or you'll never see her again," Hoben said. "We'll call back, me and *Jen*, later, when we're not busy. You better keep your cell with you, but calling the cops on it would be stupid. Same goes for Altau. You do what I tell you, and you might get your bitch back alive."

The call disconnected.

I made it to the basin before I threw up.

Chapter 43

Twenty minutes later, Alex had joined us in person.

"Focus, Amber," he said. "Hoben wants something from you. While he wants that, we've got a chance."

The 'we' helped me as much as the question itself. What did Hoben want?

"He's not just out for revenge. He's trying to set something up," David said.

Alex had gone all stiff-legged and territorial at finding David here, but, smart man that he was, David ignored it. It went away quickly and I could see them becoming a team. The trouble was, they needed me to lead them and I was having difficulty seeing the problem dispassionately. Just as Hoben had intended, no doubt.

"It's not just trying to kill you. He could have set that up in minutes," Alex said.

"Yeah, he needs time. He's gone to talk to someone," David said. "My gut says Matlal."

Pia leaned forward. "If it's Matlal, there's no chance he'd let you go. It'd just be a trap."

"It'd be a trap anyway," I said, but at least I was thinking again. "We need to know where." I tried not to look at the screen with Matt in his roomful of computers. He hadn't been able to track Hoben's call. He was spending the time setting up some more tools to give him a better chance the next time around.

Alex brought out a huge map of Denver and the surrounding area and laid it out on the coffee table. I looked down at it, willing something to leap out at me as the obvious place.

"It'd be out of town," I said.

"But Tucker—"

"No, that was Tucker's style. He got his kicks from doing everything right under everyone's nose, like being a respected business leader and heading up a criminal organization. Hoben's different. And Matlal will want to keep things hidden. This will be somewhere private, out of the way."

"Somewhere that Matlal owns?" said Tullah.

I shrugged. "Or Hoben. We know next to nothing about him."

"Hold on," David said, and suddenly looked up. "He's gotten you to leave your cell on. If you think Matlal's tracking that, it could lead him right here."

"Shit! You're right. I'm so sorry, Alex. We've gotta move."

"Stop." Alex frowned in thought and got up. "Give me a few minutes."

"We can't fight here—"

"Matlal doesn't want to come into the open," Alex said. "Like you said, he's going to want this to go down somewhere quiet. We're probably safe here. But just for insurance, let me call Felix."

Alex left us and went up into his study to make the call. I wasn't sure bringing the pack into this was going to work, but I had to trust his judgment on that.

"Tullah." I leaned close to her and spoke quietly. "Is there anything Adepts can do to find people?"

She shook her head. "Not me. Not like this."

"Mary?"

Tullah's face went stony. "I don't think so. For sure, not quickly. And not with Athanate involved."

"Amber," called Alex from the top of the stairs, "come up, please."

His study was bright and tidy. Big windows opened to the back yard. Larimer's face looked up at me out of Alex's computer screen.

"Ms. Farrell, believe me, I am truly sorry to hear of your problem," he said.

"Thank you." No reason to not be polite about it, but I had a feeling Larimer wanted to take advantage somehow. If it got Jen back, I'd listen.

"And I want to thank you for the information about our rivals. I won't bore you with the details, but it has been of benefit to us." He paused. "However, I am not accustomed to having my wishes disregarded."

Crap. Alex or Olivia must have told him about yesterday.

"I'm not in your pack, Larimer."

"We haven't really decided that, have we? But Alexander still is," he replied evenly, "and I understand from him you claim some kind of affiliation."

"To Alex," I said.

"And thus to me."

I couldn't find a snappy answer to that.

"I don't wish to benefit from misfortune," he said, which meant he was about to. "I will make the following proposal. We will guard Alexander's house. I will allow members of the pack to run errands for you today if you need it. Alexander can help you. But the pack will not get involved in fighting any Athanate, other than in defense. That includes Alexander."

"And for that, you want what?" In truth, I was in no position to negotiate with him. He would have figured out that I couldn't call on Altau at the moment, or I would have already. My small team were very vulnerable to Matlal. A few of the pack might make all the difference.

"After today, you leave Alexander alone for a while—"

"Why? And what's a while mean?"

"Because I need to be completely sure that what Alexander is doing is what he wants to do, and not what some Athanate mind-meddling is making him do." Larimer was staying calmer than I was, and I struggled to match him. "I need to be sure where his ultimate loyalty lies. As for the while—a week, two weeks should be enough. I'll still need to see you when I want as well. I'll tell you when I'm satisfied."

"What else?" I knew the bastard hadn't finished with me. My eyes flicked to Alex, but he wasn't saying anything.

"There's been another incident similar to those in your police report. I need you to find out who's doing it."

"Huh?" Not my smartest rejoinder, but I hadn't seen that one coming.

"Ms. Farrell, you have demonstrated a capability in this area." He ticked items off on his fingers. "As far as the Were are concerned, you are…" he shrugged, "a cousin, say. As an Athanate, you have advantages in detecting the truth, not as good as the Adepts, but sufficient. And I know you are motivated."

There was no need to think it through. I couldn't afford to have Matlal attack here while I was trying to put together a plan to get Jen back. I needed some defenders.

"Done," I said, and looked at his smug image on the screen. "You trust me?"

"Ms. Farrell, I'm not yet sure that I trust you. However, I am sure I do not trust the rest of the Athanate."

"Call Skylur. Talk directly to him," I said. "I'm not able to make any official statements, but I believe Altau are your friends."

Larimer made no response other than a nod.

He disconnected and I stared at the blank screen.

Alex squeezed my hand. "One problem at a time," he said.

Good advice.

I'd just gotten back downstairs when my cell rang again.

Chapter 44

"Amber—"

Jen's voice was cut off as abruptly as it had been before. She sounded hoarse and in pain, exhausted.

"Have you been enjoying the wait, Farrell? Your bitch has."

"Hoben, I swear—"

"You want to think very hard about what you say next, Farrell. You want me in a good mood, don't you?"

I didn't reply, and Jen screamed.

"Don't you, whore?" he shouted.

"Yes! Yes, I want you in a good mood." I felt sick again, but it was important to keep him on the line and it was important to stop him from hurting Jen.

"Oh, that sounds good," he said. "Ask me like you mean it. You're a whore, you can fake it, can't you?"

"Please." I forced the words out. "Please, I want you to be in a good mood. Please don't hurt her."

"Better. Turns out you're in luck. Getting me in a good mood will be easy. You're my ticket to get Matlal off my back, so you better fucking listen and do what I tell you. You come to meet me, alone. I'll have one of Matlal's vamps along. All you've got to do is tell him where the Altau house is and persuade him you're telling the truth. Do that and you can take your pretty meal ticket and walk away."

"I can't—"

"Well, you better find a way you can," he shouted. "What the fuck's your problem? Altau have screwed you over. You don't owe them. You got the deal. But you take your time, we'll enjoy your little bitch's company while you make your mind up. You got till sundown and then I hand her over to them. And you know what they want with her. Text this cell when you decide and I'll tell you where to come." He laughed. "Come on, bitch, playtime. Make me happy."

Jen screamed and the line disconnected.

I was shaking. Hoben was a dead man. Once Jen was safe, whatever it took, I would hunt him down and he would die like a rabid dog.

"Sorry. I couldn't trace the call," Matt said into the aching silence, before anyone asked. "I'm querying the main area database. That might cut it down."

I closed my eyes. Pia was right next to me, trembling with reaction to my anger. The anger that was clouding my mind, the anger that wasn't going to get Jen back. I had to work this through.

"Play the recording back please, Tullah." My voice sounded loud in my own ears.

We listened again. I refused to let the words make any sense. It was just noises.

"Again," David said. "Just before Jen screams."

Again and again. In the half-second before she screamed there was another noise, a similar noise. Tullah clipped and played it with the volume up. It was a distinctive noise, an aircraft jet engine.

"That's not a passenger plane, it's something smaller," David said. "Maybe an executive jet at full power, climbing after takeoff."

There were a half-dozen airfields in the Denver area. Matt started checking wind direction for runways in use and plotting guesses for the noise footprint.

"Someplace upwind, close to a runway big enough for a small jet," Tullah said.

"They'll have Matlal people there. If it's the base it'll be large and private." David leaned over the map. "A warehouse, maybe a locked hangar on the airfield."

"Not a hangar, too public. Someplace belonging to Tucker," I said. "Not in use, but a place that Hoben knows about. Or a place that Matlal persuaded Tucker to let him use."

"I have an idea," Alex said slowly. "Up till this all kicked off, my company handled Tucker's shipping. We were picking up and delivering to all their main offices and warehouses. There was one that stands out. It's an empty factory being refurbished up near Longmont. About an hour north of here. The deliveries didn't make sense. There were camping beds and microwaves for instance, but no office partitions or furniture." He paused, and pointed to the map on the table. "It's off the main road and it has a security fence. It's not directly under the takeoff for the airport at Longmont, but it's close enough."

"North," agreed Matt. "I can't get any further but the call was made outside city limits and to the north. That covers..." he tapped frantically before looking up to the webcam. "That covers Longmont."

"It's the best we have," I said, looking around. Everyone nodded. "We don't have much time, less than seven hours. I'm going to have to check it out."

"If we're wrong—" Tullah looked up anxiously.

"If I'm wrong about this, then it's my fault," I said.

"What if they're still tracking your cell?" David said. "If you turn it on to text them, buy some time or whatever, they'll see where you are."

"I can deal with that," Matt said. "I'll courier you some hardware, a repeater kit. It's like an auto-forward. You leave your cell at Alex's house, connected to a computer. Any call coming in will get put through to Tullah's internet phone on her laptop. You want to make a call using your cell, you just log in and take control of the cell. For anyone tracking the cell, it'll look like you're still there."

"Matt, that's fantastic."

I called Bian on her secure number. Skylur answered.

Shit.

I steeled myself.

"Amber, another situation it would seem," he said, deceptively mildly.

"I'm sorry, Skylur. No excuses. But I cannot, *will not* come in while there's a chance of getting Jen back. She's kin. And listen."

I replayed the recording.

"We think they're at a disused factory out near Longmont. We're going to investigate. Some backup against Matlal would be welcome," I said.

"It's not enough yet, Amber," he replied. "You could be completely wrong. Or Hoben could just be using Matlal's name to make his trap sound credible. I can't commit resources yet. I'll retain this phone, and if you find Hoben or Matlal's people, I will send a team. Hold on."

There were sounds in the background.

"Amber, I'm going to have to leave it there. You realize the situation you are putting me in? I believe Bian explained the political dynamics last night."

"Yes. I'm sorry. I will do everything I can not to get caught. But what about if I call back and you're busy? Shouldn't I be able to get through to Bian?"

"It seems you have been entirely too able to get through to my Diakon. I am reviewing this as we speak. You'll have to take your chances with me."

"But—" The line was dead.

Oh, crap, now I'd gotten Bian in more trouble as well. And unless something miraculous happened, we were on our own.

I was interrupted by the arrival of the Weres, in human form, of course. For all their menace and growling restraint during my previous experience on Larimer's ranch, they were more like a bunch of pups today, full of high-fives and knuckle bumps. They were positively looking forward to Matlal trying to take this place. His involvement with a rival pack had seriously pissed them off.

I ran around, organizing us into two cars to give us flexibility. As calm as things seemed with my team, I thought it was better for Pia to go with Alex and David to come with me. Plenty of sensible little decisions to keep me occupied. Anything to stop thinking about what was happening somewhere in Denver.

The repeater arrived by courier, and David helped me set it up and test it.

One last thing.

I turned to Tullah. "I need the laptop," I said.

"It stays with me," she replied. Leaving the apps running, she closed it and clutched it to her chest, glaring at me again.

Chapter 45

Tullah refused to hand over her laptop. She wasn't going to be persuaded and in the end I gave up. We were just checking at the moment anyway. I could send her back if it got dangerous, couldn't I?

David drove. It allowed me to work through the equipment we'd loaded into the car. In addition to the military equipment, we had my surveillance kit that I'd bought for Campbell Carter's case. It seemed like half a lifetime ago. I reminded myself how to set up the laser listening devices. I had a feeling we'd be needing those. If this factory was the right place. Of course it was, I told myself.

As we headed north out of Denver on I-25, the sky darkened and a light rain began to fall.

I stripped and reassembled my guns. Again and again. Tension gathered in every muscle. Time was slipping through my fingers like smoke.

At Longmont, David found the road past the factory. Alex held back a ways and we both drove past. The factory was set back, behind barrier gates, and mostly out of sight of the road. There was someone in the gatehouse, but they didn't even look up as we passed. A small twin engine plane passed over us at low altitude, heading out from the airfield.

At the end of the road, we turned and drove back slowly. The building was obscured from the road by trees. Halfway along, I got David to stop and I jumped out with a laser surveillance scope. I fixed it to a tree and aimed it at one of the windows in the right-hand building, where I'd spotted a flicker of activity.

We reversed direction again and David parked well out of sight of the factory. I fired up the main system and tuned in to the scope transmitter. It was bouncing a laser off the window and measuring any vibrations. Noises inside and outside the building were turned into electrical signals and then converted back into noises on the main system speakers.

I put a microphone outside to pick up sounds like aircraft taking off, and the system removed those noises from the stuff it was getting from the window, leaving us listening to sounds only from inside the building. Sweet. It was the kind of system Matt would approve of.

Alex and Pia joined us in the Ford.

"Athanate," Pia said as soon as we tuned into sounds of talking from the building. "House Matlal, discussing the Assembly. Amber, there's no legitimate reason for them to be here, just as there's no legitimate reason for them to want to know where the Assembly is being held." She went shades paler. "This isn't just about you. Oh God, they're actually planning to do it, they're planning to attack the Assembly."

"Call Bian's number," I said to her. "Skylur has her phone. This has to be worth some backup." I turned. "David, walk down there and find a place for this second scope. It needs to be pointing at the office building on the left. The angle needs to be almost straight on or the signal will be too weak. Keep out of sight and stay there while we try a few windows." He nodded and walked back the way we'd come. He'd put on an old jacket from his bag, which hid his black uniform, and the trees hid him from the factory.

In ten minutes we had the second scope up. The office building was quieter, and we got David to change windows until we finally picked up sounds from the top floor. The signal was much weaker, making it sound like we were listening to a badly tuned radio.

Pia couldn't get through to Skylur. I punched the seat in frustration and she laid a quieting hand on my arm. "I'll call again in five minutes. Let me listen to this first."

She frowned in concentration. Eventually, she shook her head. "It's not Athanate."

"A group of men," Tullah said. "I think they're playing cards or something like that."

That seemed right. There was a rhythm to the talking. I could visualize the cycle of a deal, bets, jokes and boasts, but the words were blurred and indecipherable.

Was that Hoben's voice? Hoarse and raspy. The building had been stripped of carpets. I could hear cheap chairs scraping against a concrete floor.

Every now and then, the tone changed. One person would call out something and the others laughed. It didn't have the feeling of lighthearted laughter. It was something darker; sexual. Nausea threatened again. I couldn't think of Jen in there. I had to focus on this as a military operation. How to assault the building, get my team and the hostage out. The hostage.

Focus. Three interconnected buildings. The hostage probably top floor of the office building. Go straight in and whoever was in the other buildings could just surround the place. But how to trap them inside?

Pia got through and spoke to Skylur. It was in Athanate and so brief my heart sank.

She turned to me, looking puzzled. "Bian is coming with a small team."

"Thank God. What's the problem?"

"It's the day of the Assembly, Amber. The delegates are being brought in now. As Diakon, Bian is in charge of security overall. She can't be out here. I don't understand what's going on."

I couldn't spend time puzzling over it. I turned my attention back to the building.

I got David to realign the first scope and we got the best signal of all from the middle building.

"Athanate again," Pia said. "Checking something. Like an inventory." She frowned. "Ammunition. Guns."

I called David back and slipped out into the trees myself. Top had always said time spent in reconnaissance was seldom wasted. What would he have done here? I would never have perfect information, so how much time did I spend before deciding?

Heavy clouds were making it darker and squalls battered at the trees. Light, cold rain was still falling. Aircraft had stopped flying from the airfield and from the color of the clouds, I suspected the rain would get heavier.

I ignored it and settled in where I could use my binoculars to look over the buildings and grounds. Most of the area inside the perimeter was given over to car parking on the left and stacked containers on the right. There was an expanse of open space in front of the buildings—far too much.

An armed security guard came out of the middle building, looked up at the sky and went back in. Good.

The mission clock was ticking in my head. Less than three hours to the deadline. There was no way I could risk getting any closer, which meant I was working on guesses.

I had one small team with no expertise in this kind of operation, and another small team yet to arrive with an agenda of their own and unknown capability.

And matters had gotten more complicated. There were now two missions here. Get Jen out *and* prevent Matlal's troops from attacking the Assembly. Mission creep.

I refused to think of the possibility that Jen was not here, captive in the left-hand office building on that top floor. Mission one was to get in there and get her out. That was for me.

Mission two was more difficult. There could be any number of Matlal's people in those buildings.

But as I lay watching and thought about it, I realized the good news was that they were treating this like a military operation. The better news was that I was good at those and they weren't.

And I knew there's nothing like gunfire to focus your mind, even if what you end up focusing on is entirely the wrong thing.

The deadline marched closer and some short cuts would need to be taken, but a plan formed. I slunk back to the cars.

"Alex," I said. "Can I buy a truck and some tools from you?"

Chapter 46

Bian arrived in a box van as Alex drove off to get my shopping list.

Without much thinking about it, I gave her a hug.

"I hope you're not in too much trouble because of me," I said.

She shook her head. Jason, Paul and Tom climbed down out of the back of the van, which had a full medical setup in the back. I guessed that Athanate healing went only so far. It was a welcome addition.

"Just the three?"

"Yes." End of that conversation. "Amber, I'm here for a specific role, not to rescue Jen. My overriding goal is to get full evidence of senior House Matlal involvement in an attack on Haven and prevent you from being taken. I can help you only if it does not conflict with those goals."

"Very specific instructions," I said. They were like Ops 4-10 objectives. "But that's a hell of an ask."

"It's what's been agreed." Bian was pale, but adamant. She refused to say any more about it.

"Okay," I said. "You're designated Group 1. I anticipated your team might need to be separate anyway."

Bian began to relax slightly as I gathered everyone and went through the plan for the first time.

Tullah listened in, but there was no way I was letting her come in with us. Even if we'd had spare weapons, she hadn't been trained in their use. She was pretty mean with her hands and feet; no daughter of Liu would be anything less, but that wouldn't help in a firefight.

As I wound down, Bian laughed softly. "And I thought you were only slightly crazy, Round-eye."

"I'm not the one running around with an oversize kitchen knife, Pussycat," I replied, and listened to the chuckles. Good. I didn't doubt the team was aware how dangerous it was, but they had to believe they could do it, to give us any chance. They had to be in good spirits.

For a unit, we were a contrast.

The Fang team had come in their black combat uniforms and Kevlar vests. But in addition, their helmets had SWAT team infrared goggles on them, and there were matching lights on their P90s. They had enough ammunition for about fifteen minutes, if they were careful. If we took longer, or they weren't careful, we were finished anyway.

Bian had none of that. She wore her close-fitting trousers and a high-necked jacket, also black. The material was silky, completely matte, and as the light began to fade her face and hands seemed to float in an inky emptiness. She carried a backpack in the same material. Her sole weapon was her katana. More suited for my role, she explained when I asked, without really explaining anything.

David and Pia were in black combats with P90s, they had Kevlar vests too, but they had no helmets, none of the Fang team's swagger and not much ammunition. I had specific tasks for them, and hopefully they wouldn't need to use the guns much.

Time. Praying Alex would get back soon, I started the plan. I sent a text to Jen's phone, saying I would tell Hoben where Altau was and asking him where I needed to show up.

He called back, hoarse, mocking.

"Get out to Cherry Creek Reservoir and call again," he said.

That was on the opposite side of Denver.

"Cherry Creek?"

"You got a problem with that?"

"No."

He ended the call.

They were all looking at me.

"We've got the wrong place," Pia said, dropping her head into her hands.

"No." Their heads came back up and tracked me. I had doubts, but I couldn't let them show. "No, this is where Jen is. Cherry Creek is where they want me. Different things. Nothing's changed."

I called Alex's house and asked one of the Were to drive my cell out to near Cherry Creek. I lost the ability to connect to calls, but it was going to be over before he got there. All I wanted was Hoben to be tracking the cell and seeing me do what he asked.

I went through the plan again, checking that everyone knew what was required.

Alex came back with one of his Mack trucks. All $150,000 of it.

I cringed, but there was no going back now.

As if I needed a distraction, I saw Alex's startled look when he saw Bian, and the almost guilty way he glanced at me. Crap, they *did* have a history. Something I would have to deal with later.

More problems; Alex told me he was coming in.

"Felix gave you a direct order, not to get involved."

"Doesn't work like that for me." He ducked his head. "I'll explain to Felix when we're done. You're wasting time. I need to know what to do."

I went through it the final time. Adding Alex in made good sense, and I could keep him with David and Pia in Group 2. Relatively safe. Or as safe as he could get in a building that would be humming with bullets.

"To recap," I ended up, "the good news is they're running this as a military-style operation, but badly. They've split up the troops in the factory on the right from the assault weapons in the warehouse in the middle and from the hostage in the left-hand office building." My heart skipped a beat over the word hostage. "The security guards are armed with light weapons, but they're not patrolling. There's one guard on the gate and others in the warehouse or factory."

We were standing in the back of the truck. Rain drummed on the metal around us. It was getting heavier.

"The tasks I've allocated are designed to exploit their mistakes and achieve the objectives despite the fact they outnumber us." I tried to catch people's eye like Top used to and *make* them believe. "Accomplish your tasks and the mission will succeed." I paused. "Any questions?"

There was a general shaking of heads. Given their inexperience, I had taken them through it enough times that I was sure they knew what had to be done, even if they were concerned at the priorities allocated to them. I couldn't help that. I was the one with training for this type of job, which meant my primary goal landed on my shoulders. I wouldn't have had it any other way. Once this was rolling, I wouldn't have time to be afraid for myself, let alone Jen. My instincts were honed with ten years of training and I had to trust them.

Tullah looked distant, but resigned. I'd given her the role of waiting outside and relaying progress to Skylur. That would be important if things went wrong, but I hadn't added that.

Pia concerned me. I stopped in front of her and she flinched.

"Being Athanate doesn't mean I'm not afraid," she whispered, looking down and fiddling with her P90.

I lifted her face gently until she was looking at me. "Being scared doesn't mean you're not brave. You'll do fine."

She took a deep breath and nodded.

I stepped back. "In the rigging, please."

As I had specified, Alex's truck had webbing, like the netting on a climbing wall, fastened down the middle. Everyone except Paul wriggled their arms in and got ready to brace. Instant crash protection. Paul just sat on the back, ready for his first task.

I pulled on my old army harness, checked that all my weapons were secure. I had the MP5 strapped to my right thigh. On the left thigh was my Tactical Assault Weapon, the brutal cannon we called the BFG in Ops 4-10.

I couldn't believe the harness had come with Top's parting gift of weapons, but there it was. It still had the Mike 6 designation inked on a strap.

I climbed into the driver's seat and drove down the road towards the gatehouse. The mission was green to go. It was too close to the deadline, but it hadn't been possible to get everything organized quicker.

Something felt unfinished, unready.

My hand strayed over my harness straps. Old familiar catches and Velcro, all fastened. And a little pocket, right there. My fingers slipped inside. My tin of camo paint was still there.

Something I'd kept chained woke in me, wanting to howl. I stabbed fingers into the tin and smeared savage lines across my face. This wasn't to hide. War paint. Let them see me coming. Let them know death's eyes were looking for them.

I was ready now.

It had gotten darker and the rain didn't help, but it was still light enough as I turned in for the guard to recognize Alex's truck livery. He came out of the gatehouse, but the gate stayed down. That was fine; all I wanted was for him to be away from any alarm buttons. He was probably swearing, once at the mix-up that sent a delivery too late to be accepted, and twice that he had to get out into the rain to send me back. He raised his arm for me to stop.

Paul had jumped off as we turned.

I kept the pedal down.

The guard's eyes went wide with panic and he stumbled back towards the gatehouse, then he jerked and fell as I swept past him. Paul had seen to it that he wouldn't be getting up.

The truck brushed aside the plastic gate and I lined up with the warehouse's delivery doors. The huge steel rollers were down. Normally, they'd roll them open for a delivery. I didn't think we'd get them to do that tonight, so I used the alternative, Amber Farrell, way of opening them.

The truck slammed into them, ripping the light steel panels like ribbons while I floored the brake and kept the rig straight. There were a couple of guards sitting smoking in the main delivery area. That was unlucky for them. Guards, chairs and tables disappeared under the truck's huge grill front.

I deliberately hadn't had the truck flat out, but the brakes still weren't good enough to stop all that momentum. I leaped from the cab and the truck smashed straight into a couple of large box vans, folding them like paper.

I rolled and came up with the HK machine gun. This wasn't my task, but I sent a couple of short bursts into a small group of bewildered Matlal troops standing by racks of guns. That caught their attention just long enough for Group 2 to untangle from the webbing and take over their task.

I left them, sprinting up the open-frame, zigzag staircase for the top floor.

At the first turn, I could see the half-dozen Matlal troops in the warehouse were down.

At the second turn, Pia had the first of Alex's industrial packing foam dispensers vomiting its contents over the racked guns. It would get down the barrels and into the trigger mechanisms. No one was going to use them in a hurry. That was her task well on the way to completion and David and Alex were on the stairs behind me. Bian and Group 1 had disappeared towards the factory where the bulk of Matlal's men were. That was their task. Mine was ahead.

The left-hand office was connected to the warehouse by a walkway on the top floor, the third floor. If they were alerted, that's where they would be watching or that's where they would come through. Although we had been quick enough to prevent any alarms being pressed yet, they had to have heard the sound of the truck breaking into the warehouse and the shots afterwards. If they ran along the passageway, they would have David and Alex shooting at them from cover. I needed to get ahead of all that, so I got out onto the roof and ran quietly along the top of the walkway and from there onto the top of the office building.

Spurred on by adrenaline and elethesine, I hit my zone. My actions became quicker and more accurate. I secured a rappel line on the roof and passed it though my brake links, estimating the length I needed, and locked the brakes.

Up here, I could hear nothing more from the warehouse. With luck, the people inside the office below me would be looking to the walkway to see what all the noise had been about. I had seconds before someone thought about Jen or realized that they were under attack.

I retrieved the BFG from the holster down my thigh harness and set the choke for wide dispersal. I pulled the pin of a stun grenade, counted two seconds and jumped off the side of the building, legs splayed wide. The rope jerked taut and I swung towards a window. Just before my boots hit the lower sill, I fired the BFG, angling it upwards.

Shatterproof glass is strong, but the BFG was designed to take out stuff like this. The expanding mass of metal particles exploded through the glass, carrying it in a ball of flame and noise right across the ceiling of the room. Behind the expanding cloud of debris was the stun grenade. It went off as I kicked the remaining glass out of the way.

I had counted down. I was expecting the noise and had my eyes screwed shut against the light at the moment it exploded, and it was still a shock. The people in the room didn't have the warning or the training and as I vaulted in, those on their feet were stumbling around, confused, blind and deaf. Most were dazed, sitting or lying on the floor.

I had the stubby HK MP5 machine gun out as well now. I sprayed bullets at the ones who seemed closest to recovery. I wanted to kill every last one of them, but I didn't have time. I'd have to deal with them on the way back.

The important thing for me was that Jen wasn't in this room. I shot those directly in my way as I ran for the doors leading to the next office.

I launched myself at the door and it burst open. I saw armed men and I rolled to one side as I brought the MP5 to bear. We all fired. After the stun grenade, it all sounded like popguns, but the bullets did what they always did. I felt a smack of one hitting my shoulder at an angle and twisting me around, but the vest took the worst of it. I'd pay for it later. The man who fired it at me paid for it now.

There had been three of them clustered around a door. All dead now. I took that as the most likely place for Jen and kicked at the lock with all my weight behind it. It was a standard office door and it splintered.

Jen was in the room, lying on the floor, naked and handcuffed. There was a man near her, struggling to get his clothes back on. He died, more cleanly than he deserved, three shots: in his groin, in his gut and through his brain.

I knelt down beside her in despair and knew I was too late.

She was covered in blood, and they had ripped her beautiful face, slashing her cheeks. I put the guns down and felt for her pulse. My hand was trembling and my vision seemed to lock down, but I felt the faintest answering pressure against my fingers.

Her eyelids moved and my heart stuttered as she became aware of me. I got out the bolt cutters that Alex had brought me from my backpack. They sheared through the handcuffs. I gently lifted her head up.

"Oh, Jen, I'm sorry."

There was nothing outside of our bubble. Her broken lips stretched in a ghost of a smile and she whispered something.

The round caught me in my back, just over my heart.

Chapter 47

The vest held the bullet, but passed on all the force of it. I fell over Jen, rolled to get away from her, struggling to clear my head and regain my breath. It felt as if I'd been hit with a sledgehammer. My left arm wasn't working. The whole shoulder was in agony. And my guns were lying on the floor on the other side of Jen.

Hoben stood in the ruined doorway, covering me with his pistol. He must have been in the walkway when I'd come through. A couple of his men stood behind him, firing rifles back at the walkway.

"You!" Hoben shouted, as he recognized me. "Shit, I win the bet. Matlal said you'd show up at Cherry Creek."

He walked in. "Makes no difference. He's got enough people for two traps. They'll wrap up whoever you've got here in two minutes. Then we can get to know you, while we wait for Matlal."

"You're getting ahead of yourself, Hoben. You haven't wrapped us up yet. Matlal's not going to be happy with you." My voice came out almost as raspy as his. I had to keep it going.

"He'll be happy as soon as I hand you over, whore."

He was close, just a few more steps.

"He hasn't got those guns in the factory anymore. They're all set in builder's foam. What's he going to use for his attack, Hoben, bad language?"

"Fucking bitch," he screamed at me. "You'll pay for that. You've screwed me over for the last time."

One more step. Just one.

Everything happened at the same time. Jen rolled to one side. He turned and fired at her. I saw his bullet hit her in the stomach. I launched myself at him. Jen came up with the BFG and fired back at him. The kickback tore it out of her hands. But the expanding mass of lead shot didn't care about that. It had swollen to an area about two feet across. It hit Hoben in the middle of his chest, and his body disintegrated into hamburger.

I landed on his tattered corpse.

The pain in my shoulder grayed out my vision. I fought it down, grunting in frustration as I wrenched the pistol from his hand. Too slow. His men would be turning, firing at us.

There were screams, shots and then with an awful finality, the wet crunch that cartilage makes when it's crushed.

I staggered to my feet. One of Hoben's men was convulsing on the floor, his life-blood gushing from the wreck of his throat. The other was face down, his head against the floor, the enormous wolf slowly releasing the death grip on the back of his neck.

"Alex," I gasped. He snarled and his head jerked. There was blood on his flanks, but he moved easily, turning to stare at the rest of the room.

I scrambled back to Jen's side. There is almost nowhere in the human body where you can be hit with a bullet without a risk. The shot to her stomach could have ruptured arteries or organs. There didn't appear to be immediate major blood loss, but I needed to get her to a hospital right now.

I'd completely lost the zone and had trouble thinking about the best way to do things.

Someone was calling my name as I struggled to gather Jen up and keep hold of my guns. My left arm didn't cooperate—my shoulder was burning in agony. I nearly dropped her when Alex reached around and took her from me. He was stark naked, of course.

"Amber, where are you hit?" I realized he'd asked me a couple of times and just shook my head and pointed urgently back the way he'd come.

"Jen. Hospital," I said, trying not to cough. My back and chest felt like they were in a vise.

"Come on then," he said, running back to where the walkway came in from the warehouse. I jammed my left arm into my harness to keep it still, then I slid the BFG back into the holster, picked up the MP5, and ran after him. Any more of Hoben's men that looked like regaining their feet I shot without a second thought.

In the warehouse, David took off down the stairs and reached the ground floor first. He started up a forklift truck that had escaped the carnage. Alex and Jen got on board and David raced it out the shattered doors and back up past the gatehouse.

"Pia!" I tossed her Alex's clothes from the stairs. "Go! Make sure they're all right," I yelled.

I sprinted across the warehouse, nearly slipping on spreading pools of gas and diesel, down the passage to the factory. At the end was Paul. He was backstop, there to stay in touch with the others in Group 1 and hold their escape route open.

I slid to a halt beside him. "This is a trap. We've got Jen. Get them back, now."

He touched the comms unit in his ear. "They heard that, they're coming," he replied. As he spoke, Jason appeared, shuffling backwards and limping, his gun wavering, but covering routes that an attack might come down. Beyond him I could see Bian, carrying an unconscious Tom, running back to us.

I shoved Jason and Paul back towards the warehouse with my good elbow. Jason's front was slick with blood, and I knew it was bad.

"I've got it here," I said. "Go. Go. Go."

Men emerged behind Bian and I fired the MP5 on full automatic at them, one handed, not bothering to aim. Bullets ricocheted off the factory machines. A few found their targets. One magazine empty, I held the gun between my knees, ripped the magazine out and slammed the next in, my last one. Bian passed me and I backpedaled after her.

More of them were coming. My tactic had worked. Being attacked from the warehouse, they simply forgot that they could get out and surround us. It worked, but I had a big problem now. I needed to disengage and get the hell out without them being right behind me.

I ran into the warehouse and waited at the end of the passage, just out of sight. All the rest of the team were clear of the warehouse now. Soon, they'd be driving back towards the turnoff. It would all go perfectly; I would run out and leap aboard and we would drive away.

Never works like that.

I slung the MP5 over my shoulder. Time to change tactics. When the first of Matlal's men were about halfway down the passage, heart-stoppingly close, I tossed a fragmentation grenade in among them. With the explosion concentrated in the confined spaces of the passage, the results were appalling, but I didn't stop to see. I fired the BFG blindly down the passage and ran.

As I cleared the gatehouse I could see that some of them had figured out what they should be doing. They were coming out of the factory. But then they made the mistake of running straight across the parking lot at me.

They had no cover and, even one-handed, I can fire an MP5 accurately enough.

But I couldn't keep that going. I was nearly out of ammunition and some of them would eventually figure out they should be going around the containers and outflanking me. Even without that, in another minute they'd all come boiling out and swarm me.

Pia and Paul and Bian had to be at the van by now, but it was too late for me. My breath rasped in my throat and my left arm and shoulder felt as if they were on fire. I couldn't run. It was over. At least Matlal's men would concentrate on me and the rest would get away.

I held the MP5 more firmly and scanned for the first of Matlal's troops to break cover. I'd take a bunch of them with me.

It was dark and the rain was falling heavily now, so she was able to walk up to me without my noticing.

"Tullah," I shouted when I finally realized she was there. "Get out of here! Get to the van."

She stood there, ignoring me and the rain cascading down her face, her eyes focused on the warehouse.

"I'll hold them. Go! Go!" I yelled, my voice fading.

She didn't move, except to frown. Then her hands, clenched in fists, lifted straight out from her sides. The night writhed above her, spiraling, slick and huge and reaching up into the clouds.

I sprayed shots across at the factory doors. A group was gathering there, working themselves up to race across that deadly open space again.

My hair streamed upwards. Tullah and I were standing at the heart of a miniature tornado. Winds buffeted us, screeching and gibbering, trying to lift us off our feet. A thousand gleaming scales shimmered above our heads, coiling and turning. We glowed a strange electric blue, and by its light, I could see Tullah's face panicking. Whatever it was she thought she was doing with her freaking dragon, it wasn't working.

Bian's van was coming. The Ford was following.

"Kaothos!" I shouted. "Stop it."

I reached out to push Tullah away towards the road.

Like pushing my arm into a bees' nest.

I touched her.

My shoulders were on fire, my skin felt as if it was rippling. Tullah's eyes went wide and staring like a madwoman. Fat hissing bolts of brilliant blue lightning crackled and stung. And she opened her hands.

The buildings exploded.

As far away as we were, we were still lifted right off our feet and thrown into the road.

The van squealed to a halt, and David dragged us into the back.

I looked up. All three buildings were gone. There was no sign of anyone alive down there.

Of course, we had run riot through the place, firing guns and tossing grenades around. The Mack truck's fuel tank had split. So had those box vans'. Something must have started burning and it had cooked the ammunition we'd covered in builder's foam. That must have been what caused the explosion. Or maybe a lightning strike, I told myself.

The back of the van was painfully bright and Alex was using the emergency medical equipment. Seeing Jen, Tom and Jason lying there cleared my mind of the fog of the last few minutes, and I knelt down to see if I could help, shucking my equipment off and making the guns safe.

Alex was examining Jen, his hands sure and gentle with experience. I understood what he was doing and didn't want to interrupt, so I turned to the other two.

Bian was attending to Tom, in her Athanate style, head bent over him. He'd been hit several times in the leg and arm, but there wasn't enough blood to indicate any artery damage. It could have been a different story if he'd been shot with one of the assault rifles that we'd destroyed. The shock of the bullets passing through his body could have destroyed vital organs. As it was, I guessed he would live, and with Athanate healing, he'd be as good as new.

That left Jason, and I turned to him with a sick certainty in my stomach. Alex and Bian had worked a triage system on the wounded, dealing with those they thought they could save rather than those they knew they couldn't. Jason's skin was white and the stench told me his muscles had loosened. There was a limp finality to the way his whole body sprawled on the floor of the van. I couldn't find a pulse or see a breath. He had only a single bullet wound through the groin, just below the Kevlar vest, but beneath him was a lake of blood where the severed artery had completed the emptying of his body. It must have taken a supreme effort for him to get back to where Paul had been waiting in the factory. He'd probably died even as Paul carried him.

I bent my head over his body. I didn't even know how old he really was. Athanate tended to look young, but maybe he'd had a good long life as humans count it. Regardless, he didn't deserve this. I touched my hand to his cooling forehead. At least he looked at peace, forever safe from our unprofitable strife.

I turned back to Alex and the concerns for the living. Working swiftly in the unfamiliar layout of the van, Alex had managed to rig up an IV drip and blood pressure monitor. His fingers were delicately probing Jen's stomach, trying to assess the damage the bullet had caused.

Beneath the professional mask of the doctor, I could feel a seething anger.

"What is it?" I asked.

"She's slipping away from me, Amber. We need to get her into an ICU." His eyes flicked across to Bian. "She says we're heading back to the Altau house."

Bian's head came back up, her eyes dark.

"Bian, I'm sorry about Jason," I said urgently. "But we have to concentrate on the living. Jen needs a hospital now."

"No," she said. "We have to return to Haven. Those are Skylur's direct orders. We have to get back now. We can't go to the hospital."

I could see she was furious about her orders, and that she wasn't going to change her mind.

"Then you have to help Jen. You did it for Mykayla when she was injured."

She turned her gaze away, closing her eyes, and her voice caught. "No, I can't," she replied.

Chapter 48

"What do you mean, Bian?" I reached across the van and pulled her around, gasping as my shoulder screamed protest. Bian moved easily, not resisting, but her eyes were bright with anger.

"You think I don't want to?" she yelled at me. "I'm a healer, I want to help her. I feel her calling out to me."

"So why don't you?" I asked, confused.

"Skylur's orders," she replied. "He was patched into our comms. He said anyone in your House gets injured, you have to heal them."

"Jen's a bystander, for heaven's sake."

Bian turned her face away again. "She's not, Amber. Even I acknowledge that. You claimed her as kin." She threw her hands up. "And we don't have time to argue."

That at least I agreed with. Rain drummed on the roof of the van, making it difficult to think. Jen needed me. I wasn't a full Athanate. I was some weird hybrid. I didn't know how to heal people, not like Bian did. Why was Skylur doing this?

"I can't do it, Bian. I don't know where to start."

It was Bian's turn to seize my shirt and pull me close. "You are fully Athanate," she shouted over the noise of the rain. "You think because you've got some crazy wolf stuff going on that you're not, but you are. I can tell. I can tell you can heal. You have to believe me, for Jen's sake." Were those tears in her eyes?

"What do I do then?"

"You're already doing it. You want to heal her. I can smell the aniatropics coming off you."

"So…"

Bian gripped my face. "Kiss her." A smile just touched her lips, a little of the playful Bian coming through. "It's not as if she would object."

She yanked me forward roughly till I was kneeling. Jen's bloodied face was pale beneath me. My heart ached to do something. Now that Bian had said it, I could taste changes in my mouth—strange flavors, acidic, almost like unripe berries. Things were happening in me, it was just I had no idea what they were.

"Need to do something soon," Alex said, his words blurred by the drumming rain, his fingers searching out a weakening pulse.

This felt all wrong. There was a risk that I would infect Jen with prions. I didn't know what agents my body was producing. But Jen was out of options. I had to trust Bian. I had to try.

I kissed her cold lips. I wanted to lift her up in my arms, protect her, keep her safe. I had failed her. It was my fault for not being there, for not concentrating on getting Hoben before the Assembly. Hoben was after me, not her. She'd taken this in my place. This was my responsibility.

"BP falling." I could hear Alex. I could feel his presence, and Bian's, urging me on to do something. Anything.

The aniatropics weren't enough.

Jen!

Cold. Hot. Hurt. Not just my shoulder, my whole body awash with pain, my mind clouded in despair. Shame. Humiliation. Everything that had been done to me. No, not my body. Jen's. As fragile as the deep sea creature I'd glimpsed, shivering on the hillside above Denver; a fleeting phantom of hopes and desires, joy and pain.

Jen! Jen, trust me.

Always.

Our translucent phantoms touched, twined together, wreathed in light until I could not see where one stopped and the other started.

Our pain, our injuries. Hearts beating as one, air rushing into our lungs, blood flowing in our veins. Heal. Together in the heart-thudding silence. Without let or limitation, *our* strength, *our* health.

"BP rising!" Alex. Far away. "Pulse steady. It's working, dammit Amber, it's working!"

I flashed back to a childhood memory. My mother lifting me when I had fallen, kissing me on the knee and elbow and magically making me all right. This wasn't the same at all, but I wanted to make everything all right again, all the damage, everything that had happened to her because of me. I didn't want to heal only the cuts and bruises. I wanted to take away the terror, these last things in the darkness, screaming and full of pain. They were mine, my responsibility.

No! Jen struggled. *You mustn't.*

They're mine. I have a place for these.

And I took them.

"Good, Amber, good. Now enough." Bian was murmuring in my ear. I was aware of her hand on my shoulder.

The lights seemed to fade and I heard the sound of thunder above the rain.

I was sitting back upright, with no recollection of moving. Jason's blood was soaking into my jeans. Tullah was next to me, peering worriedly into my face. My shoulder ached.

Alex gently took Jen's hand out of mine. She was so limp. I reached out weakly to take her back.

You can't take her away from me.

"Amber! Stop. Just relax," Bian said. "You did well. It takes a toll."

"Was it enough?" I asked. Jen looked so lifeless. Alex was carefully washing the blood from Jen's body. Horrific images of cleaning corpses for burial forced their way into my head.

"Yes," Bian replied simply, and the images left me. "She'll recover. She'll heal completely."

I slumped back against the side of the van and closed my eyes again. I'd done it. I didn't care what happened to me now. Nothing could be worse than the nightmare of this day. A little smile, tentative as a spring flower, tugged at my lips. Just rest.

"Amber." Tullah knelt next to me and shook me back to alertness. "I have to get out. I can't go anywhere near an Athanate meeting."

Bian looked at her without expression, and I had a bad feeling about this.

Alex cut across the tension. "Let her take the Ford, Bian."

"But you're House Farrell," Bian said to Tullah.

"No." Tullah and I spoke at the same time.

"Really?" Bian's eyes became heavy and calculating. "Then we must meet again, young Adept." She reached for an intercom behind her and told David to pull over.

Pia stopped behind us, on the roadside.

"Alex," I said reluctantly, "maybe you'd better…"

He shook his head. "I can't leave my patient at the moment," he said. "Or you."

"I have to go back to Ma," Tullah whispered in my ear. "She was right. Kaothos is too strong. And what happened…Ma will need to talk to you."

I snorted. "If she lets me talk before ripping my head off for putting you in danger. Yeah, okay." I reached with my good hand and squeezed her shoulder. "Thanks. And if that *was* us, at the end, then we had to do it."

"No. We broke all the rules. Kaothos used you, and she spoke to you, without telling me. I didn't tell you her name. How can I trust her?" She pulled away and jumped out into the rain.

Pia joined Paul and David in the cab. I could just make out Tullah, through the heavy rain, getting into the Ford. Bian closed the door.

"You're a fool if you don't make her House Farrell very soon," she said as we got back on the road.

"That's not how I'll work," I replied. Mary would probably kill me as it was. Trying to get her daughter to join an Athanate House would only make things worse.

"We'll see. Athanate imperatives may change the way you think." Bian sighed. "We're not finished here. We've all got to be one of two things when we arrive at Haven. House Altau or House Farrell. It's not a matter of just saying it."

Alex's head came up and his eyes shaded towards the wolf. I put a calming hand on his arm and looked quizzically at Bian.

"Skylur's had to take desperate measures. He's got…" She stumbled a bit. "He's got reserves that aren't strictly legal in the view of the Assembly. Look, we don't have time to explain this. The Lyssae are loose on the grounds," she said. "It'll be hard enough getting House Altau people through."

"What are the Lyssae?"

Bian shrugged impatiently. "You'll see. Athanate who've lost the part that keeps them sane."

"Rogues?"

"No. They're not that. Maybe we'll understand them better when we understand the prions you've told us about. We've always just said they have lost all their humanity." She rubbed her face. "They're difficult to communicate with and you can't fight them. They're just too strong and quick. They understand and defend House Altau, and they should accept House Farrell. *If* they can identify you all as House Farrell."

"Pia and David—" I started.

"They're clearly House Farrell. So's Jen with the amount of aniatropics you've just pumped into her." Her eyes swiveled to Alex.

"I don't belong to any Athanate House," Alex growled, his eyes becoming more golden with every passing moment.

"You're more than halfway there already, wolf," Bian said. "You don't smell like the Denver pack. And as for it being an Athanate marque, it's half wolf."

"I don't belong—" he repeated.

"Hmm, maybe we can fix that," Bian suddenly moved with her predatory grace and rested a hand on him.

Before Alex could react, before I had time to think of what I was doing, I shoved her away and, protesting shoulder or not, I reached around him and pulled him to me. Almost all the way.

We looked at each other from inches away. His eyes were full-on golden now and although he hadn't fought it when I grabbed him, his muscles were stiff and wary.

Mine, mine, mine yammered my brain, but I forced myself to relax. I wouldn't ever conscript anyone, and it wouldn't work with this wolf anyway. I could feel my Athanate senses straining to reach out to him, to do *something*, but I refused. My jaw felt hot, but no fangs emerged. I wasn't going to bite. That wasn't what Bian was saying anyway, I thought.

I wasn't any good at this. I certainly couldn't make myself as attractive and seductive as Bian could. I didn't even have a clear idea of what it was to bind someone. Bian seemed to think I would find my way instinctively through all these Athanate powers.

In the end I sighed, closed my eyes and waited. It was up to Alex. I couldn't, wouldn't force him.

His mouth touching mine was almost a surprise. We kissed gently and parted.

"House Farrell?" I whispered. He couldn't have heard me above the noise of the rain, but maybe he could read my lips.

"Pack Deauville," he joked back. "You can't bind a Were any more than I can bind a vamp, but if it'll keep Bian off me, why don't we try anyway."

We did just that, much less tentatively this time. I didn't know if this was what I was supposed to do, but, as he said, if it kept Bian off him…

Not lights and mists, like Jen. Darkness and commotion in the night. A sensation of sharing. To be *one,* to hunt together.

And my gradual comprehension that all the groundwork had been done already, while we'd been, ahem, distracted in his office.

Was it all working? I hadn't a clue. It just felt right.

And when we broke the kiss, Bian was grinning. Witch. She knew just what sort of reaction she was trying to provoke in me.

I scowled at her, as she slid across to Alex. My hackles came up, but she just sniffed.

"Smell's better anyway; bit more vamp over all that wet dog. I now pronounce you House Farrell." She held her hands up in surrender at Alex's look. "At least for the purposes of getting into Haven." Her eyes lingered over his naked body. "Time to get dressed again, wolf."

His clothes had been tossed in the back with us and were stained with blood. He wrinkled his nose, but started to struggle back into them. He grinned at me, clearly not understanding what had just happened. I was going to have a hell of a time explaining it when I had a chance.

"Round-eye, another couple of things you need to know before we get there."

I looked at her. The shutters had come down again. This was Bian's hard shell showing now.

"Firstly, I don't know if I'm still Diakon. Skylur went ballistic over this morning." She shrugged. "I'd do it again, and at least we achieved the objectives I told you about."

My hand rested on Jason. "At a cost," I said.

She nodded and the shell slipped a bit. "The second thing you have to understand is how important you've become." Her head turned away, her voice nearly lost in the noise of the rain. "I had a third objective I was given. In the event you were captured, I was to make every effort to kill you all, at any cost."

Shit. I opened my mouth to ask the obvious question, and the van turned and came to a jerky halt.

"Not a moment too soon," Bian said. "Playtime's over."

Chapter 49

We all got out into the pouring rain at the gates of Haven.

Thunder rumbled down from the mountains, feeling its way through the valleys like some blind, hunting monster, seeking us out, slowly getting closer.

The rain got harder. We were already wet and there's a point where you don't get any wetter. Good thing I didn't spend much on hairdos. And maybe some of that water would wash away the blood.

The gatehouse had steel shutters blocking the firing slits. Two figures emerged from inside. One was a man I had seen on the gate before and the other was Mykayla. They both embraced Bian. With Bian there to compare against, my nose told me the man was her kin. I didn't think Mykayla had been bitten by Bian yet, to my surprise, but she might as well have been.

"You should be inside already," Bian said to them, but not angrily.

"We had to wait for you," Mykayla replied. "Everyone else is in now, or well away from the boundaries." She looked over towards the dark grounds and shuddered. "They're out. And someone tried to get in on the far side."

"I know," replied Bian. "Open the gates and let us through, then close them behind us. Amber stays with me, the rest get in the van. And leave the back doors open. Same with the windows in the cab, David."

Alex started to argue, but Bian wasn't having any of it.

"You have no idea, Alex. You've just got to trust me. Get in there and do not move, whatever happens."

I touched his arm. He'd taken Bian's refusal to take Jen to the ICU. He'd worked without complaint in the back of the van while Jason's blood washed the floor. He'd submitted to Bian's requests about binding. He had been getting angrier and angrier as the night went on and I was worried about how he might react now. He'd been wolf already once tonight and I sensed that made the wolf close now. I didn't know whether there was a point when the wolf just took over.

"Please, Alex. I'll be okay. Stay with Jen."

He spoke to me quietly in my ear, disguising it with a hug.

"I'm worried about this, Amber. She's right—I don't know what's going on. Do you trust her? After what she said?"

"I don't know what's going on either," I replied. "But I trust Bian. And I'm glad you're here."

He nodded unhappily and got back in the van. Once the gates were closed behind us and everyone else was on board, we started towards the house. Bian and I walked in front. The van rolled slowly along behind us. It was like a funeral procession. In fact, I reminded myself, it was. Jason's body lay in the van.

The van's lights glared around us. It was quieter than it had been inside the van, but there was still the unceasing surf sound of the rain, the howl of the wind, and gravel crunching beneath our feet and the tires of the van.

One second, the van lights showed nothing but the falling rain, and the next, they gleamed on a huge figure blocking our way.

I gasped in shock and stumbled. Seven feet tall and dark as the void, the statue of Anubis from Skylur's dungeon stood in front of us, his breath steaming around him like an old-time locomotive.

Bian, at least, had expected this. She walked forward confidently, dwarfed by his size, and spoke to him.

She used Athanate, and touched him lightly on the arm to emphasize what she said. The sound of his breathing was louder than the rain and wind, reminding me of a laboring horse. His wet skin gleamed darkly in the lights of the van, but his eyes reflected nothing. I was happy his attention was focused on Bian.

His head bowed until it was close to Bian's and he snuffled. Bian continued to talk to him. I could see the muscles in his neck and head, the twitch of his muzzle, even the saliva dripping from his loose lips. It was difficult to believe. This wasn't some lifelike mask on a huge man's head. This was a man, seven feet tall, with the head of a jackal, who'd been a statue last time I saw him.

He stood back up and Bian turned so she could gesture to me.

"*Ykos* Altau," she said loudly, her hand on her chest. "*Ykos* Farrell." She placed a hand on my shoulder. "*Philos. Perikos.*"

I really hoped those meant good things and Anubis understood them. I couldn't see how he was taking it. How do you read expression in a jackal's face?

He stepped forward. I really, really wanted to see if I could make it back to the gatehouse and hide before Anubis caught me, but taking my cue from Bian, I stood my ground.

"No sudden movements," Bian said calmly. Easy for her to say. I was looking into the huge jackal face, inches from my own, with eyes that seemed to drink the light and slobbering lips that seemed to indicate he hadn't eaten recently. Then I caught sight of the blood on his muzzle. It made me twitch and his head twitched right along with me.

He took a long breath. A noise came from his throat which might have been *perikos*.

I reached out slowly and touched his shoulder. "*Perikos,*" I said. His flesh was hot, and this close I could see steam rising from him, even with the constant rain. His skin wasn't hard like it had been when I'd touched him in the dungeon. It was like human flesh.

He stood back up abruptly, making my heart skip, but apparently I had passed the test. He stalked past me to the van, Bian and me following. Every footfall thudded into the ground.

He thrust his head into the cab, which must have been terrifying for David, sitting in the driver's seat. But one long, bubbling breath later and he was back out and stalking towards the back.

There, he crouched down and his body seemed to fill the rear of the van. Bian squeezed in alongside him, her hand on one huge arm, murmuring *perikos*, over and over. I copied her.

Anubis wasn't happy. He ignored everyone else and fixed his gaze on Alex. His lips quivered and raised over long, sharp teeth. Saliva dribbled down onto the floor of the van. A rumble started deep in his throat, like the thunder rolling up the valley.

"Don't change, Alex. Don't even move," Bian hissed, and then switched back to Athanate and spoke to Anubis. Alex's eyes were golden again, bright even in the light of the van. He was trembling and his muscles bunching. His lips had drawn back in a snarl as well. I'd never seen it, but I knew he was moments away from turning into a wolf.

"Alex, Alex," I called quietly until his eyes left Anubis and moved to me. "I need you to stay human. Jen needs you too. Please."

Alex's eyes dimmed a little and he blinked slowly. With a visible effort, he got his muscles to release their tension, and the trembling faded.

Anubis went. One second he was there, we were leaning on him, holding him, and the next he was gone. Bian and I stumbled and then sagged down and leaned against the van, ignoring the rain streaming off us.

"Shit, that was close," Bian said hoarsely.

"We're through?" I asked.

Bian nodded. "The others leave this to him, apparently. They won't touch us now." She shivered. "I think. Time to get inside."

We trotted to the front door and between us, we got Tom and Jen covered and up the stairs to the protection of the portico. Bian carried Jason's body.

There were guards on the door, human and Athanate, and they let us in quickly. The sound of the door finally closing behind us was a little comforting, though I doubted that it would hold Anubis long if he wanted to get in.

Bian went into overdrive. A gurney was brought for Jen, and Bian put the backpack she had brought in on the shelf beneath it.

Others came and carried Jason's body away with respect and grief. I saw tears in some eyes, but Bian left no one with any time to linger.

The house was cleared, section by section, with guards running in and being checked off. I guessed we were going underground as I had advised and it made me nervous. I'd never liked being somewhere with only one way in or out.

Finally, we were gathered in a room with an elevator and, six at a time, the guards went down until there was just our party remaining.

When the elevator came back for us, Bian waved us in and picked up a house phone.

"Last elevator about to come down. Check all security systems active. Check everyone clear from the upper house." There was a pause and she waved at a security camera. "Got that? Okay, lock down and wind up the banshee."

As she walked across to us, something moaned in the night. It was almost inaudible, a rising note that I could feel behind my eyes, like a million fingernails on a blackboard.

"Banshee," she said to us. "A signal for the Lyssae. They've already defeated one attack that came up from the valley behind the house. Apparently, the banshee will hype them up even more. Anything that tries to come in now is dinner." She punched the button.

"Isn't that dangerous for other people?"

Bian shook her head. "We own the neighboring properties. The Lyssae won't leave the grounds, and there are guards outside the boundary."

She turned away from me. Something in her voice told me that some of those outside were part of her Athanate kin, and they were in danger.

"It's a good thing you know what you're doing with them."

Bian snorted, "It's the first time I've ever seen them. I knew of Lyssae in theory, I just didn't know we had any. I was working on Skylur's instructions."

I shuddered. "I'm glad you told me that afterwards." Skylur hadn't trusted anyone with his secret, not even Bian. Not really even me. I'd seen them, yes, but as far as I had been concerned they were freaky statues.

The elevator took us down to Haven's underground.

The party divided. Bian guided us through security doors into a huge room. My little House Farrell: Alex, Pia, David, Jen on the hospital gurney. And me.

Heads turned. There must have been a hundred people there and our little band, running blood and water, caused a ripple of quiet to spread out, followed by a murmur of speculation. And stares.

Hunger. Fear. And hate.

Chapter 50

Bian's presence kept us in an oasis of calm.

"No coffee and cookies. I don't feel very welcome," I said to Bian. I wanted to lie down somewhere and go to sleep, but I'd walk in hell before I let that show to these people.

"They're just Warders and advisors," Bian said. "They're not important. We'll be called into the actual meeting when they're ready."

"So we rush here, not even stopping at the hospital, and now we wait?"

"Amber, I hate it as much as you."

"Do we clean up?"

She shook her head. "I want us looking exactly like this."

Bian checked Jen's pulse and temperature. I touched the lines of her face, already healing. Her skin felt feverish.

"The scars will disappear in a day or two," Bian said. "She's sleeping deeply. It means your aniatropics are working." She paused, her hand touching mine almost shyly. "Not all Athanate can heal, you know, and very few could heal as well as you have. You're gifted."

Alex used some strapping from the supplies to immobilize my arm. So much for exceptional healing. Athanate curative or not, this shoulder was going to be a bitch tonight. I tried to distract myself from the pain. "So, Matlal knows where this place is, knows damn near everything that's going on," I said to Bian. "Who's the traitor?"

Bian's face darkened. "Skylur will deal with it."

That wasn't the same thing as saying she didn't know. She was the head of security for Altau. She had to know. She obviously had more instructions from Skylur on what she could say.

"Are you going to tell me why are there so few Altau?" I went on for pure devilry. "Every one of you I've met is working around the clock. Pia gets promoted to Mentor when she isn't ready. Mykayla gets used as security before she's learned which end of the gun to hold. How come? And how come there are Altau you don't even know about, running around Denver?"

She smiled thinly. "You'll find out the answers soon enough. Heads up."

A man and a woman approached us. He was from the Indian subcontinent from his looks, and she was Tucker's fiancée, Inez Vega Martine. The bitch who'd cold-bloodedly murdered her intended husband, sending him into crusis that he could not survive.

Tucker got no sympathy from me, but I'd rather have been joined by a rattler.

"Diakon Trang," they both said, with the slightest tilt of their heads to Bian. At least out here, if Bian had been demoted, they didn't know of it.

"Diakon Vega Martine, Diakon Chopra," Bian replied coldly, and to me: "House Matlal, House Singh."

"I am very pleased to meet you, Senorita Farrell, at last," Vega Martine said.

"I am so sorry not to have been available for a meeting before," snarked my demon. Like I would have enjoyed that. "My condolences on the death of your fiancée, Senorita Vega Martine."

She blinked. "Thank you. Please call me Inez." She glanced at Bian, then back to me. "May I speak privately to you?"

"No, I don't think so. I'm not sure enough of Athanate conventions. Diakon Trang is here to make sure I don't make any mistakes." I held her eyes and spoke mildly. "I wouldn't want to give any unintentional offense."

Bian smiled a little at my choice of words, but remained silent.

Ronit Chopra and I had spoken before, of course, but I'd take his lead on whether he wanted that known. He simply nodded formally.

"Unsure of everyday conventions and already the Mistress of your own House," Vega Martine said. "You sail in strange waters." She edged closer, as if trying to block Chopra out. "It's that very thing I want to talk to you about. You must realize you have not been fully informed about everything that's happening. I've no doubt you've been well briefed on all the shortcomings of the Basilikos party, and we admit we have faults. I wonder how much you've been told about Panethus or House Altau? Have they even told you about what's happening tonight?"

"I'm just here to swear allegiance to Altau. As to knowing more of what's happening, I had to miss my briefing today. I was busy rescuing my kin from your House."

"Oh, no. No. You are mistaken," she said. "That was Jack's son. My House did not kidnap your friend."

So neat. No Matlal involved in the kidnapping, no Matlal on that side of the building. But she knew about it all.

"There have been mistakes made, Inez, and you must admit to them," Chopra said to her. He made another little bow to me. "Not all Basilikos is your enemy. Theokos and House Singh would very much welcome you as an ally, or affiliate. But I agree with Inez in this, that you have not understood what is happening here. Altau will be a prison." He waved his hands to indicate the building above us. "A pleasant prison, but a prison nevertheless. And it is not the only prison that might be waiting for you. Theokos offers you freedom. Our mantle is beyond the reach of the federal bureaus, or our influence would be brought to bear. But we would give you the choice—"

"A limited choice is no choice at all, " Vega Martine interrupted him. "You are not fully Athanate, not fully committed." She slowed and her dark eyes narrowed. "Why not reject the Athanate entirely? Walk away from it all. The federals are only interested in you if you're Athanate. Rebuild your life. Tell me, have you not dreamed of having a child?"

Vega Martine was very good at what she did, much better than Chopra. Even with all the problems, there was no way I would give up everything here to go and hide in India, but a daughter? Like Emily? Yes, that caught my attention.

"What are you saying?" I asked, despite myself.

"What Altau will deny—there is a cure," she said. Bian snorted.

The door at the end of the hall opened and a tall figure emerged.

"The usher," murmured Bian. "He's going to take us in now."

He made his way to us at a measured pace, and my stomach tightened in anticipation. Vega Martine's hand touched my arm.

"Your last chance, Senorita Farrell. Once you're inside, you're committed. You're nothing to the Panethus cause. Don't trust Altau. You don't know what they want. They will betray you to achieve their ends without a moment's hesitation. Walk away."

Bian jerked me back to face her. Moving with her swift grace, she raised her hand to her mouth and bit down on the heel. Blood welled from her flesh. She pulled me down as if to kiss me, but instead, forced her bloody hand against my startled lips.

"*Our* Blood," she hissed, staring into my eyes. "We are one House. I swear on our Blood, I will not betray you. Trust me, Amber. Trust me with your life."

Her hands seized my face and she kissed me, quick and hard, then let me go and stood back.

The usher had arrived next to us. "The Assembly are ready. It is time," he said.

My stomach surged. My lips stung with the salty, coppery taste of Bian and her plea rang in my ears. What kind of a snakepit was I getting into this time?

"Senorita Farrell." Vega Martine gripped my arm. "This is not real. They have kept you unbalanced with oaths and protestations of how attractive you are, how they love you. You must understand, the marque does not know about love. It knows about need. It understands use. That is what you are to them. Something they need. Something to be used."

I looked sideways at her. They *had* kept me unbalanced. Skylur constantly putting me on the defensive. Bian and Diana, each in their different way. A deliberate policy by all of them? And this woman sensed so much about me. Even such a little thing that I was uncomfortable with their insistence that I was so attractive. Her warm eyes begged me to reconsider. She would be my friend. Why not go with her?

She was frighteningly good. Utterly believable.

I shook myself. "You tell me there is a cure," I said. "What was it that you told Jack Tucker?"

For an instant her composure broke and I glimpsed the rage beneath. It was a shot in the dark, but I had hit her all right. She was the one responsible for the lies that Tucker had been told. The lies that really killed him, despite the fact he'd pulled the trigger.

The anger passed from her face. There was a moment of icy calm, almost resignation, and I felt as if something cold had slithered over my shoulders and whispered in my ear.

I pulled from her grip and led my tattered little band in to face the Assembly and whatever doom they were about to decree on me.

There was a connecting chamber. Doors closed behind us with the finality of prison gates. Bian grasped my hand. The place was dark, full of Warders. Two of them came towards me. Holding manacles.

"No!" I screamed, pulling against Bian's unrelenting grip.

Chapter 51

Bian shoved me behind her without letting go.

"Stop!" she shouted. A moment away from blows, the Warders and Alex hesitated.

"No fucking way you're putting those on me," I choked. Images of restraints and windowless cells boiled up into my mind, as fresh as if it were all yesterday. I couldn't go back to that, no matter what.

"Amber, Alex, wait," Bian said. "Just wait."

Alex's hands were clawed, his fingernails like scimitars and his eyes were golden. This was all about me; I couldn't let him get into trouble with the Warders, but I couldn't reach for him. One of my hands was trapped in Bian's grip and the other strapped up and immobilized.

We teetered on the brink of disaster.

"Alex," I managed to say, "please."

He took one step back. Another. Then he and David and Pia were all around me, supporting me.

"Thank you," Bian said. She turned to the Warders and took a breath. "What do you think you're doing?"

One of them cleared his throat. "This is an instruction from House Matlal, Diakon Trang. He's within his rights."

"Why?"

"Ms. Farrell—"

"*House* Farrell," Bian interrupted.

The Warder stuttered to a halt. His eyes desperately sought support. No one wanted to help him.

The door to the Assembly chamber opened, and another Warder stepped through. Relief showed on the Warders' faces.

Ah. Boss Warder. And not my friend, from the look of him. Joy.

"What is the delay?" he said.

"Your staff don't understand the basic rules of address, Captain," Bian said. "Once we get it into their heads that this is House Farrell, you can try and explain why you're trying to put manacles on a House."

The Warder captain plainly didn't like being dictated to, but decided to try the 'orders' defense.

"I'm afraid we have no choice, Diakon," he said. "House Matlal has raised serious charges against…House Farrell, and demanded adequate security precautions."

"Where are we?"

The captain looked confused. "In House Altau." As soon as he'd said it he saw the trap, but he could hardly deny it was the truth.

"And who is responsible for security in this House?"

"You are, Diakon."

"Then I will determine what security precautions are necessary."

"I am responsible for security at the Assembly—"

"Are you? How many security issues have I raised in the last week?"

The captain clearly didn't know. One of his team came forward with a notepad, trying to be efficient. "Thirty-seven, Captain, Diakon."

"And how many have been dealt with?"

"They've all been looked into, Diakon."

"That means you've answered the phone and entered it into your database. Not a single one resolved. Not one. You've sat on your backsides and watched Matlal flood the city with his people."

"We raised it as a concern—" began the Captain.

She turned her back on them.

"They have formal guidelines on their side," she muttered in my ear. Her eyes almost pleaded with me. "There is no going back now, Amber. Not for any of us. This is just shit, but we have to compromise. What can you accept? Cuffed to me?"

She could tell my heart rate was through the roof, even if she couldn't see exactly what was causing it. For that matter, neither could I. I shouldn't react so extremely.

Get a grip!

I closed my eyes and forced myself to nod.

She turned back. "You." She pointed at one of them. "Give me those handcuffs."

"But the requirement—"

"Is dealt with if she's handcuffed to me. Or are you going to claim, here in House Altau, that I am not sufficient? That the Diakon of House Altau is not acceptable? Because if you are, I'm calling you out, right here, right now."

No one said anything. I kept my eyes closed. The chill of the metal circled my wrist, and the snap of the lock was loud in the silence.

I let Bian lead me stumbling forward. I was trying to stop the wailing inside from slipping out.

Chapter 52

They split us up. Bian and I went forward while the others were kept in the back of the Assembly room. I twisted around, but the rest were all but lost in the gloom around the entrance.

In front of us was a brightly lit arena. We sat, handcuffed together, on conference chairs at the edge of this open space in the middle of the room.

So this was the Assembly of the Athanate. Forty-two seats arranged in three tiered rows on either side of the central area. The body that had my life in its hands.

Skylur sat at the head on his peacock throne, his face completely unreadable. Matlal was in the middle on the right. That was the Basilikos side. Arvinder sat three seats away from him, still part of Basilikos.

I recognized a number of the representatives. A little of the tension leaked from me. I had danced with most of them at the charity ball. Was it just a week ago? Was that going to count in my favor?

Maybe not, the way you dance.

Thanks, Tara!

She helped. I took deep breaths and tried to focus.

Eight seats were empty. To either side of Skylur were screens for absent representatives to join the Assembly by teleconference. Three were blank. Maybe Romero and two others?

Behind us, a huge projection screen hung from the ceiling.

To our right sat an elderly couple, casually dressed and largely ignoring the proceedings. The Adepts, I assumed.

Bian nudged me and looked upwards. Cameras were mounted above the four corners of the seating, looking down onto the representatives.

"Skylur's little surprise," murmured Bian. "Secure real-time broadcast of the proceedings to every Athanate House in the world. That's why things have been delayed. He had to bulldoze it through."

I guessed that meant Basilikos couldn't misrepresent the proceedings, but it struck me as a risky move.

There was a buzz of discussion which did not die away. I felt almost every eye in the place was on me, but in here, I couldn't read the faces as I had with their staff outside. I gave them back what they gave me, fighting down the panic, keeping my face as blank as theirs.

This had gotten beyond an oath ceremony long ago, with complaints from Matlal about me. But the intensity of the inspection, here and outside, made me realize that every single one of them had heard there was something to be discussed about my Blood, and what that meant to them. I brought change to the changeless. Behind the masks, there would be the same emotions I had seen outside.

It was cold, and I shivered a little in my wet, stained clothes.

Trying to focus on what they were saying, I realized all the conversation was in Athanate. The bar just got higher.

"Basilikos are trying to disrupt this before we even start," Bian whispered to me. "It's important you don't speak until I tell you. And keep that blank face, Round-eye."

That was easy. Think court-martial.

Skylur nodded to her. Bian stood and waited while silence slowly fell.

"This issue will be discussed in English," she said and sat back down.

The place erupted. I think even her own party—our party—were affronted by her statement. I sat there and kept quiet.

When the shouting died down, a Basilikos representative spoke, in Athanate.

As soon as he finished, Bian stood. "Precedent," she said and sat down.

Before they could restart their complaints, Skylur cut in. "Diakon Trang is correct. The oath of House Karamazin to House Spasenieva, held before this assembly in 1931. That was in English at Basilikos request." He looked around and added, almost as an aside. "It's not as if you don't all speak English to each other any time you meet another House outside of this Assembly."

The representatives looked as if he'd slapped them across the face, but the first discussion ended there, and the blank faces returned.

We had made a first step, and gotten the proceedings in English. But I wondered how many Panethus Bian and Skylur had just pissed off. What were they doing?

The Basilikos representative from Brazil stood. House Correia, I remembered from the ball. She'd refused a dance. Her sleek black hair lay artfully about her shoulders and she wore the sort of elegant business suit that Jen did.

Correia looked at us, drawing everyone's eyes back to the contrast. Bian and I dripped bloody water onto the floor and stared back.

There was an absolute silence now, and despite their indifferent expressions, I had the sense that every representative was straining forward to see how this would go.

"The agenda item is the proposed oath of allegiance, from the newly proposed House Farrell to House Altau. Basilikos contend this item and advise they will expand the scope," she said.

"House Correia, there is no 'proposed' about House Farrell. In my authority, I have set up and formally approved the creation of this House. There is no discussion to be had about that. As to your other comments, linked or open scope?" Skylur asked.

Bian tensed, and Correia's eyes flicked to Matlal for confirmation. The room held its breath.

"Open," she said.

Skylur nodded and a quiet sigh flowed out from the seats.

"Anything can be discussed now," Bian breathed in my ear. "Risky. He should have restricted it."

"Then I will commence with a complaint against House Altau," Correia said. "That you infiltrated an Aspirant into the McIntire-Harriman Foundation Charity Ball for the purpose of spying on the Assembly."

"The Assembly only exists as a body when you're in a room and an Assembly is in progress," Skylur said pedantically.

"No defense," Bian whispered. "What is he trying to do?"

"The collected representatives then."

"House Farrell was not an Aspirant," Skylur countered.

"So you're at least admitting to the spying." Correia sounded exasperated, but I sensed they both played behind masks.

Skylur shifted his weight. "No. I was requested by another House to have someone attend. Obviously, that couldn't be someone from House Altau, by the rules of the Assembly. I contracted House Farrell in her capacity as an investigator."

"But she was Athanate and unregistered. That's—"

"No, not at the time." Skylur cut across her.

Correia smiled as if he'd made a mistake.

"We're all well aware you're a supporter of Emergence, but this is untenable. On your own decision, you risked exposing the entire Athanate. You've admitted that you contracted a human, not kin, not Aspirant, not Athanate and briefed her on Athanate matters to attend the ball."

Air hissed between Bian's teeth.

"No." Skylur seemed unconcerned. An usher delivered messages to him and he was scanning them before placing them in a pile.

At his denial, heads swiveled to the Truth Sensors, but they stared blandly back.

"She was in the process of becoming an Athanate," Skylur explained, putting the last of his messages aside. "But not aligned with a House, so not Aspirant. And so none of the categories you mentioned. A risk, yes, but not as you've portrayed it, and well within my rights."

I could feel the unhappiness from the Panethus side. It was all great fun for Skylur to play Correia as a fool, but his own side wanted more answers than he seemed willing to give. Maybe he wanted her to keep digging, so he could reveal Matlal's connection to Tucker.

Correia declined to pursue the thread and moved on. "So, then this Aspirant-without-a-House became Athanate. And then you established a House for her. In a week. I mean, I assume you established the House, since she can't even speak Athanate?"

"Correct." Skylur shrugged. "This is my mantle and such decisions are within my authority. There will be no discussion about that."

"I hardly need point out, there's not time for crusis in that."

"Normally, no," Skylur admitted.

The representatives rustled in their seats. A couple nodded to neighbors—so, the rumors were true. Tension ratcheted up.

Correia voiced it for them all. "The whispers about this woman's Blood would seem justified."

"Possibly, House Correia." Skylur settled back and steepled his fingers. "Is there a point to all this?"

"The point, House Altau," she snapped back, "is that you've been making questionable decisions that risk Emergence without the authority of the Assembly, and have lost control of your mantle. I propose that you be removed from your positions, both within the Assembly and within this mantle."

Skylur chuckled. "You have a long way to go before your allegations add up to any sort of grounds for the actions you suggest."

"House Farrell has been acting with your authority and approval?" She waited for him to nod. "Well, let's see what an affiliate of yours has to say."

She pressed a button on her seat controls and a screen behind Bian and me showed Oscar Jaworski, Diakon of House Romero. Crap. Altau had let him go and he enjoyed recounting all the things I'd done to him. Made him undress, tied him up. Yes, it had been in broad daylight, but to hear him you'd have thought most of the population of Denver witnessed his treatment.

Jerk.

"Is that controlling your mantle?" Correia asked.

Panethus representatives remained blank, but there was a stir of discomfort.

"What about this?"

She showed some shaky video footage of me jumping off the Nexus building and being flown off clinging on to a helicopter's landing skid.

"Demonstrating Athanate abilities," Correia claimed, her voice rising. "In front of witnesses. On camera. Risking revealing the Athanate, risking Emergence. Is that control?"

Absolute crap. I was doing that kind of thing all the time in Ops 4-10.

Bian gripped my forearm and kept me in my seat.

This wasn't a slam dunk, but again, there was more concern building on the Panethus side. Skylur had to bring out a counter.

"And now, I would like to question one of your own House," Correia said. "Marlon Pruitt. Under the protection of the Assembly and the Warders."

I frowned. What would Marlon have to say? Refusing to be brought to see Skylur by the Fang team? Surely that was nothing. Unless…unless he'd also found out about David and me compromising Altau security. He hadn't been at David's house that night, but he would have talked to the others. Bian might even have briefed him about it. But why would he do it? He was the spy? How?

Bian's head fell. She closed her eyes. "My second in command," she whispered. "I trusted him completely."

"Are you sure, House Correia?" Skylur said, his voice silky. "You want to unmask your spy before the Assembly?"

She was sensible enough to worry, but Matlal made a brusque gesture. Get on with it.

"Not our spy," he was smart enough to add.

They brought Marlon in. His face was completely relaxed, unconcerned.

Bian's hand gripped my arm. They weren't accompanying him, they were guiding him, supporting him. His face wasn't just unconcerned, it was utterly emotionless.

"We pass him to the protection of the Assembly," Skylur said. Marlon stood in the central area, swaying slightly, eyes wandering uncomprehendingly over the Assembly.

Correia recovered quickly. "What have you done to him?"

"*We* have done nothing, House Correia, except confront him with evidence of his spying. You say he's not your spy. Well, whoever managed to recruit him and program him, managed not only to control him so finely we could not detect it, but also planted a self-destruct compulsion in his brain." Skylur sat forward. "This man was second only to my Diakon. He was a good man, an honest man, who put his trust in the wrong place. Who in your Houses, my colleagues, do you trust now?"

A ripple ran through the room. All Correia's work to unsettle Panethus was swept away.

But Bian's head stayed down.

Skylur gestured to the ushers and Marlon was taken to one side and sat down on a chair between us and the Adepts.

Skylur went on to the attack. "Your main case, House Correia, which you're having difficulty setting up, seems to be that Amber Farrell is unfit to be Mistress of a House, is behaving incorrectly, and that in appointing her, I am similarly unfit. And since you've also brought up Emergence, we will discuss that in the process of this debate."

Matlal and Correia stiffened, but they recovered quickly.

"Unfit to be Athanate," Matlal said. "And thus unfit to be Mistress of a House."

Skylur snorted. "Your presentation has run aground, and I doubt you want a vote now?" He raised eyebrows at them. "What assessment of fitness would you accept? An expert?"

"Yes," Correia said, too quickly.

Skylur shrugged and indicated she should continue.

"I request the ushers bring Judicator Philippe Remy before the Assembly."

I recalled Diana saying something about trusting him only to behave as expected. My nervousness increased. I wished Diana were here to give me advice.

Remy came in and I didn't like him any more than I had before. He refused to look at me as he walked into the central area and peered at the controls for the presentation system. We swiveled to watch the screen behind us.

He got a picture of his cart of equipment up on the screen and then he spoke in bursts about what it could do and how it worked.

It was a development of the latest systems available anywhere in the world; it was almost perfect, all it needed was someone trained to interpret it. Here were some more slides.

I tried to focus. I had the feeling there was an unpleasant shock hiding in here. Correia and Matlal had been just too eager to get him in. They must know what was coming.

When it came, it started deceptively dully.

"On the left, one can see the average outline pattern for healthy Athanate. Do not worry about the shape of the pattern, simply that there is a pattern. This is gathered from many tests I have done in many Houses." A second pattern slid in from the right. "Now, on the right, one sees a different pattern, from fewer subjects, very different." He paused. "All these subjects on the right failed to pass through crusis, and became rogues, or passed and still became rogues."

I didn't like the direction this was going. Remy himself looked increasingly uncomfortable.

"One now overlays the shape obtained from Ms. Farrell." He pulled a shape to the left, then to the right.

My stomach dropped. I felt nauseous. It was closer to rogue than normal, far closer. Even I could see that.

"Judicator Remy," Skylur cut through the buzz. "Is House Farrell rogue?"

I sat there, struggling to keep my face clear, while every eye turned to me.

"No." He dragged out the word. "That is not what I am saying. Merely that there is a predilection. Statistically, she will become rogue."

"I see," said Skylur. "Statistically. Altau don't use this machine or your undoubted expertise. Tell me, are you familiar with our success rate?"

"Yes." Remy had to admit it.

Oh gods, you go Skylur!

"Well, we put our trust in our methods, and they tell us differently in this case. Still, very interesting, all these new gadgets. I shall be so impressed when you're getting as good a prediction rate as we are. Tell me, just out of interest, are Basilikos culling Aspirants on the basis of these results?"

"I do not know. I merely do the tests, sir. I am within the mantle of the Warders."

"Hmm." Skylur smiled at him like a crocodile. "And tell me, would a different set of tests or a different order of displaying produce a different result, a different shape? One which maybe everyone approximated to?"

"Yes, but—"

"Thank you. Proceed, Judicator Remy."

My stomach settled.

I forgive you everything, Skylur. Nearly everything.

"But of course, Altau did not infuse Farrell," said Matlal. "We do not know the House that did. Altau merely…adopted what had been started. There was no preliminary assessment."

Basilikos around him nodded in agreement. Panethus stared blankly back at them.

Remy stopped to wipe his brow with his handkerchief. Sweat marked his jacket. I was shivering with cold.

"The next feature I wish to present is not entirely from my own work. This equipment is starting to be used in the wider world to assess mental conditions. Using guidelines developed there, I have assessed Ms. Farrell's mental condition." Remy started to load images on the screen, his fingers clumsy on the controller.

"Ms. Farrell has an exaggerated preference for risk."

Not news to me. What did I have to worry about? Where was he going with this?

"In isolation, a concern, but regrettably, it is not in isolation." Remy bowed his head and pressed his fist to his mouth for a second, before continuing. "One does not like to use the terms schizophrenia and paranoia, because of popular misconceptions about their precise medical meaning. I shall say, rather, that Ms. Farrell manifests a predisposition to delusions."

What?

"These may be in the form of voices telling her to do things, or constant feelings of persecution. She has been relatively successful, so far, in controlling this. In order to do this, a structure for dealing with these matters pervades her mind. Without more study, one could not be absolutely definitive, but I believe she regards her Athanate state as a sort of creature in her mind, to keep chained."

Panethus stirred in their seats again.

Bian's grip on my arm tightened. I was tensing to stand. I forced myself to relax back.

Remy wiped his brow again. "And…there is evidence of memory tampering."

"What?" Even Skylur started at that.

What did they do to me? What did they do to me in that windowless cell?

I wanted to run. Anywhere. Hide. Bian's grip increased. She pulled me closer, her lips right next to my ear.

"Breathe. Calm. Breathe. He is trying to provoke you. Trust me, Amber. I will not betray you."

She put her head in front of mine as if I was whispering in her ear. She was dosing me with pacifics. Leaving me defenseless.

Trust me with your life.

I took a deep breath.

"It is possible for one to determine blocks on the memory," Remy said, "as might be performed to obscure Athanate information. This is not a technique exclusive to the Athanate and Ms. Farrell has just such a block. Alas, I can tell you no more, without more study." He looked down, and continued slowly. "But Ms. Farrell was previously in the United States army. One could say…that is, it is not inconceivable that they are responsible."

"So, Judicator Remy," Matlal said. "She is mentally unstable and may be under some form of compulsion to betray us? Or even to assassinate someone?"

"One could…one could validly draw such conclusions," Remy stuttered.

"Or she might be under a compulsion to sing the National Anthem on Independence Day," Skylur said. "The point is, you have no idea whether there is a compulsion or what it might be."

"No. The point is, Judicator Remy, would you assess that she is suitable material to be an Athanate?" Correia asked.

"Unfortunately, that decision is past." Remy dropped the presentation controller and scrabbled to pick it up. His hands were trembling. "She is already Athanate, or at least partly so. One might speculate that there is cross-infusion with Were." There were gasps from the representatives. "I speculate that she is in an indeterminate state, one could say, a perpetual crusis." He looked down and his voice dropped. "For everyone's sake, she must remain constrained. In these circumstances, in her mental state, one would recommend lobotomy, as a mercy."

Bian's pacifics weren't working well enough. "Let me go," I groaned through clenched teeth.

"Why not termination, if she's liable to go rogue at any second?" Correia said.

I would go rogue. I would take Correia and Matlal, I'd rip their throats out before anyone could stop me. And Remy. I'd do the whole world some good.

"Amber, think of the others," Bian hissed in my ear. "Jen, Alex, David, Pia. They need you to get through this."

"The Warders..." Remy blinked and looked as if he was lost for a second. "The Warders request to take responsibility. However damaged the vessel, these claims of reduction in crusis from the Blood must be investigated. The Warders' facilities are neutral and would ensure that any benefit would be available for all Athanate." His gaze wavered over the Assembly. "This investigation must include all House Farrell Athanate and kin."

"No!" I tried to shout, but Bian's pacifics robbed me of strength. It came out as a croak. Why were they doing this to me?

"We propose a vote on this immediately," Matlal said.

"A short while more," Skylur said, holding up one hand. "Where are these facilities?"

"New York," Remy mumbled.

"New York? Are you sure?"

"There are better facilities being constructed, which we would move to in due course." Remy's eyes darted as if he were looking for an escape, and now the sweat ran unheeded on his face.

"Those would be the facilities in New Mexico, would they? The ones that have just been started."

Remy stuttered incoherently.

"Paid for by Banco Armeria, which in turn is owned by...Bioteca Eztlian." Skylur's words fell into a pin-dropped silence. "That's one of yours, isn't it, House Matlal? You truly thought we would not notice? What is happening when the Warders accept gifts from Basilikos?"

Lindberg, the Panethus representative for Sweden, spoke. "Clearly, it cannot be anywhere but New York. That is the assigned neutral territory. But also clearly, this investigation must happen. Surely you agree with this, House Altau. This is too great an opportunity to waste."

"Really?" Skylur brooded for a minute before sighing. He turned back to Remy. "And all these opinions and speculations you have so uncharacteristically come out with?"

Norgaard, the Panethus representative from Denmark, stood. "I agree," she said. "It takes weeks to get an opinion from you, and here you are shoveling speculations like so much shit around a farmyard. What has happened, Remy?"

Remy said nothing.

"Who put those opinions there, Remy? What was your price?" Skylur demanded. "New facilities, no limitations on the scope of your investigation?"

"This is ridiculous," Correia said. "He works for the Warders. He is neutral. New Mexico would be in Panethus territory. This is a vote of faith on the part of Basilikos. I protest this treatment of the expert. You agreed to his determination on this matter."

"Ridiculous..." Remy echoed, sweat pouring from him. "Neutral…"

"Come, Remy. Look at the truth of your position." Skylur pointed at Marlon. "Admit it."

Remy just shook his head violently. He looked as if he might be about to throw up.

"Then I am truly sorry," Skylur said quietly, and pressed a button on his seat.

The presentation screen now showed Remy in conversation on the telephone. I heard almost nothing before Remy started shouting and waving his hands as if he could stop them from watching.

"Cease this. This is outrageous! *Scandaleux…*" He stopped, dwarfed by the Remy on the screen. *"C'est…?"* A look of bewilderment passed across his face, and for the briefest moment, sheer terror. Then it was just blank, like Marlon's. And, behind him, the screen showed him arguing the details of the diagnoses he had just made on me. Trying to argue against and simply being told what to say.

Skylur stopped the video. The room was silent as ushers removed Marlon and Remy.

I felt ill. Bian's hand remained on my arm, but I slumped in the chair, waiting for the next disaster.

Lindberg rose to his feet again. "I restate my opinion that Ms. Farrell should be placed in a protective situation, and a neutral team set up to study the effects of her Blood on crusis."

Norgaard started to argue, but Skylur cut across them both. "House Lindberg, my understanding of scientific method is that there needs to be a control subject. Perhaps you are offering for the whole of House Lindberg to go into this protective situation with House Farrell, and have your Blood studied for the benefit of the Athanate?"

"But I am…" he stopped.

"Exactly. You are Athanate, and Master of your House, and not subject to arbitrary imprisonment." He leaned back. "Just like House Farrell."

"That has not been determined," said Matlal. "Remy suggested—"

"You are surely not accepting anything Remy said?" Skylur looked astonished and raised his hands to the ceiling. "He has just been completely discredited. But I did agree to submit to expert determination, and the suborning of Remy has robbed us of one expert. But not all. Adept Emerson?"

"Oh, so very traditional, House Altau." She chuckled and stood up.

Bian whispered. "The old method of assessing fitness to be Athanate—she can assess the binding of kin and House."

"What do I do?"

"Nothing, she'll do it all."

"Do what? Is it going to—"

"Just trust, Amber." But Bian was nervous now as well.

Pia understood what was happening and brought David forward from the back of the room.

"There are others as well back there," Correia said.

The ushers helped Alex wheel Jen's gurney to the center. She was covered with a sheet to her collarbone and her golden hair was matted and flat beneath her. I was sure none of the Athanate recognized her.

Emerson came and stood in front of me. She had a bright vitality beneath her wrinkled face. Her eyes were winter sky blue, unblinking in their reading of me.

After ten years in the army, no one beats me with staring games, even as battered and tired as I was. I just stood there, trembling with the effects of the pacifics, and looked back at her.

She took my right hand, still cuffed to Bian's. Her fingers were cold, restless in their grip. Pia gave her hand. My heart skipped a beat.

"Bound," she said immediately, her voice both raspy and soft.

David gave his hand. "Bound," she said again.

Jen's gurney was pushed closer. Emerson reached for Jen's hand. Her face swayed close to mine. I could sense Bian's tension. Those cool eyes bored into me. It felt like a prickle of pins traveled up my arm. Her eyes widened slightly and her face creased into a smile.

"Oh! Twice bound," she said so softly, no one else would hear.

She reached for Alex's hand, when Correia spoke: "Were! She's brought a Were to the Assembly. This is a security—"

"Precedent," shouted Bian, leaping to her feet. "Several Basilikos Houses have enslaved Weres and Adepts. They have been brought to the Assembly. And this Were is here of his own free will."

Well, that got Alex's vote, I guessed. He ignored it all, except for a golden-eyed glance at me. His hand lay in the Adept's.

"You can't bind a Were," Correia said. "Altau's affiliates must enslave them."

Emerson laughed. It made her seem much younger.

"And thrice," she whispered.

What?

She returned to her colleague, not even looking at the Assembly. "All bound," she said, waving to encompass all of us. "None compelled."

"Well," said Skylur. "That's all clear then."

Speak for yourself, Skylur.

"And House Farrell," Skylur said, looking at me. My heart skipped another beat. "For completeness in registration, who is or was your Mentor?"

Bian squeezed my wrist and I stood again.

"Diana Ionache." I sat down in a profound silence.

Lindberg rose and made a small formal bow. "If there were any lingering doubts, that would dispel them. My apologies, House Farrell."

I made an awkward sitting bow back.

Skylur beckoned to David and Pia.

Oh gods, what now?

"I believe you have a presentation for us? I know this is not according to the schedule, but since you're here…"

A controller was handed to David. He stood there in his damp combat uniform and composed himself.

What on earth was this?

"David Thaler, House Farrell," he introduced himself, and I felt a surge of pride.

"I've been asked to present an analysis of the implications of Emergence—"

Matlal rose to his feet and interrupted. "What possible relevance has this to the oath of House Farrell?"

"You did request the scope to be opened," Skylur replied reasonably. "This is House Farrell, demonstrating why they warrant being an entity. I haven't seen this presentation, I'm eager. Aren't you?"

Matlal sat down, fuming.

"…the implications of Emergence on the financial stability of the world," David continued. He glanced nervously at Skylur, but composed himself again. "In parallel to this, we have a second analysis." He indicated Pia.

"Pia Shirazi, House Farrell," she said. "An analysis of the societal impact of Emergence."

I hadn't a clue where this was leading, but I loved them standing there, everyone just accepting the designation of House Farrell. Maybe we were through the worst.

I'd always known David was smart. He showed every one of them exactly how smart he was. He'd gathered information about the way large financial institutions invested, where and how they received the funds to invest and he made it all simple, even the way that the whole worldwide structure was interconnected. He had to have worked twenty-three hours a day this whole week to do it.

He demonstrated his analytical system by using the worldwide financial impact of the banking crisis, how it came about and how much weaker it left everything.

Pia took over and showed the societal effects of the banking crisis—the vilification of bankers, the crisis of confidence that led to the collapse of banks and financial institutions, and the fall of governments in the wake of the disasters. She gave the floor back to David.

He'd gotten into his stride earlier, but now, for the second time, he seemed nervous. I had an uncomfortable glimpse of where this was going, and many others did as well. There was a muted murmuring from the seats on both sides. Skylur made a gesture to carry on.

David resumed. "That data gives us a model to predict the impact of Emergence. In the time available, we looked only at two primary drivers: pharmaceuticals and insurance."

The two supporting parts of his graphic model became highlighted.

"Investor confidence in these areas would plummet," Pia said. A slide came up to the side showing dramatic estimates for falls in stock prices.

"This is ridiculous," said Norgaard, ahead of the rest of them. "You're implying that humans would expect Athanate to replace all medicine with healing? The post-retirement income investment companies would be crippled because humans live longer? Athanate are not numerous. We can't possibly do this."

"You are absolutely correct. But the world financial structure is built on confidence and perception, not on substance," replied David. He held up a ten dollar bill. "This piece of paper says the government of the United States owes me money. Where do I go to collect, and what will they give me? What if everyone goes there? This bill has no value except its perceived value. The effect of Emergence would be even more profound than the banking crisis." He gestured at the screen, where his three-dimensional model of the interconnected financial structure went through an animation of the pharmaceutical and insurance pillars collapsing. The whole worldwide structure followed.

"This would lead to an anarchic reaction against the perceived cause," Pia said. "We're talking worldwide riots. Lynching. Burning."

The whole Assembly sat, appalled at the picture David and Pia had painted.

Except Skylur. I was watching him, wondering what the hell he thought he was doing. An icy smile passed like a spring frost across his face and was gone.

"Well, most instructive, House Altau, House Farrell," Correia said, letting her breath ease out of her. "Emergence is a dead cause from this time forward. Excellent."

"Not exactly." Skylur reached down beside his seat and placed something in his lap. "That presentation shows the results of *unprepared* Emergence. That is what we are facing at this very moment." He looked at me and beckoned. "House Farrell, please."

Bian unlocked the handcuffs. I walked unsteadily, in a daze, every step sending jolts of dull pain through my shoulder. What next? At least no one challenged the removal of the handcuffs.

"We are here, at the heart of the most powerful and advanced human civilization the world has ever seen," Skylur addressed the room, and suddenly his voice reached out like a lash. "And you think we can hide in the shadows."

"Explain this device to them." Skylur thrust my blood test unit at me.

A bubbling glee threatened to break out in me, but I managed to control it. I turned and held the unit up for everyone to see.

"This box," I said, "belongs to the US military. And it was made to measure the change from human to Athanate."

Shouts of denial interrupted me, but I pointed at the Adepts.

"Truth," they said.

"The military know about the Athanate, and our only defense against the disaster of unprepared Emergence is to prepare for it, to control Emergence. And to do that, we must prepare with governments, secretly and at the highest levels. And for that to work, our behavior as Athanate must be—"

I couldn't proceed against the tide of protest from Basilikos. They could see where I was going, where Skylur had expertly driven us.

I returned to my chair, letting the argument rage over me like surf. The ushers had let my House reform around me, comforting me. The emotional rollercoaster, the pain and the pacifics robbed me of reaction. I sat numbly.

Eventually, a semblance of calm was restored.

One of the teleconference screens lit up with a blue bar. The unofficial representative of the Midnight Empire requested to speak and Skylur nodded.

"Tell me, House Farrell," he said, his British voice thin through the speakers, "what your Mentor thinks of this."

"Diana wants it," I replied. "She would like me to start making connections through my former military contacts to talk to the government."

I saw a raised eyebrow from the Adept, but I hadn't lied outright.

The Midnight Empire seemed to take the news as positive.

"That is irrelevant, and the Midnight Empire has no vote here," Correia said, gripping the armrests of her chair. "Not all your own side will support you in this, Altau. Maybe Emergence will need to be accepted in the future, at a time we all agree on. But Basilikos will oppose this proposal now. Put this to the vote."

"The timing of votes is my responsibility, House Correia, unless you want a vote of confidence?"

Correia backed down. Earlier, she would have taken it, but Skylur had whipped Panethus back into line now, even if not on the issue of Emergence.

"And as for the precise timing, I admit to some subterfuge." Skylur smiled. He was enjoying himself now. Matlal and Correia exchanged worried looks.

"I was truthful in saying I don't know where Diana is, when you asked earlier. But I do know where she's been." He picked up a pile of papers next to his seat and worked through them till he had the one he wanted. Pure showmanship.

"In Canada."

Bian twitched. Not what I expected at all, but at least Bian must have had an inkling of what might be coming.

"The assembled Houses of Canada," Skylur read, "etcetera, etcetera…hereby agree to the proposed terms of inclusion in the Panethus group." He looked up. "They'll be here tomorrow."

The representative of the Midnight Empire looked surprised but not shocked, on his screen. He had clearly been expecting it.

Basilikos weren't. And the balance of the Assembly had just tilted against them.

"And further," Skylur almost purred, "I have applications from thirty-six new Houses in the United States to put before the Assembly tomorrow."

Correia stood. "That's impossible. This is fantasy. Purely a delaying tactic to stop a vote on Emergence from being taken now."

"Clearly not impossible," Skylur said. "Difficult, yes. My colleagues, almost all Altau Athanate in the last ten years have been sent out across the United States. Every major city that was without a House now has one. Earlier than planned, I choose to reveal them now."

Basilikos sat shocked to silence.

I couldn't remember the formula for seats in Assembly.

"At least six seats," whispered Bian. "All right behind Altau."

"If all your House left you, how have you increased, how have you protected yourself?" said Lindberg. His frown became concerned. "Indeed, there have been rumors about Denver which I disregarded. How are we protected now?"

"Why should we need protecting, with the Warders here?" Skylur asked, and let that sink in. "Yet, I felt we did. And I reveal another secret of House Altau. We are sealed in down here for our own safety. We are protected tonight by the Lyssae."

Now faces throughout the room registered shock.

"It should be safe," Skylur said helpfully. "We don't *think* they'll break in here. And as for protection in Denver following the Assembly…" Skylur looked around. "The failure of the Warders was the trigger for my change of plan regarding the new Houses. My affiliate Houses have now provided sufficient people to ensure safety. I assure you, my colleagues, few of you were truly safe, or would have been safe departing this meeting. Even before we were sealed in, there was an attack on this house."

The shouting rose and died as he went on to speak directly to Bian.

"My apologies to my Diakon for keeping her and everyone else out of these decisions."

There was another storm of protest, led by Basilikos.

"This is ridiculous," Correia shouted. "You are accusing Basilikos—"

"Have I once said Basilikos?"

The screen showing the representative for the Empire of Heaven glowed. The room became quieter. The Empire of Heaven was not in the Assembly, but they were the largest cohesive group of Athanate in the world outside of the Assembly, and they spoke with this one voice.

"What is your purpose in establishing Houses throughout the United States, House Altau? We have never defined ourselves strictly by these human boundaries."

"Right to the point," muttered Bian.

Skylur shrugged. "It is now Altau strategy to do so. Those few Houses, of whatever creed, remaining in North America are now under notice to affiliate or leave."

The Assembly's collective breath hissed in.

"It is all to do with Emergence, then," said the Empire of Heaven. "Very well. We give equivalent notice within our territories. And what, House Altau, of New York?"

"Altau and our affiliates will hold all Athanate North America. Including New York," replied Skylur firmly.

"But that's ceded to the Warders," called out someone.

The Warder captain strode forward from the shadows in the back of the room, his face flushed with anger. "You cannot do this!"

"The terms of your charter were absolute neutrality, Captain." Skylur pressed a button and Agent Ingram's recording started to play over the speakers, a bit of the conference call I had not heard earlier. I recognized one of the voices—Marlon.

"Marlon," whispered Bian, her voice catching. "Betraying our location to the Warders."

"And from the Warders, straight to Matlal," Skylur said.

"Baseless allegations," Matlal called out. "A vote of confidence, now. Now, before you can distort this Assembly with additions that do not reflect the existing opinion."

"You call it baseless, House Matlal. You have raised an issue and I may address it first. You can have your vote of confidence after that."

"No! It's too close to call," Bian hissed quietly. "The vote of confidence will be a vote on Emergence. Too many Panethus want to stick their heads in the sand. This is too risky."

"Diakon," Skylur called. "I believe you have something to show the Assembly on the behavior of House Matlal in Denver."

Bian stood.

She took three miniature recording disks from her pocket and handed them to an usher to connect into the presentation screen system. Then, in the expectant silence, she paused and turned to me.

"House Farrell. Please, if you would say why we were at the factory in Longmont."

I got to my feet, ignoring the pain from my shoulder. This I would do.

I pulled Jen's gurney forward into the middle of the Assembly. At the far end of the room, few of the representatives would have been able to see her. Now they all could.

I trailed my fingers gently down her unconscious face. My eyes smarted and I shook my head angrily.

"This is Jennifer Anna-Marie Kingslund, one of the most prominent people in Denver. Most of you will have met her at the charity ball. My kin, as you have seen proved."

There was a murmur of surprise throughout the hall, but I was watching Matlal. He flinched. Oh yes, the bastard may not have actually kidnapped her, but he knew all about it.

He was fiddling with the communication system built into his seat, seemingly unable to contact his advisors outside. A small fault, caused by the storm no doubt. Skylur had a way of thinking of everything.

"She was kidnapped," I said. "And the price of her release was given to me. It was to betray the location of this House in time to catch the Assembly in progress."

Even Basilikos representatives hissed at that.

"But they already had the location. It was simply a trap. A trap to capture me and have me taken to House Matlal."

"Ridiculous!" Matlal shouted, joined by fewer of his supporters.

"When we rescued her," I continued, "it was from human criminals supported by heavily armed members of House Matlal, who were planning, once they had me, to attack this Assembly."

The whole meeting erupted. Panethus representatives took me at my word and shouted at the Basilikos side. The Basilikos side shouted at me—lies and proof being the main theme. And that was a problem. I believed what I said, the Adepts indicated as much, but I couldn't prove it. As if they sensed that, the shouts of 'proof' became coordinated.

Bian was standing beside me. She reached beneath Jen's gurney and retrieved the bag she'd carried in Tucker's factory.

I wondered blurrily what this was. Then I flashed back to her saying that her katana was the weapon best suited to her task, and I knew with a gut-churning certainty what was in the bag.

"Proof!" shouted the Basilikos representatives.

Bian calmly reached into the bag and pulled out a severed head.

"Pascal Medina of House Matlal." She dropped the head onto the floor and reached in to the bag again while silence fell. "Estebano Moreno of House Matlal. Vincente Herrera of House Matlal."

I shuddered. I'd had it right ages ago. My allies scared me more than my enemies.

Bian took the presentation controller and the screen at the end of the hall flickered and split into three. I realized that the military helmets that the Fang team had worn hadn't been equipped with infrared equipment at all. They were video cams.

Paul's came up first, with the time showing in the bottom right-hand corner. He was sprinting into the warehouse behind the truck I'd just crashed. He scanned the dead guards, the racks of rifles and ammunition, the short fight and the start of making the rifles unusable.

Then he and the others headed towards the factory, chasing the slim figure of Bian. Matlal's people died on the screens. Tom and Jason fired their P90s and Bian moved like a wraith, the blade flickering in her hands as she reaped her grim harvest.

She and Tom were attempting to pick the leaders, but there were too many. Tom was hit and fell; his camera lens swung wildly as Bian picked him up and headed back, Jason firing to cover their retreat.

I appeared on Paul's screen, covered in blood and gore from Hoben, yelling for them to go. Jason's camera wobbled as he was hit and started backing towards Paul, then lurched as he was picked up and carried.

They got to the van. Alex and Bian bent over Jason, and then left him. Tom's helmet came off and was tossed aside. Paul looked out from the window of the cab at the factory, just as it erupted, flaring out the image.

Basilikos inched away from Matlal, as if he had some contagious fever.

"And here, rather less dramatically," Skylur said in the silence, picking a message from his pile. "A communication from my good friend and ally, the alpha of the Denver Weres. It seems that they took it upon themselves to investigate a report of Matlal sponsoring a rival pack in Denver. A discussion was had at the Cherry Creek Reservoir. There don't appear to be any Matlal survivors."

He tossed the report aside and stood.

"Friends and colleagues, we are at the brink of a new age. Emergence may not be what we want, but it is coming whether we want it or not. We must ride the tiger. Emergence is not a cause for factions. We cannot be seen to be fighting. We cannot hold creeds that humanity will not accept. Emergence is a unifying—"

"No!" Correia was back on her feet. "Basilikos disown Matlal. You cannot use Matlal's attacks against you to force this proposal through. No to Emergence. No to expanding this Assembly. Basilikos will deal with punishment for Matlal. Enough delay. A vote of confidence now."

Skylur bowed his head. "Whether I agree or not, House Correia is correct, and I cannot delay a vote of confidence." He looked down the row of Panethus.

A half-dozen shook their heads at him. I groaned.

"See!" shouted Correia in triumph. "Those Panethus with sense abandon you. We outnumber your supporters. You are removed from office."

"This is very much not the case," a calm voice said behind her. "Theokos will support Altau to remain in position." He stood, and those closest to him stood.

Other Basilikos representatives were yelling at the Theokos representatives. Correia finally made herself heard.

"I am assuming leadership of Basilikos." She glared at Matlal. He was furious, but smart enough to see that he couldn't lead Basilikos now. Correia looked around and no one contradicted her statement. She turned back to Arvinder. "I demand you withdraw that, House Singh. Basilikos does not allow this opinion."

Arvinder remained standing, locked in a staring contest with her. Without moving his eyes, he said: "Then Theokos requests acceptance into Panethus."

"Granted," said Skylur. "And welcome."

Theokos crossed the floor with dignity while Basilikos dissolved into shouted arguments, Matlal and Correia at the center, yelling in Athanate.

Skylur beckoned me forward.

With only a few of the Panethus truly paying attention, I knelt shakily and gave my oath.

An oath that permitted Skylur to imprison me if he thought it was for the greater Athanate good.

An oath that had its counterpart, where Skylur promised loyalty for loyalty.

"Welcome." He almost smiled at me. His right eyelid drooped. Almost a wink.

He looked over at the swirling quarrel that was Basilikos. "We've gained ourselves some useful time, for which I thank you. We have to use this time well, we're not safe yet, not by a long way."

I rose and everything went dark. I nearly keeled over. Bian and Alex caught me and helped me back to the chair.

"A minute, House Farrell," called out Norgaard. "Since Diana is your Mentor, maybe you can tell us where she is?"

I struggled to focus. "I don't know. Canada was a complete surprise to me."

"Where did you think?"

"Mexico City seems empty of Athanate just now," my demon said. Not that I wanted it, but Basilikos heads turned and I had their attention again. My mind cleared at the hostile looks, but the demon rattled on. "Maybe she's gone to claim it for Panethus. Or, who knows, she could be in New Mexico. It's a trap, of course, but as House Matlal has found, traps can bite back."

Matlal screamed in rage and leaped to his feet, fighting off restraining hands.

Diana and Skylur had prepared me for this.

Matlal's attack on my mind was brutal, with nothing of the restraint of Skylur, nor the overwhelming power of Diana. Sheer direct assault, like ice picks thrusting into my head.

Diana had taught me how to defend myself, to use my buried anger as fuel to resist. It wasn't even as if it were buried now. The whole day, anger had simmered just below the surface, threatening to explode at any time.

I howled and lashed out with every fiber of my being. I screamed at the tide of pain that flashed through me: forgotten pain, remembered pain, pain gathered from Jen, all buried in an anger so violent and formless it made my whole body burn.

Matlal collapsed like a broken toy.

I knew. I knew then.

Alex caught me as I fell.

Chapter 53

Bian got us out of the Assembly, and took us to a luxurious underground suite. David and Pia were pushing Jen's gurney and Alex was holding me up.

Jen stirred as we moved her to the bed.

"She'll come around briefly, from time to time, during her recovery," Bian said. "She'll be disoriented. You have to be there for her."

Too shaky to stand, I knelt next to Jen on the bed. Alex was on the other side, checking her pulse and blood pressure again.

Jen's eyes fluttered and she frowned. "Amber?" she whispered.

I held her hand and bent over her. "I'm right here with you, Jen. You're safe. You're going to be fine."

"Pain," she mumbled.

"I can't risk giving her painkillers until I've done some tests and got her on a monitor," Alex said to me.

I shook my head. I knew that wasn't what she meant.

"No," Jen said. "Don't want. No pain. There's no pain. What happened?" Her free hand came up to her face and I felt her horror at the memory of her wounds and her confusion as she found healing flesh.

She opened her eyes wide and looked at me. And *reached*. The shock traveled down my spine. I grabbed Alex's hand for support, and that made it worse. It felt as if every emotion was shared between the three of us, raw and sharp as broken glass.

When Bian had talked about binding, I'd had a vision of what it would be. I imagined ships tied securely to a solid, concrete dock in a safe harbor, with me as some kind of pompous harbor master strutting around, in control. That may be what can be done, maybe what Bian thought we'd done, but it wasn't what we'd done.

When I'd bound us, if that's what it was, I'd done what felt right. The picture that came to mind was more of three ships lashed together out in the wide ocean. They were bound to me, but by the same means, I was bound to them. When they shifted, I shifted right along with them. Both of them.

Twice bound, and thrice.

Surprised as we were, Alex and I had a chance to figure out what had happened. Jen had just woken into it. She was panicking and it was panicking me too. Alex couldn't help; in fact, he was making it worse. As he realized what had happened, he pulled away as hard as he could.

It was Pia who understood what needed to be done. Gathering David and Alex, she pulled us all physically together and began to radiate a feeling of family, of belonging together. It washed over me, calmed me, lifted me, until I could join with her and David, broadcasting the feeling to Jen. We swept her up. I could feel the moment when she ceased to struggle and just joined with us, not understanding, but accepting.

But Alex couldn't. I could see him try, and I could also see his wolf frantic with the feeling of being trapped. He radiated a claustrophobic fear, and because we were together, he realized the hurt it was doing to us. He was trying to withdraw and trying not to hurt us, and realizing that he couldn't do one without the other. We were on the point of losing him, which would have left us forever wounded, when I felt Hana scrabble to the forefront of my mind. The others could feel her and they were shocked, but took their cue from my welcoming reaction.

Hana looked out through my eyes and captured Alex's, wolf to wolf. Speaking for the first time, addressing him through my mouth, she uttered the one, right word. "Pack."

The wolf in his eyes became calmer, less frantic, and I could breathe again. It was a long way from acceptance, but it was a start, an understanding. I looked from one set of eyes to the other—Jen's puzzled and blue and already slipping back into unconsciousness, and Alex's, wary and golden. Both so beautiful to me.

"Bian." I stopped her as she made to leave after a monitor had been delivered for Jen. Alex sat silently attaching wires.

"You must rest, Amber."

"I will. There's something I must tell you and Skylur." I was barely able to speak. My thoughts skittered around like marbles dropped on a stone floor. "Matlal…"

"You're safe, he's being held."

"No." I grimaced. If only my shoulder would stop hurting. If only my head would stop spinning. "Not that."

She pushed me gently back onto the bed, next to Jen.

"Matlal's not real," I said, slurring.

Bian frowned.

"He's really what his publicity says he is. Barrio boy made good. Not the real leader," I said carefully. I wasn't making sense. I tried to sit up, but Bian pushed me back down again. I could smell the pacifics coming off her.

"Not old enough. Not strong enough." I struggled. "A feint. To draw our attention."

"He was the leader of Basilikos, Amber."

"No," I whispered. "A puppet."

"For who?"

I felt her eyes on me. Not Bian's. Hers. The eyes that saw too much, too easily. The voice that, given time, would have turned me aside, even against my friends. A feeling like something cold had slithered over my shoulders.

"Vega Martine."

"I'll look into it," Bian said, still frowning. "I promise."

I closed my eyes for a second. She would check, but she didn't believe me. I hoped she would believe before it was too late.

When I opened my eyes, she was gone.

Alex was sitting like a statue, watching Jen's vital signs. Didn't need to. I was watching. Both of them. Our hearts thumped in lazy time together.

We'd been betrayed and we'd survived.

Things had just gotten *really* complicated.

But I'd make it work.

www.ingramcontent.com/pod-product-compliance
Lightning Source LLC
Chambersburg PA
CBHW051324250626
47155CB00007B/2439

* 9 7 8 1 9 1 2 4 9 9 1 4 4 *